Barred?

By

KEVAN POOLER

Keep Safe

Kevin

First published in Great Britain in 2016
by
The Lime Press

10 9 8 7 6 5 4 3 2

A CIP catalogue record for this book
is available from the British Library.

ISBN 978-1-9993664-2-1
Amazon Print ISBN: 9781080770465
Kindle eBook ASIN: B07V7FJH3P

Lime Press edition printed in England by
CLOC Bookprint Ltd, London N17 9QU

Published by

The Lime Press
1 Lime Grove
Retford
DN22 7YH

Barred?

Thursday March 4th

'Feckin' Polacks.' Suzanne the chambermaid at The Loseborough, was chuntering as she trundled into her third bedroom of the day, and it was still only half six. She almost wished they hadn't bothered to oil the wheels of her trolley. 'Feckin' Polacks,' she said again. She heard herself this time, and she caught herself in the mirror too. She left the cloth on the sink. Her hand made its own way to her cigarette packet. Without looking away from the mirror she slipped a co-conspirator into her mouth. She felt around for her lighter, but froze as she realised she couldn't light up in here.

The pause button was released and she tilted her head to one side. She swept her grey-streaked blonde locks all across to one side. She moved the cigarette to the corner of her mouth. She narrowed her eyes and moved in to threaten her image in best American gangster growl: 'Fackin' Paw Lacks.'

She whipped the weed back into its packet and set about the room quickly so she could to nip to across to 212, where she would get a gasp on its balcony.

Suzanne's son had told her about the Polacks when he challenged her racism. Right-on was William. 'Kick Racism out of Football' – that was her William. She still thought it was funny. Even after he had told her the American anti-Polack jokes were the worst and that as she was from Irish immigrant stock herself, she should know better. She did. She knew. It didn't make it any easier to accept the East Europeans pushing her friends out of their jobs. It did make it sillier though – because only Anya, lovely Anya, was a Pole. The others were from all over – Latvia, Estonia, France; but the one she really hated was Agnes from Glasgow.

The room looked hardly used. Mr Houldsworth said these four would probably be quite easy. The party had stayed over one night, then through the day. Because they had not stayed 'last night', she could set about them first. Do the others as people left. This one was funny though – whoever had it was very methodical – the towels were exactly as she left them fresh, except for the hand towel, which was wet through and had maybe been used to wipe out the shower. It was folded neatly and left squarely in the middle of the bath.

The bed had been stripped. Sheets and pillowcases had been folded and made the base of a pyramid beside the bed with the dressing gown and slippers on top. 'Must be a man – bet he was in the army – or prison,' she thought.

Suzanne could beat the stipulated 'Polack' nine minutes in here. She had the room done in just five.

Setting her trolley at the door, checking up and down the corridor, she dashed into 212. She stripped off the pillow cases, bundled them into the sheets, raced into the en suite, grabbed all the towels and went and - just in case anyone were to suspect she wasn't busy - threw them into the corridor.

She shut the door and leaned back on it. She'd gained herself a luxurious four minutes. Four whole minutes. She looked into her pocket and winked at her ciggies. She got one out and readied the lighter.

It's cold in here.

The French window was open.

She catwalked over to the balcony.

She stopped just before it. *Bugger that* - she wasn't going to let that spoil her gasper. She lifted her head and took a lungful of fresh morning air, blew it out and replaced it with the wonderful Molotov cocktail of nicotine filled smoke and tar. She blew it out into the fluffy pink clouds as they picked up the dawn.

'Take that Anya. They won't catch me.'

After that she had a massive two hundred and forty seconds to take in the dawn. Was it spring? The trees opposite were still dark skeletons. A magpie chackered and she spied him. He got a reply from below her. Her gaze worked its way down the trunks to the evergreen of the rhododendrons and over to the leylandii windbreak, fogged over with steam from the jacuzzi.

'Nice morning,' she mused. 'Oops!' Any early birds in the jacuzzi to spy her?

'The jacuzzi!'

The magpie flapped on the shoulders. She noticed lovely blonde hair – natural – not out of a bottle like hers. Suzanne was flushed by a rush of pity, mixed with disgust. A whole life rushed before her eyes at the moment of death – but not hers – someone else's.

She leaned over.

She rubbed her eyes.

She screamed.

She threw her cigarette and screamed out of the room.

She choked off her scream down the stairwell, but it burst out again as she slid onto the bottom and skidded round the banister.

'Somebody's …' She braked on the rail. She faltered in her scream – she couldn't shout 'jumped' – that would mean suicide, that lovely blonde. No.

Without checking anyone was there, she screamed across to Reception, 'Somebody's fallen out the window,' and she barged out of the back door.

Before
One

Leo Nicholas was spinning his redundancy notice on his desk, the point of his pen held firmly against the heart of his boss's signature – his eyes tracing the obnoxious and arrogant loops and dots that formed it. He sighed. An e-mail was open on his computer screen revealing that the ever increasingly costly red tape of Criminal Record checks had lost a pile of records. Would Leo ask certain individuals for a copy of their own?

The day had started well: he had thought of Talya's mantra – 'you never buy me any flowers' - and he had bought flowers. Shattered and headless they were mocking him from his waste bin. He had slung his bulging satchel onto the car seat and crushed them.

'Oh, talk of the Devil,' he said to Gina, his secretary. She had to remind him that he wasn't talking, he was daydreaming. He laughed and said, 'You'd better give Abe and me some space, please.' Leo always had time for a man who volunteered to work with the nation's untouchables – young drug users.

Abe Grant was a bit puffed out when he got up to Leo's office. He stuffed the last piece of his sausage roll in his mouth and inspected his jacket before deciding to use the bag to wipe his fingers. Same old tip of an office. Abe couldn't get over how badly the council provided for its employees. He could see Leo behind the partition he had made for himself inside the cavernous old knitwear factory. Poor lad – caring so much about others left no time to look after himself.

'Got a minute, Leo?' He was looking around to see if anyone else was likely to come in. He shut the door behind him. 'I know – if it's *ever open* for me, it has to be for everyone else? We need to talk.'

'Of course, Abe, sit down.'

Abe rolled the secretary's chair from under her desk to be nearer Leo.

'The Leader-in-Charge says the staff are a bit twitchy with the volunteers kind of grilling them about the increased pressure of Criminal Record checks.'

'Heard it on the telly, eh Abe?'

'Yes. Even people ferrying lads to football in their cars … they reckon about eleven million people will need police clearing.'

'Well, I for one hope someone sees sense pretty soon and realises that a huge costly bureaucratic scheme alone is not going to save children.'

'But people hate getting checked up on as if they are guilty. Aren't they even calling it 'vetting'?'

'Oh yes – and barring!' said Leo. 'The politicians are panicking and getting onto all the councils about failures in child protection. They feel Social Services took no notice of the reports after Maria Colwell, Victoria Climbie …'

'Baby P?'

'Yes, and of course the paedophile gangs – Oxford, Rochdale – and we've got our own, haven't we?'

'Jelly! We reported Jelly and his grooming of the rose sellers.'

Leo gave the bin a quick glance.

'How much notice did they take?'

'Exactly.'

Leo laughed. 'I didn't think it was a florist! Thought they told the kids heroin tastes like ice cream.'

'Ah, that as well. They see the advance guard – often Jelly himself in his posh Black Man's Wagon – then if all's clear of police, they hear two blasts on a boy racer exhaust and chase after that like it's an ice cream van.'

Leo stretched his mouth and sucked his teeth. He had not got Abe police cleared – if they vetted him, they would certainly bar him. Leo would lose his job if anybody found out. He glanced at his redundancy notice. He had not worked out how to enable Abe to carry on his great work with the most vulnerable young people.

'Abe, I'm half hoping it is just the media hyping it up. I don't think all the austerity measures will allow such expense at the same time that jobs are being slashed.'

'Jobs, Leo? Not our youth workers?'

'Ah well, that's something else I'll have to tell you about. But don't let's get drawn into all this negativity.' Leo knew that they hadn't addressed what Abe had surely come for, but he stood and looked around for Gina. 'Leave it with me, Abe. Love to Rowena.'

Gina saw Abe off, gathered up her photocopying and went back to her desk. She thought Leo was about to bash his head on the keyboard, but her gentle cough stopped him. When Leo eventually decided to take notice, he flashed one hand towards the screen and one suppliant hand at her.

'I'm not having it, I'm just not having it?'

'Gotta do it, Leo.'

'Why, because a little Hitler of an admin officer says so? What's she know about youth workers?'

'No, Leo. It's because an Ian Huntley might be in your team.'

Leo spun on his seat. 'Who? Oh him, Soham murderer ... but Gina, Gina, you know Huntley and Palmer ...'

'Behave yourself, Leo! You know it's Carr, Maxine Carr.'

'... were crackers.'

She winced.

'They were let slip though the net – social misfits who should never have been let near a school. Damn bureaucratic checks, didn't stop them. People let them in; people depending on the 'system' to do the work.

'You know you have to do it, so why resist?'

He threw himself back in his chair and stared at the ceiling.

'No, I'm not doing it. These people were all checked and cleared when they were appointed.'

'Were *you*?'

'Was I what? Well, of course I ...' He coughed. 'Well, no.'

He gave Gina a sideways look and pinched his Trotsky goatee.

'Got me. But I was in post for fifteen years before all this political correctness went mad.'

'But the checks are about *child protection*.'

'It's *job* protection, can't you see?' Leo was weary with the political correction endemic in the County's whole 'post Soham' response. Yes, Ian Huntley murdered two beautiful little girls, but what Leo saw was hundreds more lives being destroyed, by men out to exploit them in one way or another, right there on his patch, simply because there were not enough *people* out there to make a difference. Since the job freeze, he could put fewer and fewer youth workers out on the street where the kids were open to exploitation by 'Jelly' and his gang of 'taxi drivers.' It was Leo's team who had alerted the authorities and now it was they who were 'out on the street' themselves.

'But Leo, Huntley would never have been employed if the system had worked.'

'Exactly my point. Only a bureaucratic system, Gina. It won't protect kids. I won't be able to put any more youth workers out there next year, because this whole criminal record and barring palaver is costing five million. More desk jobs won't protect anybody – except the politicians' backs. You've seen this email about lost records?'

'Leo, you are going to get yourself into hot water if you carry on like this.'

He waved his 188 Redundancy Notice at her.

'Now we've got these.'

'Come on Leo, you know it's only a precautionary measure, everyone's got one. The whole service is at risk of *possible* redundancy.'

'Not damned Wyndham Leyton, I bet.'

'You've got quite a thing about him, haven't you?'

'Should never have had the job. What's he know ... or care?'

'Seriously, Leo ...'

'I am being deadly serious. We'll come back to my clearance – or lack of – but what I am mad about is that bloody admin worker – she calls herself 'an officer' - losing clearance forms; losing the most data-sensitive materials we in the youth service hold. Not just in my team, either?'

'No, they're across most teams.'

'She wants me to get three of my staff and one of Abe Grant's Drugs Team – a *volunteer* - to let her have a copy of their own forms. I refuse. I am not letting on that we are such a disorganised, inefficient service. I had to tell Abe – but I've sworn him to secrecy. I thought he was going to skin me alive!' He grabbed his chin. 'So, should I be cleared, too? Good question? Is Wyndham - how come *he* hasn't told us to?'

'No, he's not cleared. I asked Ms Admin *Officer* straight out. She is appalled, but isn't saying anything. I'm not either – keeping my powder dry.'

'Ha! Not only unqualified for the job, but not cleared to work with young people either!' Leo looked across at his secretary 'Get me a blank form Gina.' He added, 'Please? Any chance to be one up on the boss, eh?'

Leo was torn in two - as the county's lead child protection trainer he felt as if he needed to protect young people from the likes of Wyndham Leyton, a typical corrupt manager. Leyton had been appointed as Head of youth service 'by mistake' apologised the CEO, after it was revealed that Leyton did not have the 'Essential' qualification as a youth worker and possessed no management qualifications either.

Leyton was, as the Chief said, dynamic, clever and had great administrative experience, including some in a backwater, hick, county youth service somewhere in the beautiful south. He was a bean counter, a bureaucrat. He thought youth workers should be running discos and giving out darts and table tennis bats in tatty halls, 1970s style. Three years in, it became obvious to Leo that he had no empathy with what real youth work could achieve, and at the sound of the bell, had heartlessly asset-stripped the service of meaningful services that changed lives, to make cuts for his Tory masters, and to keep himself the glittering kid in their eyes. They made him Head of all services for Children and Young People. That was not equal opportunities.

Leo, on the other hand was a time served professional and managed around forty others. Dedicated and trained, they gave up their time late into the evening, night after night so young people could weather the storms of adolescence, poverty and the law. It didn't matter to him, or his team which side of the tracks they came from. They were vulnerable and in need of help. In a nutshell, that was the fundamental difference between him and the pen pusher.

Leo on the other hand felt 'more equal' than that womanising pig. He had come blinking into the light of a whole new world when Thatcher shut his pit. As 'Red Andy' Nicholas, he needed a new life, preferably one that allowed him to line up all the Thatcherites and shoot them. He wasn't exactly the shooting type – too noisy to get away with – but he had had his sock-cosh, and he had used it. He smiled at the thought of the coppers from the Met, buckling onto their shields at the Orgreave Miners' picket. The shields didn't protect their knees, and without knees...

His new life in youth work had given him equality. Equality of opportunity had been a lengthy era of political correctness, sorely needed in Britain and Leo had received it, despite his immigrant background. Like many at the time, he had received so many opportunities, that now it was not stressed so much, he felt the burning need to ensure that it was not forgotten, and that others got them. He had so much opportunity, that surely he was now more equal. About the pigs Orwell was so right he was wrong.

It was bred into Leo's very bones: The British had given a whole new life to their ex-enemies - his parents - a Ukrainian ex-prisoner of war and his Italian sweetheart. By the time Andrej Nikoluk arrived at school, he didn't notice that his name entered the register as Andrew Nicholas.

Leo didn't see himself as a violent man, but he always felt the need to handle himself. Maybe it was the 'specky-four-eyes' taunt - he always managed to wrestle his way round a bully. This developed into judo – 'The Gentle Way.' The 'Dojo' was at the miners' welfare – and so was the youth club. Sensei said the youth leader wanted a workshop to encourage some of the lads in particular, to take up something more constructive than mugging old ladies. Never having considered such a move, Leo volunteered. He couldn't believe that so far into the twentieth century, these lads' greatest wish was a job down the pit.

When the colliery closed soon after, his heart ached to hear the stories of all the lads in the village, boozing, smoking bongs, doped and lifeless, on the slag heap – and even that was redundant now.

By the time he was qualified in a second career in youth work, his fellow undergrads had christened their bushy haired, be-spectacled Socialist pal with a hint of a hippy beard, 'Leo' after his hero, Mr Trotsky.

Leo was imagining himself skulking with his sock-cosh in the black shadows of County Hall and as the man slunk into his bespoke Alpha Romeo in the floodlit car park.

'Leo!' said his secretary.

'What's up, Gina?'

'Tapping.'

His pen had stabbed through Leyton's name on the 188 Notice. No, stabbing wasn't his way, coshing was. Motive – the man was not cleared to work with children and he was putting them at risk. MO and weapon – unknown.

Leo was already more equal, and now he would love to get even.

Before
Two

Abe Grant, Chair of The Tin Tab young people's drug and alcohol team, was wondering how he could get round Rowena again. She was pretty fed up with him prioritising his youth Drug Project over their family life.

'I'm taking Ivan to look for a bed, a settee and a telly later, seeing as Marina's cleaned him out and not left him a stick.'

'What Abe, you're surely not letting her get away with it? That's our Ivan's furniture – *she* moved in with *him*.'

'Yes, but you know what he's like – he loves her and she has not got that stick.'

Rowena pursed her lips and shook her head. She had as much influence over her husband as her son had over his wife. Well, perhaps she'd credit herself with a bit more: she had turned his life around – and not a proselyte either. She had sown the seed on soil she prepared over several years of patient visiting, and it had paid off. He had done what he had done to his first girl, but Rowena McGill chose Michael Abram Grant to father her children … and no regrets. He had become her rock. Now he could walk all over her and she knew he would leave no footprints. Her guardian angel. Shame they'd had to drop the Michael – but then there already is the Archangel Michael.

Now, she felt she might be able to rescue something.

'Where exactly are you going to look? Not the Saint Vincent's furniture store, I hope.'

He stood up and took her into his arms.

'Ah now Coddy, my little Codling, sweet Cod Rowena – would I do such a thing to our own flesh and blood?'

He would. She knew he would.

Rowena knew she had to steer this in a different direction. Prisoners all wanted to be innocent. They would lead the visitor to that belief at all costs. Rowena's second client nearly cost her everything. So she learnt for herself. She learnt to enable guilt to be accepted, repented, and from there, moved on.

Abe was her major success. But even thirty years on, she knew he must not be allowed to feel guilty; so what could she hand him?

'We've still got his room full of furniture upstairs, isn't it time we sorted that into a guest room.'

'Coddy, you're brilliant. He'll probably feel good about that – ownership and all that, yes? He hasn't stayed here for a single night for … how long? Tell you what – I'll offer to buy him a big screen telly if he'll take that lot off us.'

He spun her round. As theirs was not the sort of kitchen for two people their size to tango in, that meant he spun most of the breakfast pots round, too. He put his finger in his mouth, 'the bad 'un.'

'Well, now you've got yourself an extra job, you daft 'a'p'orth. I'm off to work.' She gave him a clip him round the ear, a kiss on the pate, and flew out of the door.

Abe clicked on the kettle and looked out at his estate – a nice square of lawn with flower border right round, and a six foot fence to three sides.

If things got a bit tense for Abe, he was sure he could see that little glint of hellfire in the darkest space. No one else could see that little glint. He kept it because he felt it easier to believe in Hell than Heaven, and that bit of fire kept him upwardly mobile. Coddy didn't know he could see it, that he had purposely not buried all memory of that awful past. She would be angry to discover he had left a nail out. 'The past is the past. Michael A. Grant no longer exists. You are a new man. You have been forged anew in the fire of God's love – and mine, Holy Mother help me. Six years in the furnace and three more years under the Hammer of the God's – (that's me by the way).'

He'd teased her ever since with that. To keep a bit of fire in such a calm marriage, if ever he banged anything, he'd cry to the kids in Rowena's hearing, 'I'm Thor! I'm Thor!' taking a glimpse to see her being careful not to react.

'Now you're re-born simple Abram Grant – my Abe – and God's.'

'Not Thor's then?'

'Don't make me blaspheme, Abe Grant.'

The Tin Tab did have priority. There were not enough Coddies to go round, certainly not since the enterprise culture, health and safety, litigation culture, and all the red tape had drastically cut down on people's desire to volunteer. The criminal record checking system had given him a fright several years ago, but the parish priest knew his background, first revealed in the security of confession, then brought outside – but they had what Father Hu called a 'covenant.'

When the new youth officer arrived, and took a special interest in The Tin Tab's work, Abe felt the need to come clean. Leo made him feel whiter than white. But Abe didn't want that. He had killed his 'Missus' and that was all there was to it.

For a couple of years, Leo didn't even know exactly what Abe's 'Life' conviction was for. He felt no right to question. The Tin Tab had been running for fifteen years under Abe's lead, and if the 'system' let him out of prison after nine years over thirty years ago, who was Leo to quibble?

When both of them had become safe in each other's company, become friends even, they were having a drink and Leo was laughing about his antics in the miners' strike. He let out his own sock-cosh 'Riot Act' secret.

Abe was not a drinker, he was a strict two pints of shandy man; he couldn't risk anything stronger. He noticed that Leo had stopped dead, gaping and blushing.

Abe put his hand out. It rested on the table between them. His eyes welled up.

That took two men, well in control of their emotions, into unfamiliar territory, 'women's territory.' Leo was thinking of his wife Talya who didn't know. Abe was thinking of Rowena, his Coddy, who knew only too well.

Abe said, 'I told the parish priest.'

'That monster guy!' said Leo.

Abe laughed out loud. He took a glug of shandy and wiped his unevenly shaved lips. Abe had another little chortle before correcting Leo.

'Not the *Monsignor* - Father Hu, stupid.'

'Me no stupid, you old enough to be my father!' said Leo

Abe had sat back a relaxed man and told Leo about the 'Covenant' Father Hu, the previous priest had made with him.

Leo simply nodded and took time to smile at his friend's threadbare tweed jacket, which wouldn't meet across his bulk. He saw him squirm, only a little, before leaning forward and replacing his 'comb-over.'

'I really appreciated you not asking me at the time Leo,' Abe started. He could see that Leo knew where this was going. 'Do you want to know?'

Leo felt unable to give a direct answer.

'Things are changing with all this new disclosure ... and vetting ...' His head was shaking, '... and barring stuff.' He didn't want to have a secret to hide. 'Well Abe, only if you really want me to know. I don't have any problem with your position. You told me about your conviction, but I know your real record – the record of the last ... how many years have you been helping the drug users?' This didn't need an answer. 'We've got a covenant, too, haven't we?'

'Thanks Leo,' he said and took a look around, and one at his shandy. No it wasn't drink making him talk. It was affection, building trust. 'Go on, I'll tell you.'

Leo opened a palm and raised his brows.

'Up to you?'

'Just a stoned young man, scares his Missus to death – literally.'

Leo winced. This was worse than he expected. He had hoped manslaughter or bad luck.

Abe choked up a little but went on.

'Actually we weren't married. She was just a kid – at Tech re-sitting her A Levels. Bright young thing took to the cock o't' walk. We had one of those two up and two downs in Warsaw ...'

'Warsaw?'

'Yeah, Bond Street and Seal Street, where all the Poles are now.'

Leo wasn't about to correct the old guy's racism, so inched out a smile.

'I was a wheeler and dealer – 'dealer' you would say now, hence The Tin Tab, see?'

Leo flickered his brows.

'You mean – set a thief ... you were involved in drugs and have seen the error of your ways?'

'And how! Well, one Sunday after a long session in the pub, flushed with the success of a good deal going down, I decided to show her a good time and take her for a spin ... yeah, spin is what she got. We dropped a couple of 'blues' – 'Phet' – and jumped in my souped-up Capri.'

Car fanatic Leo wanted to follow this up, but realised this was not the time.

'That 'Think Bike!' sign hadn't been invented then – anyway I wasn't thinking. I skimmed a group of bikes on a bend, lost control and broadsided into a tree. The left side of the car met the middle – and so did I.' His voice had reduced to a moan. 'No seats belts. No air bags. No side impact bars. Janine cushioned me - she saved my life.' Abe was talking to the table. He didn't see the man across from him, drained of blood, and still. He picked a peanut off the table and unconsciously put it in his mouth. How many times had Coddy told him not to do that?

Abe looked up at Leo and added, 'She saved my life. I killed my love ...' He squeezed the tears out. '... and our baby.'

Leo coughed and shuffled in his chair.

Abe watched him for a bit, and then added in a falsetto whisper, 'Coddy forgives me. I don't.' He wanted to know if the CRB would. He didn't know how to ask. He started, 'See, see our ...' He coughed on the peanut.

'Abe?' said Leo. 'See your what?'

He coughed and spat out, 'CRB.'

Leo grabbed his chin. 'Criminal Record Bureau? What's different? It was an accident. Manslaughter at worst.' He was nodding to convince himself.

Abe was shaking his head.

'Very kind of you, Leo. Americans say 'Culpable Homicide.' I was truly, truly culpable, Leo. I call it murder, but yes, I got Manslaughter. Is that enough of a record to ... to keep between us.'

'It has done so far. I don't see what has changed.' He hoped he was convincing enough, though he could feel the increasing squeeze of the latest barring scheme making a liar of him sooner than he would hope.

Before
Three

Brien Devine was 'lost', dead heading roses in the convent garden. All was lost.

Lost, all those broken men who had filled the Monasteries, Convents, Friaries and Priories after the war and built Brien's boyhood faith.

Lost. All those innocents, lost to the sexy sixties. Brien going up to the big city was lost to them too. In Gomorrah he lost his innocence and his innocent Colleen.

He had heard a lot of talk about pornography – they reckoned the most common search of the internet was pornography. He didn't dare look himself. Even masturbation was a form of Adultery to him. He had asked Carol, the Leader of The Tin Tab youth workers, what this sort of thing was about. She was a young woman and had to be computer savvy. She had told him that the most popular sites were webcam sites where women and young girls stripped for the viewer – and even talked to them.

Dear God, what was Brien supposed to think? He had married his Ginny. He hadn't felt greatly compelled to seek a wife, but their love grew within the church – meeting at parish socials, a mutual interest in gardens and gardening – it had all blossomed into a beautiful marriage. Sex was amazing – a complete revelation to him.

He had never had the supposed Catholic angst about sex – he hadn't really been interested in it. That all changed. Ginny was so tactile. She touched him and kissed him all over. All this, a reward from God for saving themselves ... for each other.

Then came pregnancy – he was going to be a Dadda! And what joy of anticipation! That first was dashed, but they weren't the only ones whose baby was called to join the angels. A couple more followed and went with the first. Brien started to ask the Lord a few straight questions. What was his game? Was he toying with their affections? Their affections certainly were turning into something else – it was no longer 'making love', it was all about making a perfect baby. And in the end that worked: Colleen – an angel on earth. How Brien's heart ached at the beauty. But she very near killed Ginny, so no need to be making further babies.

In the early years, such creation happening in the baby was a reward in itself, then at the same time as baby's daily routine set in, Brien was in greater demand at work, for statistics for reports, to get more work for the firm. He was tired and slept.

But holidays became a nightmare. He found his thoughts turning to Ginny's boobs and her lovely bum and ...

He wanted to hold her. He thought he was going to enter her.

'Oh no, Brien, are you trying to kill me? Are you thinking of leaving Colleen motherless?'

It was a stab direct to the heart. It did not cut off his langar. It was still between his legs and too often it was not hidden, hanging, it was upstanding and proud and shouting for attention.

Contraception was out of the question, of course.

Ginny and he agreed on separate beds. Having to handle himself, Brien couldn't handle that and decided it had to be separate rooms – Ginny with Colleen, Brien by himself.

She was a great kid. They had such fun together. He had no idea about kids and used to wonder what he could do with her, but the child's own built-in quest for knowledge led them. He just played with whatever seemed to interest her and built on that. It would change and sometimes flit from one thing to another. He was such a patient man, and he had his Colleen to absorb all his waking hours, outside of work.

Colleen doted on her Dadda and would sometimes tell her Mammy that she wanted to sleep with Dadda. No problem. Didn't he love her to pieces?

'God forgive me?' Brien knew it was stupid to even ask. How could he be forgiven? Brien certainly repented. He lost his Colleen. She left. He knew why and he couldn't tell Ginny. Ginny was quiet. She was always quiet. She became cold and quiet. She could see no reason on her part why Colleen would abandon her. She accepted that Colleen was not a 'missing person' – she had left a note. It told them nothing.

The phone calls were regular, but told them nothing. If Brien took the phone, nothing was said, not a word. He put the Mammy on. At first she pleaded, but Colleen hung up. Ginny learnt. She stopped the pleading and Colleen spoke, but only a little, to say to her Mammy not to worry, she was okay. After a while she sounded excited, more in the tone of voice than what was said, because nothing at all was told. Ginny was persuaded that Colleen was happy. What more could a mother want for her daughter?

What more could a father expect of his daughter. He knew he had already expected too much.

A drop splattered on his hand shocking him into the clear blue sky ... more dropped from his cheeks.

'Brien!'

He pulled his cap in a single swipe across his whole face spoiling his hair.

'Brien!'

He coughed and taking out his secateurs shouted, 'Abe, it's you. Over here.'

Abe was shaking his head, smiling at his old friend as he approached. Brien was a thick set man, a head shorter than Abe and without a paunch. He always wore a suit and tie – even for gardening, though it would be an old one. Abe was more likely to wear his gardening clothes to church. He thought it a little odd that at their age, undefined seventyish, any man could bother to keep up appearances like Brien did, with a full head of thick wavy hair now messily Brylcreemed over his freckled forehead. Abe could see him as a red-head, the same shape in his

13

wedding photos. Fortunately it was decades since anyone could have recognised Abe from his wedding photos.

After his inspection he said, 'Brien, you have the patience of a saint.'

'It's not a saint, but the penitent pilgrim I am, Abe. Sure, aren't the real saints floating about on their clouds, and not on their knees among the rose thorns?' Brien noticed and smiled to himself how even big old Abe would not trample on the innocence of the buds.

'I was centuries away, Abe,' He thought he had better brighten himself up a bit. 'I was thinking about this great big garden and the brothers that were once here to tend it. Do you remember, Abe?'

'Before my time – just the lone secular priest since I got here.'

Brien at last noticed that his old friend had drifted, had drifted over to the pond and was peering into its murk.

'Bomb Crater,' shouted Brien.

Abe peered down at his reflection and replaced the few strands of his comb-over. His hand turned into a goldfish and cruised past his ear. He thought he heard what Brien shouted and looked around for evidence. He pointed down into the pond. 'You mean this pond is a bomb crater.'

'Yes and it was The Tin Tabernacle cre-ator too!'

Abe ambled across to Brien and gave him a very strange look. He gently swept the buds aside with his shoes, before planting himself, shoving his hands into his pockets, and looking at Brien. He sighed. He didn't know whether to follow the new train of thought pitched to him by Brien.

'Abe?'

'Mm, yes Brien.'

'What is it, Abe, you're disturbed?'

'What do you reckon to the new guy?'

Brien knew Abe had been worrying about the new parish priest – The Monsignor. He couldn't quite put his finger on why.

Brien felt affirmed by the Monsignor's more traditional approach – reminded him of his roots in the faith – and here in Spital too. But he had felt lightened by the genuinely cheerful stuff that Father Hu had used to bring in lots of new and young families. Of course some of his generation put that down as shallow, 'Happy-Clappy' stuff, and tried to inveigle him in their conspiracies against Father Hu. 'The last fellah with his Heavy Metal, his flowing locks and his Harley Davis, was bad enough,' he said feeling a twinge of betrayal, 'just a bit of a boy really. But, this one's even further away from the humble friars. He seems a bit stuck up to me, Abe. Clever man, though. I wonder if they put him in for a bit of stabilising maturity.'

'How do you mean?'

'Well I kind of wonder if they weren't a bit awe-struck by young Hu Stannton. How many fine strong handsome young men have you seen wrapped up in clerical black these many decades? Diocese could see a bishop in the making, there. One to attract the masses back into the ranks, particularly young men. There's never a one teenage lad at the mass these days.'

'What with his Rock Festivals and all?'

'Well I suppose I also was glad of the link to Saint Francis, he had.'

'How's that?' asked Abe.

'Well Father Hu used to preach, well I say preach, but I suppose he whooped and hollered, at them Heavy Metal Rock festivals, you know?'

'I never did!'

'Oh, yes. He was originally a die hard U2 fan, from the oul country,' he winked at Abe, 'but he heard of this old Franciscan Friar, Brother Caesar or something, who had a Heavy Metal band and performed up there with his flowing white beard and in full brown Franciscan habit. Reckon that's why he had the long hair to thrash around. Th'oul Friar turned Father Hu's head away from good catholic U2 into Death Metallic stuff – tall, fair and handsome, on a mission to suicidal kids. You must have heard him go on about it?'

'Come to think of it, he would always engage the lads at The Tin Tab with rock music, but I just thought he was working towards their drug use. Lot of that at them festivals. Sometimes wonder if that's what turned our Ivan's head, you know.'

Abe stopped and Brien let him muse a little before reminding him. 'The new guy?'

'What? Oh, sorry Brien. You say 'stuck up', and I do find him aloof. If you talk to him he only listens, have you noticed that?'

'What more do you want, Abe?'

'Him to talk back!'

Brien laughed, 'Of course, silly me, the 'only listens' went over my head – or should I say in one ear and out the other?' That little joke went over Abe's head – or was he just not with it today? 'Well I wouldn't rightly know about that. I don't want him to be listening to me. I've said all I need to say, I only want God to be listening.'

'Now don't go putting yourself down. We need your intelligent opinion on many matters and you're invaluable to us at The Tin Tab.'

'Well what I say is this, seeing as how you are listening now: the church, and this church, belongs to the people – us – and the priests come and go. It does not belong to the priests ... certainly not Monsignor High 'n' Mighty Green.'

Abe giggled at the outburst from the quiet man. 'Maybe you have it there, Brien. I wonder where he is going to throw his Iron Might next.'

'Like where?'

'Like The Tin Tab.'

'Seems to me he's shown a singular disinterest – not been to one meeting, but I send him all the minutes – that's around twenty sets so far. Am I wasting the paper?'

'Unlike Father Hu, I don't think the young ones would really take to the Monsignor, do you?'

'I don't think they'd take to me, meself, neither, God love 'em – and he does. They can manage without me, that's why I don't come. Mebbe he feels the same, fair play to him. Do you need him?'

'No - we - do - not!'

'Well then, you've got him in the right place.'

'That's what I'm saying.'

It was Brien's turn to smile. 'It's what you're not saying!'

Abe had his hand clamped over his mouth and gave his friend a long look from under his Santa brows. 'He knows nothing about what we do – well maybe he's read all the minutes – but he's not had a word from me, and now he's asking if we've all had our criminal records checked.'

Brien knew exactly what that was, but said it anyway, 'Vetted?'

'You know – the Criminal Record Bureau check. He's asking what we do about it.'

'I think they are calling it 'vetted', now,' said Brien, 'and if they fail you, then you get 'barred.''

'Bloody Jargon is what I call it!'

Brien was nodding. 'But it's for child protecting, that, isn't it?'

'Child Protection ... and Vulnerable Adults.'

'You have neither at The Tin Tab do you?'

Abe wondered if his friend wasn't being a little disingenuous, but nothing showed in his face, only a genuine query, so he thought he'd better explain it to the brains on his Management Committee. 'At The Tin Tab young people's drug and alcohol team we help 15-25 year olds.' He drew a line of dead-heads together with his toe. 'In CRB jargon, the under 19s,' he split the line, 'are children, and the 19-25s are adults, yes, but they're *all* vulnerable, that's what we're in business for isn't it?'

Brien stared at Abe. Abe swept the dead-heads around with his foot. Brien plucked another couple off a bush.

'Is this new, Abe?'

'No, no. Leo Nicholas has all his youth workers checked and he's checked out us volunteers.'

'Not me, Abe.'

'No, not the committee, except those who like Martin and Alice who actually come in and have contact with the young people.'

As Abe's knot tightened inside him, Brien's loosened. Abe was looking but didn't see.

'Well all's well, then, isn't it?'

'I suppose it is, but I wonder what else is he going to be poking his Holy Roman nose into.'

'The money's all straight, you have no worries, there.' Then Brien burst forth with excitement, the way he occasionally does. 'Hey! Mrs Laughton, lovely, lovely lady. Don't you know she's given us all her Winter Fuel Allowance? All of it! She's all opprobrium,' he did his hoity toity voice: 'Do they think I'm a poor beggar woman or something?'

They shared that moment of joy but Brien felt the need to end on a serious note. 'Monsignor Green might put in an appearance at the meeting, then?'

As Abe walked away, Brien noticed the pain in his knees. All good things come to the patient man. But Brien knew he was not really a patient man, so only hoped that all his penitence might just let him scrape into Heaven, even if only on the very last day.

His Father Confessor had defrocked himself. The handsome young man had held out against the womanly wiles for a good while, so maybe good things had come to him before Heaven. Brien thought he knew a patient man when he saw one. Father Hu wouldn't spoil things for him.

Before
Four

Leo Nicholas was particularly taken with the birds at the table – he had hardly noticed them before – they were Talya's birds and she let him know all he needed to about the local avian population – 'strictly for the birds' in his opinion. He watched them bobbing about in silence - double-glazing had done for the dawn chorus - thank goodness.

'Have you seen the weasel?'

He nearly jumped out of his skin. 'Sorry, Looby, what's the matter?'

Talya swept her arm gently down his back.

'What are you doing up?'

'I've been up all night,' she said, 'with your tossing turning, groaning …?'

'I was never groaning.' Leo was worried – not worried, disturbed. Yes – his sleep wasn't worried. His sleep, like him, was disturbed.

Talya turned him gently towards her and pinching the very tip of his goatee between finger and thumb, she held his gaze. His eyes welled up. Leo, well in touch with his feminine side, didn't divert his gaze.

'And they call themselves Christians.'

'Who do?'

'Ruddy Christians, who else?' They burst out laughing and banged foreheads. Now Leo's eyes had another reason to water. 'Coffee?'

'No thanks - it will keep me awake.' They shared a wry smile. 'Whassup, Leo?'

'It's this Criminal Record thing. Lots of people are sceptical about it, I understand that, what with the Big Brother an' all, and of course I see it as a matter of balance, but the God botherers of all people. The Christians think that they are all good and how could anybody question their goodness. They really object to being vetted.'

She held onto him. 'Do you want a couple of days away – I've still got that prize. It'll be out of date soon?'

'I didn't think a pampering weekend was your thing.'

'It is not! Don't want anybody feeling my fat. But I will if it'll give you a break and gets us both some sleep.'

'I don't want all that pampering, sauna stuff – country pub with a selection of Real Ales more my thing.'

'It's worth a lot of money.'

'Mm. I might ring up.'

Before
Five

Hu Stannton could not believe his luck. God made that beautiful bum jiggling about at the cooker, not the devil. He did not believe in luck, he believed in the love of his God and the goodness of human nature … and the devil stalking the earth to steer him away from it. His wife Holly had steered him away from all he held dear. Was she the devil?

He could not see that. The feeling in his heart was a good feeling. The feeling in his heart, yes it was as strong as when he was ordained a priest – all his family, cousins, aunts, half the village, up at Maynooth in their Whitsunday best. The love of God and a Just Pride bursting in his chest.

Ah, when Holly looked up into his eyes and said 'I do …'

How can he have made two opposing vows, God knows? God does know. However, his people don't know.

'My wife, my wife Holly.' Was he ever going to be able to say that without a pricking of the conscience?

It was going to take time, but there will be married priests and the church will maybe let him back in.

He had been a bit hasty though.

How come the luck had come so late? 'How come, Lord?'

Hu Stannton had come to Lady Chatterley a bit late, too, but he was right with Lawrence on the righteousness of nature, including human nature 'How come I never ever saw a bum before I saw you?'

Without turning she scratched at it with the potato peeler and giggled. Then she wiggled.

Hu was bursting out of his pants. All that is holy? Of course it is. He didn't know much about Saint Francis, but he did remember a bit of a reprimand one of his tutors in the seminary at Maynooth gave him. They were discussing conscience and the youthful Hu had asked if it was not just doing what you naturally thought was right.

'That's Pantheism, Brother Hubert,' he was told most forcefully.

Hu had remembered Saint Francis and his love of nature; and everything created by God being good. He got short shrift from the tutor for trying to open up the discussion with his peers. They couldn't have future priests thinking like that. Sex was not good.

Hu was thinking all this while fully staring at Holly's bum. Glancing over her shoulder she saw him.

She wiggled again, but turned and wagged the peeler at him. 'You just sit yourself down there, Hubert Stannton. All good things come to the patient man.'

'Is that what it is?' he thought to himself. 'I've been patient and this is my reward?' Hu thought of all the bums he may have noticed, but hadn't. Mairead had been after him all through Uni – maybe she didn't even have a bum – or tits? Nice eyes. Nice girl. Said her prayers, like him. God Almighty, it was gas to be saying tits and bums and all, even if it was only to himself.

He tried really hard to think of any girls whose bodies he'd ever noticed. 'Eileen Lafferty?' He pinched himself – the only one he could think about was the poor humpty-back thing from primary school.

Jeez, it wasn't a girl's body he saw at the junior seminary. But that was just bad luck on a couple of boys experimenting. It wasn't a couple of girls' bodies that that Brother got an eyeful of through the keyhole, neither.

Hu had a quick wonder at what he felt of Dono Donovan, as they were playing mammies and daddies on the priests' bathroom floor that day. He couldn't picture Dono's face, never mind his … tits? He certainly never saw his bum. He couldn't picture anything.

He could picture nothing except the priest's face and that creepy Brother standing beside him, pointing as the naked Dono and Hu unlocked the bathroom door.

What's a Brother doing peeping at a bathroom keyhole for, anyways? He will have seen a few of the priests' bums, that's for sure. But they hadn't kicked *him* out.

'Colcannon?' said Holly.

'Bless you.'

'Get on with you, Hu.'

'Yoo hoo!' He sidled over and grabbed her round her boobs, but she dug him in the solar plexus.

'I told you about the patient man. Now I'm asking if you want colcannon with the Irish stew.'

'But you've already got me?'

Holly turned on him as he was rubbing his stomach. 'What are you bellyaching about now?'

He had to laugh. 'If you put charms in the colcannon you can find the man you're to marry.'

'But I'd never heard of colcannon before I met you, so does that mean if I put a charm in I'll find out who I'll marry next?'

That was a step too far. He knew she had been 'married' before. Was he just a phase to Holly? She didn't mean it, but she had said it. He was cut to the quick and Holly noticed, so she threw the peeler in the sink and wrapped his head in her bosom.

Before
Six

Recently dubbed Detective Sergeant Iruna Bahadur took a look around her new CID office 'Oop Narth' in Clayford-cum-Spital ('nobody says Spital, Duck') and felt warm about the way she had been received, by men and women alike, but mostly the men. Yes she flicked and shook out her blue ebony mane and looking round, yes, they looked – 'corny, but effective, Iruna.'

She had moved up from Oxford, hoping to change her luck with men, or rather with women.

She had had no luck with men, but women found her extremely attractive. This was not a problem, she was flattered, but she needed a bloke. In fact she couldn't deny that the lesbians were a problem. She was open-minded; indeed anyone would recognise that as a Bangladeshi, it hurt to be herself in an oppressed minority, hurt so much that, her name Iruna Bahadur aside, she always hoped to be taken as a white girl.

Let's get it right – she was a white girl. Real 'white' girls, after all, are pink on the whole, or white with tan freckles, or even tanned all over. She considered herself having classic Snow White colouring – smooth white skin, jet-black hair, and cheeks she could rouge. She thought she understood what the one bloke, Justin Stoddard, had told her – she was 'too pretty.' How come he didn't fancy her, then? They had become really good pals, but never kissed. He said it was about chemistry, between them – the absence of it. She had cried, mostly in frustration.

They had been in so many clinches together, got hold of each others parts, panted fiercely into each others faces, but all and only in the dojo on Iffley Road. They had taken up judo around the same time, soon after sixth form, and progressed through the belts together. He had taken judo further, because she had moved with the force. She had achieved all her black belt grades and basically only kept up the sport for keep-fit.

They had walked down Jackdaw Lane, out along the Cherwell and Isis, but he never held her hand. They had had many a drink together – all the way from the gym to the Fir Tree –'Dojo Loco' – up to the Hobgoblin on Cowley Road where she caught her bus home to Blackbird Leys. They never had a peck, or even a Christmas kiss. (She wouldn't mention Eide, or Divali).

There had been a couple of long separations: she had been up and down the Thames Valley Force. After the mandatory couple of years on the beat in Oxford, she had served a couple more in Banbury, then plain clothes in Henley, before a final tour back in Saint Aldate's where she earned her stripes, and a move onto a fast track.

It was just not in her to make the first move, so one evening, excited but frustrated after solving the mystery of the racing boat sabotage, and getting full-on, tongue-down-throat gratitude from that bull-dyke oarswoman – the first eight's Stroke, she simply asked Justin what was wrong with her.

21

She floored him. No need to get hold of his belt, he was knocked out.

'Iruna, I'm so sorry, I didn't think you looked at me like that. I thought we were mates, pals, muckers.' He shook his head so much she thought it might fall off. He stopped and his eyes welled up. 'So, so sorry. Did you think ... I was just leading you on? So ... sorry, 'runa!' He had reached out, taken her hand and kissed it. Only her hand. The only kiss he ever gave her.

When he pulled himself together, he told her about the chemistry. She couldn't believe it and cried. She was pretty drunk - needed to have been, to have got all that out. Justin had piled her into a taxi and taken her home to Blackbird Leys, well not home ... even drunk, she knew her dad mustn't see her in that state. She would sneak up and see how the land lay. He might be on nights. Her mum would laugh.

What was wrong with the Thames Valley lads? A month after the chemistry revelation, she had a long talk with Justin and he had told her how he had been out with girls, mostly, but not only, when she had been away in Henley and Banbury. 'I wasn't betraying you 'runa! But you know what? I bet people did think we were an item. I am so, sorry, my attitude maybe did lose you some opportunities ... maybe people thought you were taken?'

'Oh, I had my opportunities all right, Justin!' She started to giggle.

'What are you saying, 'runa?' He looked hurt.

Continuing to giggle, she told him all about the lesbians. He didn't laugh or even smile for a while, but they ended up in stitches together.

'So I've made my mind up – clean break – I am moving oop Narth. I'm going to see if I can snare mesen a blork!'

Justin didn't smile at her phoney northerner impression.

She put her hand on his, but only for a moment before he withdrew it. 'Justin!'

'Iruna. We have had such a great friendship – you have been the very best mate I've ever had. It is totally ... only ... well I suppose ... I can't do anything but wish you all the very best, and ... we'll keep in touch?'

She was considering herself rather fortunate. Yes she had made a leap in the dark and now she knew it was a step into the light.

Before
Seven

Leo was standing at his office window ostensibly watching ducks mating. The legend was apparently true - ducks did appear to mate through gang rape. This offended the Safeguarder's sensibilities and he wanted to open his window and stone the drakes.

However, he was more preoccupied with his recent visit to The Tin Tab. Abe's record and lack of clearance was bearing down on him.

Now Abe was back in Gina's chair again. Again! Elbows on knees, he was looking at the floor. He had been hoping the record checks would just fade away. 'It's Simone. What have you done with her?'

'It's with HR.'

Simone Dunne was a Tin Tab youth worker. She had been in from the start of the youth service's partnership with the church. She was not however, Leo's favourite sort of worker. She came over all 'Lady Bountiful', helping the 'poor young people.' There was an unwritten dress code – casual to put the poorest of young people at ease – but she insisted on a floral print frock and high heels, and her hair in a Maggie Thatcher perm.

She knew her stuff about Benefits and always pointed it out. She was forever interrupting her colleagues while they were getting to the bottom of the issues that had taken the young people into the drug scene. After Abe, for a third time in a year, had to physically separate Simone from a colleague, he had asked Leo to see if she could fit somewhere else. Leo had naively hoped that she would welcome a 'nice office job away from the yobbos.'

Abe was hoping for a bit more. 'Come on Leo – it's me – your old mucker, Abe.'

Leo twiddled his Trotsky. 'HR have given her some reception work in an office, nothing to do with me.'

'A lot to do with me, and I think maybe you, if you're not careful.'

Leo tried to not react. A quick sideways glance may have sufficed.

'Well either you or me – preferably both of us – should be looking at replacing her.'

'I can't replace her while she's on my staffing kit and working for you.'

'But she's not working for me,' Abe pleaded.

'That's your choice.'

Abe hadn't seen this in his old friend before. 'Leo? What's the matter? You can tell old Abe.'

Leo didn't seem to be moving. 'You mean it's not your choice? You told me to take her out; she's upsetting the whole place – and the kids – with her brusque attitude, not to mention looking down her nose and her tittle-tattle.'

'I thought you had somewhere for her and we'd get someone else when she accepts.'

'When she accepts. But she's not doing. She's playing for a hand-out.'

'Never!'

'Union man's told her it's Constructive Dismissal. I'm in a bit of hot water for taking her off your hands. It's County that'll have to pay, not The Tin Tab.'

'Oh, Leo, that woman, and after all the support we've given her. We could have got rid of her years ago, but we were too nice – now she's biting our hand?'

'Yep, 'fraid so.'

Abe's laugh was completely devoid of humour. 'When I said, 'A lot to do with me, and I think maybe you,' I didn't see that at all. It's the new priest, well not so new – would you believe it's been two years?'

It had been over two years since the previous parish priest, Father Hubert Stannton a young man, a very young man in today's diminishing and ageing catholic clergy, had left and got married. He had been very keen to support the work of The Tin Tab and got involved at all levels. He regularly visited the unit in his own old parish hall, a corrugated iron Nissen hut, got to know the young people and had an annual collection at mass.

Father Hu had been replaced by Monsignor Green. He had apparently been brought out of retirement and was not a little disgruntled about that.

'But we've not seen him at The Tin Tab meetings yet, have we?'

'No,' said Abe, 'but I get this horrible feeling all that's about to change. Simone's got onto the Monsignor about Father Hu … and me.'

'Father, You … and me?'

'Leo! You've got to stop that.'

Though he could see this was not a time for levity, he didn't want Abe to be worrying himself. He felt it was his duty to save this saintly volunteer from HR Issues. Yes, he would use the term 'saintly', despite himself. In the atheist lexicon, he didn't think there was a nice word for 'saintly.'

He knew about Abe's record and he, along with Father Hu, had the secret covenant - they would ignore it. Abe had been working selflessly for the drug fixated kids of the town for nearly twenty years, and remained frustrated that no organisation would support emergency beds for youngsters. He knew for a fact that the rough sleeper numbers, even in deepest winter, would rarely drop below twenty. All five hostels had revolving doors spinning kids out at the whiff of drugs or booze. And needle exchange – the kids just wouldn't go to the clinic at the Hospital. Leo felt quite safe not needing to get Abe barred, in just the same way he didn't feel it required clearing himself. It would be an insult to insist on it.

'Simone doesn't know about …?'

'No, not at all. It's not that. She's claiming that Father Hu never supported her like a priest should, during her trouble and that was the root of her trouble with The Tin Tab.'

'She's not a Catholic, is she?'

'Not at all. Pretty anti, always was, I reckon.' Then quietly, 'worse than you.'

Leo ignored that. Abe had dropped a stone into Leo's pool. He wasn't to know what kind of a splash it would make, but tranquil it should not be. 'Bit of a mux-ip, Eh? Father Hu, you and me have an understanding. That actually shouldn't matter, but Simone's little stir wakes the sleeping giant who lashes out and hits … well he might hit us.' He straightened himself up and swivelled round to face Abe. 'Father Hu's gone, so now there's only you and me with an understanding. Understand?

'Actually Leo, I don't. Where are you going to stand and have I got to walk away?'

'I'm so sorry Abe. After all your years of service.'

'You mean I have? I have to walk away? How can I explain that?'

'Where is that Father Hu, anyway?'

'He's around here somewhere – bit brazen, if you ask me.'

'Is that him or the lass?' asked Leo.

'That hussy. She's certainly brazen. I bet she went in there and had him in the sacristy before he could get his vestments off.'

'Blimey, Abe. I bet that makes you feel bitter?' He saw Abe's jaw muscles clenching and colour rising. Was he restraining himself?

Abe looked up and gave a quick flick of the brows. 'Que sera.' He sighed. 'Seems a bit like he's having his cake and eating it, all in this life. I'd give a few bob to be there when he approaches the pearly gates – if he's got the brass neck to even bother.'

'Does not seem fair in the just rewards kind of thing.'

'Not for me to judge is it.'

'Nobody's stopping me, though. I think it abso-blinkin-lutely stinks. You deserve an explanation from the slimey slug.'

Abe didn't expect that. 'Why do you care?'

'I care a lot. You guys reckon you don't deserve your God's love and are always repenting and that. The priests keep reminding you that you are bad and you must seek forgiveness. They have not a care in the world. They only work on Sundays. Women seem to throw themselves at them, but they'd rather have little boys…'

'Leo!'

'…and after all that they just go off with the pick of the crop – I heard she is very pretty.'

'Leo, I don't want to go into all that. It's my church, not the priests'. They are simply a vessel to bring us God's Message – and some of them are a bit cracked.'

'You're too soft on him. Seeing as how he isn't going to have to do any explaining at the pearly gates, wouldn't you like to make him face up to his apostrophe?' He smiled.

'You've lost me.'

'Apostasy.'

'Nope?' Abe was blinking and shaking his head.

'It's what he's done – Apostasy – given up on his previous religious belief?'

'For an atheist, you know more about religion than I do. Anyhow, who says? We'll have married priests before so long anyway. What with the shortages and that, they may beg him to come back. In twenty years, he'll still be twenty years younger than most of the priests left in the diocese, now.'

Leo stood, then stepped across to look down on Abe. 'We need to find out exactly where we stand with your clerics, don't we Abe?'

Before
Eight

Brien had noticed the Angel – standing watching him after the weekday mass a few years before, as he was bedding out the front borders, He averted his gaze, but she sidled over, the hussy, far too overdressed in a pencil skirted navy suit, stilettos and some sort of thing on top of her stack of blonde hair. Surely not a mantilla – outmoded even in the twentieth century? He studiously split up a clump of primulas, hoping she would just go away.

'That priest of yours is wasted in a long black habit.'

Brien wasn't rising to that. He could smell her but only looked at her stilettos. Who did she think she was with her lispy, husky voice – and smoking in the church yard too.

'What's he called – the fancy Father, Eh?'

'His Holiness Cardinal Otto Von Trap, on a visitation so he is.'

'You ... you cheeky little man.'

'Well if you knew already, what're you asking for?'

He didn't look to see her nonplussed expression, but caught her ash on the back of his glove and looked up so see her sashaying back to the gate. She was an absolute corker, but he couldn't admit that to his consciousness.

Abe Grant came over. 'Where does she think she's going – Breakfast at Tiffany's?'

Brien looked at him – reading his face. 'I've written to the Bishop about having girls as Altar servers.'

Abe smiled at his old friend – the innocence of it – if it were only girls those Irish priests had been distracted by.

Brien went back to his planting. Something stirred in his head. His little Colleen had always been his angel, but she no longer wanted her disgusting father in her part of Heaven.

The joy at the thought of her was instantly smacked down by the pain of her loss. Now the church meant more to him than his angel did, on his knees in the church garden, on his knees in the muck. He plunged his hand into the well-worked soil. The muck, the Good Earth.

Before
Nine

At the next Tin Tab young people's drug and alcohol team management committee meeting, Leo was not impressed by the first words from the Monsignor's mouth.

First impressions were very important to him. The Monsignor had apparently taken no notice of the meeting at all, having his hands in the sleeves of his soutane, his already thin lips constantly pursed and only occasionally noting who was speaking. This compounded the impression Leo had already gained that the parish priest had his own agenda – a hidden one.

'Chair, may I enquire of the youth officer how this awful name 'The Tin Tab' came about? Doesn't give the church a very good name.'

Leo was wondering what kind of a name the Monsieur thought the church might have and barely restrained himself from asking. He was considering how he could deign not to answer when Abe replied from the chair anyway: 'Why would you like him to do that Father? It's nothing to do with him.'

'I'm assuming it's a youth service project we are helping with, that's all.'

'To assume,' Leo interjected, 'is to make an ass of you and me,' and he added a flourish to his doodle of a paisley crucifix.

Abe suppressed a smile and continued: 'It's named after our old, new, old, church, Father ...'

'A Tin?' The Very Reverend Monsignor Nicholas Green blustered.

Abe continued: 'The original church had been a tin hut, which the good people nick-named 'The Tin Tabernacle.' It served as the parish Hall until the new one was built and, standing empty, we begged it for the base of a service for the young drug users. The Tab bit stuck, too, because LSD tabs were all the rage and Tabs is also short for Tablets – pills, of course.'

Brien gave a little cough.

'Maybe I haven't got that right, Brien?' Abe frowned innocently.

'Not quite' swallowed Brien. 'The Convent is over a hundred years old Abe, Father, founded to serve Spital Workhouse, now also long gone. In the war a jettisoned bomb landed in the Convent garden and blasted all the church windows out – basically damaged all that side of the church. It wasn't going to be fixed for the duration, but they were flinging up Nissen huts all over the country and one of the parish grandees gave us a bit of land and bought a hut for our temporary church – 'The Tin Tabernacle.' The name stuck.'

'Thanks Brien – that's what you mentioned in the garden that day. I get it now. So, Father, the name stuck, because the clients know who we are and what we do. It's a Catholic charity. The youth service has recognised the quality of service we volunteers have offered. *They* have come in with *us*, because of the unprecedented access we can offer to the most vulnerable young people in the county.' He looked across at Brien for the nod of approval, and likewise to Leo.

'Oh, jolly good,' chortled the Monsignor mirthlessly. 'Fair enough – quite humorous. I haven't been to meetings before - for which I apologise - but I have taken an interest via the very informative minutes sent to me by Mr Divine.'

'De-*veen*,' Brien said, too quietly for the Monsignor to hear; but The Very smiled graciously at him, nevertheless.

'The title is a minor issue, though I think titles generally are not insignificant,' continued the Monsignor, whose claim to be *Very* Reverend had been lost in 1969 – well before he may have been doffed with it. 'But I have two much more serious questions … issues. The first is the question of increased stress on safeguarding by The Disclosure and Barring Scheme, and the other is the issue of Mrs Simone Dunne, about whom I would like some clarification.'

Leo, Abe and Brien felt this below the belt, each for a different reason, and each hiding the effect from the meeting. Leo also felt his collar was a little tight – he did rarely wear a tie.

Abe took the helm and shut the Monsignor down. 'They aren't items for this meeting, Father. I will come over and explain to you in the week, if that is okay?'

Afterwards Leo took the opportunity to say to Abe simply 'we've got to talk,' before scooting off home.

Abe on the other hand felt the need to avoid going home and asked his old friend Brien to have a pint with him.

Over his half of Shandy he said 'Stickler.'

After sipping his glass of tap water – with lemon and ice – Brien muttered 'Scheister.'

'Do you think he's had hold of Father Hu, yet?'

'I'd be very surprised. He'd be too worried about tarnishing his papal mitre, or whatever crowning glory he fancies for himself, to even be in the same room as that heretic. Sure I was really tickled that not a single person referred to him as Monsignor, at all.'

'I bet that Simone does.'

They both had a chuckle.

'Do you know exactly what her beef is, Abe?'

Abe cocked his head. 'It's got to be us rejecting her at The Tin Tab, I think. She is employed by the County, that's how Leo has got her a post somewhere else, but in fact her substantive post, as they call it, is with us. Leo's a bit miffed with me, because she's got her union onto HQ and Leo's managers are onto him. She's after a pay out, he reckons, and anything extra will come from county, not us.'

'Oh is that it?' mused Brien. 'I thought mebbes there was something else a bit, well, fishy?'

Abe tugged at his collar and raised his eyebrows. 'Father Hu went a bit above and beyond the call of duty. That was before he realised Simone was wheedling away at something.'

'You don't mean …'

'Not at all – not her. Mother of God bless us all. No, just a bit too much of a sensitive ear, playing at confessionals, sort of thing.'

'Is that what Monsignor Green's got hold of?'

'I don't rightly know, but it's the only thing I can guess that she can have from the church angle, especially as she was so anti-church before, remember?' Abe was back to his own predicament. 'We don't really know how Father Hu stands now, or which way he will turn if things get dirty.'

'Someone needs to cut him off at the pass.'

They looked at each other for a minute and then simultaneously said 'Leo?'

Before
Ten

Brien had made his mind up to see how Leo could support his friend Abe. Full of apprehension he tip-toed up the stairs and gave a quiet tap on the youth office door. Gina knew him of course, she knew everybody – even the ones she had never met – she indicated and let him find his way across to Leo's door. He had time to take in the poor office – worse than any he'd had, even in builders' yards.

He was impressed how attentive Leo was to him.

'Ah, Mr De-*veen* how can I help?'

'Very gracious – you did hear – Mr Nicholas ...' Brien raised his eyebrows. '... Leo?'

'Of course.' Leo, indicating the chair, smiled at the rather stiff little man. 'Bit of a stickler you've got there.'

They talked through the Monsignor at the management meeting and had a bit of a giggle about how stuffy he was. Brien had to push to get round to the Monsignor's concerns, however. As well as the two the Monsignor had stated himself, Brien had to add his concern about Father Hu – did Leo think the new parish priest may have been in touch with his predecessor?

Leo was aware that things were bad for Abe, but Brien felt the need to stress this more.

'They have never been worse, Mr Nicholas. Abe is the whole boiler-room of this great service to young people. The Committee is aware, nay afraid, that you have big cuts to make – so why should you support a unique project that other services do not?' He paused. 'Simple question. Abe is at his wit's end, and we are worried he could walk away. I personally don't think anyone can fill his shoes; and you won't give any more support – probably have to reduce?'

Brien knew this was not such a big issue as the Lottery were paying some of the staff for another two years yet, but Brien was not aware that the Barring Scheme was worrying Abe, and he was skirting round asking about himself.

Leo though, knew Abe was worried about his Criminal Record and thought Brien was too. He thought he had better clarify the new Disclosure Scheme: Only people directly in contact with young people on a more than occasional basis, or alone with them, needed to be cleared.

That excluded Brien, but he said that maybe he should become more hands-on, to support Abe in particular. Brien didn't know much about the Simone issue that the Monsignor had brought up anyway, and Leo did not enlighten him. He was shocked when Leo moved into a gratuitous attack on paedophile priests and Father Hu being one, but being an Irishman himself, Brien decided he had better take that on the chin and bear up.

Leo had accepted that graciously enough for Brien to move to ask to have himself vetted.

But there Brien really did fall down. He thought that his conviction for a minor offence almost twenty years ago, and his punishment of just two years probation, would surely be deemed to have been spent. He was shocked that a List 99 existed. Accusations, however unsubstantiated they might be, without conviction even, got some people onto the list – it was forever and he would be on it.

Almost wrong footed by Brien's disclosure, Leo recovered and using the pretext that maybe Brien might *not* be excluded, he nailed him anyway. Brien didn't lie, but he didn't tell the whole truth. 'Excellent references from my parish in London from before I came back here.'

'A conviction, then,' Leo tried affirming.

Brien went very pale now. He tried the 'doesn't every father love his daughter?' trick and, 'on the telly – sex in everything.'

Leo was adding, 'You know me - I'm that nice man who gives out Holy Communion at your church. Come along with me.'

Had Brien a hidden agenda? Did *Brien* know Abe's record? Was he thinking of threatening Leo – get himself vetted and also *not* barred? Brien struck Leo as cut from a different cloth from the run-of-the-mill paedo. He thought of him as he thought of Abe – a man who realised his mistake and was a genuine penitent. There it was again – damned religion-speak. But is a crime ever a mistake?

'So Brien, sorry to appear dogged, but if there is no record, nobody's going to bar you from helping out at The Tin Tab. Was there a conviction?'

'Several years after she had left home the daughter told people she used to sleep with me. I shrugged and said 'what's wrong with that?'' He stopped, still looking Leo in the eye. He worked hard on the inscrutable look. He had almost a couple for decades of practice. People had dirty minds. 'Sexualised, see Leo?'

Brien lifted an open palm, as well as his eyebrows and said 'I just said, to take away any pain the daughter may have had, for whatever reason, I wouldn't know, well I just said, if sleeping with my daughter is sexual assault, I am guilty, I'm guilty.' I have to tell the truth.' He checked to see if Leo believed him. 'Two years Probation was all.'

Leo was twisting his Trotsky. He took a look out of the window. Grey skies. 'Ah. Well.' He pushed his small-lensed glasses right up to his eyes. Brien felt himself under a magnifying glass. 'Now as it is a conviction, and it is for sexual anything on a minor, I have to say, it isn't worth us bothering, I'm afraid. HR just won't have it. I am so sorry.'

Brien hardly took breath before moving directly on. He needed to find Father Hu. He decided to approach by having another go about Simone: she had definitely rattled Abe. Brien felt unable ask him why. 'Now we have Simone throwing accusations … about stuff that happened over two years ago … that we can't check up about … but maybe you could, Leo?'

'I see.'

Brien was not so sure he really could see.

'I suppose I really should try to get Hu's side of the story,' Leo said. 'County is implicated by Simone's allegations.' He looked at the sky. It was a gloomy old day. 'Have you got his address?'

'I have not, sorry. I was surprised he's still round here, but Abe says he's working for the corporation housing department. You're the corporation too – so I thought you could look him up.'

So many questions were burning into Leo's head; who knew what about whom that could implicate him in a 'cover-up' if the Criminal Record Bureau really turned the screw? With all the redundancy notices out there he needed a clear mind to see to his own people.

'We need some explanation,' he said. 'I have an inkling of an idea. Fancy a bit of pampering for yourself?'

'What's that, a hare you've set running?'

'You're running with me. I'd like to get Saint Hu in a room to tell you, me and Abe what his game is.'

It had been a roller coaster ride for Brien and he left with his stomach churning: he shouldn't have been surprised that Big Brother would still be watching him after all these years, but Leo had let him down gently.

His heart sinking, Leo watched the man shamble out of his office. Brien crossed the communal area to the door to the stairs, head down, feet scuffing the carpet. It was not fair, Leo thought. This man had done something – maybe only one thing – a lot less serious than Abe – but he could never be forgiven. And here he was making a real disclosure, and only in order to support a mate.

Where was he? Leo tracked across and glimpsed Brien take out a packet, light up a black cigarette, and blow a satisfied cloud up to the heavens, one more puff, nipped it out and giving a quick blow, shot a look directly up to Leo's window – and Leo ducked. Leo ducked out of sight. Not what Leo was expecting? He took a careful peep. Brien checked the cigarette was out, blew it again, pocketed it and turning, walked nonchalantly away.

Leo's secretary was straight back at her desk: 'Eyup, Gina, what did they call those black cigarettes that were all the rage – before my time, but when you were a lass? Were they cheroots?'

'I'm not sure, Leo. Not smoked in my circle. I saw them in old films when I was a child,' she coughed. 'Weren't the black ones Gauloise? Or Sobranies?'

'Sobranies, that's it, yes,' said Leo. Gauloise are the smelly French ones – Gaul, de Gaul, of France, see? D'accord. Tres Bien. Get me Simone's file, silver plate, Gina?'

The Area youth officer, putting aside the Redundancy Notice, 'only covering their backs Leo – not you', stood contemplating his prospects of promotion: could he be the first ever County youth officer to resist the power enough to not be corrupted?

'Come the Revolution,' thought Leo. 'A coup after a popular uprising?'

Leo was wondering if the Russian Revolution was the perfect crime. The aim if not the end Stalin achieved, certainly seemed to justify the means. He found himself humming 'Lara's Theme.' People had to die – but only those who made others' lives not worth living. 'Off with their heads.' Pull down the palaces and Cathedrals. Ban the religions for opiating the masses with their masses.

He lined-up the whole Management team in front of the bin depot wall at the other side of the canal. He closed one eye. Not one of them had any track record in the field – got jobs from established secondments, or after carrying out a pet project for a Councillor. What went up never came down – except for the eventual cropper that their replacement never seemed to learn from.

He saw that the really able workers, who also knew what they were talking about, should not have done - they should not have talked! Clever talk inevitably showed up the dimwits in charge.

Leo, with his background in heavy industry, was not at all comfortable with 'meeting speak' and jargonese: 'Point of order, Madame Chair,' 'Speaking to a paper,' – what a load of cobblers.

Leo had his staff in thrall with the way he could always wrap the hooligans round his little finger. 'How is it you get them to do what they don't want to?' they would ask.

But Leo and his lions were definitely led by donkeys, 'present company excluded,' he smiled. However, he knew that even if they were the strongest, largest, most Ofstedly successful team in the county, he knew his little army would not carry out a coup.

Leo's thoughts turned to that other organisation that needed a revolution – and a bloodless, velvet one would not satisfy Comrade Nicholas. Rome and its empire had continued for over a millennium after the Vandals and Visigoths are supposed to have done for it. Just re-brand and carry on. Mesmerise the faithful with the smoke and bells; systematise the oppression of women by giving them a virgin goddess of their own; and take their virginity for themselves.

'Want to get ahead? Get a hat!' and the more stupid and useless, the better. Skull cap? Biretta – was there ever a sillier headwear outside of Halloween? Yes, the crown, the Mitre, oh and one of them with gold embroidery, jewels and tails.

Heads must roll.

The symbols of oppression – look at poor Brien and Abe, spending a lifetime on their knees, kow-towing to clerical requests that are ordained by diocesan edict, diluted from Papal Bull.

Clerics in fancy dress facing down their crimes and trusting a quiet cover-up, and a transfer out, to tend fresh fields of virginal lilies.

'More tea Vicar?' Hu Stannton was having his cake and eating it.

Leo's revolution had to start somewhere.

Before
Eleven

Simone Dunne was languishing in the office at E2E. Young people at risk with drugs and falling out with family were her mission, but the 'unemployable' layabouts in this project were scroungers to the marrow – she couldn't picture one of them making an 'Entry 2 Employment.'

The kids were rude to her, called her Maggie, Maggie Thatcher. She thought it right – there was a likeness. Simone was taller and thinner, but 'Tory streak of piss' was hurtful. She liked to keep herself presentable. State of their Mums – they wouldn't know any different. Leo, and Abe for that matter, had both asked her to dress informally for the druggie kids at The Tin Tab. But she wasn't having it. She had standards and they should have them too. And she wasn't going to let Leo get away with it, sweeping her under the carpet! The Lady's not for sweeping. She had started at the Tin Tab the first day they moved into the old tin tabernacle. She thought they ought to call it something sensible, but Abe went with what the young people called it – coming down to their level, she thought.

She had reckoned she knew that Abe of old, reckoned he used to call himself Mickey Grant, and a bit of a rotter, if she wasn't mistaken. Could be his brother she supposed. Cousin? There had been a gap of twenty years since he had given her the brush off at the Broken Wheel nightclub – tall handsome gangster that he was. When she met him again, the bald paunchy man in his glasses had a likeness she couldn't put her finger on. She said 'Abe *Grant* you say?'

A few weeks later she had broached the subject again: 'Any relation to Mickey Grant?'

He'd laughed at that; quite genial. 'Ha, Mickey Grant. He was a bit of lad wasn't he? I suppose he must've been some sort of relation.' And he had giggled some more. Abe was so genial that the resemblance faded over the years. He was a real gent, a gentle giant. He had been so sympathetic when her Jim had walked out on her. She hadn't been much use to them at The Tin Tab in that period, but he had kept her on, and he had kept the Leader-in-Charge off her back. Carol was such a bitch – tried to get Abe round her little finger. When that didn't work she had got Leo Nicholas to do the dirty work.

Simone didn't hold it against Abe, but in the end he gave up fighting for her. Well, she did think he had been a bit weak, not the Mickey Grant she remembered; or was he?

He had disappeared off the scene pretty suddenly, back then. Where to? Prison? Rang a bell. Didn't he get done for killing his wife in the end? Could Abe be a killer? That was almost laughable.

Simone daydreamed of Abe's face with a mop-top of sandy hair, sideburns and 'tache. She looked across and saw her own sixty-year-old face in the glass partition. How she had changed in … forty odd years. Could she be taken for her cousin Julia?

Mickey Grant, the first real man she'd ever danced with. He wouldn't remember her – teenybopper in a beehive.

How do you find these things out?

'Andrew Nicholas' office.' It was that Gina – Leo's Gatekeeper.

'It's Simone. Is Leo there please, Gina, I need a word?'

The line went quiet. Gina had her hand over the mouthpiece. Bound to be asking him 'if he's in.' Bound to come back and palm Simone off, yet again.

'Yes, Simone, Leo was about to call you, hang on, I'll hand you over.'

'Simone, I'm hearing good things about you from E2E – they say you're a wonder at the admin.'

She was flattered, but said, 'That's not much, coming from them though, Leo. As far as I can make out with this lot, it's the blind leading the blind. None of the workers can spell – I have to interpret what they want me to type. They can't add up – the accounts were a right mess, but I've rescued them.'

'So you're feeling really valued there, then I am so glad it's been a good move for you.'

Simone knew a wolf when she saw one. She wasn't fooled by the afghan coat. 'Leo, is Abe Grant police cleared?'

Lucky for Leo they were on the phone – she wouldn't be able to see if he had fallen off his chair. 'What's that you say, Gina?' he shouted. 'Oh, sorry, Simone, I'll have to call you back.'

Simone heard the phone click. She rang back. Engaged.

Gina put her phone down. 'That was Monsignor Green, Leo. He has asked if I can let him know who is actually police cleared at The Tin Tab.'

'Tell him to mind his own blimmin' business.' Leo chomped through a mouthful of sandwich. He had been standing at the window eating his lunch and digesting the call from Simone. Turning back to Gina he mellowed. 'I suppose he can only mean the volunteers – and the church's volunteers at that. We clear them too don't we?'

'Well I said it would be easy. I can just send it to him, can't I?'

Leo was back at the window again and appeared to have not heard.

'Leo?'

'Yes Gina?'

'You weren't listening, were you?'

'Monsieur Green,' he said. This was true. It was all he needed.

'O-kay?' she hesitated.

'Eh? Okay what?' he said shaking his head.

'Leo! I'll send the Monsignor my list of *all staff* and volunteers that we have already cleared at The Tin Tab. There can't be any harm in that. No need to wind the man up Leo, now, is there?'

Leo stared at Gina, paranoid thoughts running through his head. *'No, there is nothing wrong with that. Totally transparent, that's the jargon. Why could Gina possibly think he was frozen to the spot?'* He mumbled something, while he had a wander and wondered some more.

'Naah, I'll go and see him, see what he really wants.'

Gina was not wondering who was in charge round here, she knew she was. She took a breath and gave a look. 'You won't let me down will you?'

Leo could also wonder who was in charge, but no way could he verbalise it. If he fancied himself as a great man, he knew who the great woman behind him was.

'Now look, Gina.' He noticed the look she gave his raised finger and put it in his pocket. 'Sorry. Er, we have to clear all of our workers, obviously, but we don't *have* to clear any volunteers, but we do some.'

She assented stressing, 'we do clear *some.*'

'There's the problem - some, not all. Nostra Señor is going to be thinking *And why not?* then asking, see?'

'You do get yourself into some scrapes, Leo. I told you not to do for one what you can't do for everyone. But what Abe wants, Abe gets for his Tin Tab, eh?'

He rubbed his chin. 'OK so we now need to tell the Monsignor that with the huge increase in costs against the public sector cuts, we can no longer afford it and sorry but he *now* has to clear all his own people. And if you let on,' Leo finished, pushing his point home with a shove of some papers on Gina's desk, 'he will ask how come we can clear Alice and Martin, but not the rest.'

Gina felt she was being fobbed off with that argument, but let him off with, 'Alright, Leo, I'll wait until you've seen him, then.' She had to have the complete and final say, though, so drawing the diary towards her she asked, 'When will that be?'

What had Simone started?

Before
Twelve

It dawned on Hu that he saw this Angel first. It was the first time he could recall doing that – they always sneaked up on him – and anyway they were always fallen angels, weren't they, the devils?

No, this was an angel – and she wasn't looking at him.

When he gave her the communion, she looked at the host.

When he gave her the host he followed the host to her lips. She put the host onto her tongue and her lips closed slowly round it. Her eyes shut momentarily then opened and zapped him.

Surely not? Who zapped who?

Mrs Mahoney had to 'whisht' him to get her host. She saw him.

The Angel wasn't there. Well it wouldn't be – it had appeared – that's what they do. An apparition doesn't hang around. That didn't stop him looking around during the silent communion prayers and again after mass. He noticed that Mrs Maloney was not letting him think she hadn't noticed him standing there zapped.

But Oh God Almighty, she appeared again the next day, then not for a week.

Holly knew what she was doing. She had zapped him. This one wasn't getting away from her. She hung around after mass inspecting the Religious Pamphlets – Lives to the Saints, mostly. Is there a Saint Holly, or is the Holly sainted because it's part of Christmas? She supposed 'Holly Mary' made hers a Christian name. She laughed how her Dad would call 'Holy Mary' when he was getting round her. Of course he wouldn't say that when he was trying to get into her.

Holly was mightily pissed off with all the holy nuns and priests peering out at her. 'You'll not make me feel guilty you frumpy, frosty knickers.'

She was however distracted by the rough looking lass, Saint Maria Goretti, and jumped as the hunk, so predictably whispered, 'You don't come here often?' She nearly burst trying to keep that one in. She lifted Maria Goretti right up before her eyes and stared hard to get a grip on herself.

'A real Saint for our time, that one.'

She lowered the pamphlet slowly and turned, slowly, slowly, to give him the full on body, face and all. 'How's that Father?'

'She was strangled and stabbed because she wouldn't let her lodger have sex with him.'

'What's wrong with sex father? Aren't we all born through sex – even your mother and father had sex to beget you.'

Fr Hubert Stannton withstood that assault on his battlements. That was something to be proud of. Maybe it was because she was no angel after all. No she was no angel – she was still standing, full in body and soul, right before him. And what a body. He took a breath. He tried. It became a gasp strangled into a cough into the sleeve of his soutane. He drew out the ample handkerchief.

He started again. 'Are you new to the parish? I see you have been a few times.'

A few times. He had noticed her every time. She had been three times. Twice is not a few; three is the minimum for a few; so he had noticed her every time – every time. Her eyes thought about welling up, but she sent that idea away. She gave him a proper close up look, close upwards – he was very tall, light and handsome. Fair. A fair man. She felt she could probably count on him being fair in both senses of the word. Will he move through the fair with me? 'It will not be long love, 'til our wedding day.'

'What's that you say?'

'Not long, Father. Not long … have I been down this way?' said Holly through a giggle. She was working on a lie. 'I think I been here longer than you though, but not for a while.'

'You have me there, dear.'

'I'll have you yet,' she thought, 'but you haven't had me.' 'So I have you do I?' She said and patted the little book on his chest with a closed fist. 'Sparing your blushes Father, I think I was conceived here, but we moved away and now I'm back again. Where were you when I was …being conceived?' She knew it wasn't true, but she liked the hint at her Mammy and Dadda living there now.

Father Hu was not for crumbling. 'Well I suppose that would be Mayo?'

'Mayo. Now you could put some flavour into a woman's life if you weren't in that old black habit. That's a bad habit for a catch like you. Get out of that habit.'

How dare she? Oh, she dare. She was in Heaven. Angels do not fear to tread. He'd noticed her every move. She had him there – there in the palm of her hand.

She moved the little fist away, peeped in it, lifted it before his face and slowly unlaced the fingers; slowly moved her face to the palm; slowly pursed her lips; and slowly blew in his face.

When he opened his eyes the apparition had gone. He looked across at the Lady Altar. 'And the Angel declared unto Mary …'

As his dutiful wife laid his coffee before him, Hu pulled her to him and, looking up, narrowed his eyes and said 'Hey, Holly, did you ever pay for that Maria Goretti pamphlet?'

Before
Thirteen

Hu Stannton couldn't remember the last time he had seen Leo Nicholas, so had a little difficulty finding him in the pub. He felt that as his old parish was made up of predominantly Irish people, there was a strong possibility that he would be recognised by someone in almost any pub in town. Besides, as a priest he was not in the habit of frequenting pubs, so as a layman it was not something he felt he needed to be, either.

He pulled up his collar as he approached a head of long greying hair at the bar.

'Ah, Father Hu.' said Leo, intentionally loudly.

Hu clenched his teeth and looked around, but the pub was quiet. 'What can I do for you Mr Nicholas?'

'Get me another pint, I've nearly finished this.'

'Yes, sorry I'm a little late. What'll it be?'

'Farmer's Blonde for me and a Guinness for you I'll bet.'

Hu wasn't being pigeon-holed. 'Half of Farmer's Blonde,' he called, 'and a glass of Chardonnay - large, please?'

'One-all,' thought Leo as they sat down. 'Thanks for coming. I just wanted to go over some of the stuff to do with the church's involvement with The Tin Tab.'

'Yes I'm still in touch – with The Tin Tab, as you know - but not the church I'm afraid.'

'Okay, the new guy, Mon Senor Green's been asking some questions and I just wanted to recall how we stood – stand – on a couple of issues?'

Hu Stannton had a new job. He knew he was lucky to get this job in the Housing Department and he knew he had talked up his role with the substance abusers, particularly the homeless ones at The Tin Tab in order to get it. He didn't want the youth service giving his new managers a different impression.

Then Leo hit him below the belt. 'Simone Dunne has apparently made a complaint.'

The colour drained from Hu's face. Could the woman be insinuating something about the confessional? She wasn't a catholic, but diocese wouldn't know and she probably wouldn't tell. She had however, confided her deepest thoughts to him in his role, and in his dog collar. Not in his trousers, though. 'Complained about me? After all this time?'

'Your friends in Ireland aren't exactly helping you, are they?' This was working. What else could Leo throw into the mix? 'Then there's the suicide cult and the death metal stuff the diocese didn't like you meddling with.' Leo guessed at least some hint would have been made to Hu about this, so no lies there. The word 'meddling' had useful undertones, too.

Hu did not see this coming at all. He had peacefully walked away and, as far as he considered, he had left nothing hiding under any stones, but 'paedophile priests'? Breaking the Seal of the Confessional? Kids committing suicide, his fault? He was buckling. 'Leo,' he said, 'where is this leaving me? Why are you concerned about church stuff?'

'I'm concerned about *people*, especially young people. I am fed up with systems supposedly set up to protect them, but actually doing nothing of the sort. Then the Church and the Priests, damn the lot of you. But I bet most of you don't even believe in that packets of Bisto, mumbo jumbo, but you love the power it gives you over people, don't you?'

'Are you saying I'm ... a paedophile?' He had been accused of this, even if only after going off with a pretty girl – albeit one over thirty years old.

'Sorry to get quite so personal, I don't mean to, but you were an intrinsic part of that oppressive system. A system which objectivised children and oppressed women. I am wondering what your bishop has got hold of in your relationship with Simone Dunne?'

'Yes, Simone Dunne. What's she got to do with it?' He appeared to have forgotten that this what Leo started with.

'You tell me Hu,' said Leo, 'I have no ideas at all.'

Hu was completely adrift. He was thinking humility might be his best course, but he wasn't sure Leo Nicholas wouldn't walk all over him. He chose a spot of diversion. 'Sorry,' he said with a sudden grin, 'I was just being cheeky with that half o'bitter. Will I get you a pint, Leo?' but he didn't wait for an answer. He stayed with wine himself, but a red this time.

As Hu returned to the table he saw Leo studying three fingers placed over the table edge. He recognised a threat approaching. 'Abe Grant? This is about Abe, isn't it?'

Leo sat back and quaffed a full half pint out of his glass. 'Perfect.' he said, smacking his lips.

'What do you want, Leo?'

'Understanding.'

Hu lifted and brightened up.

'You want to keep your job,' said Leo nodding, 'and I want to keep mine.' He released the three fingers, necked the rest of his pint and stood.

They shook hands. Hu thought he was getting a genuine smile from a man whom he had great difficulty feeling comfortable with.

Before
Fourteen

Leo Nicholas was the man of the furrowed brow, today. His budget for youth work staffing had not been cut last year, 'Oh no. There will be no cut to front line services,' they said. But recruitment had been 'frozen' – for two years so far – and the average time spent as a part-timer in youth work is around five years. Leyton insisted the youth club sessions be protected so the street workers were coming inside. The boss just did not understand the work done out there on the streets where the kids were: the real diversion from disaffection happened – where the car thieving thirteens, Sexually Infected twelves and bong-puffing eleven year olds were.

His team had known for years that Social Services would do nothing about a fourteen-year-old having sex with a twenty five-year-old, because by the time they got their bureaucratic machine cranked up, the girl would be of consenting age. To say nothing of Jelly.

Leo had come away from his experience with the Street Pastors with mixed feelings – Volunteers, the saviours in the Big Society which would be left after the Tories had cut the public services to a feint memory. He was thinking of all the work that needed to be done out there, and shivering at the thought of the steam-roller remorselessly trundling towards the Professionally Qualified youth service - to crush the very people who were still left trying to do it.

Out on the Pastor session he had also seen the rose sellers for himself. It was Carol, Leo's Leader-in-Charge of The Tin Tab youth team, and Abe that had first told him. He had kept up his six-monthly attendance at the Social Service's monitoring meeting about the sexual exploitation by Jelly and his gang. ('Jelly? You're kidding me!') But he had still not seen James Leigh for himself. For several years now, Leo had heard stories from his workers of girls getting 'pimped by Jelly.' This black guy provided girls with roses to sell at a pound each round the pubs and clubs. He did this in the bigger towns and cities all over the region. Jelly would 'forget' to collect their takings sometimes and let some build up a debt. It would always be the carefully selected, vulnerable ones. Then he would persuade them of the necessity of paying off their debt. Of course, they would have spent it in their chaotic, often parentless, lives. He would then offer them an easy way to pay off the debt – in a room over the kebab shop.

Carol, had told him how two of the regular clients living in the hostels had recruited homeless girls for Jelly. They would be picked up at the YMCA by Asian guys and taken off into the country. Was there any more vulnerable cohort?

Mulling all this over in his head, he found himself chuntering to Gina about the huge reduction – and more to come, year on year – to the street workers. 'And didn't Ofsted give us 'Outstanding' for our *Detached* work – not only the quality, but that we were on each of the estates, too? Now the damn Tories want us out of schools, off the streets and back into crummy halls doing youth Clubs –

somewhere where *their* kids would not be seen dead – and nowhere to hold a gymkhana either.'

Still lost in loud thoughts, he remembered Abe telling him how important Carol and the qualified youth workers were to their joint project, The Tin Tab. He was going to be forced to pull them out – leave it to Volunteers – the Big Society.

Abe had told of how he had been out with Saint Luke's soup run; how they had a fourteen year old girl on the team and she was putting her arm round a forty year old wino and giving it 'tell me about it.' Abe had been appalled at the risk that the church was putting its volunteers at.

Leo so valued the work these volunteers were doing, but in the end there were so few of them. Their input, great as it was, could not replace the national youth service of workers trained in child and youth development, psychology, sex, drugs, counselling, relationships and more, a status that had taken 50 years to develop and appeared to be going down the tubes in less than five.

With the steamroller in front, he was feeling he had only a rock and a hard place to turn to. What did that rat do when cornered? Which neck would Leo get his teeth into? He realised he was baring his own.

Which would save the children – more workers or more forms in County Files saying who was and wasn't barred? All these creeps getting sex off vulnerable people: children, nubile pubescents, boys; vulnerable young people from the children's homes in his purview; drunken young women, carers and visitors in care homes – and what about that bloke who broke into an old folks' home and raped an inmate? 'Bloody priests, too.'

'Bloody Father Hu, eh?' What kind of a woman had he gone after? Would 'woman' be stretching it? 'Girl?' he wondered.

'No I am not thinking Ladyboy,' he told himself.

Before
Fifteen

Abe was worried about word of his record getting out. For Abe to stick around, it would put the whole thing in jeopardy. But it was his life! His family were all grown up, and lovely Coddy was still working and enjoying it. He could not go fishing forever. The shame of going back forty years. Of forty years of effort, of success in turning his life around. President of the Chamber of Commerce; respectable elder of the church – a lifer! He couldn't live it down. He knew he would not live it down.

He wasn't going to have to, either. He and Leo would come up with something. They had had some sticky times and always got through them. He had the thought of bringing someone else into the Covenant – Brien, maybe. Perhaps there would be strength in numbers.

He dropped in and found Leo at his desk. As ever, he was most welcoming to Abe and it was lovely to talk with him about family as well as Abe's life's mission – young substance users and The Tin Tab.

It took Abe a while to get to the nub of his thinking, but when he suggested Brien, the bottom nearly fell out of Leo's stomach, out of his trousers, too. Oh no, he was not going there! He had had enough of the Abe/Hu/Leo covenant. He regretted ever going there. He could think of no other way he could have done it, but he would not do it now and, basically, he was going to have to undo it somehow or other. Renege, or lose the fifteen or so years he might still get in, build up his pension, and maybe the pinnacle of the career – Head of Youth Service.

So Leo felt how it was for Father Hu and the secret of the confessional – he could not tell Abe about Brien's record. If nothing else what would it do to the man, to think that he has been sheltering a paedophile? Even Lifers in prison hate Nonces.

Leo did however feel that he could reassure Abe that their little secret was safe with Hu Stannton.

'How can you tell?'

'He's told me.' He covered his mouth with his hand. 'I did put him in a very awkward place … and he now knows he's got more to lose than to gain, in ever letting that secret out.' He fingered the side of his nose and knew that would make Abe laugh. 'I can now sweeten the pill with the pampering idea?'

Abe looked blank.

'Did Brien not tell you about the Spa weekend of pampering?'

'Aha! Yes – 'the dirty weekend'! He only told me you had an idea – I thought it was one of your little 'jokes.' You're serious?'

'Well Talya won this prize and, as you can imagine, she is not one for having her flesh felt (except by me of course!), and she has offered it to me to thank you guys with. Of course we don't have to do the pampering stuff – it's a 'weekend away' in a nice hotel – The Loseborough in Grenley. You know it?'

'No, not at all. I'm not much of a posh hotel man myself, either.'

Leo picked his teeth for a minute. 'I'm thinking of some way of consolidating our 'position,' Abe.' He had his eyebrows raised in question. He was struggling with the notion of bringing four guys together for a single purpose, when he knew that each had a different perspective on the situation and the differences were pretty much irreconcilable. 'This Criminal Record and Barring thing cranks up the expectations of statutory *and* voluntary organisations – and individuals, too – to make sure that only squeaky clean people work with children and vulnerable adults.' He gave Abe a moment to absorb his context. 'I've had my 'little chat' with Stannton,' he continued, 'and because I needed to know he would not waver, I made it that he *could* not.'

'You threatened him? What with?'

'Well Abe, it'll be no surprise to you that I could, nay would, lose my job if county found out about our little covenant …'

Abe turned and looked out of the window. The council offered Leo a picturesque view of a car park and back of a bin depot – enhanced by a luxurious view of a three metre strip of canal - even that now skulking under a doom laden sky. 'I hadn't thought about that Leo. I'm so sorry.' He turned to face him. 'Had I better go?'

Leo was biting his thumb. 'I really don't know how to proceed, Abe.'

'How might the pampering idea work?'

'I thought if we got in a relaxed atmosphere we may be able to assure ourselves. I am thinking mostly of you and I, but Stannton might need a good cop input after the grilling I gave him.' He opened his hand to Abe.

'But, Brien, too?'

Leo didn't want to give the real reason for that idea. 'Yes. I'm thinking of using the story that it's a farewell gift to Father Hu, from The Tin Tab.'

Abe Nodded.

'Carol might be a good one to have along, but I've only got four places, and I'm thinking a woman's presence might indeed make it look like a dirty weekend.' They both laughed. Leo continued, 'Brien's the next most important committee member after you, and I get the impression you two are pals?'

'Yes, he's lovely gentle soul, is Brien. He's a good Ying to my Yang.'

'Woo! Well let's yank him in then. How's Carol getting on now, without Simone's 'help'?'

'Oh don't mention Simone – to me, or Carol! You won't send her back will you? All quiet on the western front without her. Please? Yes it's really good. Young people numbers are up and more of them make return visits, even the two who complained about Simone.'

'She's got something on Father Hu, you know.' Leo wasn't ready to mention falling off his chair.

'Is that how or why the Monsignor mentioned her?'

'Yes, I think she's complained to the Bishop, not Mon Senor. She's done a good job at E2E, but she knows she's been shoved there and we've got ourselves a woman scorned. She's been with The Tin Tab a long time, hasn't she?'

'Yes, that's what hurts. She was in at the start – one of the first group of part-time youth workers, but she had been volunteering and we felt compelled to put her on the books, remember?'

'Oh yes.' He stopped. He needed to know if Simone could know about Abe's record. 'You've known her a long time, then?'

'Not so subtle, Leo,' thought Abe. 'What's he heard?' Abe grabbed his upper lip and was giving it a real tugging. 'She knew someone at church who told her about the soup kitchen we ran the Christmas before we really got going at The Tin Tab. She winds the young 'uns up. Her bloody Tory lady image don't help neither.'

Abe could see that was not enough for Leo.

'I've been really good to her, you know. I did have a bit of trouble, because she wasn't very used to men being nice to her … you know how I mean!'

'She hasn't mentioned that, not you harassing her or anything.'

'I should bloody well think not, silly woman, it just wouldn't be true – but I could say that about her, if it wouldn't make me look a right pansy.'

Leo had a chuckle. 'Does she know you're a killer?' his brain roared, but his mouth was silent. Leo knew of Abe's record – Life imprisonment for murdering his wife, forty years ago, out on license after nine years. Did people round there knew about it, remember and know him? 'Where are you from Abe?'

'Sykehouse,' he said, knowing Leo would be none the wiser. 'You?'

'Glapwell.'

Ditto.

'Does Brien know Simone of old?' asked Leo.

'No idea! Never mentioned her. So do you want him to come?'

Leo was weighing things up: Brien's a Paedo and Abe probably doesn't know; Abe's a Lifer and Brien doesn't know; Father Hu knows about Abe and almost certainly knows about Brien from the confessional; Abe knows a bit about Leo and the sock-cosh, even though that was expunged from the record. Quite a little cabal. Simone had something on Father Hu, hinted at knowing about Abe, and was trying to get money out of Leo – albeit a payoff from County.

Yes, Brien was a bona fide member. 'I think he could be a good stabilising influence if any of us get a little … tetchy,' said Leo, 'don't you think?'

Abe was fed up with this. He thought it was a proper cat and mouse game and he had to adopt his strategy for dealing with conflict – *Mickey fights, Abe runs.'*

'Gotta run – picking up the wife. Will you firm up a date? Weekdays are OK with

Brien and me, but maybe not for you workers. Give us a call, will you?'
Leo shouted after him 'it's got to be midweek – off peak offer.'
Abe waved and was glad to get into the car park.
Leo was irritated with poor progress.
Abe remembered that Tory bitch asking him about Mickey Grant.

Tuesday 2nd March

Holly Stannton knew about men and their sort of conferences – she had been to quite a lot. That dirty devil Rupert took her to a few, but she clearly remembered the one. The one where he brought his friends back to their room.

She thought they were two couples.

They had a right old party – started on the Champers and moved onto some dope, then everything started to move, including clothes and hands … and other things. Before she knew it, it was an orgy. Rupert was across the floor entangled with the two other women and a bloke was standing over her with a video camera – and he didn't need a tripod. She giggled.

Holly hadn't met any of Hu's new workmates. They might all be women.

Her hand found her crotch. She hadn't felt herself since the minute she first saw Hu. It would be adultery – he was the only one to pleasure her and she him. Alone, together, forever. She pulled her hand away.

Where was this Loseborough, and what kind of stupid name was that? Not a real one, that's what it was. He said it was at Grenley. She knew where that was – not far. You could see Gainsborough from there – 'get it?' he said. She didn't. 'Gainsborough/Loseborough!' Used to be a missionary training place or something, he thought.

Holly had got through some men, or more accurately they had got through her. They were good times, but she put them in a bubble and hoped it would float away. In a clear sky, she was okay if she saw it. It didn't hurt her, it didn't do anything, that's what was wrong with it. Meaningless. It was a stop off – just a place she had to stop off and wait between planes. A real place with everything in it, but meaning absolutely nothing for Holly.

Coming out to the sticks, she instantly found some meaning. She wondered what her parents' old place was like. Seemed alright. Her dad was always churchy – 'not holy – you know what I mean – just churchy.' Her Mum was holy, but not so churchy. Her Dad did enough church for everybody. Bloody needed too, as well, the sod. Not that her Mum would dare miss mass, though. Too scared of cheeky old Satan.

Holly stood around outside the church loads of times before she dared go in. She saw this huge rocker coming and going sometimes. Lovely body and when he took off his helmet and he shook out those beautiful golden tresses, a tingle went right through her. 'Tresses' seemed a bit girly, but any girl would be jealous of his natural blonde hair, very shiny and just a little wavy.

He didn't seem the sort of character you'd see going to weekday mass at all. Didn't seem the sort of person to be seen dead in a church, truth be told.

She eventually sneaked into a corner chapel at the back. It had a picture of some Abbess with a really old fashioned name. She couldn't remember it, and that wasn't helped by the fact that she had never, ever heard of anyone actually called it.

A bell rang and who should walk onto the altar in priestly garb, but the rocker – Father Greebo! She dropped her lit votive light and it splattered its wax over her stilettos, stinging the top of her foot. The candle had knocked itself out, so she forgot it straight away and her heart and mind floated out onto that altar.

Holly didn't know that the church would call her a proselyte in her instant conversion.

So after one year and three hundred and fifty two days together, they were now not going to sleep together for the first time. She had made sure they made love night and morning, just in case.

'Just in case what, Holly?'

Well he shouldn't get randy should he? She kept her man very satisfied, indeed. She knew it.

She had known a lot of men and didn't know one who was ever satisfied.

Hubert Stannton was not the sort of man you meet every day, or so he sang. Holly trusted Hu.

Leo had his body language considered. On the threshold of The Loseborough Hotel, he had given all three men the fiercest handshake (he noticed a little too fierce for Brien, who forced a smile but massaged his knuckles). He got them all a choice of coffee – Brien chose tea - and choice of giant cake.

'This is right generous of you, Leo,' started Abe, 'are you sure about this?'

'Completely. Unwanted present, as they say. Actually unwanted prize - Talya's, in fact. That's my wife,' he told Hu and Brien, 'Natalya. She won it. She's not the pampering type, nor the hotel type for that matter. It's all her idea. It's her gift to you, not mine. She's heard me talking about The Tin Tab for years and also about the volunteering.'

Leo felt the need to bring Hu in. He was obviously so ill at ease, sitting on the edge of his sumptuous chair and folding his hands over and over, he hadn't touched coffee or cake. 'My people, me, we're all paid and you guys do it for the love of … the kids.' He shoved the pince-nez type specs into close-up and added, '… and your God. Just lately I had been grumbling about the whole Criminal Record thing getting out of hand, Political Correctness gone mad and all that.' He made as if to share a confidence: 'there's also been some cock-ups, sorry, County have lost some Clearance forms – filled in – Data. I am *ashamed*.'

Abe leant over and gave him a pat on the elbow. 'You're a good lad Leo, but I know you're not going to blubber to us, so give over.'

They all chuckled and Hu, seeing the familiarity between Abe and Leo, sat back a bit.

'Better get it out, better shoot the elephant in the room, eh?' He started, but obviously confused Brien who was looking around. Leo went on: 'I've brought you here, most of all, as a way to thank you. Hu, *Father* Hu … I suppose I just call you Hu, now?'

Hu nodded. Abe looked out of the window and Brien looked embarrassed.

'Well you Hu,' he couldn't resist a smirk, 'left us fairly suddenly, and Brien here has pointed out to me how he and the church feel nothing but gratitude towards you. However, you've gone without a thank you.'

Hu Stannton did not know how to handle this. He gripped his large nose in praying hands, then kneaded the bridge, his eyes closed. The tone of Leo's voice did not match his words. He realised Leo Nicholas was 'quoting' Brien, who wouldn't hurt a fly.

Leo continued: 'I have been in an objective position to watch the development of our partnership of service to young Substance Users and – here's another little elephant, my hidden agenda – I am a devout …'

Abe and Brien both sat up, then smiled at each other, knowing that Father Hu wouldn't know what was coming.

'… atheist. I mean devout. I think about God, and know he doesn't think about me – because he isn't there. This is not intended to offend …'

'We know that Leo,' said Abe, 'but you want to have a bit of fun with us.' Brien thought that a novel response and Hu was obviously intrigued and yes, he did appear to be amused.

'You might not be believing in Him,' added Brien, 'But He believes in you.'

Leo was inclined to shake his head at that old platitude. Instead his wit saved him. 'Oh, I know he believes in Hu.' The laughter was polite, only, but it did focus them on Hu. Leo was pleased with progress. He didn't want to shock or alienate them, but in one way or another he was determined to make them see the stupidity of their belief. This was not in the hope of belittling them, more in the way of converting them.

Father Hu's many years of training made him well aware of this evangelistic Atheist's approach, but who was he to quibble? Did he think God would still believe in him?

Leo continued: 'I thought we could take a walk this afternoon, nothing too strenuous, maybe a pint at a country pub – non-alcoholic for you lot – and back for a freshen up in the jacuzzi before dinner?' This generated frowns from the older men, but Hu seemed to like the sound of the programme so far.

'The dinner is the real treat,' said Abe. 'I've heard great things about the chef here.'

'Have you Abe?' continued Leo, 'that's good. Not faddy any of you I hope? Don't want a good slap up meal wasted.'

'I haven't brought hiking boots,' said Brien.

Leo hoped he wasn't trying to get out of it. 'Me, neither,' he lied. 'It's only a stroll.'

'Oh that's a relief – I love a stroll in the country, but I'm no rambler.'

Leo thought the stroll went swimmingly, then wondered if swims rambled. His mind did. Luckily no one had gone in for a swim – Canal in March could be hypothermic. He had taken them down from the beacon which induced talk of the Spanish Armada and the two Irishmen, Brien and Hu, waxed lyrical over the Spanish Irish wrecked on the Irish coast.

'Oh, we had a few of those round Westport way,' said Hu.

'Not you, though,' Brien commented running his hands through his hair.

Hu laughed. He didn't think he had got many of the black haired swarthy genes. 'More of a Viking I've always thought' he said stretching to his substantial full height and swishing his blonde locks. Definitely Norman he asserted – and of course that meant Anglo Saxon.

'Not a lot of people know that' said Abe leading them down a path of name etymology.

Leo had to own up to his name change and Ukrainian and Italian roots, while Brien claimed his name was spelled the proper way after the first king of all Ireland Brien Boru. Gaelic speaking Hu smiled thinking it a good job he doesn't call himself Brian Bóroimhe.

Abe challenged the surname though – it was surely a boozer – and a French one at that – Mr de Vin! They all had a chuckle, but Abe had drawn the spotlight to himself.

'Now Abraham is an old fashioned name – Jewish I'd say,' teased Hu.

'Illiterate, too,' Abe owned up. 'It's only Abram without the ham, after Lincoln - and Grant after Cary - because my poor old mum thought my dad was an American GI, she didn't know which one and she couldn't spell!'

Leo warmed even more to the gentle, now humble giant.

Leo had led them along the canal and rounding one of the many meanders they arrived at a boat club and its many moorings. He stopped the men next to one of the long narrowboats and before leaping onto it asked Abe to undo the front rope and push off. He had the boat unlocked and chugging downstream in minutes, with the men feeling like naughty boys making off with someone's pride and joy, not to say mobile home. They eventually got him to own up to ownership – it was, 'for another few weeks', one of the many youth service facilities or opportunities that were being cut back 'under this slash and burn Tory administration.' Abe was relieved that Leo wouldn't get to embarrass himself with one of his anti-Capitalist rants as a tunnel loomed ahead. For the hell of it, Leo cut the engine.

'Onto the top, lads,' he shouted, 'you'll have to walk it through here.'

'There's no towpath!'

'Exactly! You'll have to walk it along the ceiling.'

He had the two big men, Hu and Abe, fore and aft lying on their backs on the roof of the boat, 'walking' on the roof of the tunnel, pushing the boat along. He stood Brien in the bow with a pole fending off from the sides and Leo stood aft roaring out instructions and laughing like a drain.

In the calm of the straight at the back of the Carr, he looked at the guys – there was obviously an annoying amount of affection from the old chaps for the renegade priest. As if that wasn't enough, despite both being old enough to have fathered him, they were also calling him 'Father' and showing him reverence!

He was pleased they were putting Hu at his ease though. They chattered about this and that, carefully avoiding talking 'shop' - religion, drugs, marriage, homelessness and changes in the parish.

Abe, having kids of Hu's age, could banter about rock music a bit, and of course this wasn't all string theory to the youth officer.

Swimmingly.

At Dinnertime, Leo was first surprised, then dismayed when his joke about them all having no alcohol, was beginning to bear up. Abe had half of bitter Shandy and Brien had tap water – with the ostentatious addition of lemon and ice. As Hu joined them last at the bar, Leo thought he could have stepped out of one of the cider adverts and thwack an arrow into the bar. He wasn't disappointed: Hu spied a selection of malts, gave Leo a smile, then stood across to the hand-pumps.

'Good, Eh? Are you wining, Leo? I'm okay to join you, if you like.'

'I saw you looking at anything but wine – more of a pint with a malt chaser?'

'Grand.' said Hu, rubbing his hands. 'I'll try that stout, they have – you too?'

Leo gave an 'I might have guessed' smile but said 'I'm more of a Blonde man, myself. I've tried this one before – nice. Yep, I'll have the Blonde.'

Brien and Abe smiled to each other as the younger men got on famously. They wondered if the crafty Leo would put the knife in at all. Would he give it a twist? Abe felt that the four of them had shown a bond on the walk. Though Leo had his agenda, they didn't feel he would go much beyond his usual acerbic comments.

At Dinner, Leo talked cars – all men can talk cars, but Leo could really talk cars. Brien talked about the bangers at home in Ireland and insisted they could only afford a donkey cart themselves. He was forgetting that that was fifty years ago.

Leo was a Subaru man – a big exhaust was the most important piece of equipment. Hu, as befitting the station of most of his adult life, had always had to opt for a basic model compact.

'What about that oul Harvey Daley yoke you had?' stirred Brien.

Hu smiled, then frowned. 'You saw it? Wasn't mine – just looked after it for a friend on holidays. 'Low Rider,' ' he confided to Leo, 'not so good for my long back.'

At dinner Hu took the opportunity to seek advice on four wheels with a bit more oomph, as befitting his new station – not mentioning that of course.

After dinner the men settled in the bar and talked world politics, credit crunch, fishing and footie. Brien taking a glimpse at the old country, asked Hu if he'd been a Hurling man, but no, he could play, but now it was rugby that Hu liked – he was hoping Ireland could increase their Grand Slam record – he could get his fix of that over here. They touched on County cuts, and Leo, after an aside about RBS - a nationalised bank - still affording to sponsor the Rugby, slipped in CRB, but got no takers. He didn't push it - yet.

The older men shuffled off to bed at a sensible time, leaving the younger ones to continue getting stewed together.

Brien the messenger asked Abe if he thought Leo would ever get round to Simone.

Abe felt he had known Leo forever and gave a very wise look: 'Oh, Yes. He knows what he's playing at. One side of me thinks they could come to blows if we leave them now, but the other says Leo is a very professional chap. Of course we can't underestimate Father Hu either, what with his years of training and his experience – he's the ultimate diplomat.'

In his heart he wondered if all this wouldn't stir up CRB questions and frighten Leo off supporting him any longer. He felt Leo must surely be taking this opportunity, probably his only opportunity, to sound out Father Hu on the deal - or 'covenant' as Father Hu had christened it.

While Hu and Leo snorted and snored in their drink enhanced sleep, Brien and Abe tossed and turned, churning over their separate concerns about the people stirring up a hornet's nest for them.

Abe knew the coming upgrade to child protection would definitely push him out of The Tin Tab – his life's real work. Should he jump before he's pushed? But everyone knew he was dynamic and keen – someone might smell a rat. He no longer thought of himself as that rat, thanks to his Coddy, Rowena.

Brien felt as if he had ridden the storm over his misdemeanour, and though he missed his little angel, Ginny had stood innocently by his side. The Lord would surely credit his fifteen years of total penitence and service. He wondered if The Almighty was the only judge he feared now.

Alone in his room that night, Leo fell asleep to the memory of his mother. At the funeral of his father, just two years after hers, Leo's sisters eventually told him the story of their parents' love affair.

As he knew, Arnold had 'escaped' from the British Prisoner of War Camp in Italy. Apparently he had been taken in by the local blacksmith, who had been charmed by Arnold's ever-optimistic demeanour. Despite being easily identified as POWs – Mussolini had dressed his in Black Shirts, to 'make them good Fascists'; Churchill reposted that his would be dressed in dark brown 'like good monks' - brown battle-dress with contrasting patches, Arnold still had such a swing in his stride, it was as if he wore his uniform with pride. During almost two years 'on the run', the smith had taught Arnold all he knew about his craft. Furthermore, he was pleased that his daughter Elisabetta had fallen in love with the sunny Ukrainian.

Of course Leo had heard about this and how afterwards his dad had sent for his old love. He had worked the stipulated two years on the farms, then got a better-paid job as a Colliery Blacksmith. Now he had something to offer her.

What Leo did not know about, was his mother's initial reluctance to come over. Since Arnold left, she had fallen in love with a handsome young curate, and was pleasantly surprised to find her love reciprocated, or so she thought. She had hopes of him leaving the church for her, but there was such shame in that, not only, but especially, in Italy - and at that time. As was normal in the development of priests, his diocese moved him on, and his final night in Elisabetta's village was his first spent in her arms. She never heard from him again.

Italy was trashed by war and there was not enough for people to live on. When Arnold's letter arrived with the work permit for Elisabetta, her father's heart leapt at the great prospects for his daughter and she could not resist his pressure to go.

Full of trepidation at seeing her Naldo again, everything changed when he actually swept her off her feet as she stepped off the train and they were married within the month.

When Betty gave birth to an eight pound daughter just six months later, Arnold simply shrugged off 'the war', and loved Leo's big sister Geovana – 'gift from God.'

Leo, the Safeguarding Officer, was not so forgiving. As he dreamed, that curate had a face at last. It was the face of Hubert Stannton.

Hu was awoken by his bladder in the small hours, then couldn't get back to sleep. In almost four years this was his first night alone other than the six-month hiatus with the Maynooth Mafia.

He felt like a sex addict. 'What, only one night, Hu?'

'Holly. Who is she?' Hu started to wonder. 'Nice, ordinary girl … woman. Okay - been in several relationships – open about all that. No shock to Hu – he had heard enough confessions. But she really wanted *him* – Hu Stannton.

He wanted her. He wanted to look after her. She had flown the nest; followed the sun; flown across every continent to return to … no home.

There was nothing left and she had nothing left of herself – she had flown it all away. He was glad of this. A woman with so much history might never have been his to have.

She nestled in his palm and grew back, with Hu as father, yes, and mother, brother, sister, and son. She grew and he became a son, to her. He was fine and strong, but like all women knew all men, she knew he was just a boy and she knew how to handle him. And didn't she show it?

But who was she? Who was her mother, her father? 'Cracked. Broken. Gone,' was all she had said. He imagined druggy boozers or worse and left it at that.

Hu was not cracked. He was perfect, perfect in every way. Never been naughty, done good to all. She was going to keep him perfect. He wouldn't have been able to stay perfect with no one to look after him, to look after the real Hu.

He thought of Pauline, his perfect cousin. Had she not given up her life for him? 'No – she – had – not.' She had made him her life, made him. She was nuts. But who could see that?

She was nothing. She had nothing. She had nothing to give, except him, Hu. Hu was made in her image and likeness.

He shivered. He thought it must be around dawn, but no light was breaking the winter night. He was blaspheming and lying to himself. Lying by himself.

It's all about sex.

'You're just a dried up oul virgin,' someone had once upset Pauline with. She had discussed it with Hu. 'What was wrong with being a virgin?' she wondered and, back then of course, he could find nothing wrong. It was The Ideal, Mother Mary bless her. She did.

But Holly was jealous of her. She knew what Pauline had. She knew what Pauline had to give. At first she thought, like almost everyone did, that it must be sex. What man could do without it? But Holly was so happy when she realised, believed, that it was not all about sex.

Pauline had Hu. Pauline had Hu to give, to give to the world – a perfect, unsullied golden, glowing man. A virgin priest.

Holly had asked Hu if Pauline wasn't just 'a dried up old virgin.' There it was again. It stung him. But Holly smoothed away the sting. 'Only asking,' was all she said, her lips quickly reminding him what was wrong with that.

Poor Pauline. He had walked out on her with barely a thought. Well she wasn't anything except him. She was him. He hadn't walked out on himself.

In those dead-of-night blues, he thought of her for the very first time. His big cousin. She was always there for him. When his Mammy was not; when his Daddy was away working in Glasgow that time. Pauline was there for him. She listened to his childish fears and steered his boyish dreams.

After he fell from grace, and out of the Junior Seminary, his Mammy couldn't talk to him. His Daddy couldn't listen to him. He was *not* going to his room to pray. He was *not* going to his room to play with himself.

It was Pauline who picked him up. She knew how alone he was. She called every evening after school, the couple of hours after school 'I still have the shop to shut don't I?'

They had walked and he had talked. He couldn't talk enough, until he couldn't talk at all. They had arrived at the copse and his mouth and his feet ground to a halt at last.

Pauline turned and looked at his lip trembling and his eyes brimming.

He looked up to her, still an inch or two to catch up.

'Ha!' She grabbed his balls. 'Ha!' She grabbed his neck. She laughed in his face. She shook him. 'You're – just – a – boy – Hubert – Stannton. Now get out of that!'

He was shocked and frozen.

She was shaking him. 'Come on *boy* … get out of that,' and she roared into his face.

The ache in the balls fired him up into a blind fury and they fought, and fought like tigers. They pulled and twisted, tumbled, scrabbled and tore at each other into an exhausted lock. And the quake started. Somewhere in the middle of his chest. His heart? A sobbing quake spread and spread into great rollicking laughter.

Hu was hers and she had given him back to himself.

Where was she even?

Hu was shocked that he didn't know. Had she gone back home to Ireland? The Maynooth Mafia would look after her.

No she wouldn't go home. She would be hereabouts, for him still. She was him, she couldn't be anything else.

They had never touched again after that day in the copse. They had got up smelling of fox. Would it ever wash off? He could never wash her off him. But they never needed each other's touch again. Their relationship was consummated as it was then. She had put him back together, complete and self-contained. And she was … just there. Intact.

He eventually slipped into a dream of his Guardian Angel. Light. Long. Lofty. Tinkling choir of angels.

His Angel, his Holly. His Holly smiling, smiling, her hand gently on his balls. She squeezed.

She squeezed his neck.

She shook him. Pauline shook him. Baring her teeth, she shook, snarled and spat in his face. 'You're – not – a - kid - any – more, Hubert Stannton.'

Now get out of it.

He woke in a sweat, his twisted legs and balls aching, his hand on his neck.

Wednesday 3rd March

A couple of police support officers were giggling in the squad room and Iruna did wonder how long they had been in long trousers. They were really good looking boys. They weren't men. Several men were wandering about and all gave her a genial smile. Potential! She now understood about chemistry. She realised that she indeed had not fancied Justin, or else she would have made some sort of move, wouldn't she? But she still had a mystery to solve. 'Come on Sergeant Bahadur, get solving the missing fellah mystery.'

The DCI wanted a word. She had given Bahadur an interesting week to find her way round – the office and the area.

'So you've been out with two of the lads, studied a few of our open case files, sat in on briefings each day. You've got yourself a desk – more than they let me have when I got here! Will we do?' The boss put her hands together and cocked her head.

Iruna couldn't help but smile. 'Ready for action, Ma'am,' she said. 'Do you want to point me in any particular direction?'

'It would be nice for you to pick up something of your own – next thing in is yours, Okay?'

'What, even a murder?'

'We don't murder people round here, we're too nice. See if you can see any light other than sparks in all this cable theft. We had a bloke fry himself just the week before you came, you know?'

'Yes, one of the lads showed me the transformer box. He gored it up a bit trying to yuk me!'

The DCI walked round the desk, nudged her, and in conspiratorial mode, stage whispered close to her face, 'the lads don't realise we're made of sterner stuff. We lasses need to stick together. Any hassle with them, tip me the wink. Up an' at 'em lass!'

She looked the boss in the eyes. Pretty close up. 'Thanks a lot Ma'am.'

On her desk, there was a note to contact a teacher who had rung in to say she may have evidence about a metal thief. Bahadur had rung the school and the secretary had harrumphed that she certainly hoped none of their staff had made such unprofessional accusations. Bahadur thought it was after school time, so she said that they did not think the teacher was in fact making accusations – but could Bahadur maybe speak to her? 'You'll understand just how much metal thieves are costing the country, and we do need to follow these things up.'

She was put through within the minute. It was the nursery teacher. 'One of the children said her daddy worked at the pit. Well, as you know, the pit's been shut for years, so I asked her what he did there. She said 'My Daddy gets wire and men give him money for it!' Out of the mouths of babes, eh, Inspector?'

'Sergeant, Ma'am,' she said, feeling proud, none the less, 'Detective Sergeant Iruna Bahadur. We don't want to send in the cavalry, but can you let me have the name and address of the family, for the record, please?'

'Not just now. I'm off home, sorry ... and I'm not sure I can do that over the phone anyway. Could you pop in to the office tomorrow, say? I'll leave the details with the secretary.'

Come breakfast, Brien and Abe were up prim and proper, bibs in place when Leo came a little later and tipped them both the wink. He didn't mention his strategy, though; and they didn't ask. They'd all finished the cereals when the fine young man joined them, right as rain except for a bit of pinking to the eye-whites.

Leo suggested a twenty-minute stroll before 'getting down to business.' He had booked a room for them from nine – it was quite comfy – the hotel putting on airs calling it the 'Small Conference Room.'

This gave all three of the men a jolt, but they had to go along with it.

On the walk Leo had taken Abe aside to confirm that he had shut Hu up about their little covenant. If asked he would claim no knowledge of that side of things. Abe was relieved and picked up his pace a little.

Leo met them back at the room with a tray of the drinks they'd showed a preference for on arrival – well remembered, Leo. Edinburgh Shortcakes, too.

Leo laid his hands on the table and opened: 'I want to talk religion, chaps. I know this interests you all, but I want to feel as if I can stand up ... on shifting sands.' He bit his lip, and gave Hu a warm look.

Hu graciously took the floor, and floored them all with his ingenuous look at the change he had made to his life, which he accepted, had affected them all. He explained his original calling to priesthood and his conviction that he had fulfilled any expectation people – family and parishioners – could possibly have of him: 'Seventeen years, now come on lads!'

'I love God; I have devoted thirty years of my life to his service. I truly mean devoted – not done anything at all with my life, except that it would lead to his wish for me. He made me very handsome – this had been a huge challenge actually – women, and men for that matter, have thrown themselves at me. Beauty has honestly been a cross the Lord has given me to bear. But borne it I have done.

'It fulfilled my Mother's wishes for me. My Da didn't really get it, but I know he is really proud of me. My whole village is proud of me and even on my Ordination holiday, some girls from my youth thought they would give me one last try.' He had a giggle and scratched his cheek. 'I won't go there.'

He had a look at his audience: calm and receptive he thought, though Leo was avoiding eye contact, so he carried on.

'You say you're an Atheist, Leo, but a devout one. I like that and I get it, I think.'

Leo let him continue without qualifying his own phrase.

'I know you have supported these guys – to the hilt. I know that you believe in the kids the same way they do. You just don't believe in the motivation they have for doing it.'

He was wrong there, thought Leo. He knew why Abe was doing it and he was pretty sure Brien was jumpy with fear, probably with hell's flames licking at his toes about something.

'You'll know about the Good Thief, Leo, the one crucified with Jesus?'

'Yeah yeah – Latrun – been there, got the T Shirt – really!'

'Well that could be you, Leo, don't you see?'

''s right, Father,' said Brien, 'He's the man for me, y' man, the Thief. He was forgiven.' Then he seemed to choke up a bit, but pretended to cough and got his handkerchief out.

This went right to the heart, to the heart of the matter, for Leo. He felt it jab, but restrained himself. What he said was a fraction of what he felt. 'Why …' he gritted his teeth, '…must you insist on making me one of you?' He knew he coloured up but noticed the lay-men looking to the priest for answers. So he did too.

Hu looked down at his hands, and then put them together prayerfully. That must be a habit. 'Hmm. You're right. Why should we put it that way? Well I suppose we use language like that in talking to each other, and shouldn't use it to you. So to explain it: could we say that we believe the Thief got the reward that *we* all hope for.'

'That's good, Father,' burst out Brien. 'It is. You have it nailed.' Then he looked to see if the explanation satisfied Leo. It didn't look like it. He was grinning again thinking of Jesus being nailed.

Abe, knowing Leo better, knew he was itching to turn it round to his way of thinking. He was right.

'These two men,' Leo started, 'they're good men. They serve the very bottom layer of society – the only genuine outcasts in this country – the young druggies, the ones thrown out of their own homes.'

'Don't forget what Carol told you, Leo,' interrupted Abe, with a finger, 'home is not necessarily better than home-less.'

Leo gave him an irritated look to remind him not to disrupt the flow to what they both wanted. 'These two men, and many other fine people, Simone not least among them,' Leo nodded to Abe and raised an eyebrow, 'are good people. Now then, not only Christians are good people. You can't, I know you don't, believe that. My beef …' he stopped to think about his choice of word. 'Don't you think you priests - and we have to acknowledge rather too many from your side of the water, I'm afraid Father Hu - are telling these good people one thing, but doing heinous things yourselves?' He sat back.

Hu was studying him, his face in neutral. He thought he might let Leo drive on, but decided to grip the wheel. 'I suppose my … action could be regarded as a betrayal. I accept it is disappointing – indeed back home it is yet another scandal, I'm afraid. But it is not an apostasy.'

Leo glanced at Abe who nodded back. Brien was studying Hu's face.

Hu continued, 'I have not given up my belief in Jesus, the church, anything really. In fact, our joke might bounce back on us, Leo. We might say to you, 'You don't believe in God, but he believes in you.' Well I believe in Jesus, but many in the church will have decided that he *doesn't* believe in me any more.'

'You're having your cake and eating it. Damn!' in his annoyance Leo had spilt his coffee in his lap. He ignored it and went on. 'These guys have to carry on sticking to your Holy Roman rules, but you don't and you still think Jesus will love you. I'm a fair-pay-for-a-fair-day's-work man – and that don't work.'

Hu facing down and peering up through his brow, said almost under his breath, 'I know how everybody must feel, but I don't know who knows how I feel.'

'I think you will be feeling pretty damn smug,' Leo weighed in, 'what with your floozy and dropping straight into a cushy job – and that on the back of experience you got with our project.' He stabbed his own breast with a finger. Then he jabbed it at Hu. 'You even take that from these guys,' on whom he turned a munificent smile.

Brien and Abe both thought it a twist of the knife. Brien was most uncomfortable about it; Abe thought Hu strong enough to take it. Hu wasn't sure if Leo's closing grunt was a laugh meant to lighten his blow.

Leo took a breath before rejoining in measured tones: 'but I don't want your Heaven, nice as you think it might be. I want to know, and I think these two saints should hear, why *you* can have Heaven on Earth …' and to sound a reasonable note he added, 'really.'

'So married life is Heaven, is it? Abe? Brien? You Leo?'

Leo didn't think he was showing his frustration, much, but in the end felt as if he was outgunned. This man had many years professional training in diplomacy and if the Media thought it difficult to get answers from politicians, they should meet Hu Stannton.

Leo thought about a different tack: 'The Catholic church is all about sex.'

Hu thought this might offend the older men, but smiled and picked it up, anyway. 'Virgin Birth, Celibacy, Immaculate Conception, all about sex I suppose, you mean? Yes, but let me help our current situation.'

'Yes, please,' said Leo.

'There's love and there's sex – making love, and having sex, too. Crucially different, I hope you will agree.'

'Though I see that you can differentiate, I'm not altogether sure I do agree that you should. If we are all simply highly evolved animals …'

'Ah, well,' interjected Brien, 'what about souls?'

Leo looked daggers at Brien, but what could he say? He was here to get something for Brien and he knew he didn't want to hurt him – especially not him.

He decided to carry on and hope Brien would see it all clearer. 'All animals are made using sex and talking about 'making love' simply obscures the issue.'

'And which issue is that one, Leo?' asked Hu.

'The issue of you choosing one option, having your cake, enjoying it, and then coming back and wanting the other one - *eating your cake*, I think the metaphor goes.'

'Do you never change your mind? Is that not the same? I was eating the cake of life – it hadn't run out. I then decided that I would try a piece from the other side.'

'The big slice with more icing on it.' Leo stood up and stretched himself. He stepped to the window and looked out. He could feel Abe and Brien looking at the back of his head. They were no use – except as doormats to these damned clerics.

Hu had the end of his thumb between his teeth, but still remained calm – on the outside. He took a long look at Abe. 'Who the feckin' 'ell did he think he was? Feckin' murdering bastard.' His look hardened. He turned to Leo.

Leo was enjoying this. He sat back down with his arms folded and one hand tinkering with the Trotsky beneath a big smile.

'Did the Vatican Council not get rid of Purgatory, Father?' Brien asked. 'I hope not, 'cos all I'm doing is trying to keep out of Hell, and I'm not going to Heaven for a long, long time.'

Leo was moved by this. The Catholic Church is for bad people, too eh? The repenters. All the others are saved – born again.

Hu put his hand on his throat. He felt the area covered for many years by a dog collar. It constrained him no more. 'Well I never really believed in Hell, I'm afraid.'

The older men were suitably shocked.

'No, chaps - didn't God make us all in his image and likeness? Well could any of you see your most horrible child at their most tempestuous rebelliousness … in Hell?'

Where was Brien's little Colleen? She may really be on her way to Hell, but no, she let them know she wasn't there yet. Poor Ginny. What did she do to deserve that idea?

'I don't even think Hitler is in Hell.'

'Here he goes,' thought Leo, 'Father Hu-smugness.'

'Some Angels fell, but then God made Man in his own image and likeness, yeah? He can't let us go to Hell. There can't be 'mini-gods' in Hell. It's a blasphemy.'

If Hu said so, that was okay with Brien and Abe.

'Some people think I have fallen.'

'Yes, I'm one,' muttered Leo, and Hu heard him, but was unperturbed.

'I have only fallen in love.'

Leo laughed out loud. 'What a platitude.'

'Come on Leo,' said Abe, 'give him a chance to finish.'

Hu turned to Leo. 'You will have heard the *platitude* 'God is Love'?' he said shaking his head. 'Not a platitude. We believe it. You said 'the Catholic church is all about sex.' Well it is. Sex is what God invented to be the basis of procreation. God invented it. God is Love. Sex has been degraded by the media in its typical twisted way. The Devil can and does use sex to win us away from love, away from God. And because God invented it and he created men – and the Devil for that matter – he can't make out he made a mistake.'

'Pandora's Box, eh?' said Leo. 'He can't put it back.'

'He wouldn't want to. It is perfect for its purpose, and gives huge pleasure to his greatest creation – the whole of mankind.'

'And rabbits.' Leo couldn't resist. 'And you priests buggering boys.'

'Leo. Enough. No one round here …'

'I'm sorry,' Leo said, 'but it so infuriates me. Your church does not preach the beauty of sex at all. You priests have been suppressing the people and their natural way of going on – despite saying your God created it – it's you lot that say it's dirty and it's you 'church managers' that have not been using it for procreation for centuries. I just cannot accept that Brien and Abe here who have spent … decades?' he saw Abe nodding, 'decades in community service – pretty selfless, from what I see. You have done a bit, but it all appears to be a pretty cushy life, and then you decide you can have more, with no comeuppance. You will still get Heaven.'

After that rant, Leo thought he had better suggest a break, though he noticed it was not long until lunchtime.

Once outside the room, he sensed a reluctance to return. Abe had slipped out for a smoke and Brien took the opportunity to go with him. Leo suggested a swift half to Hu, and they had a couple before lunch.

After a post-prandial stroll the two older men, uncomfortable throughout, sought the first reasonable opportunity, made their excuses and went home.

His wife Ginny anticipated well that Brien needed his comfort food when he got back from that youth officer's 'conference.' Some simple Irish stew, followed by spotted dick and custard, hit the spot. He had told her everything about the two days, except what it was about. He felt angels would not tread there, and nor was he going to. Ginny's hand was out towards him on the table. He patted it, then his flat stomach. Tilting his head and raising an eyebrow, he gave her what she would recognise as a look of apology. 'I did enjoy that, dear,' he said, 'but it followed a lot of fancy rubbish into this fine frame, so I better do a bit if I'm going to hit seventy without the paunch.'

He wasn't going the way of every man he had known in the building game – to the beer and the belly - and they recognised it. He took great pride in that stocky, but firm frame.

Rounding the top step from his little 'chapel' in the old coal cellar, the phone had startled him. But Brien took the call as usual. As usual, he waited for the other person to speak. As usual he could hear her breathing hard, but for the very first time she actually spoke to him. She said 'You raped me Dadda.' Of course he knew this, but had never said anything, never apologised, because he didn't know what Colleen thought he was doing, or more accurately, had done. Back then she would absorb all his sleeping hours and of course she was mad keen to please her Dadda. She loved the whole idea of being his 'Little Wifey.' They had enjoyed tender love making sessions together, sweet and gentle. But 'Don't tell Mammy, she might be a little jealous.'

'Course not, Dadda.'

He heard her sob before she repeated herself, then added 'You buggered me Dadda.'

But he had not. That was utterly disgusting. He was shocked she could say such a thing. The politically correct, child protection people, had turned her head, twisted what they had done. It was wrong, yes he knew that. When Colleen finally realised, the only thing he had said was a kind of plea to her, 'Yes, they could send me to prison for it.' But that was all.

Now she said, 'You never did that did you, Dadda? You loved your little wifey, didn't you? Didn't you Dadda?'

What was she talking about? He was shaking now and could not speak. Whatever he might say had firstly to make sense with what she was saying. Secondly, he did not wish to make anything worse between Colleen and himself. Yes it could be worse. Rape was worse. Buggery was much worse.

Colleen was now crying openly on the other end of the phone. He couldn't hand her over to the Mammy in that state. He listened. He looked across the front passage. He could see the television light flickering under the sitting room door. He hoped Ginny would be dozing.

'Dadda, you buggered me. It really hurt me Dadda. He was so mad with me checking up on him. He's never been angry with me before. He threw me down and ripped me up, Dadda.' And she whined. She tore his heart out.

But what was she saying? 'You buggered me,' but definitely '*he* was so mad.' He heard a noise from inside himself, but suppressed it. He couldn't speak yet. He tried a long 'Hmmm.' He heard her stop to listen.

She was listening. Then she sobbed again. 'Dadda?'

He coughed. 'Colleen?'

'You buggered me Dadda. You tore me up.'

'I am a bad man,' Brien heard himself say.

'Ach!' she exclaimed, '*you* are no way a bad man.'

He bit his lip.

'Your lovely priest buggered me, Dadda.'

'Oh God,' he prayed, scrabbling round for whatever she was saying. 'Holy Mother of God Almighty, God, God, God.' He bit his lip again. Why was she telling him after all this time, all these years? Is that why she left so suddenly without a word? 'Oh, my Dear, Darling Colleen. Oh I just wish you had told me.'

He heard what he thought was a little cry at the end of the phone and definitely 'what the fuck?' before it went dead.

He looked at the receiver like a piece of filth. He replaced it on the cradle and jumped as a new ringing hit him like an electric shock.

She was breathing hard at the other end.

He listened. As usual, he waited.

'Dadda.' This time her voice was insistent. 'Dadda, you know who I am.'

Brien felt silly. 'Of course I do dear. Aren't you my little Darling Colleen?'

'Dadda, we talked in the churchyard, that time. You were messing with the flower borders.'

A cold shiver went down his back. He always did the church garden. When was she talking about? *'Breakfast at Tiffany's?'* 'Couple of years ago?' he said.

'You told me the priest was called Von Trapp!'

'Oh God, oh God, oh God,' he prayed, breaking into a cold sweat. Hadn't that hussy put him in mind of his Colleen? 'You?'

'You knew! Yes you did.' An incredulous tone. 'You mean you didn't recognise me?' Her laugh was more of a 'Huh!'

He was crying now and looking up to Heaven, he said simply, 'I'm sorry; I just did not think I would ever see you again …'

She wasn't sure she could comprehend this, but her pain and her anger burst through again. 'Well, Dadda, I am now Mrs Hubert Stannton, and your precious fucking Holy Priest has been and gone and buggered me. Hu buggered me.' She slammed the phone down.

After the Conference, Leo had a hunch that Hu was not going home – at least not immediately. He was intrigued as to why not. Of course it was only a hunch – but where had the hunch come from; where was the fire giving off that smoke? Leo's wife Talya was not home from work. He parked his Subaru on the street. There still being light after a bright early spring day, he decided to start up the Countryman – his Dad's beloved Morris Minor, beloved not least because Dad had thought it was named after a Miner.

He dragged open the garage doors, stiff after a winter of immobility and the car started first time. He decided to take it for a spin. He felt himself drawn back to the scene of the crime, the crime he would dearly like to commit. Idling along the Grenley bypass, the beacon caught his eye and he pulled up beside it. He took a little walk up Beacon Hill and felt a little heat from the sun on its last gasp before going over the horizon.

Leo wondered if he could see the Loseborough. He could - the roof and the chimneys were gilded below him in the copse. He was drawn inexorably on.

He wandered past the first car park looking up at the hotel frontage – plain white with simple Georgian windows. He picked out the room he had slept in the night before. Stannton's would be immediately behind it. Stannton's car was not in the car park. Leo kicked up some road chippings as he mused his way along the lane to the other car park. He noticed the fire escape was on this end of the hotel with a door to each floor. Grinning at himself he contemplated sneaking in up there. The door was shut anyway – *but the one on the top floor appeared to be ever so slightly ajar.*

Leo needed some answers. In front of Abe and Brien he had not wanted to dig into the mire of clerical child abuse and sex scandals, Stannton's Irish links and his bimbo. There was always that Italian curate lurking at the back of Leo's mind – and his face was Hubert Stannton.

He looked around, and listened: nobody around and no cars running.

He ran, two stepping up the steel staircase, but quietly, to the top floor. The door was not quite to – the shadow had made it look further open than it was. He got his fingertips to the door edge and tore at it, tearing a nail, but the door came open. Sucking his finger and tasting blood, he prized the door open just a slice, to peep and see no one in the corridor.

He wiped the blood off the door and he was in with the door shut behind him.

He jumped when he noticed a corridor to left *and* right – just a couple of extra rooms on each side. No one there, either. He stepped over into the left-hand side and composed himself. Would or could Stannton still be in his room? Wasn't it a bit rich of him to be using his experience with The Tin Tab to get work with the same clientele in Civvy Street?

Assuming a casual air – play-acting was not his forte – Leo walked airily along the top floor and was undisturbed as he went down one flight of stairs.

He deemed his 'air of nonchalance' to be not of Olivier standard – he could feel his heart pumping and noticed he was actually leaning in to listen at doors. He straightened up and walked along the corridor, noting his door and immediately realising the shouting was coming from Hu's room. He could also see light under the door and darted away when he noticed movement in it. He had a hand around the back of his neck hiding his long curls and he had hunched and aged his struggle towards the fire escape.

Thursday 4th March

The next morning Iruna thought she would call past the school on her way in to Clayford - another village to add to her memory map – and she didn't know there had been any coal mines round there, either. However, before she got there, she was thrown in at the deep end – the deep end of a jacuzzi - with a missing body on her hands. She told one of the lads that, and of course he laughed at her. When she realised what she had said, and laughed, he had simply nudged her, smiled, winked and walked off. Nice bloke … blork.

Inspector Blundell was laughing inside. He was outside in a meadow which should not have been ploughed up, but which was gouged with mysterious ruts. Totally mysterious to the farmer, but they had a 'right laugh' as Blundell revealed all to him, and was even able to point across the river to what it was all about. No it wasn't cattle or sheep rustlers, it wasn't even alien abductions. (Shame - that would have gone down well at the pub).

It was metal thieves.

'But there's no metal left,' said the farmer. 'Fucking Gypos took my rusty old harrow about five years ago, came back a couple of months later with a trailer and nicked my concourse condition '42 Marshall Tractor from out the barn. I bet they scrapped that 'cos they couldn't show it – probably unique.'

Detective Inspector John 'Chocky' Blundell was not in the Politically Correct Reinforcement Squad, not today anyway. He said simply, 'Looking in the wrong place, sir – look up.'

He did. 'Never!' gasped the farmer. 'The pylons? How?'

'They actually climb the pylons and cut the wire.'

'Wow! I thought mebbes they'd be cutting out spars off the pylon, not the cable itself! Anyhow, not that there, though?'

'No, but that's what the ruts are about. Look across the river at the other pylon.'

'Ah, well,' said the farmer squinting at the sky, 'I can see the pylon, but I couldn't see the wire if it was still there! Have they had it?'

Sweeping his over-long hair under his battered trilby, and tipping it onto the back of his head, Blundell walked to the foot of the pylon. 'Look,' he said, 'mud up here where they've climbed it – two different blokes by the look of it. You didn't disturb them, or anything, did you?'

'No, sir, I don't even know when it was. Can't see this field from the 'ouse. When did it rain last – the tracks are fairly clear aren't they?'

Blundell was holding his back and peering up the pylon. 'Wonder if they only reccied it?' He turned back to the farmer. 'Anyway, sir, they definitely decided to start over there.' He pointed at the distant pylon again. 'They'd cut one of the cables right out, and cut another from one pylon and left it dangling. Could've killed man or beast.' He mused and mumbled, scratching his head, 'dame or dog.'

Blundell's buzzer went off. 'Excuse me, sir … D.I. Blundell.' He trudged between some cow-pats, oblivious to any potential spoliation of his tatty suede boots, a bit away from the farmer. He looked around and peered under his hand into the distance, away from the river. He replaced the mobile in one pocket, and taking a card out of another, he offered it to the farmer saying, 'Got a missing body. Better go and find it, sorry. We've been working the metal thieves for years and they always seem one step ahead of us – except if they electrocute themselves …'

'Y' mean one's copped it over there?'

'No, unfortunately not,' he winked. 'Call me if you have any more hassle with the metal, won't you? Got to go.'

He spun his battered trilby onto the parcel shelf and set off to Grenley. He followed the line of pylons across the landscape and wondered if there was any end to it. They went on forever and straight into his living room. But they could not police everywhere. Where is the morality in these people – two miles of cable pulled off a railway line, total disruption for days to the Great North Eastern, costing millions, and the thieves would get a few hundred pounds for it?

Upping the game a bit – in both senses – taking the copper off the pylons, but he did hear that the monkeys had got five tons of it in one haul, which would be worth about twenty-five grand. Some would blame the Chinese, but not Chocky. Yes Matt might - at least they want work, which is more than can be said for his son. He sighed thinking of his wife's tears. What could they do now – they had given their middle child everything, including a sense of justice and loving their neighbours, even if they are black?

Readying himself for the task ahead, he could not for the life of him, remember what the new sergeant called herself. What would Matt call her? He'd seen the pretty thing around the office, so he knew who it was phoning him. He hoped the DCI hadn't given her a baptism of fire in the jacuzzi. He had a little chuckle, but upbraided himself when he remembered they were investigating a death, possibly a suspicious one, definitely in unusual circumstances.

As he turned at the Beacon, he caught the sign for the Loseborough but couldn't see the Hotel, concealed as it was in a copse.

He had to wonder if it wasn't all a bit of female hysteria – missing body and all?

Very clever – nice development on the end of Grenley Hill with a view over Gainsborough, all neatly broken up by a variety of old native trees.

What was their food like?

The car park was not adequate though. It didn't seem a very big space for this size of hotel, even though it wasn't the Hilton. No emergency vehicles either. Blundell was in it before he realised there were no spaces. Not in the wrong place though - he had never heard of The Loseborough, and the young Sergeant from 'darn sarf,' had had to give him directions. Shame. So, backing out he saw the sign

'Overflow Car Park' pointing further down the lane. Two Police cars – one marked only with the blue light on top - and no ambulance. He supposed you needed no ambulance for no bodies.

From the car park he had two options – front or back. He knew the Sergeant was there, a body wasn't. There was no ambulance and no sign of the Scene Of Crime Officers either. He walked towards the back, hoping to take in the scene before he was seen.

A four story whitewashed building. Some wrought iron 'balconies' – two above each other over the tent. Not originally been a Hotel proper he didn't think. Could have been a convent or training place. Nice setting though. He walked away past the building towards the larger trees for a wider picture. The SOCO's van was on the lawn.

So someone fell out of a window. He went into the tent and showed his ID to the SOCO photographer, androgynous in the paper suit.

He looked into the small jacuzzi. 'What have you got the tent here for?'

'Prying eyes, Guv?'

'What's to pry at? The body's not here.'

'Unfortunately not, sir.'

'Unfortunately! You mean it got up and walked?'

'No sir the Ambulance took it … him.'

'Wasn't it … him … he, dead?'

'Yes sir, but …'

The look from Blundell stopped him going any further. Blundell had his hand over his mouth and was staring at the person aghast. He looked for a more sensible correspondent. No sign of the young sergeant. He saw the Pathologist scrabbling around on the grass. 'Jenks! Save me! What have you got a tent up for?'

'Hi Chocky. Not such a sweetie today? Sorry to say, the Hotel thought someone had just fallen out of the window …'

'You mean he didn't fall out of the window?'

'Wait for it … had *only* just fallen out of the window, so they called an ambulance. The Paramedics got him into the Ambulance – basically away from the mess the Hotel people had made - and away from the punters. Local Doc declared him very dead and they took him away.'

'Was he still alive when … he was found, then? Could there have been signs of life?'

'No, not at all. I know! Probably actually fell out last night.'

'Well why did they take him?'

Jenks gave Blundell a look. 'Calm down, Chocky. This isn't the sweet Inspector we all know and love. Frankly, I have no idea why they took him. The way things are, they could've been a couple of kids from St John's Ambulance Brigade Cadets. There is only one mitigating circumstance for them – at least the head was warm. He dropped his tone and looked over his specs at the Inspector. 'Imagine that cleaner mouth-to-mouthing a stone cold face? She had pulled him out of the jacuzzi – well his head at least, had been in the jacuzzi apparently – so it *was* actually warm. But keep your toupee unruffled – I have been in touch with the hospital, and give me two more minutes here and I shall proceed to inspect the body.'

'What's to see here, Jenks?' He was wondering who would use a jacuzzi in the deep midwinter.

'A highly compromised scene, I'm afraid.'

Blundell had one hand massaging his neck and the other clinking the coins in the back pocket of his cords. 'Pray, tell.' He advanced a smile.

'A cleaner doing the room, thought someone had fallen out of the window up there, ran down and dragged him out of the jacuzzi. By the time the Manager caught up with her, she was administering all the procedures she's seen on Casualty, all at once. Kitchen staff charged in after him. One says, 'don't do that', another says 'do this', - you know how it is.'

'Not like on telly, you mean?'

'That's a bit sweeter,' said the pathologist tweaking Blundell's cheek. 'I suppose you'll be going up to the room. Your delectable young Sergeant's in there somewhere.' He blew a kiss and waggled his hands around, up towards the room and back to the car park. 'Or do you want to come with me?'

'I'd better check the room,' Blundell said, going out and looking up. 'The Sergeant called me because it is such a mess, but it may actually be something suspicious. Foul play? You?'

'Well, as we sing in the trade 'Ain't got nobody, nobody but you.'' Jenks quickstepped onto the lawn and shouted back 'I'll call you with immediate first impressions, Okey Cokey?'

Shaking his head, Blundell was concerned things were being taken a little too lightly. On the other hand, he was sorry that Jenks had needed to pull him up. He was actually proud that the plods had caught onto his wife's pet-name for him. His disdain for the violent 'Sweeney' type of seventies cop had led him from thespian notions towards being a good cop. A sweetie from Thornton sounded drippy at first, but he had felt happy to be recognised for his gentle but successful detections. Chocky saw a helmet. 'Constable,' he shouted, 'were you first on the scene?'

'Yes, sir. Put up the tape and cordoned off the corridor with the room on it. Bit tricky, because some people were still in bed.'

'What time was this then?'

The Constable went to get out his pocket book.

'Oh give over Constable! Approximately what time are we talking about – lazy lie ins, or crack o'dawn?'

After a double take the PC felt safe to continue with less formality. 'Oh, seven fifteen. Cleaner came on at six thirty, had a quick tidy downstairs and the boss told her to go and do a room that hadn't been slept in.'

'Why clean it then?' said Blundell.

'Yes, does sound funny, but it's not really. It was used into the evening – kind of a two-day conference. But nobody was sleeping over the second night, and it wasn't needed for any fresh customers, so they didn't bring in a cleaner specially.'

'Fair enough,' mused Blundell. 'No it's not! You mean somebody's been lying dead out here since, what, early evening, and nobody noticed?'

The constable felt as if he had regained some ground on his superior, so he chanced a smile saying, 'Did I say 'early evening' sir?'

'Sorry, no. Tell me what you found when you got here.'

'The Paramedics had the man in the ambulance by the time I got here and I simply let them do what they thought best – they're the experts, sir. Local Doc came just after me and did the declaration bit.'

'Any clues as to how long he'd been dead?' He narrowed his eyes. Was he cold?'

The Constable just looked at Blundell.

'Curiouser and curiouser.'

'Sir?'

'What's your name, son?'

'Jason, sir.'

'Now look Constable Jason,' said Blundell, licking his finger and thumb and 'writing' on his hand, 'You have done your training – not a cadet or anything?'

'PC Jason Hancock, sorry, sir – first suspicious death sir. And very early, sir.'

Chocky chuckled. 'Alright, I won't interrupt – give me your story.'

The lad looked like he was about to cry so Blundell put an affirming hand on his shoulder.

Hancock took a deep breath. 'I came through the hotel having entered the front door. I came out the back and there was a complete mêlée round the jacuzzi – that's inside the tent sir.'

'Yes!' snapped the Inspector looking to the heavens. 'Calm down Chocky.' 'Go on.'

'I had some trouble gaining their full attention, but eventually, I discerned that the centre of attention was not the corpse, but the cleaner who had found him. She was exhausted, apparently from giving artificial resuscitation and the kiss of life, one or the other - are they the same thing? – and she was crying. I shouted and got them to take her inside. I told them not to disturb the scene any more than was necessary - to all simply walk away.

'I asked who was in charge,' he went on, 'and a rather stuffy manager came over and berated me for being the sole response from the Police.

'I declared it a crime scene. Then, realising that there was no body left at all, I looked around to see the paramedics jumping out of the back of the Ambulance ready to drive off. Sorry if I shouldn't have let them sir … Control said seeing as he was kinda like already in the ambulance, there wasn't much point taking him out and putting him a hearse, see sir?'

DI Blundell appeared to be all ears – and no nasty looks - so the constable felt safe to continue.

'As no one at all was now outside, I decided to nip in and asked the Manager,' he blinked and coughed, 'told the Manager to send someone to keep everybody well away from the jacuzzi, while I went up to sort the room. I stood at the door and sort of peeped ...'

Blundell sighed.

'I was going to do the corridor, but people were coming out of rooms in all sorts of state of undress, and the manager bloke was breathing down my neck. I realised that I would be best not entering, so I didn't, sir.'

Blundell gave a nod of approval.

'I just taped the door, sir. He was giving me and the tape the dead-eye, sir, so I thought discretion being ...'

At Reception, Blundell at last caught sight of the sergeant, evidently poring over the books.

She looked up and rushed over. 'Oh sir, I'm sorry to drag you over, but this is a fine mess someone has gotten us into.'

'I've already picked up on that, erm ...?

'Yes, sorry sir, we have met around the office. I'm DS Bahadur, sir. Just transferred from Thames Valley.'

'Welcome aboard, Sergeant,' he said offering his hand. 'Chocky Blundell. Settling in okay?'

She frowned at what he said, but thought it a sweet smile he gave her.

'So what have you got?'

'Even worse mess, sir – they don't even know who was in which room, so we don't know who the victim can be?'

'Not at all?' Blundell's voice cracked.

Bahadur bit her lip and waggled her head. 'One of four apparently.'

'Blimmin' 'eck.'

A tall obsequious looking man was hovering. Bahadur introduced him as Mr Houldsworth, the Manager, and Blundell - not bothering to shake his hand, used his own in the 'show us the way' signal. The DI was a mild mannered man, but his patience was being tried. He decided discretion was the better part of biting someone's head off.

He waved Bahadur to come and take a look, too.

The bedroom door gave Blundell another shock. 'You've taped the door, I see, Hancock. What now, do you suggest?'

The Manager said 'I hope that gaffer tape doesn't rip off all the paintwork – and you've got it on the wallpaper there, you twit. Inspector, should he have just tied a bit of that barrier tape across from the handle.'

Blundell wasn't having this Jobsworth upsetting one of 'his boys' on his first job. Giving young Jason a surreptitious wink he turned to the Manager and felt

71

John Cleese creep into his vocal chords: 'Your name, sir?'

'Houldsworth, sir.'

'Expert in Police forensic procedures are we, Mr Jobsworth? Watch a lot of CSI, do we? What else is there to tie it to? Or do you suggest a pretty bow on the handle would have done the trick? Get back down to your desk and find me as much detail as possible on every single person who has been at the hotel – staying or not, staff, guests, visiting tradesmen – from, say, yesterday morning for starters. The Sergeant will give you priorities. If you need to, bring someone in to help you, we need this soon, so I think ... yes, do bring someone in.'

Bahadur was pretty embarrassed by this carry on and stood away from it. Blundell noticed.

As Houldsworth scuttled away, Blundell shouted after him, 'and I don't suppose you know who fell out of the window?'

Houldsworth ground to a halt and turned slowly with his hand behind his head. 'Ah, now there we do have a problem.'

Blundell stepped along to him. 'Problem? You don't know who is staying in your Hotel?'

'Not quite ...'

'Sort of ... can kinda like ... guess, you mean?' He gave Hancock another wink. 'Get off, before you really embarrass yourself. When I come down in a few minutes I want your best guess as to the identity of our faller.' Turning to Bahadur, he whispered, 'get a list of at least those who *could possibly* have been in this room, Sergeant.'

Back with Hancock he said loud enough for the retreating Manager to hear, 'Rip that tape off Hancock, let's take a peep. Idiot.'

'Ignorant isn't he sir?'

Blundell laid his hand on Hancock's sleeve and looked into the Constable's eyes. 'Just peel it off – we don't want the Super moaning about having to pay for redecorating the whole flippin' hotel!' When all was clear, he flung the door open, but held the enthusiastic Constable back. 'We're not going in. Have you had your beetle crushers in there?'

'Well ... I have been in. I just went over to the window and looked out – I wanted to be sure it was this room he fell out of.'

Blundell took in as much as he could from the threshold. 'Fair enough, son. Now shut the door and *tie* some of the barrier Tape across ... maybe to that radiator – just the blue and white stuff - eh?'

Blundell thought he had better try to get the man's name right. 'Mr, er Hawksworth, was it?'

Houldsworth gave the Inspector a suspicious look as he corrected him.

'Jolly good. How's the list getting on? The top of it, I am most interested in!'

'Yes Mr Blunder, but I have to tell you that there is something a bit suspicious, and I stress that I do not think there is any fault on Loseborough's side.'

DS Bahadur had her eyebrows raised and, unseen by the manager, was shaking her head at the DI.

Blundell was pulling his lip.

'No,' continued the Manager, 'It is all a bit strange: there were four men booked in for a mini conference and had reserved their rooms for use until four p.m. – didn't clear rooms by eleven as normally expected, you see. Small extra fee.'

'Four p.m. Do you think this chap was lying out there since before dark yesterday, Mr Houldsworth?'

Houldsworth warmed a little, thinking he was gaining some of the respect his station merited. 'Almost impossible, I feel, though someone falling over the fairly high balcony, likewise, Inspector. I was on earlies yesterday, like today, sir, so I am not really sure what the booking situation was like for the evening. I can confirm that the room was not booked for the night. I cannot confirm what time the chaps left – were supposed to leave.'

Blundell took a look around. He saw the bar across the way with a man and a woman busying themselves, but ear-wigging, from there. He noticed the oddly old-fashioned prints round the place – out of place in such a modern pamper-pot. 'Anybody here who was on last night?'

'I think the barman may have been. Shall we ask him?'

'Do, please?'

Houldsworth stepped across and pushed the glass door open a bit. 'Jez! A minute? Jez, this is, er …'

'Inspector Blundell, Sergeant Badder.'

'Inspector Blundell, this is Jeremy Fylde.'

Fylde proffered a limp wrist, 'charmed, I'm sure. We could go a bundle,' and returning the crushed wrist to his hip, recovered from his grimace to size the Inspector up and down. He ignored the pretty Sergeant.

Do all he could to challenge his innate homophobia, Blundell could really not compass the OTT, camp behaviour of the 'I'm Free!' type. Particularly in someone who, for some inexplicable reason, reminded him of his son Mattie, the 'queer basher.'

Houldsworth interrupted the charade: 'Jez! You were on duty last night, Yes? What can you tell us about the poor chap who fell out of the window?'

Fylde pulled out a massive paisley handkerchief and gave big blow. 'Awful! I was overwhelmed. It's all a bit much. Don't expect stuff like that in a nice place like this.' He made to walk off back to the bar.

Houldsworth jumped to block him. 'Pull yourself together man. Have a little think.'

Seeing Fylde peeping over his hankie at him, Blundell felt sure he was laughing at him, but spoke evenly: 'Yes Jeremy, tell the nice Policeman what you know.'

Fylde saw that Blundell might actually be more fun than old Houldsworth. He returned his hankie to its place and spoke a bit of sense. 'We had a Golden Wedding in last night, and though they might have been fogies, the old guys were CAMRA buffs and could sink a few.'

'I assume we are not talking under water photography,' sneered Blundell, 'and not in the jacuzzi, out there, Mr Fylde?'

That tickled him, but Houldsworth harrumphed.

'The old girls were on Port and Lemons, and Whisky and Orange, you know…'

'People, faces, dead man, Jez – come on.'

'Yessir. Lots of … one dead. Not sure which one, what with Suzanne fainting and all. Which one was it Mr Houldsworth – not one of the Golden Couple I hope?'

'Oh Jeremy, do try to be of some help to us, here,' said the Manager. 'It's not a ruddy TV Soap. A man's dead.'

Blundell turned to frown at the Sergeant whose fingers barely concealed her gritted teeth.

The barman continued, 'Of course, sir, but as I said, I don't know who it is … was … is dead.'

'Inspector Blundell will tell you what he looked like.'

Blundell jumped. 'I will, will I?' His hand was behind his neck again and the coppers clinked. He gave Houldsworth a look-among-equals at last. 'We're all in a bit of a silly position here aren't we? But can I start here, now, again? Get your Registration Book,' and waving the Sergeant into play, 'sit yourselves down in the bar – Jeremy, Mr Houldsworth and Sergeant Badder - and see if you can't get to the bottom of this.'

Fylde whipped up a grin, but Blundell slapped it back down with narrowed eyes.

'I think I had better get down to the hospital with the pathologist and check out whether or not there is much to be suspicious about. Sergeant, you keep on, here. Tape up the whole of the back yard – across to the trees. Take a SOCO up to the room and maybe make a start there – photos and all. I hope to be back within the hour to start making some sense.'

As he got to the car, Blundell had the pathologist on the phone as he wound up the engine. 'Jenks, you got to the hospital, yes? Can you please tell me something about the dead, man? It is a man, isn't it? We've got that much?'

'Yes, Chocky, first sight. Caucasian, mid thirties, about six two or three, bit bashed about by the fall, but appears to have actually drowned. All very first impressions as you well know. Give me another hour and I should be able to clarify some of that.'

'Thanks. Identifying features?'

'Long blonde hair – bit unfashionable in his age group, I'd say. Blue eyes. Say he was a pretty handsome chap – to remark on, you know.'

'Good enough for starters, get on and let me know some detail for the 'suspicious death' file A.S.A.P. Bye.'

Returning to the Hotel staff, who all jumped to see him back so soon, Blundell said, 'Seems like something to go on. A tall man with long blonde hair…'

'Oh Dear,' cried Jeremy pulling out his hankie again and sobbing. 'Oh not Hubert! He was lovely. Oh no!'

'Sounding useful?' said Blundell to Houldsworth. 'Got a Hubert on the list?'

'Yes, Hubert, not Rupert as I first thought, and Stannton – double 'n' – in the middle.'

'Good. Address?'

'Yes. I'll make a little list for you. There were four men together …'

Jeremy sobbed again and added through the hankie, 'Two older men, plus Trotsky and the lovely Hubert – he had big, expressive, artistic hands.' He went back to his paisley.

'Come on now Jez, bear up for a bit more detail, there's a good lad.'

'Oh Officer, you're so sensitive. Yes the younger pair really liked my real ales and got through quite a few single malts, too. The older guys were costing us! One of them, out of character for an Irishman, if I may be so bold, only had tap water – with ice *and* lemon!'

'What were they doing here?'

'Spa treat, I think, wasn't it, Mr Houldsworth?'

'Yes, a Groupon thing.'

'Coupon?' asked Blundell.

'Sort of – loss leader thing we have – cheap, off season, sold in batches – groups – and people buy the coupons/Groupons. Do you follow?'

Blundell looked to Jeremy again: 'You didn't happen to pick up on anything they were on about did you, son?'

Fylde rolled his eyes and dabbed them while he had a think. 'The Golden Wedding kept me too busy to hear at night, but in the daytime, they were like ramblers – coming and going after walkies. Nothing interesting caught my attention. Marta might have caught something, I didn't.'

'Not now. What about this cleaner, Houldsworth?'

'We let her go home, Inspector. Do you want her address, too?'

'No, I think I really need her to talk and walk me through what she found. Is she usually a nervy type?'

'Not at all!' Houldsworth let slip. 'Took her opportunity to pile it on a bit I reckon.'

Blundell let a noisy breath out of his nose.

'Yes, I suppose it was quite a trauma for her. Shall I give her a call and see if she'll come in?'

'No! *Tell* her to come in, and give me her number as well. Tell her I want her here at some point, today – two o'clock, tell her. I need forensics to give their best shot on that room first, before we walk about in it. Maybe it can all come together. Get me that list and I'll call by the house. You don't happen to have taken the phone numbers of these blokes, do you?'

'Usually only the person booking,' said the Manager checking the book. 'Yes, Andrew Nicholas.'

'Name Andrew mean anything to you, Jeremy?'

Jeremy was frowning, hoping he had the right group of people. 'No, not at all. The one I call Trotsky could be him. Seemed to be 'hosting' the group - bought a lot of the drinks. The water guy never came to buy, but I heard him talking – to-be-sure he was Irish. What are the other names, sir?'

'G. Grant?' Houldsworth was stumbling over the signatures, 'Brien Divine, A, R or L Nicholas and Rupert Staunton? Stannton?'

'Ooh Hubert – it's Hubert, sir – he was *Divine!*'

'Just stop that, please Fylde. Let me see, Mr Houldsworth.'

'That's De-veen, Houldsworth – proper Irish name, though I think that says Grant. That signature doesn't say Andrew …'

'Signatures are rarely a name – just initials, aren't they Inspector?'

'Mm, but that's a capital 'L' – Len, or Lou, Leo or Larry … ideas Jez?'

'Leo! Yes Leo! Silly me. I called him Trotsky – not to his face, you know. He looked like Trotsky with one of them really tiny little goatee strips – makes you wonder why they bother.' Fylde swept his long hair all over to one side to reveal crop circles cut into the shortened patch over his right ear. He turned back to flutter at Blundell.

'Sergeant. A word.'

Bahadur followed the Inspector as he led her slowly out into the back yard again. Standing on the bar steps he didn't say anything as he again looked over the scene.

The Sergeant was becoming ever more uncomfortable. She didn't like the way it was all going. She felt stupid that everything was topsy-turvy when she arrived and she hadn't managed to straighten anything out at all. The Hotel system was not helping. Nor were Blundell's muddy suedes.

Blundell eventually turned to her and snapped his teeth together. 'Sorry to put it like this and I don't wish to give you any poor first impressions, but over the years you will have heard plenty of your colleagues refer to this situation as a right fucking mess.'

She kept a straight face and was not ready to comment, yet.

'It's like bloody Fawlty Towers,' he went on. 'And you know what?'

She didn't.

'If we don't get something right in the next hour or so, we are going to look like the bloody Keystone Cops.'

Fawlty Towers was before her time, but of course she had heard of it; unlike the Keystone Cops, but she felt she shouldn't want to look like them. She wasn't sure if the DI was blaming her at all. He was back looking over the garden with his hand on his neck. With his head he signalled to come through to the front.

He took her round the car park he had used and went all the way to his original viewpoint, hopefully well away from compromising the scene, and in the trees.

Bahadur jumped as he proffered his hand again, 'John Blundell. Let's start again.'

Her growing discomfort was probably showing in the reluctant offer of her own hand. 'Iruna. Iruna Ba-ha-dur.' She was squirming as he held onto her hand with a double handshake.

'Mmm. Nice name. Where you from Runa?'

'Blackbird Leys, sir. Thames Valley.'

'Sounds pretty.'

'Does, doesn't it sir.'

Letting go or her hand he stroked his salt and pepper beard. He kicked a pine-cone. 'What's it all look like to you, Runa? You alright with Runa?'

'Prefer I-runa,' she said hoping she wasn't coming over too primly.

He chuckled at himself. 'Fine mess, eh? Sorry, I-runa … and call me Chocky. What about this body?'

'Well, sir, dark by six o'clock. Men were supposed to be out about four. Even if he hung around for two hours before falling out, like you said, you'd think somebody would have seen something.'

'Some*body!*' chuckled the DI.

The DS was not being put at her ease. 'Sir. Can I say something, sir? I'm…'

Blundell looked at the young woman. She had incredibly white skin contrasting against her jet black hair, but now the skin was blotching with obvious embarrassment. 'Hey, Iruna, I'm not one to stand on ceremony, say whatever …'

'This is my first really serious case in my really new role as a DS and it really is looking really a bit, well, pear-shaped. I had to call you 'cos somebody's not followed procedure.'

'Well said,' he clapped. 'Exactly. Now that's in the open, what do you suggest?' He nodded, 'Your case Sergeant.'

'That's gracious, sir, but if it does turn out to be serious had it better not be our case?'

'Down to it, then – do you think a bloke's not *just fallen* out of a window?'

She looked up at the balcony and he followed her gaze.

'It looks a pretty high balcony,' Iruna said. 'I don't think I could accidentally fall over it.'

There was not much more to go on until they could find something about the group and exactly who had fallen out. They agreed that Blundell would call past the Hospital to get a good look at the body while Bahadur pulled together the limited information she could from the Hotel.

Meeting back at the station the DS had a plan ready for the DI: from the list of phone numbers she had discovered that Nicholas was the local youth officer and she had got four names, three phone numbers and one address from his office: Andrew 'Leo' Nicholas, the youth officer, with three people from a voluntary youth project – two of the management committee and the parish priest.

DI Blundell had clarified in his mind an image of the victim and it was little different from what he got on the phone – a man in his thirties, with shoulder length blonde hair, and maybe tall enough to fall over the balcony. Jenks hadn't finished his autopsy.

DS Bahadur hazarded a guess that this was probably the parish priest.

Blundell whistled at that. Catholic as he was, he hadn't come across many young parish priests, nor long-haired ones for that matter.

'The youth officer's secretary gave me a bit of thumbnail sketch of each – her officer is greying and around fifty, with a goatee; there were two old men – seventies, she thinks – and the …' She took a breath. 'He's not a priest any more, the ex-priest is in his thirties and … he had long blonde hair when he ran off with a woman a couple of years ago.'

Blundell gave out a full-breath whistle, followed by a noisy intake of breath. When Bahadur showed him her list, he dug a sandwich out of his drawer. It was the ex-priest's name that had no phone number or address against it. He had a long thoughtful chomp on his sandwich. Eventually they agreed that he would find out more on the ex-priest and his sergeant would try to winkle-out some more detail on the others from the youth office. If possible she would get out and find the full story from Nicholas, and if she had time, either or both of the other two.

'Let's hope we can decide it's not a suspicious death before we go home tonight,' Blundell asked, adding 'haven't got a date tonight, have you?'

She gave a blank look at first, then shook her head. Dark nights and her luck had not changed that quickly.

Blundell didn't want to reveal his sources to the new sergeant quite yet. He had got onto his own parish priest for the inside information on Father Stannton. Apparently the Diocese had high hopes of the young Irish priest with no blots on his copybook relative to the scandals coming across the Irish Sea. He had built up mass attendances well, particularly reaching out to the young, and succeeded in making lots of the Polish influx feel welcome and part of the parish. The old Friary Convent was only a small parish, a good starting point on the career ladder for a fresh young cleric.

However, he had succumbed to a very pretty woman who, so the word goes, absolutely gunned for him. His Alma Mater, the big Irish training college, at Maynooth, did coax him out of her clutches, but for no more than a few weeks. The source did not know Hu Stannton's address, but did think that he had not moved a long way off. He promised to make a few calls and get back to the Inspector.

As he was leaving, Blundell got a call about this morning's cable thieves, but swapped to take the incoming call from Bahadur. The youth officer's secretary had tracked down her boss who was on leave and driving round Derbyshire and he's heading straight back home. He had given Stannton's address.

Blundell decided to go straight there. He told Bahadur to meet up with the SOCOs and the Cleaner and do a walk through and he would join them as soon as.

Blundell found himself outside a semi on a new development. Pretty, but pretty small. He rang the doorbell, or more accurately set off a grand campanile.

What an apparition greeted him – a fallen angel, blonde-haired and red eyed.

'Hello,' she whimpered.

'Good Afternoon, Ma'am. Mrs Stannton?'

'Yes.'

'Hello Mrs Stannton.' Bending as if talking to a little child he said, 'I'm DI Blundell from the Police Station.'

'Do you want to come in?' she asked, but didn't move.

'I think so dear.'

Blundell put his arm round her waste and steered her gently as she veered into her lounge.

'Not more bad news, Mr Blunder, I can't stand any more.'

He sat down but she didn't. He stood again.

'No Dear.' What was he doing? This could be a murderer. He didn't do this sort of thing. She was a thing of beauty, but crushed, like a rose not quite perfect - not up to the gardener's high standards.

'I'm DI Blundell from the Police Station.'

'Yes, you said. You mean you want me to call you Deeaye?'

His daughter would say 'Ah, Bless!'

'I'm sorry, Mrs Stannton, we do so easily slip into these ways. I'm Detective Inspector John Blundell. I've …'

She looked at him horrified and a strange mewling crept up from her very core. She raised her face to the heavens, then covered it with a tissue. She almost collapsed into her chair, but pulled herself up resolutely, wiped her face and came to attention.

'Oh Detective, I am so silly. I can't think straight. What's going on? Where's my Hu?' She choked off another whimper, shook her head and flattened her hair down. After a strong blink and head shake, she continued quite calmly. 'Okay. Okay.' A breath. 'What is it I should call you?'

'Inspector, Ma'am.'

She lowered her head just a little and looked out under heavy lids. She couldn't help herself. 'Do I look like a Ma'am, to you, Inspector. Call me Holly.'

Blundell almost smiled at this. Of course she in no way brought a 'Ma'am' to mind. She was very much the lost little girl.

'Somebody said my Hu jumped out a window. He didn't. He wouldn't. He couldn't. He …'

Blundell felt his teeth clench. More cock-ups. Bahadur must have got the number. 'That wasn't fair of her, Holly. I apologise. We really don't know how he…'

She whimpered yet again, but pulled herself up short. 'My Hu died, the great lummox and it was all my fault.'

This completely threw Blundell. Green as she was, the DS had surely not said anything like this. He waited to see if Holly would elaborate, but she was gone. He followed her look to the portrait of a stunning couple laughing on their wedding day. Not a white wedding though.

In the end he had to prompt her. 'Holly. You didn't push him out of the window?'

She looked at him and if that mewling was anything, it was not this. A noise boiled out of her slowly, like a train from a very long tunnel, one long growling sigh, until all her breath was gone and she crumpled onto the floor. She didn't faint. She lay in a foetal position, snuffling, rubbing her nose red raw on an already soggy tissue.

John Blundell got down on his haunches and laid his hand on her shoulder.

And waited.

Eventually he felt able to get back to it.

'Holly you didn't push him out of the window, did you?'

She thrashed out at him. 'No I didn't push him out of the window, you stupid man.' She was on all fours now – a big cat. 'Si' down!'

She dragged herself up and slunk unsteadily into the kitchen. Drunk?

In the films Blundell would have pulled out a pack and lit himself a cigarette, peeping at all the evidence in the room. But this wasn't the films. He sat and thought of his own daughter – no images – just the feeling of unconditional love for a delicate thing.

'I suppose you'll want a slug of whisky in your tea?' she shouted from the kitchen. 'Well tough – you get a choice of milk or sugar.' Then peeping round the door with a smile, 'Well I suppose you can have milk *and* sugar.' She was gathering all her strength in there.

'Nuts, bloody nuts,' was all Blundell could think, sitting, chin in hands, looking at the wedding photo of a man - without long hair. He picked up the picture and approached Holly in the kitchen. 'Holly, this is you with your husband - your husband, Hu Stannton?'

She looked at the picture wondering what else it could be. She nodded vigorously.

'You've got blonde hair?'

'Mmm,' still nodding and looking at the photo. 'Mmm, but his is longer than mine.' She bent to give the picture a closer look and Blundell's stomach relaxed. 'Can't tell on that can you, officer?' She squeezed her eyes shut.

He couldn't smell drink on her.

Her face lit up. 'Oh, yeah, I forgot, he tied it up special for our wedding, but I don't like it like that, so he never looks like that.' She then just cried like a baby.

Blundell steered her back into the room carrying two mugs in his other hand. She wouldn't sit down.

'Holly, no one should have told you that Hu jumped out of a window.' He did not want to raise her expectations back up, but had to tell her that they did not know he was dead, or even who was dead. 'At this stage, we have found a body. It may be Hu, but we do not know who it is. But it could be Hu. It is a man in his thirties, over six-foot tall with long blonde hair.'

She sobbed.

'Until he is formally identified, we cannot be sure it is Hu.'

He got her to agree to come to see the body, but felt he needed to know who had phoned her, why she thought he had not jumped out of the window, and why she thought she killed him. Delicate a state as she was in, he knew that in effect she was not only statistically a prime suspect, but she had actually intimated that she believed he would not have jumped, as she had killed her husband.

Before they got to the mortuary the only point he had clarified was that it was not Bahadur who had phoned, 'some bloke with a funny voice' had.

He was glad to know this before he rang Bahadur and asked her to meet him at the Mortuary. He needed her to join him in observing Holly's reactions.

Holly was wrecked when he had arrived at her house. She believed her husband was dead. Did she 'know' because she killed him, accidentally or on purpose? Blundell wondered how the hell anyone had found her before they had. It had to be someone at the hotel, and someone who recognised the victim. It must have been a reporter who had rung Holly.

He checked his phone and looked at Holly. He decided that he could not take Jenks's message just yet.

DS Bahadur had left the SOCOs in the room still working but not coming up with much. She felt better leaving them to get on with it and maybe they would come up with some details later. The cleaner could not come before 3.30 anyway.

In the hospital foyer Bahadur spotted her DI and she took a few seconds to observe him with the young woman. He was at it again. He practically had his arm round their pretty prime suspect. She followed at a distance and made herself known at the Mortuary door. Blundell handed Holly over to a Mortuary assistant and asked for a minute to update his Sergeant.

He told her about the wreck he had found and the three little mysteries. He squeezed her elbow as he squeezed out of his set jaw, 'Some fucker had already told her about her husband before I got there.'

'Not me boss!'

'No, no, Badder, but this mess just keeps getting deeper.' He straightened himself up, his face needing the most work. 'We've still got to decide if we think there are any suspicious circumstances, and of course, the spouse,' he thumbed towards the door, 'is always our initial prime suspect.'

'Of course,' thought Bahadur, but silently followed Blundell into the mortuary. She didn't like that smell.

Holly continued to baffle Blundell, and the first impression she gave the Sergeant was completely mixed. Blundell stood next to Holly and Bahadur stood opposite her on the other side of the body as the technician revealed the head of the corpse.

Holly smiled. She smiled the sweetest smile as she went to stroke an invisible hair off her late husband's forehead. 'Ah, Hu, y' Lummox. What you gone an' done?' Blundell was ready to pounce if she were to make too big a move on the corpse and compromise the evidence, but she, oh so gently, holding back her own hair, kissed him a butterfly kiss on his forehead.

The formal identification was sorted. A female PC was called to take Holly home and stay with her, cautioned to not let her do any washing or changing of clothes without calling Bahadur.

Travelling in separate cars did not allow for any discussion and only a little was exchanged before the detectives found themselves on the threshold to room 212 of The Loseborough Hotel.

Blundell did listen to Jenks's message before belting up: as suspected Stannton had not died instantly from the fall, he had drowned; he had a lot of injuries – ribs, arms, toes broken, and hands, knees, etcetera scraped; he had recently had sex; he had broken some teeth.

At the Hotel, the three androgynous SOCOs had done a lot of work and there were now plenty of pointers.

Having donned overalls and galoshes, they got a SOCO to show them round. He firstly pointed out that it was already a compromised scene. The bed had been stripped, by the cleaner he believed, 'she's waiting in the bar for us,' and possibly by the first constable on the scene judging by one clear footprint.

Blundell's pursed lips were over by one ear as he let out a noisy breath.

It looked as if the victim had been in the shower – drip marks all over, right across the room to the window. 'It was pretty cold last night, maybe even a frost – you can't imagine someone getting out of the shower and standing on the balcony, but the drips do make it look as if that is what he did.'

The SOCO pointed out the marble slab used as a threshold, and the water marks, two different shoe prints and, when pointed out, an evident barefoot, or feet, slip mark. He showed some fibres on the wrought iron rail of the balcony, which Blundell gauged to be just about at the bottom of his own rib cage. It looked as if a hand may have brushed or even grabbed a door jamb. Blundell asked if there was anything on the balcony rail to show the victim may have grabbed or tried to hold on. There was a small amount of cigarette ash on the balcony – that could explain the reason for using the balcony in freezing conditions – a non-smoking hotel.

The Detectives did not stray onto the balcony. It looked to be holding most of the evidence of misadventure they were likely to find, besides maybe the shower. They took a second look there. On the way out of the room Blundell took a look at the bed – but whatever evidence it would have held, would be wrapped in the sheets.

'Where're the sheets and towels and that?' he shouted back from the threshold. The SOCOs simply looked at each other. Blundell walked the wrong way down the corridor and inspected the Fire Escape door. He did not touch it. Walking back past room 212 he charged the SOCO with taping and checking it out.

In their silent retreat down to find the cleaner, Bahadur hazarded 'Slim pickings, sir?' She did not know what to make of the lack of response. At the bottom of the stairs, Blundell spied a woman sitting in the bar, but indicated Bahadur to follow him into a restaurant area. He looked around and arriving at a window gave her a weak smile. She joined him to look out at the tent over the jacuzzi. She followed his gaze as he strained to look up to the balcony.

They sat down at a corner table and he was drumming his fingers lightly, continuing the feeble smile.

'Slim Pickens - cowboy actor. Is that a comment on this investigation, Iruna?'

She frowned at him, hoping something other than the ground would start to open up.

'Sorry about before, at the mortuary, Iruna,' he said.

'Mortuary, sir?'

'Yes, swearing and that. Not usual for me. But this is *such* a mess isn't it?'

'Oh, no probs, sir. It's fair enough to get angry. But it war'n't me what phoned her, you war'n't thinking that was you?'

'To be honest,' he began, thrown by her sudden lack of grammar, 'I did wonder, but Holly told me it was a bloke with a funny voice.'

'Funny voice?' Bahadur said. 'Disguised, you mean?'

'Well, as you saw, she's in a real state so I didn't follow that up, but possibly - probably even.' Blundell looked at his two hands smoothing out the table cloth. 'What have we got? What's your first thought on 'falling out of the window'?'

'If it were me, I'd need a running jump off a trampet to lift me over that balcony.' She had a hand showing the height almost at her neck. 'But we hear he was maybe six foot three?'

'And Holly told me it was her fault.'

'What?'

'Hold on, Runa,' he said, 'I don't think she killed him, but see those footprints and that, I was wondering if they maybe had a bit of a tussle there and he fell out. Unlikely, but we can't dismiss. I'm sitting here because I need a minute.'

Iruna thought he was composing himself again. He pulled his cardigan ('cardigan!') down under his tweedy jacket. ('Tweed!') He pushed his chair back. 'First thing we need to find out from this here cleaner is where's the bedding from the room? What she called - Susan?'

'Suzanne, sir, shall I get her in here?'

'Yeah, good idea. Let's have a talk through, before the walk through.'

Blundell opened by asking Suzanne to *talk* them through, but it was all over in three sentences so they had to take her back over it. He nodded to Bahadur to do the leading. He wanted to hear her at work.

'We need to know what exactly happened with the bedding?' was the crucial point.

'Oh yeah,' Suzanne started, 'I usually just strip out everything that has to come out and dump it in the corridor, next to my trolley.'

'Trolley?'

'Yeah, all me cleaning gear, clean sheets an' that, all on a trolley.'

'Is that what you did this morning, Suzanne?'

She did glance across the room. 'Yeah. Went in, straight into bathroom, grabbed all the towels, threw them on the bed, ripped the pillows out their cases, dragged out the sheet all round and bundled everything up in it. As I was going back to the door to dump 'em in the corridor I saw the French Window open.'

'You didn't open it?' said the DS.

Suzanne again glanced across the room. Blundell checked what at. Nowhere - not the door, windows, bar.

'No. They were open already. Pretty parky it were, in there. Should o' noticed straight away …'

'But you were rushing …'

Suzanne jumped and again glanced away. She patted her tightly permed hair, dyed that new unreal auburn. 'Always rushing here these days, Polack time. She stopped, hand on mouth. 'Sorry.'

'Polack?' said the young policewoman.

Looking a bit sheepish at the Asian, Suzanne thought of a way round this. 'Yeah, I started calling it 'Polack' time. My son said the Americans call them Polacks.'

Blundell thought he realised the hole the cleaner was trying to climb out of. 'It's alright, Suzanne, you mean the East Europeans, Poles etcetera, don't you?' he said mostly to Bahadur with a nod. 'But you said 'Polack *time*'?'

'Yes sir. Since they been coming over 'ere, they work so 'ard. I 'a'n't got anything 'gainst 'em, but we 'ave 'ad reasonable conditions for years, now it's all to be rushed and no breaks. Not fair, really sir, is it?'

Blundell was non-committal but told her to go on. 'You were rushing so didn't notice the window at first?'

'Yessir. No sir. I puts the sheets and that out in the corridor and then goes over to look at the window. Seemed alright, so I looks out, that's when I sees him sir.' She noticed that the Inspector was looking at the sergeant, so she turned to her. 'I thought it was a woman first, in the jacuzzi, well not in it exactly.'

'Not in it?' Bahadur prompted.

'No. Her 'ead was in it. Her lovely 'air floating. Well *his* hair.' She grimaced and again patted her own hair. 'He were over the side.'

'Just clarify that for me, please, Suzanne?' said Bahadur tapping her notebook with her pen. 'Just run it by me again, carefully.' It was the 'over the side' bit she wanted to clarify. It seemed he had landed on the side with his body out and his head in the water. 'Just his head, not a hand?'

Suzanne screwed up her face. 'Mmm. You know I think he may have had a hand on the side come to think of it. His arms was definitely not hanging in the water, else he woulda looked half in – half out. But he looked like just his head was sort of over the side, yeah?'

'Nice detail, well done. Then you …'

'Well I screams first, but claps me 'and over me mouth 'cos, people was still in bed. Then I runs out and runs down stairs to try to 'elp 'im.'

'You ran down stairs – didn't take the lift? Wouldn't that be quicker?' Bahadur knew it would not.

Suzanne harrumphed. 'Not this lift! An' anyway we're only allowed to use the lift to take us trolleys up an' down. Yeah, I ran down, shouted across to reception – I didn't look if anybody was there – then ran out the back of the bar – it's quicker to go out the bar Fire Escape door. The bloke was pretty big, so I grabs his ankles and pulls. Yeah, he clonked his head on the ground, but anyway I set about giving him the kiss of life an' that.'

'If I can stop you there, Suzanne?' said Bahadur. 'Take me back to *everything* you can remember before you pulled him out. Could be important things there that only *you* could have seen.' That got a nod of approval from the DI.

Suzanne explored the ceiling. 'Yes, of course. Dressing gown. He had on one of our white towel dressing gowns. That's all. I know 'cos I had to undo it and all was revealed. What a waste!'

'Slippers?'

'Mmm. Don't think so. Ours are slip-ons, mule thingies, you know. Could've fallen off. Sorry, but 'e might have had some on, an' I didn't notice, even though I pulled him by his ankles.' She put both hands on her cheeks and stared at the Sergeant, who just patted the table mouthing 'Okay, Suzanne. Go on.'

'What else? Well I 'ad a look up at the window – an' of course it was open. Somebody was looking out of the one above too – I probably woke her, sorry. But I was getting on with it, yeah?'

'Was it light?' asked Bahadur. 'What was the jacuzzi doing this time of year? Was it not covered?'

'Yes it was light. Just come light as I went round the other two rooms. Jacuzzi's a bit daft, i'n't it? Well people, not jacuzzi. They love the hot jacuzzi in the freezing weather – always go in it when there's snow about. I seen some lads jumping in and out and rolling in snow. Mad!'

'Not covered ... and warm then?'

'Yeah. No, not covered and *hot*.'

'Okay, so you pulled him out. Was he still breathing?'

'No. I tried to get him going again. They was all telling me do this an' do that, but I know, Officer, I done me First Aid, 'a'n't I? I gave him four breaths and fifteen compressions.'

'No pulse,' said Bahadur, 'no breathing?'

''s right officer. I'd shouted 'em to get an ambulance and before it got there I was getting done in, meself. People wanted me to stop, but I had to carry on. I wasn't giving up on him, oh no! Poor, lovely man.' She looked ready to cry all of a sudden. Her first sign of emotion.

Blundell interjected, 'Okay, Suzanne, well done. But before we go up and you talk us round how you found the room, just catch a breath and see if you think of *anything* that may have been a bit different, you know ...?'

She took the breath. She didn't think of anything.

As they arrived on the second floor, Blundell asked Suzanne to get a trolley out and proceed just as she had done first thing, starting at the room she left to go to 212. They watched her stop outside the room, then warned her not to dash in as she had done, but first think. Blundell indicated Bahadur to watch while he went in and got them all some gloves and galoshes from the SOCOs, still at work. He asked them to leave the room for a minute to give the cleaner as clear a view as possible.

It was a pretty fruitless exercise, all just as Suzanne had said, but Bahadur did stop her to give the bare bed a second thought. She frowned but didn't say anything.

In the pub, Blundell was surprised, but didn't comment, when Bahadur asked for half of bitter. His head was buzzing. He had started out with a significant development in the metal thefts and ended up drawn into the suspicious death of an ex-priest. The tabloids love this, and by the sound of 'a bloke with a funny voice', they might already be on to it.

'If that was only a local reporter,' he said, 'if he gets any confirmation we can expect the red tops to have a story on Sunday. We need our own story, Iruna.'

'I'm sort of sorry I called you ...'

'Now don't let's have any of that. Of course you should have called me. What I have to work out is who *I* call. How suspicious are we?'

'Well I just think that balcony was more than a bit too high for even a big man to fall over, sir.'

Blundell needed some ground rules. 'Now look, I called you Iruna just now. Can we have some civility among us if we are to work together? I came into the Police partly to make it more civilian friendly and I think we should talk naturally with each other.' He noted Bahadur's smile, so went on, 'you should call me 'sir' in any company, especially at the station, and refer to me as Inspector. None of this DI and DS stuff okay, except to other Police.'

'I'm liking the sound of that, sir,' said the sergeant, 'so do I call you 'John'?'

'Yes Mam! No,' he scoused up his accent, 'only *me Mam* calls me John still. Call me 'Chocky,' you've surely heard people calling me that?'

'Yes, but I can't assume to call you … a nickname, can I?'

'No – but I changed it by deed poll when I was at Uni! Now, Runa, let's get on and get home.'

It was a weak smile. 'Okay, sir, Chocky … I can do some time tomorrow, but I really would like to not do another twelve hours.'

'Fair enough, I-runa, sorry if I seem to miss the 'I' sometimes. How about eight 'til four-*ish*? I'll go back in now and update the Super and the Coroner's office and see if someone will set up some appointments for us in the morning. The youth officer seems an important start as he set up this party at the Loseborough. What kind of name is that? I expect they'll have to get the Home Office Pathologist to decide if cause of death was suspicious.'

'That'll certainly help us get nearer to accidental or not, sir,' said Iruna, 'Chocky.'

'Date tonight? You didn't say.'

Iruna laughed. 'My pillow.'

'Right,' said Chocky, 'bright eyed and bushy tailed. I'll get in for seven thirty and have some stuff ready for you.'

'Oh, but sir, I didn't want you to be doing more …'

'Sorry, Runa. We'll *both* get in for eight and see what there is. Now get off with you.'

Friday 5ᵗʰ March

With a nightmare of Opus Dei killers and blood dripping Knights Templar hanging over him, DI Chocky Blundell met up with DS Iruna Bahadur in the station car park. He braved a wide smile, wide apart hands and a sweep towards the door. Following her springing up the stairs he delighted in the swish of her steel blue hair. She had on a leather jacket – a feminine one though, gun metal grey with almost matching jeans. He was glad he had his wax-jacket on for this wintry day.

'Hope you slept better than me,' he said.

She shot a smile over her shoulder.

The team members on duty overnight must not have had much demand from other cases; they had built up a nice pile for them. The exhibits officer had left the HOLMES fired up on the computer. Chocky and Iruna browsed it side-by-side.

'Looks like the Pathologist will be arriving at the mortuary about now,' said Chocky. 'Let's give him until about half nine for a prompt?'

'Do you want us to split up and tackle the guys at the conference?' Iruna asked.

'Andrew Nicholas, the youth officer is tee'd up for nine o'clock. Let's both see to him.' Chocky peered at the screen. 'Great! They've got us phone numbers for the other two, and that they will both be available at home until early afternoon. Say we see what Nicholas and the Pathologist have for us by mid morning?'

They then looked over material about the four at the conference. The priest and Devine were both from Ireland – but the latter came over well before the cleric – as a kid really. They all lived around Clayford, within fifteen minutes drive of each other. The parish priest Hubert Stannton had left to marry, two years previously and caused a bit of a sensation, but the brouhaha over the Irish Child abuse has shielded him from a lot of glare.

The Tin Tab is a well-respected youth drugs charity with lots of positive interaction with the force, because the majority of their clients, addicted as they are to illegal substances, inevitably had criminal records.

Andrew Nicholas is the Area youth officer and is ex Coal Board; Abe Grant a retired local businessman; and Brien Devine was a company accountant in London, retired here years ago.

Stannton worked in Housing and has lots of local contacts.

The Hotel is privately owned and run. No issues on record.

Chocky started, 'There appear to me to be three areas overlapping, Iruna.' He was drawing a shamrock on the desk-pad. 'There's the youth service – council and that; then the church with its input; and then,' he was scrubbing round and round, 'I bet there's the ex-church - separately, left over stuff.'

'People seem to love runaway priest stories,' said Iruna, 'News of the World, People, Sunday Sport …'

Chocky groaned. 'Yes, we will probably have to issue some kind of statement before we finish today.'

They were interrupted. 'Message from a Mrs Stannton for you to call for an update, sir.'

'Yes, going to do that,' said Chocky leaving the message down on his desk.

Iruna saw it. 'It's not Holly, sir, look?'

'Pauline Stannton!' said Chocky, 'could that sound like Holly? He did say a 'Mrs' Stannton didn't he?'

Iruna called the desk and got confirmation.

'Bloody hell,' said the Inspector dragging his hands across his face, 'He hasn't got another little wifey secreted over there in the Emerald Isle, has he?'

'Could be his Mum, sir.'

'OSINTOT! Yes. This mess is panicking me.' To Iruna's giggly and quizzical look he added, 'Not heard that? Oh-Shit-I-Never-Thought-Of-That.' He didn't smile.

'Sorry, yes, heard that – but people tended not to say it to my face.'

The Inspector called the number and discovered that it was the ex-priest's maiden cousin – a heavily stressed 'Miss' - and Housekeeper. Greatly relieved, he got her to come in to talk to them later. He suggested to his Sergeant that they would get a full story from Nicholas, the youth officer. She was shocked at his expression – 'beard him in his lair.'

'You expecting him to be a fearsome lion sir?'

He flicked his eyebrows.

Bahadur felt her preconception of a 'youth officer' was pretty much borne out when a hairy hippie type in sandals – with socks – answered the door.

Blundell thought the socks a sensible measure – despite the kids' disdain, he wore socks with his sandals in winter.

Nicholas brought the officers in and didn't offer them a cup of tea, or invite them to sit down.

Blundell sat down and his sergeant followed.

Nicholas remained standing, his hands stuffed in his pockets.

After a preamble checking he had understood that Hubert Stannton had been found dead, but telling no more, Blundell asked the youth officer to tell all he knew about the Spa session he had provided.

The detectives were not at ease with his easy manner. The seriousness of the ending was not affecting the lightness of the rest of his story. After letting him go on to tell the outline, Blundell felt the need to assert, 'But someone died sir.' He waited a second then added, waving at his sergeant, 'what can you tell us about that?'

'Nothing at all. You have to tell me. I wasn't there was I?'

'Weren't you?' asked Bahadur. 'We don't know this, sir.'

Nicholas's hands came out of his pocket and one wiped the grin off his face. 'Listen Officers,' he said, 'he was nothing, nothing to me. He was everything to some of his people and he had been the chaplain of a project that I happen to share with them.'

'The Tin Tab drug project?' asked Bahadur.

'That's right. But first he runs off with a bimbo and then he gets a job on the back of his experience of *our* youth Project. He stressed this with a poke at his chest. 'Aren't you a bit fed up with these bloody priests having their cake and ...' He held out his hands and shook his head.

'Bimbo?' said Bahadur.

'Well, I hear she was a pretty thing,' his voice was tailing off as he was telling the inspector. He looked at the sergeant, 'Sorry if that is perhaps a sexist term, but it makes me very mad.'

'Mad?' said Bahadur.

'Angry. Irritated. We youth workers are supposed to be non-authoritarian and non-judgemental, but look at these supposedly holy authority figures preaching to the poor and sitting in their confession boxes judging and sentencing them ...'

'Bit harsh, that,' interrupted Blundell. 'You know what goes on in the confession box do you? Judging that are you?'

'We-ell. You can't argue the hold these Irish Priests have over the poor and the Government of those poor, can you?'

'Have?' queried Blundell. 'Not been keeping up with the press, sir?'

'Well, he's an Irish priest and product of that machine, isn't he?'

'Just lumping this young local priest in with a job lot.' Blundell coughed. He then changed gear. 'What happened at your conference ... was it a conference?'

'We conferred. Actually, it was a treat for some of the team. It was a prize my wife didn't want and she suggested I gave it Hu as a farewell present, seeing as he'd left without a by your etcetera.'

'But he was 'nothing' to you.'

'Mmm, I did have an ulterior motive.' He looked down and back up. His own choice of word shocked him. 'Not a motive to kill him - but I thought it would be enlightening for them, and fun for me, to let him reveal his true self - as a snake, rather than the saint they seem to still regard him as. Well did ...'

Blundell really wanted his Sergeant to carry out this interview, but Nicholas never taking his eyes off him, he couldn't help being drawn in. 'You just told us that you are non-judgemental but it sounds like you are slipping a bit – 'saints' - or serpents would that be, sir?'

Nicholas took a sharp intake of breath through gritted teeth and started to jab a finger, but pulled back. 'Look. We had a lovely couple of days – Brien and Abe, Hu and me - whoops, there it goes again – lovely place, great food and drink, nice surroundings and walkies, but he was just so complacent.'

'Got you 'mad'?' said Bahadur.

'Yes it did.'

'Mad enough to throw him out of the window?'

The youth officer stuffed his hands back in his pockets and walked into his bay window. The Detectives took a glance at each other. Nothing was revealed.

Nicholas turned back. 'Is that what happened?' he asked the sergeant at last.

'You tell us.'

Nicholas huffed.

Feminine Bahadur decided she was probably Good Cop, and so steered away from the direction things were going. 'Can you tell us about the other people at the conference, please sir? We know nothing about them. Any of your youth workers?'

'Good question. We should really have brought my youth Leader-in-Charge. She worked with the project, day in, day out and knew Abe at least, very well - friends even. But she is a woman and we thought it maybe best as an all blokes affair.'

Bahadur was amused by his choice of phrase, 'blokes affair', but tried to hide it. She got the Leader's name and carried on, 'We thought?'

'Well, Abe and I. We have got very close since I took over the district some years ago. He is a real saint.' His face curled up.

'What's that sir?'

'Saint! I keep catching myself using these religious terms and hate myself.'

'Abe,' she checked her notes, 'Grant, sir. Good friend, good man?'

'Yes. Great man. Decided to do something for these poor kids, not like the preachers up in the pulpit. One of his sons came unstuck - 'got in with the wrong crowd', as parents always say - but Abe found nothing was there for his lad, so he set something up. The lad's doing pretty okay now – well you can't take the heroin out of them … ever, you know. And what's more, Abe's carried on doing it for thousands of kids since.'

'Thousands!' gasped both detectives at once.

Andrew Nicholas gave them both a long look. 'Detectives? Surprised? Fifteen years, about five hundred a year. 'Do the Math.''

Blundell whistled and his sergeant said: 'Wow. Hidden problem, eh?'

'Yep. District Council claims there are no rough sleepers in their town – make sure their wardens sweep them under a dirty doormat. But once on drugs, there's not much out there for young people. Their families throw them out when they don't get Child Allowance for them any more. They've got nowhere to go – sleep under a bridge for a few nights, try to - then if they take something, they find they don't notice the cold or lack of sleep – or the rats biting them. Give them three weeks and they're hooked.'

'What,' said Blundell consulting his pad 'and five hundred a year sleep rough for three weeks? My 'math' tells me that makes 30 sleeping rough in any one week?'

'Yes. Sort of. They aren't all sleeping rough, but they aren't in their own bed for sure. Heard of 'sofa-surfing'?' Nicholas felt the Police were not convinced, and he needed to feel believed. 'Never less than ten actually sleeping rough – sheds, under bridges, derelict buildings, some have tents. Our outreach and detached youth workers try to find them very quickly – intervene – to stop them getting to the hard drugs.'

Bahadur checked with her boss before saying, 'fair enough, I suppose. Horrible statistics though aren't they?'

The youth officer smiled and nodded at her. 'Tell the Tories that.'

'Abe's the man?' asked Blundell.

'He – is – the – man,' said Nicholas.

'What do you know about him?'

'Retired businessman. Shops. His wife's family had a small chain of painting and decorating shops in the region. I think he ended up more-or-less running them. Comfortably off. Loves his wife and four kids, who have all done well – all considered, with Ivan's little weakness.'

'And the other man,' Bahadur checked her notes, 'Brien Divine?'

'De-*veen*, Miss. He really does not regard himself as divine. He's forever praying, 'God forgive us' and all that.'

'What for? Forgive what?'

'He's Irish, too, you know, but a real big fan of Father Hu. He's a nice gentle man. He was an accountant, money man of some sort in the building trade, I think. He wasn't an Irish Navvy I don't reckon. That's what he does for Abe – the books. I said he could do mine if he wanted.'

'Family?'

'Don't know about that, sorry. Don't socialise with these guys, you know – except for this little treat.'

After a difficult silence, Blundell felt that Nicholas had decided to put up the shutters, so he decided to sum up. 'You run, jointly run, The Tin Tab, and there is a long standing member who happens to be the parish priest, who leaves without notice. He leaves your partners high and dry. You decide to get him to explain himself to the Chair and Treasurer of the committee on the pretext of treating them all to a 'pampering weekend.''

Nicholas was following, but was expressionless, though Bahadur noted his high colour. She took over. 'At the end you all went home except Hu Stannton … you three went and left him still there. Did you travel together?'

'No. We each brought our own car. Not very environmental was it?'

'Who went first?' she said.

'Well I went last, if that's what you're getting at.'

After ascertaining the time he left and what he did next, they asked if he would be willing to give fingerprints and DNA for elimination purposes. They agreed Monday for that.

Chocky looked back at the house. 'Bit of a weekend hippie, I reckon. Nice pad, man.'

'Nice man, sir?' asked Iruna.

They looked at each other.

'I'll call Jenks – the Pathologist – see if he's got anything for us.'

For the second time in a couple of days, as Brien came up from the cellar the phone attacked him. He had been down there doing a couple of miles on the rowing machine followed by his Matins - his morning prayers. He had regained some calm. But nobody called in a morning.

The Police had never called before.

He had slammed the phone down on Colleen. He couldn't slam the phone down on the police. He watched his hand settling in slow motion. He had done the right thing by his daughter at long last. He had never apologised to her because he knew that what he had done was unforgiveable. All his praying and service of repentance would maybe only just keep him out of Hell – but he would be in Purgatory until the very last day. Poor Father Hu, he didn't deserve that, but who was Brien to judge? Judge not, lest … .

But what else could Brien do – he could, would and did respond when at last Colleen did ask him for … for anything at all?

Abe Grant was fishing when he got his call. He had needed to be alone after the tension between Leo and Father Hu. He could not, he really could not let himself get riled. Of course he knew where Leo was coming from. Of course he pretty much agreed with him. Of course Father Hu had set himself above, above Abe for sure, but Abe didn't really see anything wrong with that. Before. Abe had, once upon a time, taken some stuff and that led to his taking a life. But he didn't end up with anything. Hu Stannton took it all and had it all. Abe's grip on the fishing rod had been ominous. Had to relax.

Now what? His Coddy had told him that something had happened to Father Hu. The Police would obviously want to talk to him.

He didn't get that. 'If he's been in a car crash or something, what's it to do with me?' He realised that was evasive and would sound bad to Coddy. Why didn't he just ask her what had happened? He thought it might just be the word 'police': he had had nothing, nothing to do with them since the day he walked out and into the strong arm of Coddy – not even a parking ticket. Nothing? Well not on the wrong side – loads to do with poor Ivan, his son, and of course almost everyone who ever sought the help of The Tin Tab.

'They seemed to think you would know that he had died at that hotel where you had that drugs conference.'

'What drug conference?' he let slip, but recovered himself and added, 'Oh Leo's thing. Eyup! What? Father Hu Dead? Never. Mistake, Coddy.'

She seemed to be sniffling.

He looked at his float. It disappeared. He let it. 'What am I going to do, Coddy?'

'You're going to get back here and be ready to talk to the nice policeman, Abe. I'm sure it's nothing to worry about.'

'Coddy, I'm too old for this.'

He whipped his rod and the line snapped.

His life wasn't quite passing before his eyes, but he felt a sinking feeling about The Tin Tab. That was going to have to pass him, or rather he was going to have to pass on that. No way could he do that if his record returns to public knowledge ... and to haunt him. Can he *never* serve enough time?

'Drugs conference'? Is that what the police had said to Coddy? Did they mean he had been drugged up, or overdosed or something? Who was that Sloan Ranger Father Hu had set up with? Coke was their drug of choice. Had he had a snort of some dodgy stuff?

But what did they want Abe for? His record! No escaping it. Hu didn't die of old age ... so something fishy.

He looked at the lake: cold, deep.

Why didn't he ask Coddy some more, some simple stuff. 'Oh yes? What happened to him? How awful? Course, yes, I'll get straight back?'

But no – all suspicious silly jabber. 'What am I going to do Coddy?'

Bet she thought 'It's not all about you Abe.'

His record, though. Abe is a lifer, a killer walking free.

Abe couldn't get away from thinking violence, killing, murder, but Coddy had indicated nothing of the sort.

Bastard did have his cake and eat it. Eating Abe's cake too, if Hu were to keep a job with the homeless druggies and Abe were to lose his vocation to them ... the police would gun straight for Abe.

'Talk to the nice policeman' eh, Coddy? He bit his lip and it hurt.

'And that bugger's taken me bait, hook, line and sinker,' he mumbled as he abandoned his station.

DS Iruna Bahadur had started on the flipchart – bit old fashioned – but she wasn't questioning her new boss - yet. She had put the names of the Conference group and Holly and Pauline on it under a photo of the Loseborough Hotel that she had taken with her phone. It included the balcony and the jacuzzi visible through the tent flap.

Her DI joined her with information from the pathologist. He looked agitated and talked excitedly.

'The fall didn't kill him, Runa! And he didn't die straight away – but he did drown.'

'Sir?'

'Look at this.'

She leaned over his notes, but looked straight back at him with a rye smile.

'Yeah, okay, sorry,' he said. He pointed at his scribble. 'He wasn't killed by the fall – instantly I mean. Apparently he bled slowly into his lungs for some time and then they filled up with water. But here's the bit: Jenks says that both his feet, a knee and a hand show signs of a struggle on concrete.'

'Jacuzzi,' said Bahadur. 'Carpet and polished marble in the room and balcony.' She took another look at the notes.

Blundell read them. 'It looks like he landed against the jacuzzi side,' he laid his hand across his chest at armpit height. 'His head and one arm landed over the side, and the other arm was badly broken by the bath side. Several ribs broken, puncturing his lung. Couple of teeth broken, maybe as chin hit side. Couldn't have been very nice for that cleaner,' he said looking into Bahadur's eyes.

She bared her clenched teeth automatically. 'Not brilliant for him, neither,' she said. 'Anyway if he wasn't dead, he maybe spat them out himself.'

Blundell pointed at her as she mouthed 'SOCO!' 'Yes – have they sieved that pool do we know?'

'Their report's not in the evidence log yet, sir, Chocky, sir.'

'Anyhow, this scrabbling about on the concrete's a bit intriguing. If most of him is on the outside, you'd think it wouldn't take much effort to sort of flop himself out of the pool.'

The detectives stared at each other.

Bahadur thought Blundell's eyebrows would meet his chin, then realised hers were more likely to touch the ceiling. She was wriggling her shoulders trying to work that one out. 'I'll chase SOCO,' she said.

'Friday today.' He rubbed his hands together. 'So what do we need to do Detective Sergeant?'

'Not a simple accident is it sir? Do you have to let the Superintendent know?'

'Yes - better get the Super to make a Crime Plan. We want more stuff from SOCO, some people to help us and the Super'll have to sort the Coroner.'

'Inquest, sir?'

'Well, open and adjourn it before the weekend.' He pointed at her. 'We are agreed it's a suspicious death aren't we?'

'Bloody weird! Er, very suspicious sir.'

'I don't think they'll be happy with Jenks's Post Mortem – it's a suspicious one so they'll want Home Office in on it.' He stood and looked down at the very young lass. 'You seem okay Iruna, yes?'

'Yes sir. Interesting first case, innit?'

He smiled at her. 'I'll go down to the Super. You want to get the rest of the 'conference' lined up on your … I'm not calling it a 'whiteboard'? Let's see what they've got to say for themselves.'

After taking a copy, Blundell put the picture of Hu Stannton on his flipchart and named the happy couple.

Sergeant Bahadur was almost shocked by the meticulous precision of the little front garden of the old semi – it reminded her of her Grandma's. Not much colour yet, but she knew it would burst forth in the first spring sun. She asked the big Detective Constable to introduce them – she didn't let him know that she still felt people would not believe she was a detective, let alone a sergeant – 'still a schoolgirl!'

A little old lady came to the door and wasn't at all put about at police asking for her husband. 'A nice cup of tea?' was of course on offer.

Brien was sitting in the front room, his wife's 'best room', dewy eyed and wringing his hands. He couldn't stand and felt bad about that. He pointed the settee for the two officers and gave a weak smile. They both held the antimacassars in place as they sat, neither of them knowing that that was what they were. The fire was made up, but not lit, not been lit for a long time judging by the fusty smell of the room and the dust on the coals. Winter?

Bahadur sat forward, checked that Mr Divine ('De-veen') knew Hubert Stannton had been found dead at the Hotel, but nothing more, and asked him to tell all he could about the Conference and how Mr Stannton had been.

Brien's hands continued to wring, slowly, and his eyes fixed on her every word, welled up slowly and brimmed over - just one tear.

He took a long time, looking at the fingers rolling over thumbs, palm, backs of his hands. Iruna could wait. But she caught herself wringing her own hands and stopped it.

'He was a good man,' was his opening line.

'So why did you kill him?' was not the first response Bahadur felt as appropriate response to that statement.

'What happened to him?' was his next line.

The sergeant carefully side-stepped that preferring Brien, 'May I call you Brien?' to tell her all he knew first. She was pleased how the big DC merged into the background with his notebook.

Brien ran through his version of events. It was as meticulous as his garden and slowly, carefully put together. He nodded each of his own points home before moving on.

He agreed to come by the station on Monday to give prints and swab 'for elimination purposes'.

The only animation he showed made Bahadur jump back and the DC to stand to defend her. When she told how Hu seemed to have fallen out of the window, Brien had leapt up and become even more agitated, lots of cursing/prayers in an even deeper Irish accent than his main story. Iruna was familiar with this reaction.

'The poor man threw himself out of the window!' It was a statement, more than a question.

'We do not know this, sir,' said Bahadur. 'We are trying to find out how he died. At this stage all we know is that he probably fell from the balcony onto the jacuzzi …'

'What kind o' mad yoke is that at this time o' year at all?'

'… but we really do not know how or why he fell, and whether or not it was an accident.'

Brien looked from one to the other of the officers while he thought that through. He shook his head.

'Sir?'

'Drownded I suppose he was?'

'Why is that sir?'

'You said he fell in the stupid pool thingy.'

'Did I sir?'

'Sure she did didn't she officer?'

The constable looked to his sergeant.

On the way out she wiped Brien's cold sweat from her hands and took a fleeting moment to note the sprinkling of colour – just a few primulas dotted here and there. Though her Grandma never had any of those blue ones when Iruna was a little girl, sweet thoughts helped her recover from the somewhat sour time spent in that cold old semi.

Coddy stood guard while the rather pleasant informally dressed Inspector Blundell interviewed her husband. He was much too agitated to leave alone. She didn't know why, as he was on very good terms with the police with his Tin Tab clients, but thought she could guess that a personal intervention was something else altogether.

When it came to Father Hu meeting a violent end, she was herself shocked. As it gradually became clear that it perhaps was a suspicious end too, a large knot tightened in her stomach. Abe always told her you could never take the heroin out of an addict. What about killing from a killer?

When the officers had gone, Abe and Coddy just held each other, or rather Rowena held her husband tight until she felt all the pain ease out of his body and soak away into her big, big heart.

When he was back in the car with the constable, Chocky rang Iruna. 'How was he?'

'Strange, sir. Can't say why, though. And Grant, sir? Chocky, sir?'

'Yeah, don't know. Had any lunch? Get some then we'll compare notes.'

Chocky weighed straight in with his news. 'Course, I had to tell the Super that it is a suspicious death, Runa. You okay with that?'

'Oh yes sir. Coroner, too yeah?'

'Yes – apparently she had already alerted her. But Super wants me to run through it with her?'

'Super or Coroner, er, Chocky?'

'Sorry, yeah, Coroner's a woman too.'

Iruna rolled a hand. 'Run over it for me please, will you …?'

Chocky sat her down with a fresh piece of paper between them and went over the findings so far, pointing out the details that did not seem to add up. 'So a fine young man in the prime of life has everything going for him. And the wife thinks suicide's not in him.'

'Even a big bloke wouldn't easily fall over that balcony …'

'That's not for us, but that is a suspicious element, see – there is a slide mark on that slippery marble?'

Iruna fingered her chin and gave her head a shake.

'But we can't say it's murder either, can we?'

'Yebbut, there's loads of domestics that aren't quite murder, i'n't there?'

'Yes it could be a row and within that an accident – a shove, maybe?'

'We 'an't got enough to talk about motives have we Chocky?'

'No we haven't, but we still haven't talked about our two guys.'

Iruna grinned at Chocky. 'Haven't exactly given me a chance for that sir.'

Brought up just a little short, Chocky reassured her that they would come to that, but he needed to get over to the Coroner's officer 'PDQ.' Super would no doubt fight with the Coroner about suicide versus murder, misadventure and time delays, force costs mounting, etcetera. He didn't want Iruna and himself caught in the crossfire.

While the Inspector went off to the Coroner, the sergeant wrote up her notes and set about the whiteboard. She cut the 'lovely couple's' photo in two, spaced and named them and using Hubert Stannton as the centre she drew three neat and different male silhouettes to the left of him and named them Andrew 'Leo' Nicholas, Abraham Grant and Brien Devine. To the right she put Mrs Stannton's photo along with a silhouette representing Hubert's cousin Pauline and, slightly out of that circle, one line to a box on the right and another to the left.

Across the bottom she put a row of Post-it notes, 'Church, Family, Hotel, Random, Friends.'

She stood back and explored her map for a good quarter of an hour, touching up her silhouettes and wiping blotches with a finger as she went.

Her compadre on the interview sidled up at one point, commended her presentation and, beaming his most charming, asked her if she was all right with Chocky. She nodded and smiled but went back to her musing. The DC hung around only a little longer.

Neither Chocky nor Iruna were impressed with their line-up as a list of potential murderers.

'Well we probably don't think it's a murder, do we sir, Chocky?' said Iruna, gradually becoming comfortable with using the familiar with her boss.

'Nah!' but he screwed up his mouth. 'But we do have to try to find out what actually happened. So neither of us thought anything much about Grant or Divine …?'

'It's De-veen, sir.'

'Yes, sorry – *I* told *you* that didn't I? Just to run with it – could you possibly see him as a murderer or, say, angry perp?'

'Summink creepy about him, but just a regular old bloke, I thought, really. He is very religious.'

Chocky did a double take on that word to see how much she weighted it. Not much. 'Do you think religious people are necessarily good people, Iruna?'

She twisted the side of her mouth. 'Why not, sir? What, like compared to not religious murderers and that?' She had a little think, and then added, 'Well all this Irish priest stuff ...' and she choked, laughed and looked at Hubert Stannton's photo.

'Not suggesting one of your blanks could be someone he sexually abused then Iruna? That could ratchet things up for us.' Clinking his coins he added, 'Grant, neither. Gentle giant of a man. We've got three people who purport to like the man – two parishioners and the wife.'

'We've got to suspect the wife as general first principal haven't we sir?'

He was uncomfortable with the reality of that, but assented anyway. 'But we are not rushing, are we? Neither of us were very comfortable with that Leo character, were we? His attitude anyway?'

Iruna had thought that was a bit of man-to-man thing, but kept it to herself. 'What do you reckon to my two blanks and the list across the bottom. Want to move any of them up?'

'We need some background I think ... and more forensics.' Chocky turned and looked at Iruna. 'We're only at the start. We've got the Housekeeper soon. Could give us a much broader view – known him a good deal longer than the wife, eh? We need Mrs Stannton, Ahem,' he smiled, 'the actual Holly, to give us her dabs. Maybe call on her and see if she's up to coming in for ID suite, or if they need to get out to her. Might be nice to offer to bring her in yourself? And do you want to get background on your names and I'll scrutinise the forensics, so far?'

Though she wasn't so sure she should ever, would ever, say a word about it at all - while he was living at least - Pauline Stannton felt absolved of that responsibility in the circumstances – what with him being dead and all.

'I don't know how it is with ye Gards, but like I seen on the telly, it may have some bearing on the case ...'

Blundell smiled at her Irishism, didn't say anything. He knew it was pushing at the dam and it would burst out of the poor woman soon enough.

'That's what you say, is it not – 'has a bearing on the case'?'

He thought his silly idea of a secret wife, could actually be used to open up the discussion. 'We do if it does, Mrs ...'

'All of a do-dah-day, eh, Officer?' She paused. He didn't smile. 'Miss,' she said.

'Miss what?'

'All of a do-dah, as I said.' She took a look around the scruffy interview room with its cream gloss painted walls. 'I'm not after being in many Garda Stations. What's your name sir?'

'My name is Inspector John Blundell,' he said through gritted teeth, 'and your name is what?'

She noticed his frustration at last. 'I am Pauline Stannton.'

'Mrs Stannton,' he thought maybe more productive than her already corrected status.

'Not at all! You're not after thinking I'm poor Hu's wife.' With a shake of her head she permitted herself a proud smile. 'I'm his cousin and his housekeeper – was.'

'I see.'

'Now do you see at all? It's not like a lot of yeez think, I am not his secret wife …'

Blundell coughed. 'I'm a Catholic, myself, ma'am, I would not be having such thoughts.' How did *that* Irishism sneak into his own dialogue? Uncle Seamus?

Pauline looked at him in a whole new light. An English Policeman and a Catholic. 'You're not from the North?'

'Yes.' He smiled at his own conceit. 'Liverpool. But Miss Stannton, we are not getting far, very fast, here. I have to try to find out what happened to your cousin, Hubert Stannton and you surely wish to help me.'

'It's that woman,' she blurted.

'At last, we start' thought Blundell. 'Go on.'

'That woman tempted the poor lad right out of the Garden of Eden.'

'Would that make Holly the snake and you Mr Stannton's Eve?'

Pauline blushed deeply. Could it appear like that, or was he being a bit devious, for a Catholic? He didn't look like a real policeman with his shaggy hair and beard. Was it a beard or was he just a scruff?

'Anyway, let's not be having any Bible fairy stories, what real things can you tell me?'

Though she was shocked at the implied heresy, she knew she should not be shocked at what a real Gard would say. She steeled herself. 'Something I thought no one else could tell you, except me.' She let that sink in. 'Which may have a bearing on the case …is this …' She took a look around to check the walls weren't listening. 'When he was a boy, Hu slipped off the rails. Just the once.'

Blundell sat up.

'Now Hu was always a lovely lad and everyone said he'd make a fine priest. He'd been taken with the African Missions – save a black baby an' all – and as soon as he could he was off to Ballinafad.'

'Not Africa?'

'Not at all, y'ommadawn! Oh, sorry officer. No, no, it was a Junior Seminary – a school …'

'I know what a Junior Seminary is.'

'Of course you do. Well you'll mebbe know they took boys pretty young to be priests in them days – they don't no more. Eleven he was. Well he's a big lad, so he is, and by the time he was thirteen, weren't the boys discovering new things about their bodies an' all, boys being boys? Unfortunately a group of them was caught fiddling and having a bit of practice and they was t'rown out – no ifs, no buts.'

John Blundell looked at Pauline expecting some more.

'Well?'

'Well what, Miss Stannton?'

'Well, don't you see - he never ever looked at a girl until that t'ing t'rew herself at him.'

'Are you telling me he was gay?'

'I am saying nothing of the sort – why do you have to be a...' she took a look around, '... a homo-sexual if you don't want sex with girls?'

'Fair enough,' said Blundell, 'but *are* you saying he simply didn't want to have sex with girls?'

'I am.'

'And you think this has a bearing on the case?'

'I do so. I think his almighty sin may have got to him, and like yer man Judas, the poor boy could do nothing but end it all.'

Blundell spun his Parker on the desk and clicked it a few times. 'We have, of course, to consider all possibilities, and suicide has to be one.'

Pauline burst into tears.

With her coming to tell him about suicide, he hadn't been expecting the upset, but he supposed it had never actually come past her lips. He gave her a minute.

'Tell me about Hu, your cousin.' Blundell knew he was risking a long haul with this woman, but he wasn't sure who else could actually know the man. 'Give me a picture of the real Hubert Stannton.'

Pauline looked at Inspector Blundell and appreciated him asking her that question. She looked in her handbag and rattled across to him, 'A Tic Tac?'

He took a couple of the sweets and dashed them into his mouth. He had to blink at the shock of sour orange when he was expecting mint, but he puckered a smile.

'Like I was saying, he was a lovely lad, loved by everybody – even the girls mind - but he steadfastly stuck to the notion of saving black babies. Despite being summarily dismissed from Ballinafad, he told me he was not put off. Within only a couple of years, he knew it was only boys' stuff and put it behind him. He also thought the church would too. The church changed its mind about Junior Seminaries after the Vatican Council, annyways...'

'Yes. There aren't any at all in Britain now. I was toying with the idea myself as a boy.'

'Well bless you Inspector, you'll know how it was. He stayed a regular mass goer – not everyday – but how many young ones even go every week? He did well at school and went off to the University at Dublin, there. He got involved with the chaplaincy – great influence on the young ones, what with all the sex and drinking and that.'

Blundell suppressed the smile considering the future priest giving instructions.

'I'm not saying he was a saint or anything … well I am reelly.' She got out a tissue again, but saw Blundell's look.

She continued, 'None of us are saints are we? No. But he was a very good man, had a couple of pints with the lads and with the lasses, was always popular, always gangs calling round for him when home on holidays. Course he was quite the man with the Hurling stick, and they'd have him for a ringer sometimes - for the cup matches. But Officer, I do need to say that he betrayed his heritage a little when he came over here – he went over the to the other side – the Brits,' she waggled her head. She thought the Inspector interested. 'Rugby, y' see.'

Blundell stuck to his own train of thoughts. 'He never had real girl-friends?'

'Whether he did there up in Dublin, I couldn't say, but not at all round Westport.'

Blundell stood up. 'That is all very useful Miss Stannton. If I can some up: you think he was a generally good man, with a sound, happy up-bringing. He didn't drink much, or go out with girls, had a normal schooling, on to university and … then onto the priesthood?'

'Yes he applied with time still to go at College, but Maynooth told him to finish his degree, then come on to them and he did – got a first.'

'What in?'

'Music.'

'So he became a priest,' Blundell continued, 'his lifelong wish, and you supported him - as housekeeper?'

She nodded.

'As his cousin you were no temptation to him?' Thinking of her has no temptation to any man - except maybe to a strangling - Blundell had to restrain a smile. 'For some years a model priest.'

'Seven, Officer.'

'The Seven Year Itch? Then, out of the blue, he falls.'

'I'm after reporting him to Maynooth straight away. Well wasn't he leaving me in the lurch, too?'

Blundell tapped the pen on his teeth. 'Hu falls from grace, and you, you his cousin, you think of the shame and disgrace. You think he has to take another fall and jumps out of the window.'

Pauline looked up aghast – was that what she was saying? Was she placing him in eternal Hellfire? Despair? Her Hu?

'Suicide, Miss Stannton?'

Pauline stood, mouth agape, eyes streaming.

Blundell looked around for the tissue box and offered it to her.

Pauline was incoherent. Recognising the significance of the tissue box, she took one, sat down and pulled herself together. 'No, not my Hu. It was her. It was she med him do it. It's not his fault. Never. He would not jump into hell's flames. She turned his head.'

'Almost as good as pushing him?' he asked, telling himself 'bit naughty that, Chocky, putting words into her mouth.'

Pauline was not stupid. She thought he maybe did not realise that. She could not accept suicide – killing himself - but she realised she was sort of saying he took his only option and that was to take his own life. How to put that across? 'Pushing him, you say. Now that could be metaphorical, could it not, Inspector?'

He smiled and the eyebrow told her to go on.

'I cannot accept that he lost hope in God, so literally killing himself is difficult for me. You're a Catholic, you say. What do you think I am trying to say?'

Clever. 'We have quite a few categories of 'killing,' ' Blundell said. 'Self murder is a strange concept, but self-homicide or self-manslaughter? I don't know. Usually it's called 'while the balance of the mind is disturbed', if maybe there was no intent to kill...'

'Yes.' They looked at each other, aware that each was thinking it through. 'I don't like the idea that he went mad or cracked up, though, sir.'

'You did seem to indicate that someone else was involved – turning his head?' he said. 'It is sort of saying someone else caused his death – a bit like pushing him?'

Again Pauline sat looking at him. She could hear the blood pumping in her ears. 'Maynooth,' she mused.

He thrust a lip out and frowned.

She pushed the corners of her lips back with her fingers, then tapped her teeth together. 'Maynooth did not like him going off with her in the first place. Mebbe they could not accept completely losing him. I'm not sure I could.'

'What exactly do you mean when you say 'Maynooth'?' Blundell said. 'I know it's the seminary...'

She looked at him, then down and back up before committing. Would he believe her? No, stick with the hussy. 'That woman did for him. She took away all his life, everything that had gone before, his ambition, his vocation, his successful career, his God - and his faith in Him ... and his family. So she took his life from him, don't you see?'

He did see and nodded. But she had wriggled. 'Maynooth. You said Maynooth. Why? What is that about? It could be very important, Miss Stannton. Please tell me about that.'

She fell for the flattery, but narrowed her eyes before rushing in.

Blundell prompted: 'How did Maynooth show its displeasure at him 'going off with her?''

'Well they came for him I heard, and took him back to sort his head out. Couple of months they took and he did come back to me, but she had her claws into him. Poor Hu only lasted another few weeks before he left us for good. Went in the middle of the night. I had heard the phone, but at the time thought I was dreaming. I've never spoken to him since.' She sobbed.

Blundell underlined 'Maynooth' on his pad. 'So you are suggesting two possibilities of him being pushed: his wife 'pushed' him into it – I don't think you are saying she actually pushed him?'

Pauline shook her head then stopped and said with a dip of the head towards him, 'Was he pushed? I don't actually know ... but you might. I hadn't thought to ask?'

'We are exploring all possibilities, Miss.'

She sneered at his creeping about. Was that reely a cardy he had on?

'But are you saying 'Maynooth' may have actually pushed him?'

She stared at him. She wasn't saying anything. She made to leave.

'You are also not saying that you pushed him.'

Pauline dropped back into her chair. 'What? Where the hell has that come from, you little creep?' Not so little, but she wanted to wither him.

'We have to explore all possibilities, you see.'

Her eyes welled up in fury and she was breathing hard, stuck for words. What possibilities could implicate her?

'You must have been very close to Hu.' Blundell held his voice back the several semitones he felt it climbing in a kind of plea. 'His closest relative? You lived with him alone for, what, seven years?'

She turned a cold shoulder to him and told the window, 'sly, very sly piece of twisting. And me only coming in to share with them some details which could reely have a bearing on the case and they start accusing me of murder.' She clammed up and refused to say another word until he showed her the door.

'Mm. Thank you again,' he said to her back retreating down the corridor. Either he had lost it, or she was hiding something. 'I can obviously depend on your support if I have any more queries?'

She turned, glared and went.

He tapped out an ellipsis at end of his notes...

While Blundell was interviewing, Bahadur had contacted Holly. The Family liaison answered and in a hushed whisper said that she thought Holly strangely calm, then loudly called Holly to ask if she was well enough to call into the station to give her details, fingerprints, etc. The DS heard a stout affirmation and agreed the Family Liaison would drive her in.

Bahadur joined them, finding Holly assiduously filling in forms. She was in a smart black trouser-suit and her blonde hair looked well in a centre-parted, longish bob. She gave Iruna a swift smile of recognition and straight back to the forms. Iruna sat and watched.

'Murder suspect?' she wondered. She saw Holly pondering over what to write in some of the boxes and decided to step over and see what the hold-ups were: names and addresses.

Holly noticed and said 'Does five years seem like a long time to you? Or the twinkling of an eye?'

The sergeant gave a knowing smile. They were of an age, she guessed. But she was careful to not engage Holly in anything that could be deemed 'Interview.' Much as she could imagine any 'parish priest' relating fully with the other three men at the 'conference', she could picture no way Holly could have any relationship with any of them – except maybe as wayward daughter.

She could more readily see her as a voluptuous temptress from whom to avert their gaze … and feel very bad about her.

Bahadur collected up the forms and agreed to keep Holly informed of developments and nodded the Liaison to see her home.

She rushed back to the team office to load in the information, only to draw a complete blank: The National Insurance number belonged to a forty-two year old man. The last London address was in the hundreds for a street of less than eighty. Her maiden name and date of birth did belong to people, but didn't seem to be hers. This was so much misinformation that Sergeant Bahadur had a rapid change of opinion on the sweet Ms Stannton – they couldn't all be mistakes.

Back at a flipchart in his own office on a quiet Friday afternoon, Chocky was scratching his head and clinking his coppers, when he suddenly recalled the 'recently had sex' comments from the pathologist.

'How could you tell if he's just had a shower?' he asked.

'Who said he just had a shower?' said Jenks.

'But that's why he fell out of the window.'

'Who says?'

Blundell was flabbergasted. His hand slowly sank the receiver onto its cradle. While he was still thinking, he even more ponderously tapped in the digits to call Jenks back. His opening was a noisy breath, then 'Stop trying to distract me!' burst out of him. 'I rang to ask you how you know he recently had sex.'

Jenks was expecting some sort of apology, so he also took time over a noisy breath. 'Ex-Priest wasn't he? Why 'Ex'? Paedo? Gay?'

'No, none of these … you're trying to distract me again. How could you tell he recently had sex if he's just come out of the shower?'

'Because he hadn't just come out of the shower. As a matter of fact, I shouldn't think he'd had a shower for a couple of days.'

'But you said he probably slipped because his feet were wet and he was in a shower robe.'

'I said nothing of the sort.'

'Who did then?'

Jenks took a little cough before he replied, 'you're the Detective, I'm merely the Forensic Pathologist.'

Blundell gave the receiver the dead-eye before slamming it back down. He immediately picked it up and punched the digits back in again so hard he hurt his finger. 'Okay, Okay,' he barked, 'but you still haven't told me how you know he recently had sex.'

Silence, except for breathing and background music. Then a husky female voice said, 'I beg your pardon?'

'Oh. Sorry. Where's the pathologist I was just speaking to?'

The voice moved away from the phone. 'Any of you naughty girls just been on this blower telling tales out of school?'

Blundell listened intently to the phone, realised his mistake and again slammed it down. 'How come I didn't just press redial?' he asked himself. Then he did.

'Hooters! I know I can help you.'

Blundell threw the phone at the wall and gave the waste paper bin an almighty kick, immediately looking round to see no one was observing this uncharacteristic – he hoped – behaviour.

He sank to the floor to massage the ankle the bin had bitten.

Back at his desk with a cup of coffee he stared at the blank wall for a while. Then he turned and looked Hu Stannton in the eye. He squinted at him. Blundell was used to looking at mug-shots and seeing baddies – he could tell them. He didn't think he was looking at one. He had to remind himself that Jack the Ripper maybe looked good on his wedding photo. He realised that if someone snapped John 'Chocky' Blundell right now, they would have a grey-faced, glowering, wholly unlovable character in the frame.

He didn't regard himself as a devout Catholic, he did realise he was a superstitious one. He needed an angel. He had his lucky charm, a gold Lourdes medal his mother had given him. He touched it and started a Hail Mary, but extended it into the longer Hail Holy Queen, '... mourning and weeping in this vale of tears.' Pathetic. He smiled at last, when he couldn't find his phone. He picked up the receiver from the desk behind his, but couldn't see the number over on his desk. Ashamed, he could see his own phone on the floor. He returned the receiver to its place.

He stood erect, stretched himself rotating his neck, and took a breath.

He sat down, gathered his phone off the floor, assembled it, patted it, raised the receiver and listened for a dial tone. He replaced it. He put his pad with the correct number beside it. He straightened other things, then redialled ... and got the answer machine.

'Blinking nine-to-fivers.' A considered thought, not an angry outburst. 'Your prayers are answered, but not necessarily with the answer you want. So what is the answer?'

Thoughts of Mattie and his 'National Front' homies facing up to Iruna distracted him. He shook them away. Their son was tearing his mother's heart to pieces.

'My original question was flawed,' thought Blundell. 'How could you tell if he's recently had sex, if he's just had a shower?' and Jenks says he hasn't had a shower. Where'd I get that notion?'

His mind wandered back over the hotel room. It was a SOCO – white suited as Jenks had been. But there were drips from the shower to the balcony and wetness and slip marks on there. So who had a shower?

But the victim recently had sex. Could it be the other person who had the shower? Could they have had a tussle on the balcony and Hu lost out?

Blundell got up and looked Holly in the eye. He tapped the flipchart with his pen. He didn't like that camp barman. Any less than Mattie would?

'The Home Office Pathologist will shed more light in the morning.'

Bahadur with her bundle of papers in her arms, toed Blundell's door open and stood looking at him. She felt the need to assess him … and to let him speak first. He didn't, he raised an eyebrow.

She didn't respond.

He pointed at the paperwork.

She looked at it nestling in her folded arms.

He stood up.

She held the papers out and lifted the file open.

'Well Badder?'

Her turn to raise an eyebrow.

'Sorry Runa, what you got?'

'Mrs Stannton has told me a pack of lies.'

'What?' Chocky got excited and rushed over to look at the papers. 'Show me.'

'She's been in to give us her forensics and details. No problem, all helpful and co-operative. But her stats don't add up.'

'Stats?'

'Well, yes, it is the stats – her figures are all wrong.' Iruna caught him smirk at 'figure.'

He coughed, looking at her pointing. 'Numbers, figures, yes. All wrong?'

'Well sir, do you know your NI number off by heart?' she said. 'I suppose the vast majority of us don't. Well Holly Stannton, if that's even her name…'

Blundell whistled.

'… she doesn't know hers … or where she lived and …. Well you can make a mistake with some of them, but I think she has put us off sir.'

The Inspector scratched his beard, then grabbed the notes and Iruna's elbow. They sat down and tried to make sense of Holly's nonsense.

'I get the impression you think she has intentionally, culpably, fobbed us off, Iruna,' Chocky started. 'Is that right?'

'Like I said – anyone can get some of it wrong, but she's not fooling us all of the time – is she now sir?'

He was fingering items from Mrs Stannton's forms. 'Which of these do we know to be true? Is she even Mrs Stannton?'

The sergeant smiled. 'Well *you* would probably say not …' She coughed a laugh. 'Catholic aren't you sir?'

He nodded with a frown.

'Well the priest was married to Holly Spiro in, wait for it – Vegas.'

'No?'

'Well that's what she said. It gets worse. They haven't bothered to have it recorded in the UK. She's given us her maiden name of Holly Spiro. I think – just a guess – that that was her married name from divorce papers. Got to be some sort of real name hasn't it sir?'

'It does make sense that – for us a priest is always a priest, and he couldn't get married in a church – he wouldn't believe he was properly married anyway.' He rubbed his chin. 'What's your general impression of her as a person, Runa?'

Iruna was hoping he would tell her what he thought, first.

'She was a wreck at the house, but you should have seen her today – glammed up in a smart suit – hair lovely and that. Leopard. Know what I mean?'

'Chameleon?'

'Nice one sir – yeah – chameleon.' She chuckled. 'Yeah, Leopard's can't change their spots.'

Chocky thought her colouring up was cute. He smiled. He sat back and tapped his pen on the papers.

Blundell thought of Bahadur's skin – no spots, but strange colouring. Funny way of talking too.

'Sir?' she said. ''Chocky'? Kinda hard for me. Do you mind…?'

'Ha! Childish?'

She smiled.

He nodded. 'That's Plods for you, isn't it?'

'Childish?' she wondered, but said 'Ploddish?'

He chuckled. 'Naa, they catch onto something that'll embarrass and stick to it like…'

'I get it, sir, yeah, but come on, you'll have to tell me now – what did you do?'

'I married a lovely Librarian whom I met at Liverpool Uni. I was from the 'pool, but she wasn't. She's never heard of my part – Thornton…!'

'Chocky's from Thornton – Brill!'

'I dunno. The Plods heard her call me Chocky at a Christmas party…'

'And it stuck. Okay. It's cute. I can handle that.'

They sat and smiled at each other.

'Right,' he said. 'My turn ... From Oxford you said. What about this west country accent you keep slipping into?'

Iruna was shaking her head. 'Town and Gown! That ruddy 'Oxford Accent' they talk about is nothing of the sort. It's what's spoke by the people who *come* there, not what *lives* there! Public school toffs!'

He leant forward conspiratorially. 'Come on then – have you ever seen

Morse?'

'Course I have, loads o'times - on telly, same as you!'

They laughed.

'Where were we? Mmm, yes, chameleons change colour for camouflage. Do you think Holly Stannton's hiding from us?'

'Better get her back in, eh, sir?'

'Got a date tonight, Iruna – it's Friday?'

She coloured up even more but didn't say anything.

'I think we should call in unannounced.' He looked at his watch; she didn't. 'Got time?'

'Sir? Chocky, sir, you haven't told me what the cousin had to say.'

'Shit, sorry, no I haven't. Hey, nor old Jenks.' He looked at his watch again. 'Bugger. Oh sorry. What say we drive up to the Stannton place, we only need a couple of minutes to make Missy jump, and I can bring you up to speed on the way?'

The sergeant laughed at the familiarity and decided to take it as paternal rather than chat-up. 'Want a spin in my new Mini sir?' She thought the intended 'sir' would sustain a professional relationship.

Inspector Blundell's lips pouted.

'Hold on a minute,' said Blundell leaping back out of the mini.

Bahadur frowned as she saw him size up the car. 'Wassup?' she shouted.

He jumped back in and snuggled into his seat belt. 'I was just checking – you said 'Mini', then I realised when I got in that I must have misheard you. I had a real mini when I was a student and you felt like your bottom was dragging along the floor.' He was nodding. 'Very nice.'

'Yes, my Dad made it for me – going away present.' She chuckled at her own curve ball.

Blundell turned a look on her.

'He makes them sir – at the Cowley factory – geddit?'

'Aah. Sweet.' He got his notepad out.

He caught her look at him.

'What was our Mrs Stannton like?'

'Not as green as she's cabbage looking.' Bahadur wasn't asking.

'No. She played a kind of daft Irish woman, but didn't like it when I treated her like one and then turned tables and treated me as the daft one. Then finally I got her cornered and she clammed up.'

'Not enough information among that lot, Chocky,' she chuckled, breaking hard for someone fed up of waiting for a turn to pull out.

Chocky picked up his pad. 'Ye-es.' He gave her a quick synopsis of his conversation with Pauline Stannton before slowing down to the issues as he saw them: Pauline accusing others of 'pushing' the priest, then panicking that maybe she could also be one who pushed. 'It's all very well her working out people who had a motive, but hers is just as strong.'

'Have we decided he was pushed, then? What'd the pathologist say?'

Chocky rubbed his ankle. 'Ah, now that gets a bit more interesting – he recently had sex.'

Iruna snorted.

'Nah...' and he laughed with her. He continued, 'steady on. You didn't hear me – *Stannton* had recently had sex.'

The steering took a wobble. 'Woops! Hey, you should've told me. Sorry. Yeah. That's something! Not Holly?'

'Don't know. Bloody office-wallah packed up. It's Friday, isn't it?' Blundell packed his notepad between his knees and rubbed his hands. 'Yes, mmm. Better pull over a minute.'

She did and turned towards him.

'Switch the engine off. We need to get this together before we see the wife.' He cleared his throat. 'Sorry I should have told you this, but I had a difficult conversation with Jenks and it looks like I must be having some senior moments or something. This shit is deep enough and I seem only to be adding to it.'

Bahadur tapped her Christmas tree car deodoriser dangling from the mirror.

Her Inspector groaned and brushed down the back of his head. 'Can I ask you to tell me what we saw in the room – Stannton's room at the hotel? I want to see where I went off track.'

She frowned and stopped the little tree swinging. 'What, right through?'

Blundell was flicking pages of his pad. 'No, er, no, just the state of the room, I think.'

'What? Window open, bed stripped, shower used, dripped over to window ... oh, cleaner's trolley had been put away.' She thought maybe this latter was what he was getting at.

'Yes, that's what I put together. Now here's the thing. Stannton had *not* had a shower!' He raised his eyebrows and stared at Bahadur.

She whistled.

'There's more – he recently had sex...'

'You...'

He held a finger up. 'When is 'recent' to you?'

She stretched her mouth out and waggled her head. 'Yeah, and when had he not had a shower, since?' She looked at Blundell conducting an unknown symphony with his finger. She waited.

'Okay, I took 'recently' to mean just before he died? Is that not fair enough?'

Bahadur was pursing her lips. She looked at her watch. 'It's all news to me sir, so put it together again – he recently had sex and he had not recently had a shower. How's that?'

'Fair enough, we better know what we need to know from Holly, because she's the one he's *supposed* to have sex with. Was *she* there?'

'Timings, sir. I didn't think she knew he was dead until the man with the funny voice told her, did you?'

'Ahah! Just thought – what man? She may have made that up. She was totally distressed when we got there. But she would be if she'd shoved her husband out of a window, accidentally or on purpose, wouldn't she?'

'I definitely think she's made up some of her details, sir.' She revved the engine.

Chocky hadn't heard it even start. 'Yes, need to get on. But just to clarify: Holly Stannton's husband – if they were married and if that is her name – is found dead having had a struggle. The shower appears to have been used and there are drips across to a balcony that he has 'fallen' from. But he has not had a shower and he has had sex 'recently.'' He rushed in another sentence before the sergeant moved the car into gear, 'We must be careful that *she* tells us things and we only *ask*.'

The Family Liaison opened the door to them and took them to Holly in the lounge. She was dressed in the same two piece but no longer looked smart and composed. She was slumped sideways in the chair from the pristine suite. Back to the lost child again.

Blundell nodded Bahadur into the settee and elbowed the liaison to stay back with him.

Bahadur opened the file of forms and handed one over to Holly. She awoke slowly to it, inspecting it before taking it.

'What is it?'

'It's the form you filled in this afternoon.'

'Who? Me?' Holly looked at it again. She was still slumped and it was down beside her. She was studying it. 'Writing's a bit squiggly.' She very carefully moved herself up. She squeezed her eyes shut then re-focussed on the page. She looked at Bahadur. 'Officer?'

'Now, Mrs Stannton…'

'Holly, please?'

'Mrs Stannton, you will know that we need the information on these forms to put on computer for it to tell us more about a person.' She stopped.

Holly looked at her and her face appeared to harden, just a little. She sat up some more. 'You want me to tell you, or your computer?' She looked across at the Inspector. He looked at Bahadur.

The sergeant went on, 'Talk me through your details, please, Mrs Stannton? From the top. Your full name.

'Just Holly Stannton. It's got two 'n's, well three really. I told Hu I didn't need all of them.' It was a wan smile.

'I couldn't find a record of your marriage…'

'Vegas. We got married in Las Vegas.'

'Okay. And did you register it over here when you came back.' He looked at the photo.

'Hu did that.'

'Do you know he did?'

Holly looked sad. 'Hu said he did.'

'Alright. Now your maiden name?'

'Holly Spiro.'

'Spiro? Unusual name.'

'Yeah, my 'orrible ex's. I was glad to get rid of that name.'

'Got it! Thanks Holly,' said Iruna with a sigh of relief, 'so Spiro's not your maiden name is it?'

Holly squeezed away a big tear and at last sat up properly. 'No,' she said, as if she had just made a big discovery. 'No it's not is it?'

Bahadur looked her full in the face, waiting. 'What is your maiden name, Holly?'

Holly fainted away.

Blundell rushed over to her.

The Liaison ran to the sink.

Bahadur got up, then stomped out and stood by the front door. She opened it and hands on hips, took some deep breaths.

They were a mile or so away when Iruna slapped the steering wheel and said, 'I'm not having it sir. Why are you giving her such an easy ride? Sorry, but that's how it looks to me.'

Her Inspector was watching the road. 'Mmm. I don't know. I'm not a doctor, see. She didn't properly come round did she?'

Saturday 6th March

Blundell had been in a while and got up to date with some intelligence traffic. He did look over some updates on the metal and cable gang, but had to let his colleague know that the suspicious death of the priest was to be his priority, at least for a few days.

The new sergeant had actually started the case and Blundell invited her in to take up residence in the second desk in his office – at least for a few days. She didn't look hung over, indeed her reply to his query of a 'good night out?' was simply '*sleeeeeep.*'

He could tell. 'Though I don't think I slept that well, I have had the chance to sort out my son … my head – and its contents – with a nice glass of red and the wife snoozing along to her Cliff records.' He noticed Iruna's frown. 'You don't want to know. Hey, telly's rubbish on Fridays isn't it? Anyhow, Jenks emailed through his report and it makes even more exciting reading. It also makes sense of the 'recent' bit.'

DS Bahadur was sitting at the desk, looking serene, pen and pad at the ready.

DI Blundell noticed and chuckled.

'What?'

He shook his head and went on, 'This, er, *appears,* to be it: Leaving the fall injuries aside for a minute, Stannton appears to have not died instantly – but to have drowned over maybe a half hour period. He appears to have struggled on concrete, which as *you* noticed, is not in the room, but beside the jacuzzi.

'Now this is it: He had *not* had a shower, that day, maybe not the day before even.'

'Yucky.'

''Recently' – in the context of his having had sex – was not long before death and, wait for it…' Chocky looked at the 'little girl's' face and adjusted his own demeanour to deadly serious. 'It was anal sex.'

She blinked. She raised her eyebrows a little. She was not shocked.

'It was anal sex evidenced by both faecal matter and … blood.' He sat back and tapped his pad with his pen.

There was a gleam, verging on a smile in Iruna's eyes. 'Hotting up sir, Chocky.'

'You appear alright with this er…'

'Sir. I have *risen* to Sergeant – I didn't walk in off the street yesterday.'

Chocky coughed and sat up. 'No, no sorry Iruna, but it does sound a bit gory. Most real murders are not like telly. But anal sex, blood, dying man struggling for life – against what? Yes?'

'Yeah, yeah. Against who?'

'Whom?' he said, but instantly swallowed it with another cough. He stood next to the flipchart. 'Need a few more of your little Post-its, here. I want one for our barman.'

'Jez?'

'That's it,' he said as they both riffled through their pads. 'Here, Jeremy Fylde. Let's get him in.'

Looking up he saw Iruna cringe just a little. She thought a second before drawing the boss into the other area – fall. 'Did he jump or was he pushed, then?'

'Or did he simply fall? Don't let's leave that out. Yes, not so much Jenks can help us with. He is well battered, so separating out injuries from what may have made him fall ... from those caused by the fall...' he waggled his hand, '... is not so easy.'

'And this struggle don't forget, sir.'

'No I'm coming to that. Suzanne said he definitely was not half-in, half-out, didn't she. His head over just the side.'

'So if he struggled, how come he didn't manage to *slip...?*' Iruna was lying on the desk, only her head and shoulders on it, the rest down the side.

Chocky stood over her. 'Get your hand up to the side of the desk Runa.'

She did. 'He's broken a knee, you said.' She was kneeling on the floor. 'And some toes.' She swung her feet about. 'Why didn't he even slump out?'

'Held?'

'Held. And drowned.' Iruna stayed with her head on the desk and looked at her hand practising holds on the jacuzzi side of the desk.

'He's a big lad. Could his length have held him up – straight back – as he couldn't really push on that broken knee.'

Iruna dropped down onto her haunches. Up straight she was head and shoulders above the desk-edge. Now she could just get her chin on it.

'But he must have been a foot taller than you...'

Iruna elbowed the kneecap standing next to her.

'Aggregated spine length *and* thigh length ... and anyway who's saying the jacuzzi was that high?'

'Or low sir – pretty low to step into, yeah?' Chocky helped her up and she rubbed her knees. 'Must admit it gives us some idea, sir.'

The DI scooted his chair over to the flipchart and wrote 'Pushed,' 'Slipped,' and 'Held'. underneath Stannton's picture. He smiled up at Hu. 'Only surmises at this stage, sir.'

Abe Grant was criss-crossing his tiny patch of beautifully manicured lawn weighing his phone in his hand. He snuffed out the life of a new-born dandelion. He brought up Leo's mobile number – workaholic as he was, he might just be off on a Saturday morning. He thought that the three of them should maybe reconvene. He jumped as the phone buzzed in his hand. Brien.

'Now then Brien,' he said. 'Bad news, eh?' He heard a deep breath at the other end.

'Abe, what's happened?'

'Don't you know – Father Hu's fallen out of a window.'

'Yes, yes, of course I heard that, but how? How did he fall out of the window?'

Abe's hand automatically sized up an imaginary balcony. 'Yes, that is the question. I suppose the police will tell us.'

There was a gap before Brien continued, 'they didn't tell you, then?'

'Nor you by the sound of it.'

There was a slight gasp at the other end before the line went dead. 'Eyup, Brien?' Abe saw that Brien had hung up. He was relieved that he didn't have to put his idea to him first. Abe needed Leo.

Leo was cogitating all round his Dad's old Morris Minor Traveller. He had taken a back door and all the wheels off, had the bonnet up and a spanner in his hand. He had purposely wiped some dirty oil on his hands for evidence. He was wondering what Abe and Brien were up to. He reckoned to be musing on how the idea of these 'Woodies' came about. But he knew it all backwards. His heart was beating a bit too quickly for such mundane considerations.

He thought they would be looking for him. Talya, too.

A rare weekend without any youth service events. Well, always fewer in winter; and even less as the cuts strip away the workers who put the events on. Caving? All year round sport – ambient temperature underground about nine degrees, winter and summer. Health and Safety Risk Assessment was a war of attrition, defeating youth workers who had even set up a club for such demand.

Who was it that Hu had been arguing, rowing with? Hiding at the end of the corridor, pretending to check a fire extinguisher, Leo had heard a door shut but missed whoever it was that rushed down the stairs. Might not have even come out of Hu's room.

If the pigs asked him what he knew, he couldn't let them know he had gone back there.

Leo's concern for the abused had turned his focus towards abusers.

Regarding rape, it was common to regard it as an exercise of power, of dominance. The 'thrill' for the rapist is to win, to get one over. Leo could imagine a rapist, after the act, punching the air as an Olympian would after crossing the line. It was just that child abuse was now defined clearly as rape.

He was realising that this concern was merging with his adult long affection, yes 'affection' is what it was, it was not dewy-eyed nostalgia, for old-fashioned communism. He had once wondered if it was Anarchy that he espoused, but no, he did believe in order. He believed in a systematised exercise of power but shared among equals. Equality was key. All Animals are equal, but….

It was dawning on him more and more, that his cases in Safeguarding young people almost always arose out of individuals seizing power over the vulnerable from within a system. The system of churches and mosques cloaked, and sometimes consciously sheltered, members who abused children or killed to be martyrs; Masonic Orders sheltered their own – seemingly from accusation from whatever wrong they did; the Police consistently closed ranks round their own racists and torturers; Management was full of nepotism, sleaze and covered up scandal; when his beloved communist system broke down in the Balkans, then Yugoslavia and of course in the mother Union of Soviet, Socialist Republics, always, always, individuals corruptly stole power. Oligarchs rule!

Leo had consistently shrugged off being accused of being naïve – were these not all examples of nations breaking out from under oppression, and individuals, as dictators, oppressing huge populaces. Individuals were always sneaking into power vacuums. It was great that the Czar was shot, but millions were killed by those wanting the fill the vacuum and in the end a worse Czar, Stalin, fought his way to the top, then struck an ice-pick through the brain of Leo's beloved Leon.

He knew this, but Leo always focussed on the individuals, all equal in his sight, the ones who suffered, the little ones who cried and who died, and who died in their millions. 'What were the world wars all about?' was his cry.

Conversely, who knows Gavrilo Princip or Adolf 'Schicklgruber', the individuals who caused these millions and millions of gallons of blood to pour into Europe's soil? Gavrilo who fired the shot that started the first world war, killing the Archduke Ferdinand; and Adolf was the son of the illegitimate wife-beater Alois Schicklgruber, who had changed his name to Hitler.

Leo had long harboured murderous intent on his own corrupt managers, but currently he was more intent on someone else who seemed to have had everything he wanted, but still wanted more. He saw two others who showed by their deeds that they regretted taking what was not theirs and spent many years giving it back.

What was the difference between them? How did he differ? They had all done evil, he had not. He knew his means justified his end. He was equal to the task. He was more than equal. How would he choose to see it through?

So Hu Stannton was dead. Who could have killed him? Were Abe or Brien more up to the task than Leo himself?

He saw the light from the kitchen door move and grabbed a rag.

Talya shouted in, 'Abe on the phone for you, Leo. You coming or shall I say...'

'Yes Looby. Just tell him I'm wiping my hands.' He prepared his words.

The Bishop had been disturbed by a call from Monsignor Green, who in turn had been irritated by several calls from parishioners and one from a newspaper.

The Bishop asked him what he had said.

'I told them I had nothing to say.'

The Bishop didn't suppose that satisfied the curious. 'You will need to say something – you have a Saturday evening mass, don't you?'

'Yes Bishop. Could do with something before six o'clock.'

'I'll get on to the Police and have a Press Release along with something to read to the people. To you for five o'clock, is that enough? Now Father, you will have to use your email. Can you do it, or get someone to help you?'

'Yes, yes I can do it,' the Monsignor lied. He wasn't having that whipper-snapper patronising him – Bishop or no Bishop.

The Super had recognised the growing complexity of the case, so by the afternoon Chocky and Iruna had a couple of DCs to brief. Chocky, insensitive to anybody's personal space, had four of them sharing too little air. He did notice something was not quite right, so he rushed, sweating, through the issues as he saw them.

After introducing 'Mike' Gatting - 'I won't mention your real name shall I Alfred?' – and Alan Prisco to Iruna 'Badder', he dived straight in by saying that the case had so far been a complete cock-up from beginning to end, and that the guys were brought in to help Chocky and Badder sort it out.

Iruna coughed.

'I didn't mean cocked up by us, no Badder, but the situation we found at the Hotel and what other elements have shown up.'

He wanted to say at the beginning, that the suspicious death of an ex-priest was sure to be a sensation, and that great care was needed to not fan that flame. All they had was that the body of Stannton had been found. He had died of drowning and the police were looking into the circumstances of his death.

That the meeting was disturbed several times with messages and queries underlined this point, so Chocky set Alan on to take all incoming calls on the case.

He was aware of the weekend getting in the way, but Sunday had a special poignancy in this case. It involved an ex priest, so the Sunday Red Tops would want it, and a *local* ex-priest, so there were issues with the church, Sunday Mass and parishioners, some of whom were involved in the case.

'Most sensationally – and this must not leave this room, yet – we have an ex-priest who has recently had anal sex, involving faeces and blood.'

Alan coughed and held up a finger. 'Not semen, sir?'

Chocky was nonplussed and Iruna dropped her jaw. 'Of course semen,' said the DI blinking feverishly.

He continued with the need to get Holly's details sorted out, to find the towels and bedding from the cleaner's trolley, especially Stannton's, and to get the forensics scrutinising them and the balcony.

He wanted the barman bringing in, under caution. He counted off: to get full information and background on Leo Nicholas, Brien Devine and Abe Grant; plus the Golden Wedding couple needed to be contacted to find which of the hotel guests were theirs. 'The Hotel will a have record of any who stayed and we need anything useful witnessed – especially from rooms round about – rowing and that. And did *nobody* hear him fall? If not, why not?'

'Did they have a disco or anything, sir?' asked Gatting.

'Find out,' he smiled. 'Now look, it's weekend. How are we fixed?'

Bahadur just couldn't work Sunday – her parents were coming up and bringing some more of her stuff – but she could maybe do a couple of hours in the evening; Prisco agreed to join her then; Chocky himself would come in and do a

117

couple of hours Sunday afternoon; Gatting was unforthcoming over why he couldn't do anything before Monday morning. Chocky didn't tell them that he would be attending both the Saturday evening and Sunday morning masses at the Friary Convent.

Finally, though he felt he must not patronise the pretty sergeant, he stressed the need to recognise the chain of command, and for the DCs to bring stuff to Bahadur and she to him.

After the DCs had left, he got Iruna to *copy* their materials from the flipchart and, if she could, set up a fresh space on a white board in the briefing room – 'try to get one of the white whiteboards will you Duck, I flipping hate those see through things.'

She smiled as she turned away, but it immediately dropped off her face. She turned back, and shut the door again. 'Sir, semen, sir?'

'Ye-es?'

'We are clear that Stannton had anal sex with someone else…'

'Aha! Yes, Prisco's observation was not quite so stupid. Clear it up with him, will you?'

'Erm … I have it from you sir and, not being really well up on the finer points of male homosexual procedure, I assumed that Jenks meant he had …penetrated someone else…'

Chocky had his hand over his mouth.

Iruna had to finish her own sentence, 'and not had someone penetrating him … and leaving…'

'Semen! Osintot!' Chocky was shaking his head. 'We can't go on like this, Runa. Well done. That is correct … and of course I could have mislead the constables in not making that clear. Shit.' He laughed. 'When Jenks told me 'he had anal sex' – it was simply that he had … buggered, sorry, someone else, and not vice versa. Of course it was an assumption on my part that the lads would get that meaning too. Stupid?'

'Not really – it was clear to me, but as Prisco showed – he maybe thought the opposite.'

'Sorry, but it is so murky Iruna.'

'Sir.' She took a deep breath. 'I have been in the force for coming on fifteen years.'

He placed his hand on her forearm and looked into her eyes: 'Forgive an old … er, older man his chauvinism, please Iruna? I'll get it double checked straight away.'

Sunday 7th March

As well as all that was buzzing round in his head, rather too much Sunday lunch was gurgling round Chocky's stomach, but he valiantly persevered in sorting something out for the new week ahead in the investigation of the death of Hubert Stannton. He had decided that it was a suspicious death and he knew it was a mess. Investigations were always a puzzle to be worked through piece by piece, but he felt the pieces of this puzzle needed firstly to be pulled out of a mire.

He had arrived with the good intention of initially sorting out what he had encountered since the team last met, but was tempted to look at what was left for him. He was very impressed that Prisco had got stuck in and obviously worked into late evening. Bahadur had visited Holly and made some progress, while Gatting had found out Fylde's shift pattern at the bar of the Loseborough, but no news about the trolley.

Nothing new had a great bearing on the case. He smiled at the thought of Cousin Pauline.

On the other hand his own updates did: he was correct in assuming that Stannton had penetrated someone else, but had to put up with more stick from Jenks – albeit only in a text message – that of course there was semen – Stannton's own. He parried a repost to Jenks about being a nine-to-fiver and not getting an actual report to them yet ... and DNA of the bodily fluids wouldn't be revealing its secrets until Monday.

Church had been interesting, though he didn't manage to take in any messages from the Holy Books. He got there early for both Saturday night and Sunday morning services at the unfamiliar Friary Convent, his own parish being Our Lady's on the other side of town. He secured an inconspicuous vantage point across from the convent to observe the arrival of any of the protagonists in the unfolding drama. He thought that sticking together might indicate collusion, whilst separation might show suspicion of others. He had gleaned that Devine and Grant were friends but didn't know whether Pauline Stannton might associate with them.

He was rewarded by the two men attending separate masses.

Big Abe Grant arrived with his equally imposing lady, but while she went ahead, he stopped outside to finish a cigarette and do a bit of cheery backslapping. Lots of nods and tipping of caps indicated a leader among men. Blundell waited a little before following into the church, deciding an exit route and viewing point, but choosing a pew near the back.

He was not impressed with the Monsignor – he thought him an old-school stuffed-shirt. The parish priest followed a different routine on Saturday and Sunday for informing the faithful about their ex-parish priest. Blundell realised why: on Saturday he will have decided to not cause a disturbance to the majority who would know nothing of Stannton's mishap; whereas on Sunday the pastor said he realised many will have read about it in their Sunday paper and went straight into it as he arrived on the sanctuary.

He of course opened about the sad and distressing news, 'and many of you who won't have heard', but it was his sad duty and, fortunately, he stoked no fires for the police. Father Hubert had been found dead in mysterious circumstances and the police are trying to find out what happened. 'Our prayers are with him, God rest him, and of course with his family.'

Blundell hid a smirk that the Monsignor didn't say '*Wife* and family.' He saw that Grant and his wife were sitting half way down the small, simple chapel with its cream walls, plain windows with only a few small stained glass motifs. They stared straight ahead making no movement during The Monsignor's statement.

On the other hand, at Sunday's mass, Devine and his wife scuttled in as the priest came out of the sacristy and took a place against the wall, near the front where there were more empty seats. Mrs Devine appeared to be crying on-and-off throughout the mass, and her husband kept his head down except when the priest raised the host and the bell rang.

After the masses, from a fresh vantage point each time, Blundell noticed Grant seemed to be at ease chatting to a few people, and though he assumed it would have been about Stannton, he rebuked himself for making any more assumptions. On Sunday he thought he had missed the Devines' departure, but they had obviously hung back inside so as not to have to talk to anybody. The way Brien looked around before stepping out of the door convinced Blundell of this, though he had to turn away and whip up his coat collar, as he was one of only a few stragglers left to be seen.

Monday 8th March

Sergeant Iruna Bahadur had been first to arrive at the station. She got a message that Leo Nicholas wasn't going to make the nine o'clock appointment that she had made with him - he was at the hospital.

She looked through the glass screen to the single side ward. She held a finger and her warrant card up to the constable on guard at the door and watched as the scene inside unfolded.

The youth officer was engrossed as he gently stroked the forehead of the tattooed young man in the bed. Along with the red and blue of the tattoos, there was the more vibrant red of a cut under the eye, which in turn was closed up with purple swelling.

Nicholas pulled at his goatee as he stood musing over the lad.

Bahadur went quietly in.

Nicholas barely registered her. He was not disturbed.

Eventually she hushed 'What's this about, sir?'

Nicholas came round from the other side of the bed and stood with his back to the patient. He looked across the room. 'Where's his Mum?' He looked towards the door. 'Where's his Dad? … his sister? … his mates?'

He looked at Bahadur, his eyes moist. 'The needle has been all of these to him. But now he's got a … wife. And she's having a baby. He's going to be a Dad. He's going to get clean. But his 'wife's' not going to have *him* in her baby's life, oh, no.' He grabbed his mouth with a full hand.

'So where's that family now? No, it's not the needle – not having that any more. So what's he got?'

The sergeant knew he wasn't asking her.

He went on addressing a chair, and the guard outside the door. 'He's got himself. Who is that? He is alone; he is angry. *What* is that? He is a loner; he is anger.'

Leo now turned his attention to the detective. He laid a hand on her shoulder, looked across at the patient and back to her eyes. 'He's stabbed the baby in his girl's tummy.' He held her gaze.

She couldn't hold his. Looking down she was ashamed of the notepad in her hand and slipped it into her jeans. She looked back and nodded at Nicholas, turned and, giving her card to the constable saying 'ask him to call me,' she slipped out of the hospital.

The team was gathered at 'her' transparent whiteboard and was intrigued by her late entrance, knowing she had in fact been first-in.

'We'll be talking to Nicholas … later,' she said, sitting and opening her hands for an update.

The three men completed a circle with her and the board.

Chocky opened, 'you and Alan got stuck in for a couple of hours yesterday, well done.'

He told of his feelings – it was all he had – about the church observation. The several possible Grants, Devines and Nicholases left a suspicious amount of scope for more details from all of them. 'And what about Holly Stannton – if that's who she is even?'

'Maybe, maybe not,' said Alan.

'Sounds messy,' said Gatting.

Iruna looked at him thinking he was blaming her. 'Well we may be getting somewhere. Spiro *was* her previous name – she was actually officially married to a Rupert Spiro. Yeah I know. And actually divorced. She said her maiden name was Holly Dean and 'Sexy Spiro' called her 'Bush.''

Gatting was smirking.

She ignored him.

'We couldn't get *anything* on the computer sir,' said Alan.

'Well today we've *got* to nail her.' Chocky turned to Iruna. 'Was she still playing broken widow?'

'Yes, sir. Is it real, you gonnar ask? I really do not think so.'

The DI pulled a long face.

'Well I *don't* sir, sorry. I know she is sweet and pretty and was definitely very distressed, but I'm wondering what she was actually distressed about, see?'

They all looked at Blundell. He swept an imaginary stone with his foot. 'Prime Suspect isn't she?' Bahadur was surprised to hear him verbalise that. 'She almost certainly is not a calculating murderer, so she would be distressed in any of the three counts.'

'Sir?' chimed Prisco and Gatting.

'Well,' he counted off the fingers, 'if he fell; if she pushed him; if someone else pushed him.'

They were all nodding now. Iruna was pleased that her boss really was open to all suggestions.

'Yes, yes,' she said, standing and taking the helm. Alan stood in her way, so as she elbowed him out of the way she breathed 'gormless' into his ear. 'So the three counts,' she continued making three columns. 'This one is small – if he fell, no one else is in it.'

'She might sue the hotel for health and safety,' grumbled Gatting.

'Central for us has got to be that - if he was pushed - who could or would push him? And over here we maybe have to ask who would have made him jump.' She looked around tapping the felt-tip on her hand.

Chocky gave the coup de grâce, 'and under all three, who drowned him?'

Gatting looked to Prisco and Bahadur and pulled the 'who's-being-stupid-now' face.

Alan asked the open question, 'What is it we, well me 'n' Mike, don't know sir?'

'I think you do, boys. Wasn't he drowned, i.e. someone drowned him?'

Gatting's face got more exaggerated, one cheek almost taking over his eye socket.

Somewhat surprised herself by the fourth scenario, Iruna realised she shouldn't be, so she decided to tell him as she drew the line underneath, 'in all these three, a fall from the window is not what killed Stannton – drowning did.'

As Blundell nodded, Gatting's finger of understanding rose up. 'A conspiracy?'

Eyebrows all round. That word hadn't been used in the investigation, so far.

Chocky chuckled and sat the team down. 'Plenty to go at, then.'

They shared the morning's tasks out and they each set about them with, 'The Conspiracy theory is for homework: who could or would have conspired with whom to kill off the ex-parish priest?'

'There's a Mrs Stannton in reception.'

'Holly?' asked Alan.

'No, that's not what she said,' said the desk.

'I'll be down.'

DC Prisco shouted across to DS Bahadur by the board, 'a Mrs Stannton at the desk, Sarge.'

'Another one?' she giggled.

'Wadya mean?'

'You mean Holly, don't you?'

'No.'

'Exactly!' Now she laughed and stood up. 'The Boss said 'another one' when the victim's cousin Mrs Stannton turned up, thinking the priest had a secret wife hidden away. Turned out she was a *Miss*. So this time we might be right, eh?'

'His Mum, Sarge?'

She winked at him and turned towards the office. 'Go and find out for us, eh?' She handed Jenks's emails to Blundell.

'What've we got, Iruna?'

'Faeces is a bit messy, sir.'

He frowned. 'Nah. Not the wife's?'

'Can't tell ... contaminated and that.' She stood behind Chocky and pointed at sections. 'If he last had ordinary sex with Holly, she would be on him, wouldn't she. But when was that?'

'Did she go to the Loseborough?' he said. 'Blood?'

'Yes, hers. Could be her period?'

'Icky. Alright, then, but who is she? Have we found that out yet?'

'Alan's on it sir. But I think we need to get her in under caution, don't you sir?'

'Too damn right, Runa, but we don't want her playing the mad woman, do we?' He had a think before asking, 'What's Gatting up to? Get him to bring her in. She hasn't seen him yet, has she? Might come quietly.'

The DS sucked on her pen. 'Dunno. Opposite, maybe? He's working on the hotel – the laundry trolley, your friend Jez…'

'Send Gatting for our Jez, that's it. What was *he* up to? Bloody tears for the *lovely Hubert.*'

Iruna frowned. She wasn't happy about the anal sex and jumping to any conclusions. She didn't want to be challenging her new boss, but she did always wonder about the systemic homophobia in the police, along with the racism of course. She let it be. 'So I'll go for Holly and you and me will talk to her?'

'Good shout,' he said, 'and send Alan in with everything he's got so far, please.'

DC Alan Prisco tapped his papers on the sergeant's desk. 'Me and Badder got the specifics on the three guys last night, sir.'

'Badder, Alan?'

'Yessir.'

'It's Ba-ha-dur, to you Alan.'

'Eh?' He shook his head. 'Sorry sir, but you introduced her to us. I didn't hear that.'

'We've got to be politically correct, these days haven't we constable?' He then mumbled to himself, 'Badder, Bahdur, Bahadur, Ba'ader. Mmm, sorry Alan. If I say it quickly. I apologise and I'll have a word with her, too.'

Alan smiled. 'Nicholas, Divine and Grant, sir. All got records, sir.'

'Swearing at nuns?' he chuckled. He thought he had better not correct the DC again.

'No sir – serious stuff. All of them.'

DC Mike Gatting had got up to speed and changed his mind about the Black Mass of the Cabal of Catholics. It did look like this could be an interesting case after all. He had a woman constable with him and he set about grilling Abram Grant.

'You know why you are here sir?'

'Father Hu, Hu Stannton,' he said.

'What can you tell us about him?'

'He used to be our parish priest and he left. He got married, and you people tell me he is dead, and oh, so did the new parish priest.'

'About you and him, sir.'

'Suspicious circumstances, *he* said. What does that mean?'

Gatting felt like doing his Gestapo voice, but being eyeball to eyeball with a very big man, bigger than him, whose record he knew, he thought better of it. 'Can I ask the questions please, sir?'

Abe raised his eyebrows a flicker. 'Me and him, eh?'

'Yes sir. What was your relationship to him?'

Abe frowned. 'Okay, I know what you mean. He was our parish priest, and a very good one too. I liked him. He happened to fall in love and left.'

'Is that it?'

'No, wait on. I mainly liked him because he was young.'

'A boy, sort of?'

Abe didn't like the tone of that. 'Well, I run a charity for young people, and he wasn't much older than them, you see?' He smiled. He felt he had nailed that one. 'Father Hu, as he was, took a great interest and was ... well, wonderful with them. I think his replacement - I am sad to say - might well shun our clients. The 'Druggies' might smell.'

'Druggies?' said Gatting.

'It's a charity for young people who come unstuck through drugs ... and their families.'

'Ah, I see. And you are...'

'I am the Chair of the Management Committee.'

'Come at it through personal experience, do we?'

'I don't know. Do you?'

'Ahem. You? You do this sort of thing because of your personal experience of drugs?'

Abe thought he would let the stupid detective run away with it.

'Yes.'

Gatting sat upright. It didn't give him any height advantage, tall though he was. He tapped his file. It didn't mention drugs, but why else did Grant kill his wife, but in drug crazed frenzy? 'You got into trouble, for it, did you?'

'No.'

'Come on sir, I have your record here.'

Abe knew that the record should not include any such detail. 'Needle's stuck I reckon.'

Swinging one knee over the other and turning to point at the recorder Gatting said, 'Lifer.'

Abe blanched just a little but held it. 'Okay.'

'Murderer.'

'No.'

Gatting uncrossed his legs and opened the file. 'Life imprisonment.'

'Minimum tariff, excellent conduct.' He was not going to help the oaf with any detail. Could he even read?

The DC coughed again and said, 'You and Hubert Standing – tell me about the way you related to him. When did you last see him?'

'Never seen him in my life. Don't know who you are talking about.'

'What?' he shouted. 'Don't try and pratt me about.'

Abe gave him the most innocent of looks. 'Who did you say?'

The detective checked the file and fingered the name. 'Clever clogs. I've only just come onto this case, so ... Hubert *Stannton?*'

'Ah, you do know who you are talking about, but you don't know who you are talking to ... yet.'

Gatting knew he was floundering so he sat back and said, 'So please put me straight, will you, sir? I'm particularly interested in what you did last week.'

Abe was not intending to be obstructive, so he told the story of the 'conference' - short and to the point. He had nothing to hide, except his record, and now that was out in the open with the detective. He watched the detective's reaction closely. He knew mention of friction could implicate any of his friends, so he took his time over it with lots of ceiling inspection and chin scratching.

Gatting made the assistant take notes, so that he could keep his eyes on the Lifer. Grant didn't give him much to go on, so he felt pressured to talk around his record for any similarity: had he pushed his victim out of the window?

Abe wanted to give as little detail as possible, so he felt that being able to say he had caused a death through reckless driving – 'and that almost forty years ago, Officer' - should leave him in the clear.

'Not so hasty, Mr Grant! How were drugs involved in the case?'

Abe thought that the detail that he had 'popped a few' before setting off, would probably not be mentioned in the synopsis in the detective's file, so he pulled a 'Don't ask me face', with his hands wide open.

'What's that supposed to mean?'

'It does mean, 'what has that got to do with poor Father Hu?' Am I supposed to guess he was stoned or something? Was I supposed to have supplied him with some LSD? Did he think he could fly?'

'You do run a drugs project.'

Abe laughed. 'Ha – *'drugs'* project! Sounds like a drug supplying project. Did you choose the plural on purpose?'

'Well okay, sorry, but both you and he would – through your contacts – have ready access to drugs. Or rather, Mr Stannton did while he was with your project.'

'What - and he came to me for a fresh supply?'

'Is that a statement for the record?'

Abe almost stood up. The chair scraped back, but he decided to stay, inspecting the table, drumming his fingers on it. He looked up at the detective.

Gatting was inscrutable.

'Now then, officer, tell me: have my record or drugs got any bearing on the case? That would indicate a way forward with this line … and my willingness to continue this discussion.'

Gatting knew Grant was not under arrest. 'Of course you can go, sir, but you are under caution and you have stated, on the record, 'he came to me for a fresh supply.''

Abe sneered at the officer. 'That won't stick and you know it.' He stood up.

Gatting also stood. He had all he thought he could get for now, but did add, 'You will allow us to take your finger prints and DNA, sir, won't you?'

The barman Jeremy Fylde was in the cells. DI Blundell was appalled when he found out and got on to the desk, who passed him on to the PC who brought him in.

'Oh, Sir, what a palaver. I see why you got someone else to bring him in.'

'Er...'

'He absolutely bloody loved it!'

Blundell laughed and stroked his chin. He was not actually surprised. 'But in a cell, Constable? He does know he's not under arrest, doesn't he?'

'Oh yeah! He bloody insisted, sorry sir an' that, but you shoulda been there.' He was encouraged by the obvious enjoyment of the DI, so went on, 'He insisted we put him in a *Man*-acle, giving it 'Ooh, Lovely butch bracelet.''

Chocky snorted. 'Quite clever. Man-acle. Haven't heard that before. But the cells?'

'Hey, ask the desk Sergeant about that. 'Ooh, I love your stripes. Oh come on let me try your Jacket on. Oh, go on.'' He roared with laughter. 'You should 'a' seen the Sarge backing away from him.' He calmed down. 'Well, Monday sir, innit – not busy. Think Sarge thought it'd be best way to get him out of reception and whatever mayhem he might cause to the public an' that, yeah?'

Chocky shook his head and wandered down to the cells. He was not light hearted about Fylde camping it up all the time, so readied himself to put on the frighteners. The barman was meek as a lamb walking to a reception room after an eyeballing from the DI. 'Simple stuff Jez – don't be digging yourself into a hole – *or wasting my time.*'

'Okay sir.' The most normal of voices.

'You were on duty cleaning the bar when we came the morning after the incident, but you were on bar duty the night before. Heavy hours?'

'Well I was cleaning up my own mess, but no, it's cool.'

'So you were on duty the whole of the night that we suspect Hubert Stannton fell out of the window.' He raised a finger.

Fylde took a breath. Seeing the finger, he took another. 'Yes sir.'

'So give me some thoughts and timings please Jez.'

Fylde could not elaborate on the details he gave on the first occasion, so Blundell moved into his hidden agenda – anal sex.

'So no breaks?'

'Oh! Oh yes, breaks. Sorry, yes I took me breaks. Well one actually, when the Golden Oldies had their buffet I had an hour. Oh...!'

'Oh, indeed. Tell me.'

'I took a bit of buffet from the kitchen up to room thirteen and put my feet up. Watched a bit of telly. Maybe nodded off.'

'Room thirteen?'

'Yes, the one they can't let! Kind of hotel tradition to have it available for staff use. I did stay overnight, too.'

'Did you have company?'

Fylde slapped the table between them, reverting to type. 'Oh you are awful!'

'Jez!'

'No.'

'On the break? And what time was that?'

'No … and buffet eight-thirty to nine-thirty.'

'So where is room thirteen?'

'One, three – first floor room three. Get it?'

'First floor, mm.' Chocky checked his notes. 'Can anyone corroborate that?'

'Ooh, I need an alibi, do I? Why, was the lovely Hu pushed?' Fylde put his finger over his lips. 'You're not tellin' are you?'

'Would that be no, then, Jez?'

'Well I think maybe a few people should be able to, but no one was in the room *with* me.' He scratched his head and looked around the room. 'I don't know how I can back that up.'

'You'll let us have your prints and DNA for elimination purposes, won't you?'

Standing up as Kenneth Williams, hands flapping, Jez squawked 'Ooh me dabs and me DNA. Lead the way, eh?'

Chocky side-stepped past, swinging his hip – he wouldn't put it past Fylde to give even his bottom a little slap.

Holly felt it drain away. It was like a dirty bath emptying from every one of her veins leaving her fresh and clean, inside and out. But where was she and what had happened? She knew, yes she knew, but why? And really she didn't know what. She went upstairs and looked out of their bedroom window. She turned and looked back at the bed: just her bedroom now.

What did her Hu do? He did not jump out of a window. He just did not jump out of any window.

That Policeman. Daddy. He was lovely, she remembered. That kid he had with him. Funny colour – white?

Holly did not push Hu out of the window.

Somebody must've pushed him. Bloody Maynooth mafia. The mad priests, madder'n Father Ted and his cronies. 'Seriously though, Hol,' she told herself, 'you don't know anybody who knows him. Better find out though, Girl.'

She pulled out his sock drawer, patted the contents and closed it again.

She went over the wardrobe and pushed a few of his suits aside. She pulled up the last one she remembered him wearing and breathed it in. She dropped it again, slid the door to and went downstairs. She found a pad in a kitchen drawer and made herself a list. She had a sudden thought and went into the study – supposed dining room – and saw that Hu's laptop was there in its usual place. Before Googling 'youth office' to find that Leo bloke, she realised he would be in Hu's address book – and maybe some emails.

Gina, the youth officer's secretary, was worrying about her boy. News was trickling through, but he hadn't shared anything with her yet. She tracked him down and told him. He apologised but was a little too terse for her liking, telling her that he didn't really know anything himself – except that Father Hu had been found dead of course – and at the Loseborough where he, Leo, had taken him.

'I just don't know Gina,' he snapped before hanging up.

But people were ringing up and asking her and she was not happy about admitting she didn't know something. She was doodling a sociogram of who knew who, as far as she knew: The Tin Tab team including her youth workers and some of the volunteers; the priests – she recalled the new one was Monsieur Green – and Bishop; the women; Hu's wife – didn't know her name – Leo's Talya, Abe and Brien must have wives; Hu's colleagues in Housing. All lines pointed to Leo.

'*Simone!* Simone Dunne.' Gina pointed at her refection in the sleeping monitor and browsed the sheet to see where to insert her. She linked Simone up, first to Hu, then to Leo and to Abram Grant. Yes, she had something on each of them. Gina underlined Simone.

The phone rang. The Leader-in-Charge at The Tin Tab was ringing to ask where everybody was.

'Everybody?' asked Gina thinking the assistant youth workers had not turned up.

'Leo. Abe. The Volunteers – I 'an't seen any on 'em for a week.'

'Your youth workers are my only concern, Carol. Have they all turned up for work.'

'Yes, but…'

'Well I suggest you get on with it then.'

She thought of them cussing about her in The Tin Tab office and smiled.

She thought that no one else would be thinking about Simone, so decided to do some research of her own – ring the Entry to Employment youth officer and see if he was happy with his temporary clerical at Harcote E2E, blah, blah…

She jumped when the phone rang as soon as the receiver touched base.

'How can I help you Miz Stannton.'

'It's Mrs, Mrs Holly Stannton.'

'Mmm. Sorry, how can I help you Mrs Stannton.'

'Don't give me that guff,' said Holly.

'I beg your pardon! A complete stranger does not come on my phone and speak to me like that. Goodbye.' Gina put the phone down, stood up, and looked down at it.

It rang again. 'Sorry, sorry…' said Gina.

'What are you sorry about, Gina, it's not like you to get it wrong – anything.'

She was going to take that at face value. 'Well thank you, Gill.'

But Gill was only ringing up about some pay advice and Gina needed her to get off the phone so that poor Hu's wife could hear Gina's apology.

As she thought, she soon had the opportunity and in her most pleasant manner also gave her Leo's contact details. She thought there would be no problem there, but was not going to be forthcoming about anyone else at The Tin Tab. Leo could see to any of that. She put a ring of dots round Leo's name. What was he thinking right now?

'My Dad made that.'

Leo looked at the mirage before him. A thing of beauty. With his Dad's old car that made two things of beauty in his garage. He was intrigued by the latest arrival, the young detective sergeant.

She saw him smiling at her and a shyness she wasn't used to, made her stroke the wood of the old car. He said nothing so she had to break the ice. 'Morris Countryman innit?'

He continued to smile and wonder just how old she could be, or was she the child of aged parents after a night of gin? 'In the right area, it's a Morris Minor Traveller, it was the minis they called Countryman…'

'Yes, I got one.'

'Really?'

She found herself enjoying a tease, but in the end added 'Yes a new BMW Mini Countryman.'

He snorted, thinking they weren't out yet, but sustained his smile as he was rather taken with the lass.

Patting the Traveller she mumbled dreamily, 'Yes, my dad did make it for me.' Noting the wheels and one of the back doors were off she added, 'I think he maybe made this too.'

Deciding she really did not seem old enough, he said 'old enough to be *my* dad, then. You sure?'

Doubt swept across her face. She grabbed her chin. 'Our first new car was a Countryman, but I was only a nipper.'

'Montego,' Leo affirmed.

'Oh Yeah. Montego Countryman. 'She stroked the old Woody again. 'Di'n't 'ave no wood, though. Oy 'ad to sit lookin' ewt the bark.'

Leo was moved yet again. She seemed to have reverted to being a country yokel. 'He *made* it you say?' He imagined a tractor with a cardboard car body.

'Yeah, at Kyew-lee. The car worrrks.'

'Ah, Cowley. Yes. So, er, you from Oxford, then?' If that were the case, he expected her to be posh.

'Wow, nearboy – Blackbirrrd Leys.'

Leo knew his cars. He really knew his cars. 'Hand-break-turn?'

'Oh Don't!' She had to laugh. 'Not many people know that – and I wanna keep it that way in my particular choice of career.' Blackbird Leys had only hit the headlines once in her lifetime as far as she could remember, and that was its notoriety as the ghetto estate for the car workers at Cowley. It was also where the boy racers had found the Montego's brother - the Maestro - was *the* car for a hand-break turn. The police crack down had caused rioting that was reported internationally.

She grew more serious. And she returned to Received Pronunciation. 'Boy in my class got killed by one of the Boy Racers. And the driver never got done neither.' She coughed. 'Never thought about it before, but I felt really bad about nobody getting nabbed, and I now wonder if that led me to being a police officer.'

That note restrained Leo, too, but he did say 'and that brings you here?'

It was a wan smile she gave him. 'Yes it is I'm afraid. You organised this 'do' which led to Hubert Stannton's death...'

'I'm not sure our 'do', as you call it, led to his death. How are you making that out?'

She had her notepad out and tapped it with her pencil. 'Time wise, it did. He died at the end of your ... what would *you* call it, sir?'

'Conference. Yes conference is what we called it. It was a 'Pampering Weekend', but it was neither a weekend, nor were we pampered, so as we were conferring that's what we called it.'

'Okay, that's useful. So can you tell me what you were conferring about?'

'We were all involved in a youth drug project – The Tin Tab. It's what we call a 'Voluntary-Statutory Partnership', they were volunteers and I was the statutory – Local Authority bit - you see? Father Hu had,' he coughed, 'left somewhat peremptorily. My wife had this unwanted prize of a 'Pampering Weekend', and she said I could use it to thank the guys, the volunteers.'

'So it was your wife's idea,' said Bahadur, 'the Conference?'

'No, not strictly like that. Abe, Abram Grant the Chair of Tin Tab wanted to mark Father Hu's departure, to thank him, but didn't rightly know how to. Talya, my wife, told me about the coupon for this pampering being due to run out and maybe give it to some of my team.'

The DS wandered around to the front of the car so they weren't quite confronting each other across the bonnet. 'So how did it go? You realise that we may consider that it did indeed lead to Mr Stannton's death?'

With one hand clenched in his pocket, the other pinching his 'Trotsky' too fiercely, Leo knew he had to tread carefully. 'Well we took it for what it was – our sort of pampering, nice food in a nice place in a nice area. Oh and nice drink too. Hu liked his pint with a whiskey chaser – real ales and single malts every time.' He thought this detail might be lost on the pretty police-person, but not the seed he sowed about drink - maybe lots of.

She noted that. 'What did you ... do, by way of pampering?'

'Oh, walking ... and narrowboating.'

'Narrowboating?'

'Yes, I don't know for how much longer, but the youth service has a narrowboat – a barge – on the canal. It's a very nice walking area and I took them along the canal and 'Da-da! Boat ride.' They loved it, especially walking it through the tunnel – on the ceiling.'

Bahadur decided she didn't need to explore this detail. 'Everything go smoothly?'

Leo uncharacteristically realised there had been enough levity. 'Yes...' He had to think about the next bit. 'Well the other guys might tell you, and I haven't anything to hide,' He peeped under his brows, 'but I did goad Father Hu a bit.'

'Goad?' said Bahadur. 'Get him mad did you?'

'Well that was what I was kind of hoping for.' He was aware of body language and personal space, so he sidled up to the sergeant's side. He looked her in the eye. He pinched his goatee. He smiled. 'I'm a Child Protection Officer, Detective. This guy is, was, an Irish Catholic priest.'

She raised a brow, but didn't engage fully.

'He goes off with a floozy, sorry, a woman.'

'But you did say floozy, sir.'

'Yes, sorry, sexist of me, but it's part of my anger, you see?'

'Anger. Towards Hu?'

'Yes, well, yes I have to tell you it would not rest easily with any of my team of youth workers, even the least aware of the wiles of these paedophiles...'

'Paedophiles!' she said turning to face him, but immediately stepping back. 'Stannton, a paedophile? I suppose you had to record this didn't you, but not tell anyone?'

This frightened Leo. 'No, no,' he said. 'Sorry, that was stupid. I don't mean him, but I do mean Irish priests and I, now with hindsight, do wonder about *Father Hu*.' He was half-hoping this would appear reasonable to the young detective.

She sucked her teeth and took a note. 'It would be significant to our investigation of a mysterious death if there were anything, any record, or even not recorded, any *hint* of abuse by our victim...'

'No, no,' he hastened, 'I really don't have anything. In fact almost the opposite: he was squeaky clean and even pretty good, excellent in fact, with our spaced-out users. He was a heavy rock fan and really empathised with the lads in particular. He wasn't phased out by their drug use or, more seriously, their criminal records. He was gentle and supportive to the young women too.'

'Young women, eh?'

'Yes. Of course I watched him. He was completely neutral, like my workers – non-authoritarian, non-judgemental – and very supportive. They loved him. Yes, I know, but like I say - I watched. He took no advantage, none at all. I know about this, it is too easy.'

She nodded and looked at her notes.

'Goaded him. You hoped to make him ... 'mad'? Why? And did you?'

'No.'

'So that frustrated you...'

'... and I came back and pushed him out of the window.' He clapped his hand over his mouth.

'Did you?'

Leo let his hand slip away from his mouth and looked over his glasses at Bahadur. 'Do I need to say, 'no I didn't'? But I know that's what you might think, especially after you talk to Brien and Abe.'

'You think they'll suspect you? You think they saw your angry frustration?'

They had travelled a long way from their nostalgic discussion of Countrymen. He decided that his garage was not the place for anything this formal and … incriminating. He wanted to lead DS Bahadur away. He took her to the door and looked out at her car. He was right. 'That's not a Countryman I don't think?'

She did a double take at her own vehicle and laughed. 'Ah, no it's not, not that one. That's last year's model – the big plods don't like it, so me Dad's got me the big Countryman on order – going away present, like - for when it comes out – September, I hope.'

'Loves his daughter, eh?'

She was tickled.

'Well I'll just say there was nothing at all unpleasant about my goading and *teasing* of Father Hu, but I mention it because it was indeed goading. The chaps will mention it, so I have already told you. I have nothing really to add.'

'Except maybe your DNA?'

Leo coughed. 'Yes of course.' He waggled his fingers.

She nodded and made the arrangements.

As Brien Devine's wife confirmed on the phone, DI Blundell found the man on his knees in the convent garden. It was pretty bleak out there on this March morning but there was a little heat in the early Spring sun. The Detective watched him for a few minutes – it was the second day running he had watched a man on his knees. He purposely clanged the gate so he wouldn't frighten him with his approach.

Brien looked up, then stood up at the approach of the stranger.

The formalities over with, Blundell got the man's story of the conference. Devine seemed to have great affection for the priest, but Blundell picked up at the point of interaction between Stannton and the youth officer. 'You felt Mr Nicholas was deliberately getting at Mr Stannton?'

'Well, I didn't know Leo really, Inspector, but I had great affection for Father Hu, despite him leaving us, and I wasn't very comfortable with Leo getting at the poor man.'

'But 'poor man', sir? Father Hu?'

'Well not then, but now, now he's dead he's pretty poor, you see. I didn't think of him as poor before. Not at all; not at all; fine strong man – and charismatic you could say.'

'You would say 'charismatic' sir?'

'Indeed I would. He turned our parish around, filled the church with fine young families and … well he breathed new life into it.'

'I know exactly what you mean. I'm a Catholic myself. May I call you Brien?'

Brien did a double take. 'Surely. Sure I seen you at mass? At the Jays?'

'Yes the Jesuits, my parish.'

'I sometimes come over for a dacent sermon. This fella's a bit stuffy, even for an old stager like meself, 'specially after Father Hu.'

'So Brien, getting back to the argument between Leo and Hu: would you call it a row?'

'Would I call it a row?' Brien stroked his chin and looked across at the pond. 'Mebbe I would, sir.'

'Angry.'

'I suppose you could say so – Leo, not Hu – that's what got Leo mad.'

'Mad?'

Brien thought about it then nodded.

'Mad enough to … kill him?'

Brien jumped back as if he had been struck. 'God Almighty … Holy Mother o' God, yer not saying Father Hu was killt?' The colour had completely drained from him.

Chocky thought everybody must know this by now. 'Have you no idea how he died, Brien?'

'Sure the Monsignor said he'd fallen out of a window.'

Blundell knew this was not true. 'Did he really?'

'He did.'

'Are you sure he said he 'fell out of a window'?'

Brien mused. 'Did he say 'balcony'?'

'I actually meant, did the Monsignor give the idea that he *'fell'* from a window or balcony?'

Brien was nonplussed, because he knew what happened. He scratched his head, rubbed his chin. 'He said he was found dead…' He stopped.

Blundell was pretty sure that, even though Brien had seen him at his own church, he will not have noticed him spying at his Convent mass the day before. He knew that Monsignor Green had not said where or how Stannton had died.

'He said he was found dead…' Brien repeated. He was evidently racking his brain. '… and because it was on Thursday … and because you are here with me … and been onto Abe … well I mebbes made two and two make five did I Inspector?'

Blundell was not comfortable with the way Brien was taking him. The Monsignor had not mentioned when, where or how. Abe Grant maybe had got some details. The DI decided to formalise the next part of this interview. 'Hubert Stannton was found dead in mysterious circumstances, sir. That was on Thursday and you, having been at the 'conference', are correct in thinking that you were one of the last people to see him alive.' He let that sink in as he watched Devine.

Impassive.

'So you'll understand that we could do with your fingerprints and, er, DNA, to eliminate you from our enquiries.'

'Oh, certainly sir. Now? I can come now.'

'No desperate rush Brien, but maybe you could come down the police station this afternoon, or tomorrow...'

'Oh, I'll be down, pronto. Nothing to hide, me.'

Telling Brien to call ahead when he was coming, Blundell left him his card. As he closed the gate behind him he saw that Brien was still apparently studying the card.

Chocky told the team he wanted them all to hear what Alan had found out before they went any further.

Gatting didn't want to be upstaged by his junior, so just put in a quick word about a murderer in the pack needing very close scrutiny.

Though his frown did show some annoyance, Chocky didn't want any acrimony. 'Yes. We've all got bits, but at the moment things are hotting up. Alan...'

'I asked the DI if we could all be together to have a few thoughts on this piece of news – *all* the guys at the conference have got serious records...' Alan enjoyed the moment, especially the amazed look on Badder's face. He went on, 'Abram Grant got life for killing his Missus; Brien Devine's a kiddy fiddler and Andrew Nicholas is a commie agitator who got exiled under the Riot Act.'

'Exiled?' said Gatting with an incredulous smirk on his face, 'what, to the Gulag Archipelago?'

Badder and Alan both gave him a sneer.

Alan referred to his notes. 'No, north of Scotland, then London – as far as possible from any coalfield. He was caught when the Riot Act was read at a picket during the Miners' Strike.' Looking at Badder he added, 'There was a great deal of violence...' he looked at his DI, '...on both sides, it does have to be said ... during the Miners' Strike and I think it's worth a note that only a few decades ago this was serious enough stuff to have carried a death penalty...'

'So was sheep stealing!' Gatting said.

Alan was not phased. 'So we have a man possibly thrown out of a window and the three men he had spent the whole of the previous two days with have got ... previous,' he sent round a smile, 'that we all need to have in mind. How *did* your interview with Grant go, Mike?'

Chocky covered his smile with his hand and turned to see Mike checking the notes. 'He's a big strong man. Killed his wife. Made out that nine years behind bars was only a token punishment for a man who just made a slip. Leads a drug project and suggested he may have supplied LSD that could make our victim think he could fly.'

Alan whistled, but immediately realised that this was just *stuff* from Mike. 'So ... almost a confession, then Mike?'

'Killed his wife?' said Badder.

'Yep. Got life.'

'And that's not all, is it Alan?' said Chocky. 'More detail, please – I'm not sure we should be using the term 'kiddie fiddler', eh?'

'No sir, and he only got two years probation, nearly twenty years ago, but these days Devine would definitely have been sent down. Sexually abused a boy and a girl. After the case, his daughter also opened a case, but backed out.'

Badder seemed to be itching to speak, so Chocky gave her the nod. She edged the team over to the whiteboard. 'Could all of these be put in our main column? Could any of them have a motive for … well at least violence against the priest?'

'Who knows about these records Alan's come up with?' said Mike. 'If they all were attempting to hide, maybe the priest knew – the confession box? But when he packed it in, did he take their secrets…?'

Chocky was biting his finger and nodding.

Badder said, 'Not the youth officer, Mike. No way a Catholic. Anti, if anything. But that could be a sort of motive?'

'So you did get to see him in the end, Iruna?' asked Chocky.

'Yes sir. Complex guy. I tried to build up some relationship, kind of get a place of entry. He's a car fan and my dad makes them 'n' that. The worrying thing is that he did play with the notion of killing Stannton.'

'I think I get you,' said Chocky.

Alan's look showed that he did not.

Badder went on, 'he actually used the words 'and I came back and pushed him out of the window.''

Alan gasped.

She continued, 'yebbut – he clapped his hand over his mouth. Yeah it was kinda jokey – hamming it up an' that.'

Chocky's intake of breath turned all their attention to him. 'Mmm.' He kicked around the imaginary stone again. They waited. He looked around them all. 'Do you think people know he fell out of the window?'

They all hummed and hawed.

'The papers said so, didn't they?' said Mike.

'Damned papers!' said Chocky. 'I was thinking, and maybe you were Iruna, that maybe I had something on Devine when he let slip about the Monsignor telling them that Stannton fell out of a window, and I know the Monsignor said no such thing.'

'Kind of, sir,' said Iruna. 'Nicholas did the same thing, see?'

'You said, but you added about clapping his hand over his mouth … and Devine was decidedly sheepish about it.' Turning to the younger DC he said, 'Alan, we've got the papers haven't we? Take a look over them and see what we and the public should know and what *they* shouldn't – we're looking for detail that the perp may let slip.'

'Yes sir, and just to say that Stannton's mother is going to be staying in town. She hasn't got much for us, but if we have to widen the net to people who may have known him...'

'Good man. Mike, Alan, tell Bahadur and me all we need to know about Grant, please?'

Alan deferred to Mike who set off, 'I thought his life conviction could indicate someone who, nice as he maybe most of the time, could lose it and throw someone out of a window. He's a very big man.'

They all looked at Mike's hand just above his forehead – head and shoulders above Iruna's.

Alan chipped in, 'he killed his girlfriend in a car crash – not *wife* Mike. You know how they say 'The Missus.''

Mike sucked his teeth before continuing, 'The police had been watching him as they suspected him of being the kingpin of a small drug racket – speed, dance drugs, etcetera. He was a really cool guy and the girl was the local Sloan Ranger...'

'Lone Ranger?' asked Iruna.

'Sorry, Badder, Sarge, posh kid – expensive class of drug, Cocaine, daddy lord of the manor.'

Mike looked to Chocky, and told Alan and Iruna, 'a bit before either of your times, Sloane Square, Chelsea, Lady Di...'

'We get it, Mike,' said Chocky. 'Carry on with what we *need* to know.'

'Yes the drug link is something I tried to follow up. He is the chair of a drug project – The Tin Tab, awful pun on Tabs, LSD mostly – and if, *if* there are any drugs hints...'

'Are there any drugs hints, Mike?' asked the DI.

'Not yet sir, but we are having to use some imagination – we might know how he died, but don't know how he was killed, do we?'

Chocky was nodding. 'Fair play Mike, well done. Tell us more.'

'Well he actually said it – Stannton 'maybe thought he could fly'! He went through a little list for me opening a few avenues for us. I hit a nerve calling his project a drugs – plural – project and reckoned he was making out he maybe supplied drugs.' He snorted.

Iruna was smiling at him.

He was encouraged. 'I couldn't tell if he knew anything about the death – papers or not. *He* wanted to get info out of *me*.' He turned to Alan. 'Al, where'd you get the drug stuff on him, I only had the basic record?'

'Yes. Drug squad have done a few busts of Tin Tab regliers, and their management team have kind of withdrawn their previous support. I looked at Grant's record because of it. Kinda-like set-a-thief - thought he might have previous. What I did find was that they were after him before his trial, but couldn't pin anything on him.'

'Mr Big doesn't get his hands dirty?'

'Mm. But his conviction was based on him being totally reckless. The girl was completely pilled up, but by the time they had found that out from the autopsy, it was too late for Grant to be still showing anything.'

'Wa'n't 'e in 'ospital or anyfin?' asked Iruna slipping into her own vernacular.

'No – she saved his life. He crashed the car sideways into a tree or pillar kinda thing, and without a seatbelt on, he crushed her. He walked away with a few bruises.'

Mike pitched back in. 'Well I tell you what, he didn't want me to know any of that. He kept on about it being nothing to do with Stannton.'

Chocky's look stopped him.

'Sir?'

'You think it might have been, Mike. Alan? Runa?'

Iruna shrugged.

'Slim possibility,' said Alan. 'Need it on the chart somewhere.'

Iruna posted it on a small note at the bottom of the left column.

Chocky nodded. 'My turn …' He pulled his phone out. 'Mary?' He nodded to the team, whispered 'talk amongst yourselves,' and stood out.

Mike spoke to Alan but Iruna was listening to Chocky.

'Mary … now Mary … Mary! Stop!' He saw Badder's look and turned away. 'Mattie's his own man, now, Love. You've done more than any mother. Let him go. Catch you soon.'

All blood drained from him, he returned to the group. 'Sorry about that. Kids! Who'd have 'em? Where were we?'

'You okay, sir?' said Badder.

'Yes, yes!' He huffed. 'My turn. Yes.' He coughed, grabbed a finger. 'Devine. Brien Devine is seemingly a devout Irish Catholic who loved his Father Hu.'

Alan coughed.

'Yes, I'll come to that, Alan. I followed both Devine and Grant to church, you know?'

Iruna nodded. The other two smiled.

'I have to say Grant was as calm as a cucumber, had a fag outside church, obviously a very popular guy. Lots of backslapping, that sort of thing. He was at the Saturday mass – papers not out yet. During the mass – the service – he, and the Missus, both stared straight ahead the whole time, not reacting to the announcement at all. Now after the mass, I thought there maybe a queue asking him if he knew what went on. But of course no one would have known about the conference, or Stannton still having anything to do with The Tin Tab.'

They were all listening.

'But Devine I was not comfortable with. He scuttled in at the last minute and held back before leaving at the end. During the mass he had his head bowed the whole time, looking down; the wife appeared to be snivelling throughout.' He lowered his head and his voice. 'I wanted to see if they were *any* kind of guilty, see?'

'Sort of returning to scene of crime, thing, sir?' asked Mike.

Chocky laughed. 'Well I suppose … sort of. It is where Devine, Grant and Stannton did most of their interaction, I think.'

'But definitely not Nicholas, sir!' said the DS.

'No Iruna. Tell us.'

'He doesn't like the churchy stuff one bit. Despite telling me that he did, I don't think he really liked Stannton. Sorta protested too much if you get me?'

'Hamlet – 'doth protest too much' raising suspicions, eh?' said Chocky.

'Ooh I didn't know I was that posh,' she exclaimed, giggling. 'You know what…' she looked round all three men, '… is it the same with you? I'm getting four good blokes all got summink to hide, yeah?'

They seemed to be assenting.

'Well this youth officer, I'd say he was really good at his job, really popular an' that. Like, really cares about child abuse – he's some kinda big knob in the whole Child Protection service, too. He hates, *hates* the Irish priest scandal.'

'Who doesn't?' said Mike, but pulled up short from saying more by a look from his DI.

Iruna continued describing her interview with Andrew 'Leo' Nicholas, concluding, 'he basically insinuated that Hu Stannton was a paedophile and he was, well, yeah, goading him to admit it…'

The men took a minute to absorb this.

'And he didn't like him enough to … well, kill him?' said Alan.

'Arr, wow,' she said, coughing, 'yes well, he did want to tell me that the others might split on him,' she smiled.

'They did,' said Chocky. 'Devine did, at least. He said he seemed to be trying to make Father Hu mad.'

'That's it, he admitted he was goading him and actually trying to get him 'mad', he said. He then back-tracked and said how good he was actually, great with the youths in their project - over Heavy Metal and that – Heavy Metal fan apparently.'

'Reminds me of our lead thieves,' quipped the DI.

Mike smiled but Iruna went on, 'Don't get many priests into that, do you sir? Death Metal, Thrash, Chocky? He, what was it, 'protesteth too much' in the end? I thought he was wriggling.'

'Yes and quite interesting what Devine noticed: he said Hu straight batted Leo's goading' – he looked at Gatting who remained impassive – 'got him mad.'

'Leo, sir?' said Alan.

Chocky flustered.

Badder rescued him. 'Andrew Nicholas is known as Leo – don' ask me why?'

'Trotsky,' said Alan. 'He's a Commie who's made himself look like Leon Trotsky, apparently.'

'Oh yeah,' she said looking at the ceiling and smiling. 'He does, too.'

'He's also a Russian, and changed his name from…' he looked at his notes, '… from Andrej Nikoluk.'

'Curiouser and curiouser,' said Chocky.

'And they tals me orf fer not speaking proper,' said Badder.

The two constables threw her a look of admiration; Alan's may have been affection.

Chocky laughed and nudged her, continuing, 'Leo Nicholas admits he goaded Stannton; Devine confirms that indeed he did, but nearly fell over protestething when I asked if he thought Nicholas mad enough to kill Stannton.'

'Somebody did, though,' said Mike tapping the chart with his pen.

This was matched by a rapping at the door. 'Mrs Stannton in Reception, sir,' said a PC.

'Which one?' shouted Iruna.

Chocky laughed, the constable was irritated. He looked at his paper. 'Mrs Holly Stannton, *sir.*'

Chocky raised his brows at Iruna and called over, 'Ooh yes, we want to see her. Get her a cuppa will you please, Constable, and we'll be down in a minute.' He turned to the team. 'We need to get some sense out of her and she's maybe ready if she's come by herself, eh, Runa?'

She nodded vigorously.

'Just one more thing to catch up with, gang: anal sex.' Nobody smirked. 'I've had that barman Jez Fylde in, bent as a five bob note.'

'Sir?'

'Sorry Runa,' he patted her arm. 'Openly gay barman, had the Desk on his back foot…'

'Interesting position, sir?' tried Gatting.

'No seriously, he doesn't think anybody will be able to corroborate him being alone in his room, well room thirteen, just below Stannton, between eight thirty and nine thirty – possible time Stannton fell. Let's sleep on that. Come on Runa.'

In the corridor, he pulled her back.

'I-runa … I may have done you a disservice, sorry. Apparently I introduced you to the boys as 'Badder'…'

''s alroyt sir.'

'… said it quickly, sorry.'

She put her hand on his arm and looked him in the eyes. 'Sir! It's alright. I'ad it all me loyf – me an' me bruvvers.' She chuckled. 'They was known as 'Badder' and 'Worse' at school until the Political Correctness brigade stopped them. In my first year at Comp I got caught sucking up to a teacher and got 'Goody Badder.'' She laughed again. 'Bloody stupid names what wi' me dad and me mum.'

He chuckled a question mark.

'Yeah, me Dad wanted us to have Indian names, but me Mum did the registering – and she's…' she checked herself, 'well, she's Irish and gave me bruvvers Mekhal and … Padman?'

'No-o! Not Paddy?' he laughed.

'… and Mick. Yes.'

'You're not Biddy, though?'

'Luckily, not! But Mammy still had a laugh – the last laugh. I shoulda been named after the god of the dawn - A-runa…'

'Ha! Ire-una. Brilliant – and a bit more unique?'

'Yebbut nobody's ever said the I or the A – so Runa it is, and Badder at work.'

'Okay then. I do apologise, but if you are alright with it … well I've said it. I will also try to make sure I get your I-runa too. Come on.'

The two detectives did not know who was doing the interviewing.

At different points Holly Stannton had each of them by their lapels and gave them a good shaking. This was, however, after she had received them both with sweetness and light.

DI Blundell was itching to find her sober and sane after the madness induced by the shock of her husband's death.

DS Bahadur was worried that her boss would continue to treat their number one suspect as a sad little girl.

After her pleasant introductory moves, Holly weighed into them. She had no notion she was being interviewed. She had come looking for answers; she was asking the questions.

She told them that of course they knew that she would have been like a woman beaten up; that she had been in shock; but 'what the fuck?' She demanded that 'some bugger' tell her what had happened.

The detectives had not come down expecting the interrogation so they had not conferred.

DS Bahadur deferred to her superior officer.

Inspector Blundell thought he would play for time and arrive at a safe destination – one where he hadn't told the prime suspect what they were assuming. '*Remember ASS of U and ME*', he told himself. He did the introductions: husband, dead in suspicious circumstances.

'Why?' she burst in, 'what's suspicious … please?'

They looked at each other. Chocky wanted the tape to run. Badder wanted her cautioned. Neither did either.

Chocky thought he would slowly tell her. 'He was found partly … in the jacuzzi below his bedroom window at the Loseborough Hotel where he…'

'I know about the Loseborough,' Holly snapped. 'What does 'partly' mean?'

'He was over the side with his head in it.'

Holly bit her lip and tried to imagine it. 'Like he fell out of the window and landed across the side kind of thing?'

All three were nodding.

'Yes okay, I've got that, but what is suspicious about it?'

The detectives looked at each other.

'What does that mean?' she shouted.

'Sorry Mrs Stannton, but it is suspicious on several counts...'

'Well come on, tell me them.'

'Firstly we have to consider whether he ... slipped, jumped ... or was pushed.'

Holly harrumphed.

'We are investigating; you do want us to investigate and find out don't you, er, Holly. We okay with Holly.'

'Yes of course, don't give me any of this 'Missus' nonsense, I'm not an old granny. So what happened then?'

'We are looking into precisely that.'

'Don't try to fuck me around with your bullshit. What do you know so far?'

Chocky looked at Badder who took over. 'Holly, it is very mysterious and we really need your help. Now you are feeling better...'

Holly did seem to respond immediately to the feminine touch.

'... you are the one we most need help from. How *are* you feeling?'

'My head is thumping. I can hear my own blood pumping. My eyes are stinging like mad. I suppose I feel like I've got a massive hangover, but I got to get up and go to work. Ever felt like that, er...?'

'Iruna.'

'Iruna. That's a nice name. What sort of name is that, Iruna?'

She shot an embarrassed glance at Chocky. 'A made up one, I'm afraid.'

'Oh well, fair enough; lot more of them about these days. What do you need?' She looked from one to the other detective. Calm and reasonable.

Chocky thought he could put that in neutral enough tones. 'We need to know if you know of anyone who might wish ... your Hu harm?'

'Maynooth Mafia!' she said.

Afterwards both detectives wanted a picture of their faces when they heard that.

They both sat back.

'The Mafia?' asked Chocky, rumours of the involvement of the Cosa Nostra in the Vatican racing into his brain.

'Maynooth Mafia, yes. Came for him before, tried to brain wash him, they did.'

'Wow!' said Badder. 'We said we needed you. We didn't suspect the Mafia's involvement did we sir?'

Chocky gave her the strangest look but let her continue.

Holly cut back in, 'ah not exactly *The* Mafia, but that's what we called them.'

Badder felt herself pinking up. 'Ah, so…'

'Priests. Bloody black priests in their black suits, their black Police shades, their black limo.' Holly sat back and looked at the ceiling; dragged her hands across her face. 'The fucking black bastards!' She slapped her hands onto the table and cried, looking straight at the detectives. She panted for several breaths then calm swept over her. She stabbed the table with a finger. 'I thought I had shed all my tears over them. Couldn't let go, eh? Like the Mafia, they won't let you leave. I didn't really believe Hu after he came back to me. I thought he had got out of their … miserable – black – clutches. Oh no! He was right and I was wrong.'

She turned away and bent right over her knees.

The detectives gave her the moment.

She saw the tear drop from her eyes and fingered its splatter on the floor. She wrote 'Hu' with it. Another tear fell and she put a 'smiley' under his name and sighed. 'Not in your … Heaven, eh Hu?' She put a cross over his name, or was it a kiss?

She sat up and ran her tongue over her teeth. 'Maynooth is this college he trained at in Ireland,' she said.

'Seminary,' said Chocky.

'That's it Officer, you know about it?'

'Well I've heard of it, but tell us more. Was it his … college?'

'He went to Dublin Uni, but Maynooth was the religious college. Religious my arse,' she cackled. 'I think it's where they get men, suck their brains out, and fill their skulls with their fucking bollocks. I'm sorry about my language, but you'll have to put up with it. I gave up all the swearing when I got with Hu, but it's done me no good has it, so tough titties!' She gave a quiet roar.

'They fucking came back for him didn't they? Realised they lost him for good so threw him out the fucking winder. Hey! … Hey …?' She had to swallow hard. She stood up. She jabbed her finger at DI Blundell. 'You know fucking what? I bet they then went down and checked they had fucking killed him, finish him off.' She swung round and stomped along under the window.

Chocky was stumped. This was such a big and unexpected turn that he felt they needed time, a lot of time to fit all that into the perspective they thought they were just beginning to bring into focus. He had really enjoyed 'The Da Vinci Code', but knew from the start that it was all hokum. Yes he knew there was 'Opus Dei' and religious orders which had their own way of behaving, of enabling their devotees to enter the kingdom, but secret societies?

He was pretty sure the Mafia would have over centuries done their utmost to get the endorsement of the Vatican to legitimise some of their business. He knew that the church had haemorrhaged priests, brothers and nuns since he was at school. His mother had told him the brothers had handed over his old college in Liverpool to the laity, there were so few of them remaining.

He couldn't see them coming and brain washing just one who wanted to leave – unless he was something special; unless he had something on them.

Holly seemed to have something. They asked her for details of the Mafia connection, but needed her to address the issues that they already had. They knew they would get nowhere at that moment.

Feeling that they had taken great note of her suggestions, Holly was placated and agreed to come in the following day to explore all the wider issues.

Back at his desk, Chocky decided, reluctantly, to use the Old School connection. 'Hello, Bishop. John Blundell here. My brother Matt, Matthew Blundell, was in your year, your class I think, at Sim's.'

The Bishop made out he remembered Matt and they went over old times and families, a bit. 'So, how can I help you, er…?'

'John, My Lord. I'm a Detective Inspector now, and we're looking into a suspicious death of a priest…'

'Mm, Hu Stannton, would that be?'

'Yes My Lord…'

'Call me Brendan, for goodness sake – we're old schoolmates. Not my Diocese, but word of poor Father Hu's demise has got round clerical circles, as you can imagine. Was there something suspicious about it?'

'Thanks Brendan. Looking that way. We can't put our finger on it, so it remains suspicious. He was found having apparently fallen out of a window, over a rather high balcony.'

'Go on.'

'Did you know him, Brendan?'

'I did not, but I'm sure I will have met him.'

'Quite striking – tall, very handsome with long blonde hair – not many priests like that.'

'Not at all. How old?'

'Mid thirties…'

'Oh Dear.'

'Now here's the thing My Lord … you do know he left the priesthood and got married?'

'That's on the grapevine, John.'

'Well the wife seems to think what she calls … the 'Maynooth Mafia' may be to blame.' He heard a snort at the other end of the line. 'Well that was my initial reaction, Brendan, but I have to explore all avenues.'

There was a long intake of breath at the other end. 'Yes, you do, don't you? but that's a funny one – very funny indeed. I don't rightly know how to answer it.'

'Well, first off, have you ever heard of such a thing?'

'Tricky, see? Yes I have, but,' he raised his voice, 'I have always taken it to be an inter … er … rivalry, between priests from different backgrounds, seminaries etcetera, you understand – like Oxford v. Cambridge - but Ushaw in England v.

Maynooth in Ireland. Old Maynooth guys would stick up for one another and ... well you know.'

'Yeah, yeah, Everton/Liverpool, Rangers/Celtic, of course.'

'Mmm but you wouldn't be ringing me...'

'... no, My Lord, I probably wouldn't. So let me run over the wife's story to you.'

The Bishop listened and concluded 'A bit Da Vinci Code, that John?'

'My thought entirely, but, *but*, could there be anything in it?'

'Well let's look at what might realistically have happened, shall we, somewhat dramatised by his wife? The pope has to absolve a priest of his ... duties. He doesn't do it lightly, indeed one of the sterner chaps who will remain nameless, let them hang on for up to eight years, I heard – backlog of ... lots.'

'It was bad in the seventies.'

'Indeed. Well he, the candidate, would reasonably have to explore his vocation, and his tutors would, reasonably, want to explore it with him. Does that seem ... reasonable to you, John?'

'It does Brendan, but, she really did reckon a 'gang' of them came for him and frog-marched him off.'

The bishop remained silent.

'I know it's a bit strong, My Lord, but ... anything in it, please?'

The bishop sucked his teeth audibly. 'It's not our way of carrying on, John, but I don't know the circumstances of Father Hu's apostasy. If it were sudden and dramatic, maybe it engendered a dramatic response in his old ... friends? I really can't say. And all that 'black' stuff – well we do all wear all-black do we not?'

Chocky's turn to remain silent – he was rubbing his jaw vigorously.

'You've no doubt heard the Opus Dei rumours, John? All baloney – Maynooth guys would say 'Blarney',' chuckled the Bishop.

'Well okay, Brendan, you've given me plenty to chew on. It's much as I was thinking myself, but I thought I would ask someone with the 'Gospel' – sorry about that,' now Chocky laughed. 'I am really glad I did.' He thanked the bishop and hung up. He was not gladdened.

He got Alan to surf for all he could find about the Irish seminary.

DS Bahadur decided she didn't want an anonymous assistant to help her with Brien Devine, and she would want some maturity in the exploration of the record of a child sexual abuser. She reluctantly asked Mike Gatting, but did tell him that she wanted to take the lead and to chip-in only if she gave him the nod.

'Mr Devine, may I call you Brien?'

'Mr Devine, please?'

'Okay sir. Our investigation into Hubert Stannton's death is now getting serious, as it is not an open and shut case. We've brought you in under caution for several reasons.'

Brien's intake of breath was so shaky it was almost a sob.

'It seems very unlikely that he simply fell from that window. Several of you were with him in the hours immediately before his death. You were one and your DNA was in his room.'

It was almost a whimper that emanated from him now. He clutched his mouth.

'We want to explore your relationship with … Father Hu.' Iruna looked steadily into his watery eyes and smiled.

Brien blinked hard, coughed and said 'poor Father Hu.' He shook his head. 'He was a lovely young man.'

'We picked up that you felt very strongly about the … young man.'

'Indeed I did. Caring. Big but gentle…'

'A deep affection, sir? Love, even, sir?'

Brien was alarmed at last. 'What, what are you saying?'

'I am asking what was the nature of your relationship with Hubert Stannton, sir.'

'Dirty, filthy thinking. Always digging for dirt…' he stopped.

'Is there dirt, sir?' She opened the file and turned pages studiously.

Brien leaned forward; she leaned back. Brien coughed but sat back again.

'Dirt, sir? On you, sir?' She tapped the papers with her pen.

Brien's eyes welled up again. 'Ah, God have mercy on me! How long has this to go on? How much can a man put up with? You people … as God is my Judge …'

'What would he say, sir?'

Brien came over calm and collected. 'I've been asking him for forty years…'

Badder rushed back to the papers. 'Forty, sir?'

'He took all them babbies off the Missus and then she took herself away from me. 'I'm only a man!' I shouted at Him, 'You made me this way.'' He looked at the young woman and saw no consolation there. He turned to DC Gatting. 'You know how it is, don't you sir. A man's a man for all that?'

Gatting leaned forward and thumped the desk with his fist, but his sergeant swept hers in front of him and sat him back.

This was new territory for the new sergeant and she wanted to get it right. She needed the man to tell her how it was for him.

'Ah, well, a bit of drink to help out. To get to sleep without … well without…' He looked at the Constable. 'Without sex! There you are, that's what you want, isn't it?'

'You turned to drink, sir?' said Badder.

Brien bit his lip. 'Turned? Well unlike most, all the lads I worked with, I didn't. I didn't drink at all. Pioneer. I took the pledge. Drink took me Dadda, and that killed Mammy. But I gev in. And that led me to get it where I could.' And he sat and sobbed like a baby.

Iruna was pleased by the way she held on long enough to lead to her present case. 'Thanks for being so honest sir, and though we do not condone it, we can all maybe understand the pressure.' She cringed a little as she thought she was probably still a virgin in these matters. She was however a very experienced police officer, Detective Sergeant. 'So, sorry sir, but could that bring you to your relationship with the priest?'

A look of horror swept over the wet face of Brien Devine. He went as if to stand, but Gatting's move put him back. 'My relationship wit Father Hu was one of utmost respect for a man of the clot!'

Badder looked at her notes and almost whispered 'Confession, sir?'

Brien nodded. 'Of course.'

'You said 'forty years', so would you be confessing … that, still to Father Hu?'

Brien continued to nod. 'Well, you're not a catholic yourself, like?'

'Not unfamiliar with the faith sir…'

'You'll know we have to confess, and repent, then.'

She nodded.

'Well I been confessing for forty years. Little stuff to start with but it got worse and worse until I … got caught. I've been repenting hard for almost twenty years, now.'

'But confessing, Sir? Confessing to Father Hu.'

He was swept into the moment. 'Oh indeed, confessing being the baddest, worstest, worst man that God ever let live. It'll be me and Hitler in hell together.'

'What about forgiveness, sir?'

'No, not for me, unforgivable.'

Gatting was nodding. 'So on your way to hell with nothing to lose?'

The DS looked at him but nodded and turned back to Devine.

Brien had a finger nail between his teeth and shook it. 'Mmm, Interesting. Interesting how you turned that round on me.'

'Well sir?' said Badder.

Brien was quite calm now and thought through what they had put to him. 'Well I suppose you have to do that sort of thing, but I don't think I've got annyting to say about it … at all.'

The sergeant felt the need to wind up. 'So to conclude: you confirm that Father Hu, Hubert Stannton, knew your secret and took it away with him; you do not wish us to conclude that in your desperate need for sex, already leading to a conviction for the most heinous of crimes against children, you did not turn to…' she referred to her notes, ''a lovely young man', for whom you had 'very strong feelings.''

Brien gulped and blinked away a tear. He needed some calm before he said anything else that might incriminate him.

Gina felt the need to know more about what had happened at her boss's little pampering session. Unusually, Leo had not shared anything with her about the planning of the session, simply told her he was off for a couple of days, but would answer his mobile phone. His silence on the matter did indeed raise her curiosity.

She had no doubts about her 'boy', but it was only natural to be inquisitive in her situation. Her phone was now red hot and of course no one was actually ringing about something that didn't concern them – except maybe Carol, the Leader-in-Charge of The Tin Tab, and she could get her info first hand from Abe Grant.

Leo was at his improvised desk along the kitchen work-top from her, apparently engrossed in his Annual Service Plan for next year. It had been sent back for some corrections.

She hoped her clicking pen would work into his consciousness. It did but he didn't turn. 'I thought we clicked years ago, Gina. Let me concentrate on this.'

'Do you want me to go over it for you, Leo?'

'Nah. It's not so much mistakes, as my shuffling of posts that Wyndham doesn't like. Won't let me advertise, but I can't end up with workers going out on the streets on their own, can I? Then he says I can't just restructure my team as I feel like it – people have got posts and there they should be. It's becoming a nightmare. I might have to abandon all our street work and bring the odds and sods – sods, mostly…'

'Leo!'

'… into the youth Clubs. Wyndham won't want me shutting youth Clubs.'

Gina thought she could sneak towards The Tin Tab. First she felt the need to remind him of his team meeting that night.

He pooh-poohed it as an 'as read' – 'They've read their redundancy notices – what more can I say?'

'I think you might find they expect a lot more. So anyway, what about project staff?'

'Yeah, that's another story. Wyndham hates that – doesn't see what drug work and sexual health has got to do with blimmin' table tennis bats.'

'Does he want you to pull out of Tin Tab?'

'Probably, but hasn't said as much - yet. Brings us – and him - a lot of kudos.' He was still focussed on the screen.

'Simone's still on your budget, isn't she?'

Leo turned to his secretary. 'Simone Dunne? What you mean - get Lady Thatcher hand-bagging the roughs and scruffs out on the estates?'

'Seriously, is she still not paid from that budget?'

'Indeed she is, Gina, don't I know it.'

'But she's Tin Tab and you're paying additional to Carol and her team to cover for her.'

'Blimey, Gina, what're you doing to me? I said 'don't I know it?' She keeps blimmin' stirring it. Got onto a bishop apparently.'

'That's better' thought Gina. 'Bishop, Leo?'

'Yes that Monster guy got onto us about her and Father Hu. Some blinkin' 'Father'!'

'Monsignor Green?'

'Yes, him. 'Not a bit comfortable about insinuations she was making about the sanctity of the confessional'! Confessional – her! She hated any of the Packets of Bisto brigade getting holy with the down and dirty. She would even attack Father Hu in meetings if he said things like 'God forbid', or 'Bless them.'' He chortled. ''We'll have less o' that!' she'd tell him.'

'Bishop, Leo?'

He looked at her. He pinched his Trotsky. 'She … apparently … has complained … to his nibs, well Gina, she's trying to get more out of us, a big pay-off and lashing out wherever she can.'

'Got it – she got on to the Bishop. But what has he to do with it - us?'

'Ah – there's the crafty bit. She's cottoned on to the fact that confession is sacred to the big-hat brigade. Well it is, and she's insinuated that her move away from The Tin Tab has got something to do with Father Hu maybe breaking the secret of the confessional?'

'With pagan-britches Dunne?'

'My sentiments entirely. But it worked. They're onto me about her relationship – relationship, no less – with Hu Stannton. Did he have her before he had his floozy?' Leo laughed out loud and looked out of the partition to the general offices. He cackled in a stage whisper, 'did he have an affair with Madame Stuffy Bum?'

Gina held him in a smile. 'Well did he?'

Leo roared again, but stopped short. In mock horror he said, 'But Gina, you're not speaking ill of the dead…'

She raised her brows. 'Leo, please … what happened?'

'You've seen the papers, Gina.'

'You were there, Leo.'

'Gina! What are your saying?'

She was poker faced.

'I was at the hotel. Yes I was with him during the week, at the same Loseborough Hotel. I gave him, Abe and The Tin Tab treasurer Brien Devine, a little treat – to say goodbye properly to their revered priest.'

'Bit magnanimous of you toward a sworn enemy!'

'What Abe Grant? No better man walks the earth.'

'Hu Stannton! You never did like him, did you?'

He wasn't denying it. 'Saying I wanted to kill him?'

'Ah now – was he killed?'

Leo took off his specs and gave them a breath before rubbing them on a shirt tail. 'The Police are saying the circumstances are suspicious.'

'They haven't accused you of anything?'

'Good as.'

'Really?'

'No. But you watch telly – you know how they carry on. Not comfortable I can tell you.' He adjusted the specs better. 'But you know what – they've set on one of their own – bloody Detective, well the boss, is one of them, a Catholic.'

'You smell cover up?'

'I do not know, Gina – it's all just a bit creepy.' He smacked his lips. 'Woman detective is interesting.'

'Leo!'

'Not like that. Well could be. She is stunningly pretty…'

'Blonde, then.'

'Gina! Opposite – Jet, blue-black hair, white, chalk-white skin, but I reckon she's Asian. Called Badder or something – great name for a cop!'

'You noticed. What colour's my hair, Leo?'

'Oh shut up, Gina. Well what happens now – with Simone, Gina, we are at work – is a conundrum. I can't let her back. I'm trying to get a deal from E2E – see if they'll keep her – she is so good for them. If they take her on, I quietly keep her hours and Abe will be so chuffed with me.'

'She's not happy with him, either. He's a Catholic isn't he?'

Leo smiled. 'Yes he is, unfortunately. It's not that that makes him a good man. Well he's the Chair of Tin Tab. Carol's the Leader – you of all people know what her team think of Simone – could we let her back?'

'No smoke, Leo – what has she got on Father Hu, or Abe – or you?'

'Nothing – on any of us I hope.' He turned and ran a finger across his Excel doc and murmured 'I just wish she'd crawl under a stone.'

Gina was getting nowhere. She wanted to know if the police suspected someone of killing – murdering – Father Hu, and if they did she wondered if they had thought of that bitter and twisted Simone Dunne. Poison would be her weapon.

Hu's Mother had tracked down her son's … wife. She didn't want to call her that, but if the hussy was that to her son, she was no less than a wife. She had to be a nice girl. As far as Mrs Stannton knew, no other woman – or girl – had ever turned his head. She had talked to Pauline first – not quite a daughter to her, she never felt sure of her motives, but her Hu had been devoted to his cousin – yet abandoned her just as he had abandoned his own mother.

She was met at the door of Hu's house, their house.

Not a word was said.

They went into the lounge and they sat for a long time and cried. They cried together and they cried apart. Like laughing, when one set off keening the other did; sniffling, the other wiped her nose; sob and they were off again.

In the end, Mrs Stannton took herself off to explore the kitchen and came back with the teas. Her daughter-in-law was away with her head up in the wing of a chair, red-eyed. A watery smile greeted the cup.

'Tell me about my Hu…' Mrs Stannton decided to be gracious for the first time, 'our Hu. How was it between you?'

The first sound out of Holly was a squeak, but she coughed it through and nodded. 'Yeah, it was lovely.' She nodded and nodded. She squeezed a final tear out. She hoped it was the final tear. She sat up and took a sip. 'A lovely cuppa, eh?'

'Nothing better. Was my boy, good to you? Did he treat you right?'

Of course he did, yes he did. Well he did. They had lovely times – all the time was lovely, right to the end. But, you don't measure anything by its end. She decided that was just stupid. You can't tell how long a piece of string is by only looking at the end. 'Missus – he was a fine, strong, handsome man – the very best I ever had, or could have ever wished for.' She thought of randy Rupert Spiro and felt even better about what she had just said.

Mrs Stannton knew all of these things. It wasn't what she was asking. 'How did he treat you, er, Holly?'

'Yes, Holly.'

'Well, Holly, how did Hu treat you?'

Holly wanted to say something about the lovely gentle sex they had, caressing, kissing, 'canooooodling.' She chuckled.

Mrs Stannton smiled at that. 'Looks nice.'

Holly nodded. 'It was nice.'

'He looked after you, sure?'

'He did, yes he did.'

'Holly. Yes Holly, we are both very sad, but, sorry Holly … Holly … ah, Holly, what *happened* to him?'

Holly sat bolt upright. '*I* don't know!' She shook her head. 'How should I know, they haven't told me a fucking thing! Oh…' and she burst out crying.

Only one of them was a mother and she came and cradled the little girl in her arms. The child at first rigid, eventually melted into her arms. 'I'm so sorry. Mammy's sorry,' she whispered. 'There, shush, there, my colleen bahn.' She felt Holly freeze again in her arms. 'I know, I know, I sang that to him – my 'storeen bahn' – my white haired boy, but you are a white haired girl – a 'colleen bahn.'' She brushed Holly's hair off her forehead and kissed it. She felt her melt again.

DC Alan Prisco popped his head round Chocky's door. 'Sir, the hotel at last sorted the trolley, but forensics are not very happy about having to sort through it. There's six sets – sort of – of bedding and that, and they don't know what we want them to look for. That Jenks bloke…'

'Oh Jenks! Jenks is okay, just always complains a bit, what's he moaning about, now?'

'Well sir, I wasn't sure what we are looking for.'

'Alan! What forensics have we got so far? Match?'

'Oh yeah. Sorry sir. Semen, faeces, blood an' that. They know about that sir, they told us…'

'Alan!' Chocky sighed and drummed his fingers on the desk.

Alan shuffled in the doorway and hitched up his trousers. 'Sir?'

'Where?'

'On his genitals. Sorry, sir, I don't get you?'

Chocky stood and looked down at himself. 'That's so far, Alan. Is there some anywhere else? Must be.'

Alan quietly pulled the DI's door to and went to ask Jenks if he can find any blood, semen or faeces on the sheets, then added the towels, and get any matches with maybe … anything. He put the phone down and held his head in his hands.

A shiver went down his spine as a tender hand stroked the back of his head. 'Are we okay there, constable?'

The team needed to do more background searching to get at any motives. They needed help with the MO – how was Hubert Stannton killed, if it wasn't an accident? That Holly for instance – is she from outer space – someone must know her? What about that ex - Rupert Spiro? Any kids? Why is she here?

'I found Rupert Spiro, sir, - Holly's ex - dead easy – name like that and he wants celebrity status I think – got a website, Facebook, Twitter, LinkedIn. Some sort of fashionista-lite. Anyway, he was tickled to be asked and obviously forgot about her as she walked out the door, but reckoned he had 'followed her progress', modelling a bit and ending up a partner in the rag trade with a very nice little concern, then nothing. I suppose that's when she came up here.'

'Why did she come up here?' Chocky looked around the team for a notion. 'Why did you come up here, Iruna?'

The DS felt rather put on the spot. 'To get away from Lesbians' might not be the answer, nor would 'to find a bloke' be much better. 'Broaden my horizon. Pastures new. Thought it could but help the career.' She saw the look on Mike's face. 'Anything wrong with that?'

'Not at all. Wholly admirable. But what's Holly done up here?'

'Part-time in a flower shop,' said Alan. 'Don't think she felt she needed to work.'

'I repeat: why?' said Chocky looking at the whiteboard. 'Has she got any family, any friends …roots, history, here.'

'Born, brought up, married and worked in London for ever,' said Alan.

'So why, here? Was she running away – hiding?'

'You mean could someone have come after her – and hers, Sir?' said Alan.

'It's an idea,' said Mike. 'Badder?'

'Okay, I'm the woman - how does a woman feel?' She tapped her perfect teeth with a fingernail. All the men watched. 'I've been wondering about a complete change.' She turned to the boss. 'See how she reverted to a foul mouthed street-girl with us, sir? Could we have gained the impression that the Spiro guy had more or less pimped her? She is very pretty. Pimps don't like to lose them while there is any money left to be made.'

Gatting seemed to have blushed, while Prisco was smiling and inspecting his shoes.

'They can get nasty too,' said Chocky. 'Maybe wanted to take her prize off her – her innocent and holy priest? Nice idea, Runa.'

Alan noticed the DI's hand on Badder's shoulder.

'Bit dramatic, though. We're not in a TV thriller here, are we? More likely she got fed up with the rat race – and maybe being used. Wanted to be ... to do ... something for herself.'

Alan was nodding at her.

She smiled at him.

'Alright', said Chocky, 'Badder, divi up between you: the conference guys and their wives; the youth office; the hotel and the guests – including Jez Fylde, and hit the phones for alibis. We don't seem to be getting any warmer, so put some heat under everyone to show proof of alibi, etcetera. We should be ready to arrest somebody – boy does that sound lame, sorry, but it's all a great imbroglio, isn't it?'

'If you say so,' said Badder patting his arm.

'We may have a situation, Inspector. Would you like to come down and discuss it?'

'Can you not tell me on the phone, Mr ... Houldsworth?' Chocky had to restrain himself from the 'Jobsworth' notion.

'Well I really would like to *walk* it through with you. I think you would get the picture better. I do realise we didn't get a very clear picture at the offset.'

Chocky thought he could benefit from another exposure to the scene of the crime. En route he made a point of looking out for any cameras. He forgot for a couple of miles as Mattie impinged on his consciousness. And Mary's. It wasn't what she was saying, it was what she wasn't saying. And she didn't want Chocky saying anything to upset their son. Chocky was upset.

Now he was disappointed. He walked all the way round to hotel looking for ... anything, before going in. The light was fading. He hoped that Jobsworth wanted to show him something indoors.

The Manager took the DI straight up to the second floor. Chocky thought they were going to the room, but Houldsworth put his mind at rest. They went past the room and Chocky saw that they had 'tastefully' secured the room with a polite notice surrounded by a barrier tape frame. Just before the end of the corridor, Houldsworth swung his bunch of keys at a door and pushed it open.

'Ah – the cleaner's cupboard.'

'Yes sir. I wanted you to see how we do things here and appreciate the delicate nature of our *situation*.' He hemmed and wiggled an index finger in the air. 'This is *the* trolley.'

'I assume these are not *the* sheets, Mr Houldsworth?'

'Correctly, Inspector. Your people have some, but here's the rub: theft is a great problem for the hospitality trade – people will steal the light bulbs...'

'The gold out of your teeth.'

'Precisely, sir. Well as you would expect us to – but the staff do not like it – oh, no, we mustn't suspect them, or it'll be straight off to the Unions.'

'If you take the gold from…'

Houldsworth huffed and planted the backs of his wrists on his waist. He regained his composure. 'We have inventoried this floor. Each floor has a full set – in and out – of each item to and from each room on the floor.'

'Very efficient, sir.'

'My own system,' Houldsworth lied. He didn't expect the Inspector to be have a degree in Hospitality. 'The delicate nature … Suzanne, officer. We are missing an item.'

'Pertinent I hope.'

'Oh yes, I think you will agree. I have not dragged you all the way out here on a wild goose chase.'

'Exactly what is missing?'

Houldsworth held the DI's gaze. A sheet sir. A bottom sheet to be precise.'

'Well I am impressed – you can tell if it's a bottom or top-sheet.'

Houldsworth didn't notice the sarcastic tone. He primped his hair. 'Totally different – bottom ones are fitted - elasticated; top ones are a simple rectangle – tastefully trimmed in our case, of course.'

Chocky actually was impressed. He didn't make the beds at home, but he did recognise what Houldsworth was talking about. He was nodding. He sidled up to the trolley, looking it over. He clapped his hands. 'Good! Very good indeed Mr Houldsworth.' Then he had a thought. 'You haven't been in the room to search for it though, I hope.'

That split second gap.

'Tell me you haven't.'

'I haven't sir…'

'But you can't vouch for Suzanne?'

'Exactly. But I do have to say that the chambermaid herself brought it to my attention. She could of course have found a way round it – pinched one from another floor, say – but that would have got someone else into trouble. So I have to say it was very fair of her, and not a little sensible, to come to tell me. It gave me confidence that she was genuine.'

'Sensible?'

'Yes Inspector. She actually considered that it might be pertinent to the case.'

'Her exact words?'

Houldsworth smiled at the DI.

'So you conclude…?'

'I think she realised correctly that a missing sheet in these sad circumstances we find ourselves with is, shall we say, suspicious, Inspector?'

'Indeed. I do think you are right. So, more disruption I'm afraid. I will have to get Forensics to try to find it in the room.'

'Not a problem, sir.'

As they were at the end of the corridor, Chocky took another look around. He pushed the fire escape door open and surveyed the overflow car park. He was chinking his coins. As he leaned out to look directly below, the Manager felt compelled to lean over and grab his coat-tail, and immediately apologise.

'In the circumstances, Inspector...'

Chocky laughed and gave Houldsworth an almost playful thump to the arm. Then he looked up ... and getting a good grip in the rail, leaned again. He beckoned the manager to join him and pointed at the escape door on the top floor. 'That look closed to you?' and he set off up the steel staircase.

'A -a!' he said restraining the manager from pushing the door.

'Oh...' said the Manager, wide-eyed.

Tuesday 9th March

Chocky was not happy about the atmosphere in the room for the Tuesday morning briefing. He noticed the body language was leaving too large a personal space between the team members and all were leaning back waiting for his lead. He knew – he felt it himself – this was not an open and shut case. It was a mess – and it was continuing to be. He had not managed to clean it up and give the team something fruitful to follow up.

'Nice weather for the time of year. Did you see it actually rained fish in Australia last week?' Chocky was smiling.

Alan looked at Mike.

'Not cats and…'

'… cows!' cut in Iruna and laughed.

'Cows?' They all turned on her.

'Yeah, in Twister…'

'Oh Yeah,' said Alan, 'They had a cow sucked up and dumped like it rained down! Saw that. Rubbish film though.'

Iruna rather enjoyed it, but agreed with him nevertheless.

'What was it like here last week?' Chocky asked.

Not a very good move - it seemed a silly question - as if he was quizzing them. Everyone knew it was cold but dry – pretty typical for time of year – no snow, though.

'What about mist?'

'I get you sir – the car park video!' said Alan. He turned to the other two. 'Boss had me checking the hotel videos and the overflow car park one is pretty creepy. It seemed to have mist drifting across it every now and then. Sometimes it completely steamed up the camera lens.'

'I wanted to see if we could vouch for coming and going of our protagonists – any of them,' said Chocky, 'but yet again our resource is worse than useless. We can see plenty of ghostly shapes coming and going, along with crisp and clear images of people we don't know.'

'Before or after dark?' asked Mike.

'Both… What we need to know is if any stayed behind or returned to sort out Stannton.'

'Nicholas!'

'Well, yes, but not just Andrew Nicholas.'

'Leo?'

'Come on Mike – Andrew 'Leo' Nicholas.'

'Bit confusing when his Christian name, his nickname and his surname are all first names. Like the twins Iain and Duncan Smith.'

Alan and Iruna were shaking their heads at Mike, but it got Chocky where he wanted to be – a lighter mood. 'Yes – the first identical twins to lead the Tories. Paul Merton wasn't it?'

They all chuckled. It was good to see that Mike had a sense of humour.

'But…'

'Not Big Butt?'

'Calm down, calm down,' Chocky only needed a small slip for his scouse to show through. 'But, we have got another little bit from where the video was leading me. When we did the first walk through with the cleaner…'

'Suzanne the Chambermaid,' inserted Iruna.

'Yes, her,' Chocky went on; 'I checked the fire escape door at the end of the corridor and had got forensics onto it. Nada. But yesterday … I found that the top floor door was not quite shut. Old Houldsworth – the Manager – was just about to sort that when I held him back. I thought there was blood on it. Got SOCO straight out and yes there is blood. It looks like someone has tried to pull the door open – it's busted, doesn't quite shut properly, only a quarter inch – what's that in new money, Runa?'

'Five mil?'

'Yeah. Hard to get a grip on, but maybe, *maybe*, our perp tried hard enough to snag a nail or something.'

'Prints too, then?' said Alan.

'No, but suspicion aroused nevertheless, because it was wiped - only a cuff or something – it smeared the blood, but left it there; should get analysis later today.' Chocky sat himself upright. 'Another thing I got was a missing sheet…'

'What, like Badder arrived to find a missing body?' Mike elbowed her.

'You know some hotels don't have a top sheet any more?'

'No-o,' said Alan.

'Just the quilt, duvet and a bottom sheet.'

'Yes sir, I've noticed that,' said Mike. 'I have wondered at either the hygiene or the environmental impact of laundering the quilt covers.'

'Well Houldsworth is right with you on that.' Chocky suspected as much. 'They use two sheets…'

'And one of them is missing, sir?' said Iruna. 'Brill! Who noticed that?'

'Suzanne did. We're pretty lucky, because she is scared of old Jobsworth, but overcame her fear as she recognised that this was significant to our enquiry.'

'Offered her a job, sir?' said Alan. 'Watch yourself Badder.' He was disappointed that Iruna did not think it funny.

'It's very neat really,' the DI continued, 'I didn't really know it myself, but bottom sheets are different to top ones.'

'Mine aren't' said Alan.

'Haven't got any?' Iruna stumped him.

'Children!' Chocky admonished. 'A bottom fitted sheet is missing. It's not on the evidence inventory of forensics' collection – remember Suzanne stripped the room and that bundle went to forensics. They didn't think to ask about a second sheet – because like I said…'

'Not all hotels use them.'

'You're catching up, Alan,' Iruna smiled.

'How come it's only just shown up?'

'She didn't have them, did she, Mike?' said Iruna.

'That's not it – neither forensics nor her could notice … until they were brought together. Forensics released them back because there was nothing of interest on the bedding except – everything - all and only the guys at the conference!'

'That sounds bad in itself, sir,' said Mike. 'How come all the blokes were on Stannton's bed?'

'They were all over the place – carpet, bathroom, toiletries, cups, bedding, window.'

'What? All of them? That is a bit weird?'

'How could that be explained?' said Iruna but went on, 'except if maybe they sort of held the conference in there.'

There was nodding, pursing of lips, and exasperation.

'Look,' said Chocky, 'this Leo guy and Stannton's wife have got to be our prime suspects, but there is so much more, including the flaming Mafia … you told them Runa?'

'Yessir, an' the bollocking we got from Holly!'

The men chuckled.

'You may larf!'

They did.

'Well look,' Chocky drew in the reins, 'you found the wives backed up the supposed alibis, didn't you?'

They all nodded. 'But not many guests done yet, sir,' said Mike.

'Not surprisingly, I don't suppose. Nobody's suspecting Jack the Ripper has returned. We need to turn the heat up on the youth officer and the wife. He organised this shindig and I don't really get why. He did not like the priest one little bit. I want you boys to bring Nicholas in under caution. Don't arrest him, but give him the words and say we need to check a number of things he has already told us – mention forensics, but not specific – and sling him in an interview room alone until we get back.'

'What if he refuses?' said Mike.

'Don't let him – you're a big lad. After what she did to us, Badder and I will go and grill Holly on *her* turf, eh Runa?'

Leo Nicholas was at his desk still smarting from the pasting his own team had given him the previous evening.

He needed to lead his team through the implications of their *Section 188* redundancy notices. He wasn't feeling ultra-secure himself: in a massively reduced service, it's inevitable that Area Officers have less responsibility and merit less pay. That having been said, almost everyone in the youth service was at risk of redundancy as the cuts were swingeing. More obviously they are likely to get someone else to do a similar job to his – 'Oh no Leo, not the same job as you!' – for less pay.

So girding his loin with empathy, he wanted to put the very best slant on things – they had *all* had notice of possible redundancy. He of course knew that almost everyone who wanted to go – for any reason – retirement, ill-health, better prospects – had taken Voluntary Redundancy the previous year. Yes there was a similar, but reduced package available – 'reduced Leo!' they had shouted at him.

Nobody wanted to go. 'We do this for the love of young people Leo.'

'I can't do anything else after all these years, Leo.'

'I can't retire yet, I haven't got enough stamps.'

'It's al-fucking-right for some…'

'We love this job, Leo.'

Who said it was alright for some? Did they think he was getting away with it? He felt the breath of his line-manager, the Assistant County Officer, on his neck.

'Gina – they think I'm getting away with it.'

His secretary turned slowly towards him. She removed her glasses. She looked him in the eye. She raised the back of her chair a little. 'Leo?'

'Gina…'

'Leo, what *is* the matter with you? How - long – have – you - been – in *Management?*'

He took a breath as if to start. 'Oh Christ almighty,' he said and pulled his hand across his face. He dropped his arms down beside him and stared at the ceiling. 'Aw, no Gina. Of course – but not *my* team, not *me!*'

'You're the *boss*, Leo, not one of them. You're doing this *to* them.' She pointed to her left: 'Wyndham – rock.'

She nodded at Leo.

She pointed to her right: 'Team – hard place.'

She raised her eyebrows.

He let out a long slow breath. 'You're dead right,' he told the spider on the ceiling. 'I tried to tell them how much I had been fighting with Wyndham and the other bosses to try to squeeze another few thousand out of them, especially after the recognition we got for spending all the Knife-Crime money on umpteen projects … and you know what they said?'

'Wasting your breath?'

'Well, yes some inevitably said that, but this is what hurt – this is what really kills – they told me to stop upsetting management and keep my head down, and they might not look at us!'

Gina waggled her head. 'Mm, a bit naughty. I bet I can guess who started that one.'

'Yes, yes, but it wasn't the start that hurt – it was the following he got. It was almost a rabble at me. I was so shocked I was probably cowed and didn't fight back. It's almost as if I'm an enemy of my own people.'

The phone rang. Gina answered it.

Leo went for a wander down the corridor.

He thought of the men he led back to work at the pit, marching behind the band – victorious or defeated. His men hadn't betrayed him and scabbed. But thousands had. And his men's hands immediately shot out and took the redundancy – that did shut his pit.

188 Redundancy Notice – 'Et tu Leo?'

When he eventually came back Gina said 'That was Charlie on the phone. He was asking - rather too brusquely for my liking - whether or not you are going to apply a 'last-in-first-out' process.'

'Ha! It'd be alright if it were last to work and first off home – I'd get rid of that idle … sorry Gina, I think I've done my swearing for today. I do apologise.'

A bunch of flowers made a world of difference to Holly's lounge. Chocky couldn't put his finger on it, but was pleased to see that she was transformed in herself, so much so that he did look around for changes in her environment.

'Thanks for seeing us at home – and at short notice, too.'

'Hey, I'm on this case as much as you are.'

Chocky looked to Badder who ran through a catch-up routine to clear the air over their 'rather heated' exchange the previous day.

Holly made no apologies and was calm.

'Holly we can't pull the wool over your eyes, so we know you understand that we are looking at you and your movements very closely.'

'Absolutely – but I hope not exclusively. I don't want the trail of the real killer running cold.'

'Not at all,' said Chocky, 'we've got four of us full-time on the case, but…'

'We calmly… ' Badder held both hands up a little, '… need to look at all the aspects relevant to you, today if possible.'

'It is possible, but have you got anyone following up on the Maynooth thing I told you about?'

'Indeed, I have done so myself, Holly,' said the DI. 'I've been onto a Bishop I know and got some very useful detail.'

Holly seemed suitably impressed. 'Okay – me?'

The detectives relaxed back into the settee. She sat forward on the chair.

Badder led with 'we need to account for your every movement last Thursday, and into Friday, please Holly?'

The detectives had discussed the problem of not recording the interview, but six days into the investigation, they needed her to give her story, and they had singularly failed on their own turf.

'Well I was around the house most of the day, nipped out for some shopping – groceries and some cleaning stuff – and I had my lunch in the Supermarket café. Bit of a treat – Hu thinks that's a bit below him, and I can have a bowl of chips without feeling guilty, too!' She grinned at Badder.

'I thought Hu had said he was going to be home at four, but I did think that was a bit early – maybe finished at four and he would be home after, you see?'

They did.

'Then I thought I couldn't remember, so I texted him to ask. Anyway he didn't reply and by four thirty I was beginning to get worried. I waited another ten minutes – well I wanted him to come home to a nice tea; but I thought he would have been well fed at the conference...' She bit her lip. She shook her shoulders.

'I thought I would do our 'Saturday special' – nice breads, cheese, olives, nibbles and that – you can have as much or as little as you want with that, can't you? He loves his Hummus and dips.' She bit her lip again. She was not going to say 'loved.'

'Saturday?' prompted Badder.

'Yes, well you know what I mean – it's what we'd usually have Saturdays with a bottle of wine.' She stroked imaginary crumbs off the arm of the chair and rubbed her hands before continuing, 'We've never had a row ... you married, er?' She looked at Badder.

'Sergeant Bahadur, Holly. No I'm not.' She looked down at the back of her hands.

'Well it can be quite nice, Sergeant. I have experienced one horrible one and one idyllic ... and that seems to have been cut short.' She blinked hard. 'Me and Hu never had a row, but he did not want me 'checking up on him' – he was fucking ... he was livid with me. I've never seen that side of him.' She looked from one to the other detective. 'What happened to him?'

'You think something had happened to him at the Hotel?'

'Yes, Miss.' She was biting her lip and looking into Badder's eyes, nodding.

'So you had a row? On the phone?'

Holly slapped and rubbed her knees. 'He was furious. He didn't swear – he hasn't learnt to yet,' she smiled ruefully, 'but it was pure bile that spewed out of his mouth. It really frightened me.'

'Was there anything in what he said that gave you any idea what had, well changed him, Holly?'

'No Miss, Sergeant, sorry. It was all about me – me not trusting him; me not giving him a minute to himself; me demanding; me ... fuck!' She hammered her knee with her fist. Some tears escaped.

Chocky spied the tissue box and stretched it over to her.

She gave him a weak smile.

'That's excellent Holly,' said Badder. 'Do you think you can go on ... tell us what you did next ... Holly?'

She pursed her lips and nodded. 'I went for a drive, well not straight away – I was shaking and that, but after I calmed down.'

'Fine. So where did you drive to Holly?'

'Oh? I don't know. Oh that sounds silly, doesn't it? I didn't drive anywhere. Oh that sounds even sillier,' and she started to cry.

The detectives glanced at each other and Chocky gave a flick of the brows.

Badder didn't know what that meant and pulled a long face.

'I don't come from round here – it's all countrified, isn't it. I hardly been out of London 'til I came here.' She shrugged her shoulders.

Chocky ascertained that she went in the little Daihatsu outside and realised they hadn't taken a note of her husband's transport. 'Did Hu drive to the Loseborough, Holly?'

'I don't know where he went, officer. Oh you mean the hotel. Yes, yes the hotel, yes he did.'

'So what kind of car did he drive, Holly?'

She looked blank at him, and opened her hands to give some idea of size. 'A silver one – bigger than mine. Oh where is it?' She was looking round the lounge.

'Where's what, Holly?'

She stood and looked out towards the drive. 'Hu's car, of course, where is it?'

Chocky raised his eyebrows at Badder yet again and told Holly 'I suppose it's still at the hotel, my dear. But Hu must have some papers for it...'

She mewled and stood up. She headed for the door. She turned back to a sideboard and pulled out a drawer. She handed Chocky a pack and he snapped the two registration documents with his phone.

'That's brilliant, Holly, thanks a lot.' Badder nodded Holly to take her seat again.

She did.

'So just a couple of more bits for us Holly, you're doing brill. Can you give us any idea where you went and how long you were driving for?'

Holly twisted a tissue round and round a finger. She mewled again.

'Did you think of going to the hotel, Holly?'

She nodded but didn't look up.

'Did you? Did you go to the hotel?'

She shook her head.

Badder looked at Chocky who nodded towards the door. They stood and flipped their notebooks shut.

They thanked her and she followed them to the door. Chocky was down the drive but Badder was at the door and patted Holly on the sleeve.

Holly was looking into her eyes and murmured 'I couldn't find it.'

Badder nodded and joined Chocky.

'His car!' Chocky slapped his forehead.

'Yeah and you pulled us out before...'

'... before she told us some new evidence – that she had been to the Loseborough.'

Meanwhile DC Mike Gatting was having some success chasing up Hu's contacts – particularly his clients. He had driven over to the Council Housing office where one of Stannton's colleagues, Bill Littlewood – his supervisor actually – took him through Hu's case files to find as much background as possible.

'Yes officer, I thought there maybe something in this.' Bill flipped opened a folder and slid a page towards Mike. 'What Hu had to offer us was a sympathy ... no *empathy* with our most intractable cases...' He checked Mike, 'the druggies?'

'Yes I can see they can be problematic – not the rarest of our clients, either.'

'See this guy, Nathan Helliwell. Hu was really keyed into him. He was one of the first ones he worked with when he came to us a couple of years ago – he apparently knew him from The Tin Tab?'

Mike nodded that he knew of the youth Drug Charity. 'Interesting. Go on.'

'Well he soon got busted – thieving for his habit, you know? He was kicked out of the YMCA, and unfortunately so was his Missus.'

'Both users?'

'In the end he got sent down and she found herself pregnant.'

'Sorry to butt in,' said the DC tapping the desk, 'but this sounds a long story and you said you thought it might...'

Littlewood pursed his lips and took a breath. 'I did not call you in here to waste either of our times, Constable.'

'Sorry sir, carry on.'

'I had to tell Hu to not forget his other cases and he took notice – but – he spent some of his own time, I know, sorting out the girlfriend.'

'Missus?'

'Aye, well he called her that. Hu got her a little flat, then she told, well asked, Hu to not let Nathan know where she was. Her pregnancy had brought her to her senses – I'm not sure she was as deep into the drugs as Nate was anyway – she didn't 'want a bag-head in the life of her baby', even if it was his baby too.' He held up a finger, then pointed to the top sheet. 'Now see this, the last entry in the file – last Monday. I saw this happen.'

Bill gathered his thoughts and went on, 'Nathan was let out of jail a couple of weeks ago. Hu went to meet him and took him to a hostel. All very nice and much appreciated. But he wasn't telling Nathan where Lisa – that's the 'Missus' – where she was.

'It all came to a head last Monday...'

'Can I just pinpoint that date?' said Mike squinting up at a calendar. 'So not yesterday, but 3rd March.'

'Yes, that'd be it. Nathan, hardly up to Hu's navel, got him pinned against the wall. Well Hu was grinning, arms out, in his lovely peaceable way, 'come on Nathan' and all that, and it worked. Nathan backed off, but he gave Hu such a look and stormed out. Days later Hu Stannton is dead ... and in mysterious circumstances, I believe.'

'Oh, well done, Mister Littlewood,' said Mike, standing and offering his hand to the housing officer. He was very pleased with this piece of intelligence and asked to be able to take the file.

'Confidential, of course, but that's a set of copies I made for you. Oh and er ... just thought – receptionist told me Nathan did come back in, looking for Hu on ... Wednesday,' he looked at the calendar, 'yes Wednesday morning. She just told him Hu was on leave.'

Mike pumped his hand and went. He felt as if he had got the case sewn up.

Back at the office after he and Mike had left Nicholas in a cell, DC Alan Prisco was perusing the list of guests at the hotel. He had already noted that only three couples from the 'Golden Wedding' group had stayed. For one of the couples he had only the name Rich Lambert. He rang The Loseborough to see if he could get any more information as the number he had been given seemed to be a wrong one. The woman on reception had a look back at the list and gave three variants of the number which was not clear.

'I'm slightly mystified why I have got Mr Lambert as a couple.' He heard a snigger at the other end.

'Have you anything else I can go on – we really need to eliminate all guests from our enquiries.' He wasn't comfortable being laughed at. 'What's funny, Miss?'

'Oh, not you sir.' Her voice dropped. 'It's Mister 'ouldsworth, sir. He talked to me about him - them. He weren't right 'appy wi' Richard Lambert and his *friend*. He was lisping it an' that sir, get my meaning?'

'We're not in the dark ages any more, Miss,' Alan huffed, 'are you saying they were a gay couple?'

'Not saying anything, sir – just telling you what the manager said and ... how he said it. That was funny to me officer, sorry, but it was.'

Prisco felt caught out by the receptionist. Of course he thought it was funny, but he wasn't telling her he thought so. He noted the three variants, that they didn't have a name for the other member of the couple, 'no, that's not unusual – 'aven't got the Missuses 'ave we, either?'

He was irritated by the secretary, but shrugged that off and got a ringing-out on one of the variants. No reply or answer machine. Still he felt pleased to add yet another little tit-bit that Chocky would be interested in.

Chocky prevaricated over whether Badder should join him interviewing Andrew 'Leo' Nicholas. He had gained a sense that he was a tricky customer. Probably a bit of a man's man as an ex-collier, but as a youth worker also maybe 'in touch with his feminine side' – how Chocky hated that term - thrown off the macho mantle and adopted an airy fairy hippie afghan coat? Sandals *and* socks: Chocky's daughter would never let him get away with that. He thought maybe Mike Gatting would make the best partner at the crease. However, he would have to let Badder down lightly.

Lead balloon was more like it. It was not meant to be a convincing smile she gave him before turning back to her desk. She felt she should get the chance to build on the groundwork she had done with Leo in his garage, but in a more formal context.

She slapped a file down and hissed. 'Sorry, Chocky, but it's not right.' She turned. 'I have got through to this man and I am not at all sure *Alfred* Gatting has got anything like the sense ... *itivity* ... for this clever customer.'

'But this man only narrowly escaped life imprisonment for rioting – against coppers, Runa.'

'Think he's gonna get me sir? Know what my lifetime's hobby is?'

Chocky started to smile. He did like her pluck. 'I maybe slipped up not reading your CV on my way over to find not-a-body.'

'Judo, sir – I got up to sixth grade – that's above all the black-belts – before I eased off to concentrate on my sergeant grades!' She leaned into her boss and tapped her chest. 'I could throw Stannton off that balcony – no sweat.'

'Fair play to you, Iruna,' said Chocky holding out his hand, but pulling it away as she went for it.

'Don't tell the men sir – it's not how I like to appear - to pull rank.'

'Come on then Dan Badder, let's go and throw this youth officer guy around a bit.' And he bashed Badder out of the door.

Chocky could immediately feel some empathy between Badder and Leo Nicholas, from which he also inferred that he could feel some enmity towards himself – a man. From what he had gathered so far, he had felt that there were some significant areas of agreement between the aims of Nicholas and himself – some kind of aim to change the system from within. He was careful to note that, mean as the Met had been, they would not have set up the few colliers they did for the ultimate trial of law and order of the day – a Life Sentence as ultimate sanction – without real cause.

Nicholas was wiry. Wiry was not strong enough. He was a man of iron, of steel, fit and lithe – a coiled spring maybe. His body was set, but relaxed – his eyes were bright and shouted 'bring it on.'

Chocky had no intentions of listening to that. If Badder had insisted like she did, she could start. He smiled at her smiling at Nicholas. He did not look to see if Nicholas was smiling back – he knew he wouldn't be.

'I know you won't mind me calling you Leo, but this is my Inspector, John Blundell, who is helping me to clear up this mess. It is a mess isn't it, Leo?'

'Not clean and tidy for sure.'

'We need to get a little more formal, but you do understand that we are not charging you with anything and you are free to go at any time. However...'

'However!' said Leo leaning forward to Chocky but keeping his eyes on Badder.

'Let's not beat about the bush, Leo, a man has died, we don't know how or why. It is looking increasingly likely that he did not kill himself or fall accidentally. We feel some others must have been involved in some way with his death. And Leo ... you are our most important key.'

'Key doesn't sound like 'suspect' does it Sergeant? Nice choice. Yes, nice – I may be able to unlock your mystery.' He sort of chuckled but it was nearer to a harrumph.

'Go on then Leo.'

'So you think I goaded him so much he threw himself about with wild irritation, slipped and maybe fell out of the window ... maybe?'

Neither detective responded but both were watching him intently.

Leo twiddled his goatee and threw out another idea. 'Or *maybe* my goading brought out such a bad side in him that Brien saw what he was really like and came back and shoved him out? Brien looks the wild eyed killer doesn't he?' He was nodding smugly at his conceit.

Badder agreed with the notion that sarcasm was a low form of wit. 'We need you to tell us a tinsy-winsy bit more about yourself, Leo. What else did *you* do on your 'conference' and after it?'

'Ooh, alibi is it? Now look at this – I know it wasn't my money, but effectively I gave this bloke – and Brien and Abe - the equivalent of a couple of hundred pounds a piece. You try and get a jam butty in a place like that - they don't even sell nuts and crisps – evening meal main courses start at twenty eight quid – we had three courses plus drinkies, as well as full breakfast – English and otherwise. All that to then go killing the guy? Give me a break.'

She took a breath; scrutinised her notes.

Chocky said 'You are a Safeguarder – a custodian of children's safety, are you not?'

'Where do they get this stuff from?' he wondered. 'That's core to my job, but I am a Safeguarding Trainer for the County.'

'But you were involved in a lot of violence during the Miners' strike?'

'Bashed with riot shields and truncheons; trampled by horses and Bobbies' boots ... oh I was involved in nearly as much violence as you lot.'

'Arraigned under the Riot Act and banished to a place of safety, away from causing any more violence and disorder, in distant exile ...' Chocky thought he had made that point clearly enough.

'You know about this do you Inspector?' He said. 'How about you Sergeant?'

'I suppose Inspector Blundell is trying to clarify whether or not you are a peaceable man or a violent man – if pushed.' She smiled sweetly at him.

'So you're letting him push me now?'

'I can push you if I want to ... Sandan?' she tried, smiling '... Shodan?'

Leo wondered where she had got that from – his judo experience wasn't part of the criminal record - that he *didn't* have. So how good was she? She seemed quite a good cop to have got that far into his background. He did wonder if the rioting indictment had arisen for him more than others, because his years of judo had earmarked him as a handy fighter. She had credited him as only getting to third grade – Sandan, but that sarcastic return to basic Shodan first grade niggled him a bit.

She noticed.

He had a smile at her and calmly went down to looking at his hands.

Chocky looked at Badder with a mix of admiration and quizzing.

They waited.

'So what are you, Sensei,' he asked Badder, 'five-four, five? But you, you could throw a six footer over a high balcony?'

'We're not talking about me, Leo,' she smiled. 'I think you can at least guess that we do not know how Hubert Stannton came to be at the foot of the balcony of his room. You can probably take from that that we are thinking: yes he could have been thrown...'

'... and you are thinking how you can fit up a likely candidate. Well versed as you seem to be in judo, you will know that as a martial art it is the *gentle* way. Do you want to try another angle,' turning to Chocky, 'Inspector?'

'Okay, Mister Nicholas, did you return to the hotel to conclude your goading of Hu and it got out of hand?'

'No.'

'So take us through your movements from just before you left the Loseborough Hotel in the afternoon of Thursday last.'

'Just before? Just before – that would be at four o'clock, the time we had agreed to tell our partners our 'conference' finished – we had got our stuff from our rooms and met in the bar area to say goodbye. We left our bags in the reception area, but one of us noted Hu hadn't brought his down – Abe or Brien, I don't remember, but I do remember that Hu said he was staying on for a bit, would maybe take a swim. I think we were all a bit surprised, but he was alright from the hotel's angle.'

'In the bar area?' said Chocky, 'Did you have a drink?'

'No, Abe and I didn't because we were driving, nor Brien – who doesn't. Drink, not drive.' He laughed. 'Sorry, he drives but doesn't drink.' He shook his head. 'But the barman had eyeballed Hu – think he fancied Hu, I know he did; he was like a giddy schoolgirl round him. Anyway, he pointed to one of the beer pumps and got a nod from Hu. Hu stopped and at least had that beer.'

'So you knew Hu could still be found at the hotel if you returned, or didn't even go away?'

'Ye-es, along with Brien, Abe and the barman, at the very least.' He then exaggeratedly stroked his chin. He put fingers to count off. 'So let's see – that's four of us to suspect. How are you doing?'

'You are not doing very well, Mister Nicholas. Politician not answering the question – did they teach you that in Commie School?'

'Ooh we have read our stuff haven't we? The sergeant here knows about my judo and you know about my Political leanings – well done.'

'We are not fishing for compliments – we want your answer please: what did you do?'

'I went home, made the tea and plated it up and went to do my job – a youth club visit.'

'Very good,' said Chocky, 'now expand on that for us with some timings, details and ways you can corroborate them.'

'There's a clue in the first point – doesn't help me. I made us a curry, but it's the wife's late night – meeting after work - so I plated both of them up to reheat in the microwave when we both got back. So, home about four-forty, had to defrost the meat – beef, for a Madras, tomatoes, onions, pestle my own spice mix, pressure cooked the...'

'Get on with it, please Leo?' said Badder who thought he was possibly having a dig at her saying he made a curry of all things. 'What time did you leave the house, and can anyone verify it?'

Leo looked at the recorder for a minute, thinking. 'Yes, I had a call on the landline. Most people use the mobile these days. The Leader of the club I was visiting wanted to be sure I was coming and exactly when, because the Chair of his Management Committee wanted to talk to me about us cutting the funding for his paid youth workers.' He put his hand over his mouth and nose and sniffed. 'Bit of a mess. I had to go back and clean the phone as I had garlic on my hands and Talya, that's the wife, she'd have smelt a rat, no, sorry, garlic.'

The detectives were not smiling.

'So what time did I say I got in?'

'It had better be the time you actually did get in, Mr Nicholas.'

'Well I had better leave it to you to get it exactly right from my phone records, eh?'

'Oh come on...'

'About five or thereabouts.'

Chocky was worried about his own exasperation. They hadn't arrested Leo, after all, so they really needed to let him dig himself a hole. That was their only hope at this stage of the enquiry. So there was more of this filibustering going on as Leo told them about his drive through the pretty villages at dusk, the sky clear and the air still, no leaves left to be blown about. How he visited one of his favourite village clubs, one that had consistently appealed to good number of young people – more than thirty a night – with a varied and challenging programme. He was just angry that Cameron and his cronies in the county had deemed that the Big Society and not Leo's youth workers would have to run the club from the first of April ... and that actually spelled the end of it.

Chocky noted that something else 'angered' his suspect. He casually noted which club Leo visited – Masterton, but Badder of course, pointedly asked what time he had been at the club; for how long; who were the Leader and Chair; what time he had returned home and by which route – 'as I'm new to the area.'

There was a knock at the door and DC Alan Prisco passed a note to his Sergeant. She took a quick look at it and showed no reaction.

'Thanks for all that, Leo – very helpful,' she said, passing the note Chocky. 'Can we explore some of the wider areas with you please? Can you give us a bit more detail about the Tinto Drug Project – Hu Stannton was involved in it, and in his new job he will have probably used some expertise that he gained there?'

'Probably? Blinking definitely! Stinks! What use is a priest to anything but priesting? I ask you. He walks out of his church and straight into a job in the housing department – bet that's run by Catholics – worse than the Masons.' He turned a cold shoulder to the detectives and crossed his legs.

'Very useful, Leo,' said Badder. 'Sounds like he could have built up some resentment – not least in you?'

Leo coughed. 'And Simone Dunne.'

'Who?' said both detectives at once, leaning forward.

Leo smirked. He savoured the moment. 'Simone Dunne was a youth worker at the ... *Tin Tab,* Sergeant, but she set a few backs up and...' he stopped a second thinking how he would *not* like to implicate his good friend Abe Grant in the nefarious deeds. 'Well I had to move her out for the good of everyone – including herself. But she didn't see it that way. She has apparently been on to anyone who will listen – including the Bishop – insinuating that Father Hu has broken the silence of the confessional.'

'She's a Catholic, too, then?' said Chocky.

'Spot on Inspector – no she is not!'

The DI frowned. 'Spell that out for us, then.'

'She doesn't like where we have placed her – well so she says – but really I think she is angling for a payout for Constructive Dismissal.'

'But she's still in a job?'

'Precisely. She hasn't got a leg to stand on, but that doesn't stop her kicking out.'

He had no idea that it might have been Simone's voice he could hear in Hu's room that fateful night, but it was now coming to him as a distinct possibility. The only thing he gleaned from the fleeting glance from the fleeing person, was that the person bobbing out and down the stairs was generically female. He did not suspect her, but was warming to the idea of getting her some much wanted attention, but not from where she was expecting it.

'But wouldn't she kick out at you?'

'Well no I don't think so, see: she blames the people in house, at The Tin Tab project, who complained about her. That isn't much to go on, so she is stoking the fire with something pretty serious – to the church powers that be – saying Hu pretended to give her support when her husband battered her and cleared off, but in fact he put it round The Tin Tab staff. They in turn gossiped and giggled about her, really enjoying her suffering. She omitted to tell the Bishop, that she's never been inside the church never mind the confessional box. So he couldn't tell the

Monsieur – the new *old* parish priest who's taken over from Hu. Only thing we've got in common, Simone and me – hatred of that child abusers' front organisation.'

Chocky's hand went over his mouth.

Useful as all this appeared to be, it was not the direction that Badder was hoping to lead after she had read the note. She had felt that it pointed far too much to something which otherwise would be a real coincidence. 'Okay, be that as it may, Leo, I would like to hear some more about the partnership The Tin Tab and you the youth service may have had with Hu as a Housing officer.'

Leo felt the heat of the spotlight turn away from himself. 'Well I think he milked it, to be honest. He was down there more often, much more often, than when he was with us. I bet he was down there most weeks. Don't get me wrong – it was a brilliant partnership – such an improvement. District Council only cares about image – getting the druggies and winos off their pretty streets. Hu changed all that and in a fairly short time they really appreciated him – and so did our team. The Users are in a constant revolving door situation: they can't give up their habits, but as soon as any sign of use is noticed by the hostels, they are out. District have to house them, but couldn't see that shoving them in doss house boarding houses did not sweep them under a carpet. Out they pop as a problem again. Hu has changed that with nurture and care.'

'Well it's nice to hear you speak well of him after all.'

Leo huffed.

'So, we are looking for anyone who may have not been so happy with Hu – recently, that is.'

Realisation swept across Leo's face. 'Oh well done, Inspector,' he said, winking at Blundell but offering his hand to his sergeant. 'Nate!' He nodded as he shook her hand. He sat back down. 'In a bad way after the kicking the plod gave him, eh?'

'Come off it, Leo, his Missus is a proper alley cat and nearly did for him.'

'Even in her pregnant state, bleeding from his knife wound, I have no doubt she might well have fended off her drunk and stoned boyfriend, but three broken ribs, a closed up eye and a broken jaw – not to mention the state of his gonads – give me a break!'

Chocky could do without the Police Complaints Commission entering the fray, so let that go. 'But he wasn't very happy with Hu, we hear.'

'Oh you do, do you? Well I don't.'

With only a scribbled note from Alan to go on, they couldn't really follow it up. They were satisfied that Nathan Helliwell was known to Leo and that there was a connection to Hu. The link between the three was most satisfactory. Badder knew why Nathan was in Hospital. She knew Leo cared about him. The note told her that Hu also cared about Nathan, but he had turned on his benefactor … she checked the note … the day before the conference.

DS Iruna Bahadur was taking a few minutes updating the whiteboard before the boys returned from lunch. She was using a bit of quiet to try to get into the mind of anyone they were considering for 'perp.'

She was staring Hu Stannton in the eyes. 'Who did you wind up my boy? That Leo wanted to wind you up didn't he? Poor Nathan warnt too impressed neither.'

She wasn't very happy with her boss's homophobia – a bit too taken up with anal sex. She wondered if that was a Catholic hang-up. She shivered – not her idea of anything lovely, either.

Holly was looking at Hu too. 'She was thinking she got a nice boy there, wasn't she Hu? She was right wasn't she? Well wasn't she?' Leo obviously did not think so.

Badder wiped away her original columns and redrew the outer two like theatrical curtains. She wrote 'accident' behind the left one and 'suicide' behind the right one – both were becoming less and less likely as the investigation progressed.

She left a 'caption' for the whole piece across the bottom: 'WHO DROUND HIM!'

She was considering three columns still – but fresh ones. The 'Conference' guys had to be in the centre. Holly's picture was to the right of Hu so she decided the right side would need to hold the family and church connections.

That left the left for Chocky's suspicions including Jeremy Fylde, the Hotel and guests – known and unknown, Hu's work colleagues and clients including the lad in hospital – Nathan Helliwell.

She rang down to the desk to see who was with Nathan now, and what the status of the case was: Uniform were still guarding him at hospital and as far as the Desk knew, they had not been able to interview him formally yet. She got the name of the officer in charge of the case, but he was out, possibly at lunch.

She went back to her desk and found Nathan's record in a twinkling. She printed it off, along with a good picture.

As she turned to stick it up, she found Alan at the board. He turned with one naughty finger in his mouth and the other pointing at 'DROUND.' She did a double take, chuckled and corrected it whispering 'Ta!' as she leaned in.

'You alright with me bringing that note in Sarge?'

'Iruna – or Badder if you insist – when it's just us, Alan,' she said. 'Yeah, course – it was brill. Amazing coincidence that it was him who had been in the hospital yesterday morning when I found Nicholas, eh?'

'Coincidence, er, Runa?'

'Well, not so much coincidence … how do you mean, Alan?'

'I'm thinking it's all a bit inbred. Here we've got a completely new, but fully credible suspect, but he's kinda run onto the pitch from nowhere, yet everybody knows him.'

'I see what you mean, it's not a coincidence that the perp is part of the network of contacts of the victim.' She put her hand on his arm and looked in his eyes. 'Well is it Alan?'

He breathed her sweet breath and looked at Nathan. 'No, no, you're right, Iruna.' He pursed his lips and nodded.

As Mike Gatting walked in Badder asked him straight out, 'How tall are you Mike?'

'Six two,' he smiled. 'Why?'

She craned to smile up at him as he stood right next to her. She shook her head.

He rested his elbow on it. 'Things hotting up, then?' he said rubbing his hands and looking from Alan to Badder.

'Indeed they are!' said Chocky coming up behind him. 'Oh well done Badder, having a bit of a sort out, eh?'

'On'y just got going sir. That Nathan was an interesting turn up for the books.'

'Oh yes – *Sensei!* Where did he get that from?' He winked at the men. 'We have a Japanese talking marshal arts expert, among us men – better watch yourself.'

'Naah – on'y a hobby…'

'Come off it, you wrong footed our prime suspect, I would say. How did you know?'

'Well it was Alan.'

Alan looked surprised.

'It was part of the background stuff you brought up for us. Never wondered how a coal miner became a youth officer? I wondered and found it – he used to help out at the Miner's Welfare youth Club when his pit shut. I wondered why and more importantly what a coal-miner had to offer to a youth club. Sport - he had been doing judo most of his life – and so have I. I just took a guess that I would have had more time – and energy – to take it further than a man who slogged his guts out a mile underground, and I bluffed it.'

'It worked!' said Chocky. 'Tell them what you see as the significance.'

'So you are around the same height as Hu Stannton, see, Mike. I'm gonna see if *I* could throw you over one o' them balconies at the Loseborough.'

He looked at Alan for support and got a smirk.

'If *I* can, basically anybody in our ring of suspects could,' she said sweeping across the board. 'More to the point, Mister Calm-as-a-cucumber Nicholas – a judo black-belt, four inches taller than me – could easily do it.'

'And so, for that matter, could Jez Fylde,' added Chocky.

Alan hoped Chocky wasn't going to get on about the anal sex again. 'Or the Missus?' he asked.

They were all nodding now.

'Updates, then,' said Chocky and pointed at the board-writer in Badder's hand.

Mike clapped his hands. He could have been applauding himself ahead of his clincher. The team were suitably impressed, but Alan had already taken some of the shine off. Mike thought he might improve his angle by suggesting that Nicholas had set up Nathan to nobble the priest. His point was noted, somewhat reluctantly, he felt.

They had a Round-Robin of all the material they had so far. They concluded that they were actually further away from a conclusion with each passing day. Chocky bit his lip and Gatting spent some time irritatingly patting his ribs.

The gay couple seemed like another red herring to Iruna but knew Chocky would follow it up – he told Alan to do so.

Alan pointed to the 'WHO DROWNED HIM!' and surreptitiously wiped out the exclamation mark.

'Yes Alan,' said Chocky. 'You thinking there may be more than one person?' He was nodding. He hated the Maynooth Mafia bit but could not ignore it. He felt that the smoke must indicate a fire. 'Could we put any two of our suspects together – one to push, the other the finish off?'

'It would be a bit much for the pusher...' Mike coughed. 'Excuse the term in these circumstances, but it seems a bit much for someone to shove him out of the window, maybe look down to see if he was dead, then run down to make sure and hold him under water.'

They were all looking at him.

'Well wouldn't it?'

'Not impossible, but unlikely.'

'More unlikely than say that Nicholas,' said Alan pointing at the photo and then at Nathan's, 'shoved him out of the window and had Nathan down below to make sure he was finished off.'

'Or Devine...'

'Or Grant ... or bloody Simone Dunne.' Iruna wiped her face and turned to Chocky. 'We couldn' arf do wi' some evidence, sir.'

'The sheet. You boys know about the sheet. What is the significance of it being missing?'

'Yeah ...' breathed Alan, 'hidden because it would give something away!'

'The perpetrator must've taken it away because it held some sort of clue?' queried Mike.

Chocky looked at him and held up a finger. 'Blood. Anal sex. Where?'

Alan chuckled.

'Alan, please! On the bed! On the sheet! Evidence. We've got to find it.'

'Shall I get SOCO to go back and search for it, sir?' said Badder.

'Maybe we four should go out there and have a search of the room – we haven't given it back yet have we?'

Mike shook his head.

173

'... and we'll take a look around the area – those trees at the back of the lawn, for instance. Damn CCTV is rubbish too, isn't it? It's amazing how many places spend a small fortune on this tackle and either it's such poor quality - Marley's ghost was clearer to Scrooge - or they don't maintain it – spiders live on the lens...'

'... and this one's over a steam vent,' completed Alan.

'One?' said Mike.

'Almost,' said Alan, 'they've got one other onto reception – it's not exactly the Hilton.'

'We are building a long list of suspects...'

'... several with strong-ish motives,' Mike blurted across his boss.

'Indeed; so we can implicate Uncle Tom Cobley, but to nail the real perp we need some evidence, don't we?' Chocky was almost pleading with his team.

'Okay,' said Badder, 'we need the sheet. We need the blood on the fire escape door. We need some video of cars coming and going – are there any private ones in the locality – neighbours and that? And the car!' Chocky held up a finger. Iruna carried on, 'Hu's car – is it in the car park?'

'What?' said Mike. 'Haven't we sorted that? What the fuck? Sorry Sarge – you mean he's got a bloody car and it may or may not be in the car park and we haven't...' he petered out shaking his head.

'S'okay Mike – I'm on it. The Missus has only just told them. I've rung the hotel and they are looking now.'

Badder was relieved and went on, 'Won't the Reception video have some of the comers and goers, too? Can you cut out pics of all the people on our list who signed in?'

Alan nodded and noted that for action.

'And I don't recall receiving anything from Jenks about the contents of the jacuzzi or its environs,' said the Boss. 'Let's get back and spend an hour on all we've got so far and Mike, you make us an appointment to look for this damn sheet before it gets dark – not long!'

Ginny Devine had of course used Father Hu as a confessor and was always seeking support for her abstinence despite loving - and fancying - her husband. He had encouraged her and made no hint of maybe using contraception - 'You've got to follow your conscience.' She did – but Hu didn't.

Ginny was livid with him and constantly got onto Brien about his betrayal of all that was innocent. She looked at Brien, her poor sad man, working at his faith and working off his urges in the old convent garden. She knew that when Colleen left, she took away the bond between Ginny and Brien. They never spoke about it. They never spoke about sex either.

When Father Hu had betrayed them all, she certainly found something to talk about – and that *was* about sex – not their own of course. That remained an elephant in her front parlour.

Brien had been with them all at the Conference and he had been mightily furtive since his return. What had gone on there? She had asked – in a voice several notes higher than her normal pitch, but attempting to sound simply interested.

Just talking and walking was all she got – and the funny old boat trip. That was a bit weird. Who the hell can walk out a door with the lads and just hitch them all a lift along the canal?

He had told her he would be meeting up with Abe at lunch-time. Abe wanted to know that everything – everything – was above board with The Tin Tab accounts and minutes, what with the police poking their noses into anything at all. She knew poor Brien wouldn't be liking the police sniffing around, not after his run-in with them over what those horrible kids said – and he'd been let off hadn't he?

Had Brien something else to be worried about? Surely he didn't go and bump him off for her, bless him? Could he do it? She thought of his little gym in the cellar – his 'chapel'; how he always kept fit, right back from the days long before they met when would take no stick from the navvies and would beat them at their own game – bare-knuckle fighting. He didn't need to beat many, just be the good sport. Did she herself not see the fine figure of a man, nicely topped out with a fine roman nose – 'Busted Ginny, it's a busted nose!' Ever humble he had to insist, but she wouldn't have it. She kissed it – regularly.

Holly had taken to watching the house. She knew what he was capable of – and what he was capable of covering up. She had rung him up for help but he hadn't helped her in the right way before. She wondered if she might have got something out of him at last. She needed to blame someone for killing her man, and why shouldn't it be the man who killed the woman in her? She was pretty sure he would not even know what she looked like. He hadn't recognised her at the church – he was on his knees in the garden – well he said he hadn't.

She walked casually along after him and saw him join a big man in a pub. It was a good old fashioned one and she could spy on them unseen through the clear glass of the word 'Snug', yet be hidden by the ground glass of the rest of the window.

They were conspiring. The bastards – head to head over a pint of beer for him and a G&T for Dadda. He was a bear of a man. She didn't like the look of him at all. And she didn't like the nervous looks they took in turns to make sure no one was watching them.

That was enough for her.

Frustration was so deeply felt that despite the SOCOs' doubtless great effort, the squad decided to have another search in every nook and cranny in the room at the Loseborough. They lifted the mattress, pulled off the bath side, behind drawers, above the wardrobe, Mike even had the idea it could be under the ironing board cover. They looked behind the stupid 'Not Gainsborough' painting and even had a conversation about it. The older two didn't get it, but the young ones bonded over the naughtiness of what the couple were smirking about: the faces of the young couple had been doctored into repressed laughing and a naked couple were frolicking by the lake in the background were surely 'Photoshopped' in – especially in the 'Honeymoon suite.'

'Hey – the ruddy sheet hasn't been turned into a canvas,' was Chocky's way of finding a funny side way out, before leading them out to search the grounds.

'Wait a minute boys!' shouted Badder. 'Mike! Here!' She waved him over to the window she was opening.'

'Uh, oh! Be gentle on me Miss!'

Alan and Chocky looked back at them from the door and laughed.

Iruna ran through several scenarios which might fit the idea that anybody with a bit of martial art skill could topple a six footer over the balcony: the doors are open and Hu (Mike) rushes in anger at the perp (Badder) standing goading by the rail – a pushover; perp pretends to see something interesting in the jacuzzi and flips an arm under legs and twist – easy; Hu has got the window open....

'Why, though Iru … Sarge?'

She ignores that and tells Mike to stand with his back to the balcony; she gives a mock push to the chest, tells Mike to lift a leg and she goes through the motion of grabbing the ankles and flipping; she has Mike worried for a minute there.

She turned to Chocky and Alan standing either side of the windows. She stroked her chin. 'Did the pathologist have a favourite way of falling – like forward or backwards?'

Chocky reminded her how both back and front were bruised and could be from either the balcony and/or the jacuzzi side, plus the housemaid had dragged him out of the jacuzzi and turned him on the concrete. There were hand-marks on both the door jambs, and on the balcony rail where Stannton had tried to save himself.

'Wouldn't be doing that if he was jumping … or flying, would he?' said Alan.

'Any of you feel very strongly about either of those options?' asked Chocky shaking his head.

They gathered at the jacuzzi side and stared at it as if it were going to tell them what happened.

'Cig and Cigar?' said Mike to no response.

They looked around the immediate vicinity, and then spread out to the full garden and all the way through the trees to the fence, all to no avail.

Chocky took them for a drink in the Blue Bell and explored the possible significance of the sheet: why was it hidden and by whom?

The team sipped their drinks and waited for the boss to answer his own questions.

'It's significantly different if Stannton hid it or someone else, see?'

'What would Stannton hide it for?' dared Alan.

'Exactly! We must ask that question.' Alan obviously did not see why, so Chocky had to continue. 'Blood...'

'... and faeces! I get you sir. Guilty priest got blood and shi ... well, I get you. So...' Alan suddenly got excited. 'Hey! If it were 'im, he couldn't take it home could he, so it's got to be at the hotel still!'

'But it's not is it?' said Mike.

'A-a! – can't completely conclude that. So the other option seems more obvious – or is it?'

'The perpetrator took it?' said Badder. 'But *'why?'* is our question if we want to explore that, yeah?'

'So if it's got blood on it and it matches that on him – who else – it's got to be Holly, hasn't it?'

'Yebbut, she's explained that away...' Iruna realised she was trapping herself. '... or she lied. Of course!'

Mike looked at Alan and opened his hands to Chocky and Badder saying, 'can you two tell me and Alan what you think are the ramifications as you see them, of the blood and faeces, please?'

Iruna knew she had to leave that to Chocky. He sighed and bit his lip. He scratched his head. 'Relevant to us needing some evidence, Mike ... the sheet will almost certainly implicate somebody, otherwise why has it been hidden? Secondly: it is possible that Stannton hid it, but after our search it is looking unlikely, so someone else has. That is more than likely going to be our perpetrator, isn't it? So what might the sheet show? Sex usually takes place on a bed,' he smiled, *'but not always*, Alan...'* Alan looked shocked and checked Iruna frowning at him, '... so the missing sheet will show some evidence. How am I doing Badder?'

She pursed her lips, nodding.

'Now as you know, I have some concerns about the faeces implicating Hu in a homosexual act, and I know you all think I'm being a bit old fashioned in this,' his voice had risen in pitch and he realised so lowered the volume, 'but Jez Fylde can't corroborate his alibi...'

'And there's the gay couple at the Golden Wedding,' Alan butted in.

'Threesome gone wrong, leaving one upstairs and one at the jacuzzi...?' added Mike.

'Hey, come on boys, this is going a step too far!'

'Yes Runa, but still to be considered. But more crucially, Holly has told us that she had sex with Hu before he left and that yes, she had started her period. The blood, Mike.'

That irritated Mike. He showed it but didn't say anything.

Badder rounded it back off, 'so as we just said, if it's her blood on the sheet then she's lying.'

Mike thanked them. They all took a drink.

Alan smiled at Badder. Then his phone buzzed. He jumped up and his stool fell over 'Fuck! The car's gone. Hu Stannton's car's not at the Loseborough!'

'Wha-at?' Chocky looked at his watch. 'I'll take you guys back to your cars and I'll get traffic onto it.' They downed their drinks.

In the car Chocky reminded them of the other blood on the Fire Escape door. 'We'll know about that in the morning, I hope. It seems a bit much, but we may have to consider searches of, well, Nicholas's car ... house. And maybe Jez's...'

'Room thirteen, sir!'

Chocky groaned. 'If Jez took it, we've had it – he'll have found some way of getting it mixed up in the hotel laundry, won't he?'

Leo Nicholas was challenging his own preconceptions. He hated religion – most institutions in fact – and he knew he was an anarchist at heart. However, he thought that within the institutions which we have to put up with, individuals could shine. That was part of his mission – there it goes again, a religious term – to give poor kids, poor in body or soul – come on Leo, not soul: mind? Spirit? – well, not got their act together *socially*. Yes Social Education was his game.

Abe and Brien shine – both really good blokes who were doing loads of stuff for other people and they didn't want a penny for doing it.

Leo knew they were flawed – most people would not forgive them for what they did – ever. Most would have Abe hung; and even the murderers in prison would give Brien a poke with a shiv. He was lucky to have avoided prison himself, even a few months. Leo wasn't sure what he had done, but he knew that whatever they accused him of, it was likely to have been only the tip of the iceberg of what he really did - that was Leo's experience of bringing any sex criminals to book.

Leo felt more about Abe than any members of even his own team. Abe made Leo raise his own game in the caring stakes. Abe always wanted more – and never for himself. Leo knew the pigs would be snorting round and would have Abe's record. They would be looking for easy solutions and Leo felt safe that they would look more closely at Abe than himself. He regretted that.

He didn't feel the same about Brien – another priest worshipping Paddy who probably followed the example of his deities. But what Leo did know was that Brien served his time, time and time again. He seemed to be heavily involved in charity work - presumably as some form of repentance.

Did Leo believe in repentance and forgiveness? He had to. He knew that some people would forgive Stalin, or worse – Hitler. They said that Hitler was only the way he was because of some example they had been given, so don't blame Brien, blame the Irish priests.

He thought he had better get Brien and Abe together with him, because he *knew* they couldn't have done for their Father Hu and he wanted them to know *he* couldn't do it either. They were closer to Stannton than he was and would know who could be implicated. Leo realised it could be a risky strategy – it could backfire with the old lads, and the pigs could think they were conspiring.

Wednesday 10th March

Leo reconvened the 'conference' delegates over breakfast in a café in Worksop, well away from what he thought would be prying eyes. Brien felt them searching each other through the windows to their souls, not much said, lots of nerves on show in hands and bodies, though Leo was pretty much his steely, watchful self.

Abe felt he had nothing to fear, but he knew that this was unrealistic. Of course one of them was a very likely prime suspect, but which one? He didn't know anything about Brien's background, except that he had come over from Ireland to the parish as a kid for ... he didn't know how long ... but not beyond working age.

Leo knew none of them wanted to be suspected, so his strategy was to directly act as if none of them could have done it and work towards helping the police get the right man – and that would be nobody they knew.

'Cards on the table, chaps,' he started, 'the police are bound to suspect one of *us* and we know we didn't do it, yeah? So let's get our heads together and try to work out some likely stones for the police to look under, eh?'

Brien and Abe looked at each other and back to Leo. 'Sounds about right,' said Abe, 'thanks Leo. I wasn't right enjoying us sitting at home suspecting each other.'

'Well, not really, surely, Abe?' said Brien.

'No, no, I don't mean actually suspecting,' he opened his hands out, 'but we know where the police are going to look don't we.'

'On with it,' said Leo slapping his knee. 'The Council – Housing Department – his mates, and ... ahem, the Church. What do we know?' He didn't stop to listen until he had added, 'of course I needn't say that all three are combined in The Tin Tab, in which each of us also has a stake. So let's move the spotlight away from us, right? Abe - you first?'

Leo's gamble seemed to work. All three of them noticeably relaxed into their seats, but each of them also took surreptitious looks to see if anyone was watching. Brien was fingering the condensation on his glass of iced water.

Abe started with Simone Dunne having a grievance against Father Hu, but queried whether or not she might feel similarly about Leo. Leo had to point out that it was Abe who wanted her moved. They agreed that, bitter and twisted as she was, they couldn't think how she might find Hu at the Hotel.

He moved onto the clients at The Tin Tab, many of whom had violent tendencies and records. To both Abe and Leo's chagrin, Hu 'took' a good number of them as his clients. Leo was familiar with this beef of Abe's – stealing Tin Tab's clients - but it enabled him to mention Nathan Helliwell.

'Is he out?'

'So you didn't know? ' said Leo. 'Well you won't be so pleased to know that Hu did – and found him a place from prison.'

'No Leo, I am pleased for the lad; but what about his Missus? She's been coming in to see us while he's been banged up.'

Leo grabbed his mouth and looked over his specs at Abe. He checked what Brien needed to know. 'Ah … well…'

'Spit it out.'

'You know Father Hu found her a place. Well she swore him to secrecy as to her whereabouts and he kept to it. After a couple of weeks, Nathan was back on the gear and raving mad – literally raving – at Hu. He went to his office and pinned him up against the wall…'

'When was this?'

'… wait for it – last Monday.'

Abe calculated and swung his head. 'The day before Loseborough?'

'The day before, yes. But! By the weekend Nathan had found out from some of his homies and, drunk *and* stoned, he attacked her.'

'What?' gasped Abe, 'is she alright? The baby?' Someone was walking over … her grave.

'Yes she'll be okay, I think. Nathan slashed her trying to stab the baby, but it only took a few stitches. She gave him a right kicking and he was too out of it to fight back. That having been said, I think his actual injuries were as a result of a very severe pasting from the boys in blue.'

Abe frowned. 'You've seen him?'

'Yes - went into the Infirmary on Monday morning. They had him in an induced coma because of head injuries. Poor lad, he's got absolutely nobody – except his Missus, see?'

'Yes, I think we've all got a soft spot for our Nathan? He'll survive, though?'

'Oh Yeah, coma's just a precaution – probably have him eased out of it by now.' Leo looked at a very green Brien.

'I'm used to a few black eyes among the lads in the building game,' said Brien, 'but the whole drugs thingy gives me the willies altogedder. Committee man will do me.'

Leo wondered how Brien felt about his Criminal Record Disclosure. 'So over to you Brien: your bit in all this is how you see him interacting with church people. Is there anything there?'

'Well there always will be people who like this about a priest and others hate that very same thing – his was always bulling up young people - 'Jewels in the crown' he called them. 'Bring the children out'; 'Bless all these young scholars', he'd say; 'Lovely to see all the young families here.' Well lots of fogies – sorry Abe – they decamped to the Jays – the Jesuits, across town. He ruffled a few feathers when he came, sure, but doesn't every new broom be sweeping clean?'

'Not exactly killing motive. Any bitter feuds arise out of this stuff?'

'There was bad feeling over stopping the bingo, but it was no longer for the parish, was it Abe?'

Abe was lost in his own thoughts and jumped. 'What's that, Brien?'

'Do we know anybody who felt real bad about Father Hu – you know, to kill him, like?'

'Ah Holy Mother, Brien, we can't be going there.'

'Where, exactly, Abe?' said Leo. 'Maybe that's where we should be going.' He glanced round the café. ' Here. Today.'

Abe was shaking his head fiercely. 'No, no, Leo, I don't mean that there's *anywhere* to go. I mean we can't be just dragging out names and casting aspersions about our fellow parishioners. Not on. Not me any road.' He narrowed his eyes at Brien, a stare under which he visibly shrivelled.

'Fine, fine, sorry, but I simply wondered if there was anything. So, how about the Missus?'

'What Nathan's?'

'No, sorry Abe, I'm moving on - Hu's floozy.'

Brien tutted. He shook his head slowly and massaged his knuckles, then moved up to his wrist.

Leo complimented himself on how sensitive he was to Brien's discomfort.

Thinking he was speaking for Brien, Abe said 'we think a woman who was good enough to draw Father Hu away from his vocation probably was not a … well, *floozy,* Leo. More to our point, she is more than likely a very strong willed, bright young thing. I've seen her – she is stunningly beautiful, isn't she Brien?'

Brien jumped this time. 'Er, well … I'm not rightly sure I can recall. You mean the one … the Tiffany girl?'

'That's the one Brien, we seen her lots of times after that.'

'Tiffany? Is that her name?'

Abe Laughed. Brien didn't.

Abe stopped laughing and said, 'Naah, first time I saw her she was dolled up to the nines – bit old fashioned to my mind, but also to my mind - very pretty – in a pencil skirted suit, sunglasses and one of them silly hats that doesn't cover your head – gorgeous. Well I says to Brien 'She think she's in Breakfast at Tiffany's?' Put me in mind of Audrey Hepburn.' He smacked his lips.

Brien was now massaging his other wrist. 'Don't reckon I ever noticed,' he muttered.

'So neither of you can say whether or not the relationship worked; whether or not she maybe had a temper; could have felt like throttling him?'

Abe looked at Brien who didn't look up, but did say 'bet his clergy pals weren't too happy.'

Abe and Leo gave him time to develop that thought.

He lifted his gaze. 'It'll cost the church a pretty penny to put a man through all that training – and a lot of care and attention, too, I have to say. Well they won't be wanting it to be whipped from under their noses by a pretty young thing, will they?'

Leo swept a hand across the table.

Abe finished his shandy and pointed to the dregs in each of his friends' glasses. Brien shook his head and Leo asked for the same again. Abe wondered about his driving. Leo assured him it was only a very light beer.

Leo didn't know about Brien's personal situation so tried, 'Family alright, Brien?' Brien's positive monosyllable reminded Leo why he taught his youth workers to ask open ended questions. He had to sit quietly, but he slipped in, 'we alright about what you told me?' and he put his thumbs up.

The picture of Brien's face spoke no words. After a few seconds he coughed, and moving closer to Leo he almost whispered, 'But you goaded Hu. I said you were only having a laugh, winding him up like.'

Leo shuddered. 'You *said*, Brien?'

Abe returned with the drinks and noticed a guilty way the others looked up at him.

Leo took the 'blame': 'I was just mentioning to Brien about me goading Hu. Having a laugh … winding him up like.' He widened his eyes at Brien and went on, 'that's how it was, well I'm asking you, both of you, is that how it seemed?'

Brien lay his hand on the table. 'The Police are going to be asking us who we think done it, are they not? I did think it would come up and I didn't want them to be suspecting you Leo, so I told them it was just a bit of joshing.'

Leo wasn't convinced by that or the bit of colour Abe seemed to have gained. However, he had to accept that his goading was genuinely aggressive and if the guys had played it down to the police, what more could he expect? So what Leo needed to ascertain was if it was Hu's wife he had seen scooting away from his room that fateful night. He brought the topic back round to her. 'So neither of you have any intelligence – sorry, slipping into detective mode, here – any idea whether or not Hu had any reason to regret his move; or her for that matter?'

Brien had heard that the priests had come and taken Hu to be rewired or something. He knew that he had returned. The Church's story was simply that Hu had to go on a training course. When he had first gone away, some thought he had run off with a woman but nobody really believed it.

Abe had nobbled any Tin Tab clients Hu had spoken to at any length to see if he could find out anything about him. The 'kids' had no qualms about asking Hu straight – 'everything alright with the Missus?' accompanied by the raising fist under the other arm; or looking at his fly area 'Worn him out yet, Hu?'; 'No seriously, sir, you didn't have a wife when you were priesting did you? What's it like?' Abe had to hide behind the kitchen door to smother his snigger. Hu was ultra professional and always managed to divert attention away from his private life and to allow the clients to seek what they needed from him.

Abe at last said 'I did try to find out – he never let anything slip to the kids at Tin Tab. Sorry Leo.'

'Just a thought. The Police are going to have these thoughts whether we like it or not though, aren't they?'

That shook Brien a little so he again mentioned the priests and Hu's first 'break.' 'Only a rumour mind!'

'A very interesting one, too. Opus Dei?'

'Da Vinci Code was fiction,' asserted Brien.

'Bollocks, too,' laughed Abe.

Leo thought he had succeeded with his plan – mainly to remove any suspicion held by his 'co-conspirators' away from him, but also to think he had none for them, nor they for each other. He could handle the 'goading' situation. He felt the police could suspect Nathan and would be looking at 'Tiffany' - Mrs Stannton – they always suspect the wife. He wondered how he could let them know about the rowing he heard coming from Hu's room – that was definitely a woman. Surely a guest at the hotel will have heard them. But it was a funny time – tea time – people weren't in their rooms much. But they would have been coming and going. But, but, Leo felt fairly confident in his hope that none had seen him there as there wasn't that much coming and going.

Opus Dei? Leo decided to ask Brien if he would try to remember who he heard the rumour from, track them down and get at the fire that gave off the smoke.

Brien was just as keen to divert any attention away from himself so readily agreed to do that. He went straight home and got on the phone.

Both Brien and Leo went home by different routes from those taken on the way.

A week had almost passed and The Superintendent wanted an update from Chocky. She knew that the case had not yet turned into a murder inquiry, but felt he should at least be able to indicate a few likelihoods beyond mere accident. She didn't like the press sniffing round Irish Priest and child abuse issues, so wanted to hear about a potential motive that steered clear of that. The press would shut up if it was only a domestic.

She couldn't afford the resources for four in the team and really wanted Chocky to leave a simple case to the sergeant who was making a good impression round the office, with maybe the more mature Gatting over Prisco as support.

A traveller had been found severely battered and the Super was worried that a turf war may have broken out among the local metal thieves.

Chocky attempted to pre-empt any close-down by asking if he could have a permit to go over to Maynooth, a search warrant for Nicholas's house and car, and support for more forensic work. He succeeded: she was amazed that the case had taken on such a complexion and that there seemed to be deeper rumblings requiring his superiority on the case.

She tried to get out of paying for him to fly to Ireland asking why a few phone calls and or emails couldn't sort it.

'I've tried all that Ma'am, but – yes I know it's not Da Vinci Code – but no one actually knows one way or the other over here. The Priest was from Ireland –

raised and ordained – and basically 'loaned' to this Diocese, which knows little about the man or the system he comes from.'

'Still the Catholic Church, *universal* though Chocky?'

'Yes but they do things a bit differently over there.'

She laughed. 'I have heard.'

He laughed too. 'Yes, dropped myself in that one didn't I? What I mean is they train their people up differently. When I was a lad, kids from my school went off to the Irish Christian Brothers' and Salesian priests' seminaries when they were only eleven. There were maybe a hundred of these schools in the British Isles, but his Junior Seminary – Maynooth - is the only left.'

She laughed some more, shaking her head this time.

'Yes, well.' He punched a finger on her desk.

She was not impressed.

He looked at his finger and grabbed it with his other hand. 'Sorry, but that is an indicator to me that they will have invested a whole lot more in training and preparing this guy to let him go very easily ... or for that very reasonable assumption that he will fairly easily be made to see the error of his ways. In fact, from what I can gather they may have succeeded and were let down by the Brits.'

'Okay Chocky I'm still listening...'

'Thanks, Ma'am.' He held his mouth while he framed his clincher. Should he mention the word 'Mafia'? 'The thing is, we may have hit upon a conspiracy that got a bit out of hand.'

The Superintendent's eyes were wide.

'I have clarified that what at first came to us a rumour is actually true – well has some truth in it - and I think I need to go across to speak to Stannton's own people to be able to move forward.'

'Sounds fascinating, but are you chasing rumours without any evidence?'

'Sorry to say, I am following up an allegation because we haven't got any evidence at all yet.'

'What – none?'

He sucked his teeth. 'Sorry,' he was doing too much apologising, '... we've got several *bits* of evidence, but they don't tie to anybody. We need to find out if someone had motive and MO to be able to kill him, in order for us to conclude that he was indeed murdered or ... definitely didn't simply fall.'

'Simply fall!' she spun right round with her arms in the air and faced back to him both hands on her head.

'Ma'am, Ma'am, it was a mess,' he went for a charming smile, 'that's why you put me on the case, yes? Well, it still is a mess, but of the suspicious criminal nature, and we are not even near being able to let it drop ... without serious questions being asked.'

'Okay Chocky, but I'm only letting it go on 'til the weekend without some real evidence of crime. The mother's been on about the body, you know.'

He took Saturday to be included in the week, and decided three days after today was as good as he could expect with practically no evidence.

The forensics were in: the blood on the Fire Escape door was Leo Nicholas's. Chocky was relieved and had grounds to immediately arrest him.

There were some other interesting little bits – mainly from the jacuzzi: a half burnt cigarette with lipstick on – DNA not discernible; a weird singe to the back of Stannton's dressing gown, close analysis - 'bit bloody tricky this one Chocky', said Jenks – it appeared to be a cigar burn, not a cigarette; and useless confirmation that they never received a second sheet.

Alan set about chasing up the car with Traffic and further scouting for CCTV while Mike went back out to the hotel again calling past the hospital to get a first hand impression of Helliwell's status.

What a slippery customer Leo Nicholas was turning out to be. Chocky had a snake in mind, but Badder was keeping hers more open, sustaining her 'innocent until proved' position.

Chocky wanted Leo to implicate himself so made him go over his movements after the 'conference' again. This proved particularly fruitless as Nicholas repeated his original story more-or-less verbatim. He also appeared very calm sitting back in his chair the whole time. Too calm – he must be lying, thought Chocky. He offered not one bit of extraneous detail for Chocky and Badder to open out the investigation.

Leo was obviously aware that they must have found something further, but he wasn't going to tell them anything, he would wait for them to tell him. He told himself to stay calm. He was not. He had Stannton's face seducing his own mother back in Italy and it riled him that he didn't know until too late to do anything for her. He was on the mission now. But it was not difficult for him to engage his poker-faced Union negotiation training and was pretty happy with the image he was putting over. He was waiting for his moment to get onto the pigs about being agents of the oppressive state, but knew he could only do this if he was not seriously suspected of anything.

When he had finished his story and the Inspector seemed to really have nothing more to go on, he waited a moment, checked out the sergeant – hardly a 'pig' to be fair – he decided to spread a little 'chaff' to throw off any missile they had sent after him.

'How can you go on with all this investigating, Inspector, when you must surely accept that a louse has been removed from society?'

'The man was a priest Mister Nicholas. There is no acceptable way anyone can refer to him as a 'louse.''

Leo looked at Badder and saw that at least she didn't appear to be wildly removed from his own point of view.

She was leaving this argument to her boss. She still didn't know what to think of the whole child abuse scandal – whether individuals within a system can all be tarred with the same brush.

'Anyway, that has nothing to do with why we have brought you here today,' Chocky added.

'Says who? Have you found out who has done for him and why? No, else you wouldn't have me cringing here.' He pulled a timorous face then smirked at his play. 'The guy was a cheat – to everything he reckoned to stand for. He didn't need to be found out – he presumably, well he *did* stand for it. So what else was false about the man? Who else had he hurt along the way? Like I said last time: why would I give him the good time, and then go killing the perv? You are agents of the state and like me you should be trying to protect women and children from the likes of this slime-ball.'

Chocky was developing a head of steam at these distractions but calculated that if Nicholas could get himself worked up about what he cared about, he may slip and reveal a chink in his armour ... Chocky kept the bloodstain dry for a moment more.

Leo went on, 'What can we over here do to help the victims of these paedophile priests? If I *had* done for Stannton would you not sympathise with me, in so much that I had done this one little thing, cracked this louse between my thumb-nails,' he cracked them, 'for the happiness for the greater number of people?'

Chocky burst. 'One little thing? Murder a man? All based on assumptions.'

'Assumptions?' he shouted, 'that he was a cheat ... a liar, a seducer, a double-crosser? Come on. All sorts of people would have had it in for the guy. I'm just a handy straw you are clutching at.'

There was Chocky's straw: 'So tell us why your blood is on the fire escape door at the Loseborough Hotel?'

Leo smiled down at the still throbbing nail. He had a slight suspicion they might find him out. He thought he had wiped the blood off, but now supposed a nylon cuff was not a very absorbent cleaner. He held the finger up.

'That the incriminating item, then Leo?'

'Why incriminating – my finger, my blood on a door I used...'

'But what for?'

'Usual.'

'Usual!'

Leo sat back as Chocky headed towards him. He was enjoying himself now.

'Usual.' Leo nodded to Badder to remind her what doors were for.

'Mr Nicholas, this is possibly a murder enquiry and we are working on the idea that you set a trap for our victim. You did so and cleverly covered our potential evidence with lots of, well 'chaff' as you call it, to distract us. Unfortunately for you, blood on a door which you should *not* have used looks very incriminating.'

'I was a patron of this hotel and the Fire Escape was there for my fully legitimate use.'

'An emergency?'

'Why emergency?'

'Because it's an emergency door.'

'Who says?'

'A sign saying 'Only to be used in emergency.'

'Does it say that?'

'It always says that.'

Leo slumped as if devastated. 'Ah well, you are the police, you check your facts of course.'

Chocky looked at Badder whose face was a dead giveaway to Leo.

'Are you insinuating …? No, stop messing about. Accepting as you must, that it is your blood, tell us why, how and when you it got on that door?'

'Though it doesn't actually excuse me, your assumptions will be undermined by a quick perusal of the foot of the fire escape staircase.'

'Leo,' breathed Badder at last, 'help us and help yourself please? If you think you shouldn't be here now, let's all go home, eh?'

Leo gave her a long look.

'… and what will we find that won't excuse you…' said Chocky, 'and what will?'

'Um. Dog-ends.'

Chocky caught on. 'You are saying the fire escape is used by smokers – well I suppose it is to be expected. It's private and easily accessed. But … er?'

'I don't smoke.'

'So what is your excuse then?'

'What smoking doesn't provide – a bit of fresh air.'

'Oh give over,' gasped Chocky, 'there are windows in every room.'

'However, unlike Father Hu's, mine had no balcony and looked onto the road. So here's my story…'

'We don't want a story, we want the truth.'

Leo pouted to pull in his smile, akin to poking his tongue out, before continuing, 'I wanted a bit of air after our session in the bar and I was also a little, only a little, curious to see the view from out there.'

'So you went out of the door on your corridor,' and thinking to entrap Nicholas Chocky said, 'and caught your finger on it?'

Leo wagged his finger at the Inspector and started to chuckle. He looked out over his specs.

'Leo!' warned Badder.

'Yeah well, nice move Inspector, but as you know, no I didn't.'

Chocky was crestfallen, but hoped it didn't show. 'Tell me?'

Still chuckling Leo said, 'The door blew to, didn't it? As you will know I was on the second floor and the blood is on the third floor door, eh? Only a little of that fresh air – deep midwinter – was enough, so to get back in I would have had to go down two flights of stairs …' he looked at Badder whom he didn't really want to upset. 'Anyway you get me, so – probably just like you – I looked around and up and noticed a chink of light showing at the door above me. I thought it was open and went a tried and …' He held up the finger again 'Da-dah!'

Chocky looked at Badder who shrugged at him. He called an end, stopped the tape, and told Leo they would look into the matter while he thought about taking the matter a little more seriously – in his cell.

'Not much for you to think about, Inspector, so … ' Leo looked at his watch.

Holly was coming out of her door as Alan arrived to get the vehicle log book for Hu's car. He didn't tell her a burnt out car had been found, simply that they needed a full description. Something about the way she narrowed her eyes intrigued him, but he had nothing to say as she rushed the full pack of car details into his hands and set off in her own car.

He had a report back from traffic that a vehicle of Hu's make and probable model had been burnt out on Wednesday. The Fire Brigade had reported it, but because of a prevalence of burnouts in the area – particularly in Top Wood, Spital, the Police wouldn't do anything until they could tie up a car like it having been reported missing. They also gave him a contact in the Brigade who would help with location etcetera. He followed that up.

What was Holly rushing about at?

Mike decided to accept a 'small half' served up by Jez Fylde. He put on his best nonchalant face and made no attempt to open a conversation. Fylde was obviously uncomfortable, constantly looking around to see if Mike was looking at him – he was – and seeking anything to divert his own activity.

The DC had had no luck in his informal search of room 13. Houldsworth had told him that Suzanne was due 'momentarily' (another Americanism creeping in!) so he was waiting to pick her brain for other ideas around the sheet and the laundry system. She hadn't any.

Instead of simply telephoning, he decided to get a real impression as to Nathan Helliwell's status by creeping up to the ward, trying to see him and get a personal update from the Staff Nurse. The PC on guard recognised him and, being the same rank wasn't going to be pushed round by Gatting's lack of a Uniform. However Mike, while chatting with his unhelpful colleague, got the chance to see that Nathan was well enough to be surfing the TV channels. Back at the station Mike went directly to the DI on Nathan's case and secured an appointment for somebody – 'not the whole gang of you' - to have a quiet – 'gentle Mike, or else' - word with the lad, later in the afternoon.

The team were gathered in the briefing room.

'If Nicholas pushed Stannton out of the window, it's looking unlikely that it wasn't him who, er … Iruna?'

'Drowned him sir, Chocky, 'cos he doesn't smoke – cigarettes or cigars?'

This was news to Mike and Alan, but all of them had a little to show for their morning's work: Alan was excited that Stannton's car had been burnt out and it could be the getaway from the killing.

'Steady on Alan,' said Chocky, 'one step at a time. Do you know when it was burnt out?'

Disappointingly for Iruna, he had to check his notes. 'Wednesday 3rd March sir.'

The boss stretched his mouth wide across her teeth. 'One step, eh Alan? The day before Stannton was, as you say, 'killed.''

Alan deflated.

'Not a complete waste, though son, it's a bit much to be happening to our unfortunate priest without there being some connection, isn't it?'

Alan felt better and got his thinking cap on to work out the connections.

Mike ignored how much time he had wasted, to enthuse about Helliwell's availability and his information from the DI that Helliwell was his own mini-crime wave.

'Got it!' said Alan, 'he's one of that Spital Hill mob who are always burning out cars – sometimes wonder if they aren't working to order for your other gang, sir?'

'Ha – the Metal thieves! Yes. Well that is another step, somewhat in the dark, Alan, and it could be how he got away from The Loseborough. Did he get there in another stolen car – it's their usual form of transport – hotwiring and hopping!'

'Straight on it sir. I'll see if the hotel can get someone out to check the car park for unlocked cars.' The golden wedding guests were also on his mind, but as he hadn't found the gay couple yet, he thought it best to avoid the subject in the meeting and get his facts together.

'They might get Jez Fylde to do it for you,' smirked Mike.

Chocky moved forward. 'Tell the lads about how we got on with Leo Nicholas, eh Badder?'

'He's digging his way to prime suspect,' she opened to the DI's obvious surprise. 'Well he's trying to make out that our prime piece of evidence – his blood on the door – is completely above board.' She repeated the youth officer's story. 'But I think it's far more likely that he came back to finish Stannton off. He sneaks in through the back car park, up the Fire Escape to the door he's already left open – but maybe not quite as far, or easy enough to open as he plans – and breaks his nail getting in.'

'But if he did that,' asked Alan, 'it'd show up on the CCTV over the car park wouldn't it Alan?'

Alan wondered if he purposely put him on the spot there – Gatting knew the video was rubbish and steamed up. 'Well I can have another look,' he appealed to Chocky, 'but as I said before, it *is* crap footage.'

'You can see vehicles coming and going – and maybe people, even if we can't see number plates and who exactly … get some idea to back-up or refute the man's story?'

Grinning, Iruna said '… and bringing us back round to smoke – there's no smoke without fire an' that – what can we make of, firstly the cigarette, and that the burn on the dressing gown is probably from a cigar? Who are our smokers? Leo says he's not – not that I'm just taking his word for it.'

'Should be easy enough to find out.'

'Gonna smell all their breaths, Mike?' said Alan.

'Children!' Chocky waved a paper. 'Search warrant – Nicholas's house and car. Get on with it you two. Now. Sheet and smoking, any incriminating research – computer – that Leo's done on Stannton. We've kept him in the cells and we still haven't got much to go on.'

The constables were both open mouthed, but snapped them to and set off.

Chocky nudged Badder towards the whiteboard, one hand on his chin the other chinking coppers. They both stood looking at it, but Badder's mind wasn't on it. She was thinking about Alan and had a warm feeling that she was not familiar with.

'I don't see Holly as a cigar smoker, do you?'

She didn't say anything but blinked hard to regain focus.

'Any of the blokes, though. Time we got some back up on alibis – from the womenfolk, Badder?'

'Me?' She felt this was a little sexist even for Chocky – little lady sees to the little ladies!

'Super's…' he wanted to ensure he didn't appear to be swanning off and leaving the work to his minions. 'Super's letting me fly over to Ireland - good job Ryan Air is an Irish set-up - and clear out the Maynooth notion. I think it is very unlikely, but that we ignore it at our peril. You couldn't make it up, could you?'

'Dan Brown did!'

Chocky laughed at the truth of it. 'What I mean is - it's too silly to make up so it, well, might be true. It also has the element of a conspiracy, which we do appear to have, in more than one person being involved.' He pointed at Leo then Nathan. 'I can't see a bright lad like Nicholas setting on a druggie like Helliwell to help him out. Besides, Helliwell's only just come out of prison and I'm sure there's not enough of a relationship for even Helliwell to help in such a stupid venture. Besides, Nathan liked Hu – he'd done a lot for him. I know he was miffed at Hu because he wouldn't tell him where the missus was, but that was probably only drunken – druggy – emotion.'

'What about the car, though? That's got to be Nathan, hasn't it?'

'Oh Runa, don't do an Alan.'

Despite the negative in there, she was quite pleased with the association. 'But you said yourself that there must be some connection.'

He nodded; he clinked; he fumed. 'We need something – something to actually go on. I'm going to get this bloody Catholic conspiracy off my chest.' He turned to face Iruna. 'You know I'm a Catholic, don't you lovey?'

She smiled. 'Yes I think so. It means a lot to you.' She raised her voice a little. 'I don't think it compromises you, if that's what you're saying sir.'

He double checked that. 'No. No, thanks Iruna. Have you got a religious anything, er?'

'Oh yes sir!' bringing her hands into prayer, waggling her head in best Gandhi style and with a mockney Indian accent she said 'pretty much bladdy everyting, sahib.' Then she blessed herself Catholic style.

'Nice one, Runa – and thanks.' He patted her on the shoulder. It'll probably be a twenty four hour turnaround, though. Keep in phone contact – I don't suppose it'll work on the plane – but it can be like we are doing it together. Sorry she won't pay for both of us...'

She grounded herself in her Oxford accent. ''s alroyt surr. Oil get to the WAAGs an' 'at.' She coughed and moved back to RP. 'We've got a bit of foot-slogging to do. Shall me and Mike see to Nicholas and let him go at tea time unless they find something – and if they, then do keep him overnight?'

'Yes, that's about it. Oh something's got to turn up.' He shook his head. 'I feel like Mister bloody Micawber here.'

She blinked but let him go. It came to her - she shouted after him 'Dickens!'

Suzanne had already realised that she could be in trouble – firstly for smoking on duty, and in the hotel, but secondly in not letting on to the detectives that that was why she was at the window – and where was her bloody cigarette? When Badder simply asks if she smokes – she lies – well she doesn't any more, not now, so it's not a lie.

Ginny innocently said her husband Brien doesn't smoke. She only thought of cigarettes. He had smoked so few of the little cigars – ever – that she didn't think he still did. It was pretty obvious to Badder that loving as they were, it was more in the way of brother sister, and she felt that Ginny didn't actually know when and where her husband was at the crucial times. She was so horrendously nervous though – shivering the whole time. Badder tried to let her know that it wasn't so bad to feel nervous.

'Well I don't want you to think I'm lying and trying to cover for him, Sergeant.'

'Far from it,' she laughed, 'your *inability* to cover for him, but obvious deep affection – well that's enough for me.'

Rowena told of Abe smoking roll-ups – dirty things but his only bad habit. She was completely open about his criminal background and life sentence – 'and knowing his history as you do, that's pretty damn good isn't it, detective?' Badder was very taken with Mrs Grant – big, warm earth mother. She was in awe of her taking on a killer with a life-sentence as a husband and was impressed that she definitely seemed to have made a success of it. Surely she hadn't got it wrong and he could still have the killer instinct?

'Coddy he calls me, stupid bloody name – Ro – Cod Roe, get it?'

Badder did.

'Wraps me in his arms and ...' she breathed deeply, '... I'm home.'

Badder's eyes welled up. She had never felt like that about a man – well except her Dad. She wrapped her own arms around herself and just looked at Coddy standing with her eyes shut.

Alan texted her that he and Mike had drawn a complete blank on the Leo Nicholas search, but the burn-out was Stannton's and there was a 'pool car' left in the Loseborough car park. He followed that up with another text saying that Nathan Helliwell had just owned up to the burnout. Typical – didn't care – but she supposed it was nothing to what he was going to have to go back down for.

Chocky texted Iruna from a bar on O'Connell Street to confirm his appointment at Maynooth first thing – but he couldn't get a flight back until evening so Thursday was down to her and 'the boys.' She felt good about that, then realised that maybe it was a bit of a poison chalice Chocky was offering. Ha Ha – another Catholic symbol. She thought of her mother and knew she was proud of her little daughter being in charge of a complex 'murder' case. Well it had been in the paper.

Hu Stannton's mother, Sheila, was staying with her niece Pauline. She didn't have that much choice, but she did have a great deal of time for her - was it not her who had 'looked after' their Hu for the family? She had a lot to catch up with as, in many ways, the family had considered Pauline and Hu 'an item' in one sense of the term. In that context, as ever, they didn't want to know about the invisible housekeeper - all they wanted to know about was Hu. Pauline had to live with that.

Hu was now dead and there was a whole chunk missing from his mother's life and that now included an interest in his actual work as a priest over here in England.

Pauline rose to the occasion and in her own self estimation – they wanted to know about her at last. She upbraided herself for feeling she could gain anything from the poor boy's death – 'but there you are Sheila.' She gave a glowing report for all he had done: the great increase in mass attendance; the large number of families; bringing the Poles back to mass (though she wasn't so sure they weren't just a bunch of tinkers); redecorating the church and Presbytery; and of the praise from the Bishop. She added that she had built herself a nice little circle of

Women's Guild Ladies that laid down the *'infer-a-structure'* that poor Hu had to build on. What lovely Christmas and Easter festivals they had – the flowers, the Calvary, the Crib…

Sheila wanted to know how a woman had got her claws into her son. She took a while to think how she could get round to it, without blaming Pauline.

She was saved by Pauline bringing it up herself. 'I never saw it coming, Auntie, or should I say 'her'? I saw her coming back right enough, but no, I missed how she originally got him.'

That lost Mrs Stannton.

Pauline registered and grabbed her mouth. 'Oh Auntie! I'm so sorry. Sorry I let that out – they told me never to.' She choked up and jammed her hands between her knees and rocked. Re-opening on a sob, she said, 'Well I suppose it'll all come out now, annyways.'

Sheila was on the edge of her chair.

'It's like this, Auntie: Hu left for her before, but they came for him and sorted him out. They brought him back to me but he only lasted another eleven weeks and two days…'

'He left!'

Pauline blinked some tears and brushed them away with a cuff. 'Yes we had to have a story and of course it was Gospel – he'd been on a training course – that was true I suppose.'

'Now who's 'they' and 'we' Pauline?'

'Oh his team – his bosses I suppose – over from Maynooth. They came and persuaded him to not throw it all away, but to take a considered view. Course, it's no shock to have priests leaving and marrying, but they get a dispensation from the Pope, do they not?'

'They do – sure we know plenty of them, do we not?'

'We do Auntie, but like that Dermot O'Neill fell in love with a woman out on the missions and came back for two whole years at the seminary – serving a Hospital I think,'

'It was – a whole two years before he left with a dispensation, keeping the faith an' all. Sure I don't know if he actually married the first girl in the end, though marry he did. We see him round the town when he visits with the kids even.'

'And fair play to him, don't you think Auntie?'

'But not my Hu, Pauline…?'

She looked out of the window a while. 'Not my Hu' she thought. 'No Auntie, it was all very sudden.' Pauline got a tissue and twiddled with it. She saw Sheila needed one too.

'You say he came back for … weeks.'

'Ah Jaysis I counted the days Auntie – seventy nine days and he was gone.' She let out a howl and her body was racked. The pain had been bottled up in her body. 'He never…'

Sheila swapped over to the settee and hugged her sister's daughter like she hadn't done since she was a little girl. The headstrong child had grown into a powerful woman who couldn't bear to be touched, would cringe from a hug from her own Mammy, so Hu was safe with her. She eventually managed to calm Pauline and discover that she had held up with never another word from Hu. He didn't come back for anything he took his few 'civvies' and toiletries in a small bag and left everything for Pauline to sort ... 'except Auntie, he did take his picture of Uncle Dan and yourself on your wedding day – he did. The only picture he did take.'

Sheila took a great long breath. Hu had not spoken to her at all, either, but he had written, written several times – apologies, but...no explanations, then a few bits of news, a very short description of Holly and how she would like her, but he understood maybe not yet. So had Holly killed him? 'I'm thinking maybe I know a little more about Hol ... his wife, than you do, Pauline, by the sounds of it.'

That was a bit of a shock. Pauline had had to live with it, live with the knowledge that the pair of them were cavorting somewhere in the vicinity. The colour drained from her and she suddenly felt cold. She snuggled up to her aunt who increased her grip. They sat for a while in silence – except for sniffs and sobs – lit only by a street light now.

Sheila relaxed her grip and went into the kitchen to make a brew. As she held a cup and saucer out to her niece they smiled at each other – maybe it was the first time either of them had smiled in a week. Perhaps they were ready to move into an investigation.

'Do you ... do you Pauline, I mean can you, er ... the Gards will be asking about who might want Hu dead.'

'They will sure enough, Auntie, but I haven't known,' she sobbed at the thought, 'I haven't known anything at all about ... Hu for over two years. They seemed to be wondering why he ... why he ... if he ... well killed himself!' She wailed to the sky. 'I wouldn't have it. I wouldn't let them ... the only thing ever – ever, Auntie – that I could think of at all bad or anything, well, you know, even naughty was, you know...'

Sheila obviously did not know.

Pauline whispered 'Ballinafad.'

Sheila couldn't understand or believe her ears. 'What's that you're saying, at all, Pauline?'

'Ball-in-a-fad!'

She couldn't believe her ears, she stood up and took a look out into the street. 'Pauline, you have lived with him all his life nearly and the only bad thing your can think of is, what? Was he even into his teens? Jay-sis!' She stood over her niece and held her shoulders. The honest plea in Pauline's eyes forced Sheila to restrain some cynicism. She released her grip and took another turn round the room. Hu will have had disagreements with tutors; fights at Uni; furious rows with other seminarians over matters of faith; close brushes (worse!) with women;

parishioners falling out with him – especially the 'parish mafia' when he came – there's one in every parish; but she realised that Pauline saw no wrong in her man, until he was no longer her man. 'He was a good man, a very good man, indeed he was. But look it Pauline, the Devil does not like a good man.' She let that sink in.

'Ah, now Auntie, here's me thinking that if I mentioned anyone that Hu upset, well I'd be saying he did something wrong. But the devils! We had a few of them over the years – kids bricked the windows, the Tinkers had the lead, beggars always wanted more next time, then they only wanted money and Hu wouldn't – he said they'd spend it on drugs and the sup.' Something came to her.

'What is it, Pauline?'

She was standing up. 'Jimmy Tobin!' she whispered. A bit louder to her Aunt, 'The Tobin Gang – well it was a few years ago now. No couldn't be. Surely not?'

'Try me.'

She did.

Thursday 11th March

There was a real kerfuffle at the Desk as Iruna came in to work. Pauline recognised her and pressed her to get them a room. 'Now Inspector, now!'

Badder had two very excited - and scared - women in front of her. They were straightening themselves and looking round to make sure no one was watching them.

'We've come up with something, Inspector,' gasped Pauline.

'Sergeant, Ma'am, Sergeant Bahadur.'

'Of course,' she told her Aunt, 'Yer man's the Inspector,' she flicked her fingers, 'Bundle is it, Miss? Where is he?'

She felt two answers were like a forked stick – one bit funny but not admissible and the deadly serious and probably also inadmissible.

'Inspector John Blundell is out of the office, today.' She thought better of telling them he was in Ireland. The fact may bring some more out of them, but this was them coming to tell her something. 'Please tell me what's excited you – we do need to check every lead.'

Sheila put her arm round Pauline's back. 'Go on *Alanna.*'

Like the little child, she blurted out her story of the Tobin gang that had a racket going in parish halls - all round the region as it turned out. Father Hu had come to the parish to find he could hardly use the hall as it was booked out most of the time for Bingo. It was 'the parish bingo' he was told. He spent several nights in there to find himself rarely recognised and certainly not by the people running it. He had got on to the people in the parish who seemed to have anything to do with money, and Brien Devine – 'him being a retired accountant' - had worked out they were taking over two hundred pounds a night, in 'our' small hall, three nights a week and handing over a paltry twenty pounds – not even the price of a letting for a children's party, because it was 'a parish event.'

Mr Devine had made a few enquiries in the area and found out that this fella Jimmy Tobin had a gang of men running bingo in many parishes, having the Ladies of the parish setting up, doing the door, the tickets, the teas and clearing up – all voluntarily. One of Tobin's men would bring the prizes, do the calling and take the money. Mr Devine calculated they were creaming off thousands of pounds a week.

'Well it came to Hu to put an end to it. And the Tobin gang didn't give up without a fight.'

'A fight?'

'A real fight. Ahem, *cac* through the letter box, slashed tyres, a garden bush set fire all by itself; and they stopped his car the one time - a man in front, one each side, swinging bats and … brandished? Swung 'em …'

'Yes brandished, Pauline.'

'… and busted his mirrors off that time. Well I never, *never* seen Hu so scared. Annways, he pulled himself together and the police took it on. Tobin got jail – massive fraud – not just the bingo – he was smuggling booze and ciggies, even the prizes were mostly counterfeit, too.'

Badder hadn't needed to say a word so far. 'When was this Miss Stannton?'

'I'd say it'd be six years ago by the time they had it all sorted. The day after they 'prisoned him, we got a brick through the presbytery window … but thank the Lord, that was the last we heard of it.'

Badder thought there might be something serious to go on, took as much detail of Tobin and only one other name and calmed the women down with profuse gratitude.

Badder was frankly irritated by the women's intervention. Chocky was frustrated by the mess, but Badder thought he was checking out all the trifling mess and not focussing on the most likely culprits, Hu's wife Holly Stannton – if that's who she was – and Leo Nicholas. If she gave any credibility to Chocky's notion that more than one – a conspiracy! – was in action, who were the other conspirators?

While the cat was away she set Alan and Mike onto finding out their possible assistants in drowning Hu Stannton – finishing him off. Holly surely must have some reason for leaving London for these parts, and most likely that would be someone, some people with whom she had some relationship. She surely couldn't be totally alone in the world outside the City.

Nicholas was a team leader, a popular man, but they hadn't looked into his wider circle – a loyal deputy, an adoring trainee?

She was not alone in her frustration at the boss's obsession with 'Opus Dei.' After seeing off Hu's relatives she found that the two DCs had sought her out. Alan had been on the computers and found a Facebook Page had been started up in support of Leo Nicholas. Of course it was mostly youths, 'Hands off our youth workers' and lots of great support for Leo as a caring bloke who had given the ones 'no fucker cares about' time and opportunities. It looked like he had a wide international circle who provided exchange opportunities…

'Alan – not another conspiracy, please!' she cried.

'No but where to, Sarge? Not France, Germany, Italy, Holland or owt, but Russia … Cuba … China … Czechoslovakia… communist countries, Sarge!'

'No such place,' said Mike, ploughing straight on, 'Holly's been out and about herself, difficult to get hold of. I can't see what she's doing round here, Ma'am.'

'Oh pack in the Ma'am!'

'No such place as Russia?'

'Czechoslovakia! It's now The Czech Republic! Come to think of it, I think it wasn't Russia he took them too but Belarus and … not China, but Mongolia, wasn't it?'

'Same difference – commie!'

'Yes Alan,' she said, her hands on his arm restraining him from letting Gatting wind him up. He took it as affection. 'But you're both with me I think. Are you not both thinking we need to focus a bit more on our two prime suspects – Holly and Nicholas.'

Gatting smiled at the apparent sexism of his female Sergeant – calling the woman by her first name and the man by his surname – despite that even being a Christian name. 'Thanks Sarge – yes,' he checked with Alan, 'we're both with you on that.'

'Leo Nicholas himself isn't on Facebook,' said Alan, 'but his wife is and I was looking through their friends. She's a foreigner too don't forget – Natalya's not Natalie is it? They've got a friend called Jan who is in a picture with Nicholas doing a 'cheers', and no other mention or pic of our man. Several other foreign names, but probably her extended family.'

'She's not an immigrant herself, is she, Alan? First or second generation – like you.'

Alan was getting mightily fed up with Mike's constant digs, but he could see they cut no ice with Badder who he really was showing quite some affection. 'Like us Italians, a lot of Poles and Ukrainians settled round here after the war – she could be one of them.'

'Yeah. Good. How about you get out to her and maybe see if this Jan is his buddy-pal an' that. I've got to do a little bit to check out the family's story – that was Hu's mother and cousin nobbled me as I came in. Yet another conspiracy I won't bore you with, but I can easily clear it – I hope. Mike – how about you make an informal on Holly to update her – don't tell her anything, like – but see what she is up to and ask the things we need to know. Okay?'

They split up. Both men picked up their coats and left.

Badder got the desk into gear. She soon found Tobin and his list of convictions, a few news items and then she held her head: Tobin had been released from prison three weeks ago.

Mike found Holly's house and mobile phone numbers. Both went to answer machine. He decided to go straight to the house and when she wasn't in, he decided to stake it out. He immediately realised how stupid that was and that she might be doing the same as them – watching for likely suspects. He went to Brien Devine's house and again reduced his wife to a gibbering wreck. He wondered if her being so jumpy was because she was scared of what she knew – or what she suspected. He invited himself in, and going straight to the kitchen he switched on the kettle. He told her to calm down, she hadn't anything to fear.

She wondered how he could say that. 'But you're onto my man – you're suspecting him, I know. It's all happening again – one little thing – it's a spark, it is. It sets fire to all sorts of things and innocent people get burnt.'

Mike agreed with her – there were lots of innocent victims of criminals – including their own loved ones. But her husband was a convicted paedo – he wasn't having her covering for him. He wondered if Devine would have meddled with his own kids if he had any. 'How come you live round here, Mrs Devine?'

'Brien, my husband, was brought up here and he wanted to retire away from London and we like it – not too big and not a village in the middle of nowhere – the people are dead friendly aren't they?'

Mike thought he didn't agree with any of that. Devine was born in Ireland and spoke with an Irish accent. He thought the town was a bit of a dump and the people miserable. 'We understand Mr Devine's Irish though, Ma'am.'

'Well he is ... was born there.'

'He speaks with an Irish accent.'

She laughed. 'Yes he does. I've always thought that a bit funny, but it's simply explained: other than a few years in secondary school hereabouts, he has spent his entire life among Irish folk – Irish parents, Irish firms full of Irish workers in the building and civil engineering business.'

'Like Murphy's and Clancy's.'

'Gallaghers built Birmingham's drains – sure we rebuilt Britain for you after the war – and dug the tunnel to France too! My parents are Irish, too, by the way.'

'You don't allow smoking in the house Mrs Devine – er, either of you?'

'Oh God no officer, sorry.'

'It's quite the thing now, Ma'am, isn't it; people don't even smoke inside their own house.' He looked towards the garden, 'but outside, yes?'

'No.'

Mike was chuffed with his subtle ruse. 'Family still round here then?'

'No sir. No Family.'

'Children?' He hit the spot again.

Her eyes welled up. 'Ten. I lost them all.'

He couldn't cope with that. The wife would always make it difficult for him to see his own kids. At least they were still alive – but *ten*!

He complimented her on the tea and real Hobnobs and needed to be on his way. 'Where is Brien, by the way?'

'He's at the convent.' She was smiling now. 'If you were a real detective you wouldn't need to ask me that – he's always at the convent.'

'Or The Tin Tab?'

'No I don't think so. He's not ... only the committee meetings. He does it for Abe, Abe Grant. What a lovely man.'

''He's not', you were saying?'

She stumbled over saying, 'Not a volunteer – doesn't feel very comfortable with the young ones – just the committee. Well that's his volunteering bit – along with the grounds and garden, fences, walls, gutters ... of the Friary Convent.' She gave a damp smile. 'That's all.'

'You do a lot together – you and the Grants.'

'No I don't do anything with them – just see them at 'parish dos' – and at church of course. His wife, Rowena, is very devout. Brien goes to mass most days and often says he saw her there.

As she saw him out he was thinking how comfortable Brien had once made himself 'with the young ones.'

Gatting set off to find Abe Grant, but tried Holly's landline first – answer machine again.

Alan needed Nicholas's wife first of all. He thought she would probably work and rang the house to be sure. Leo picked up and not recognising the name, assumed it was one of his partners in the police. 'I was just about to set off Alan. Are we still on?'

'Sorry sir?'

'Safer City?'

'Wish it was sir. I wouldn't have to be finding out who had *killed a local parish priest*, sir.'

It gave Leo a shock but he was glad he was on the phone. 'You are my closest working colleagues you know?'

Alan did not.

'The politicians mostly think we in the youth service are in the business of keeping the kids off the streets, so it's Anti-Social Behaviour, Gangs of youths, Positive Activities for kids who want to spoil them for others, knife crime. Knife Crime – would you believe I was told I had to accept knife crime money – round here! Last time anybody was knifed round here was in the Mods and Rockers era.

'Lot of drugs though sir.'

'Oh, plenty of crime, but knives were the flavour of the month last year.' He chuckled at all his mixed metaphors. 'And priests get thrown out of windows – that's what you want to know about, eh?'

'Well … er … well, yes of course sir.'

'What now, then?' He thought of the time and that he should be gone. He realised that the detective probably didn't expect to find him not at work, didn't realise that the brunt of youth work is done in the evening. 'You were after the wife, weren't you?'

'No but, yeah, maybe,' spluttered Alan. He cleared his throat. 'We are checking alibis and whatnot and, well yeah, I would like to speak to her … if possible.'

'Anything's possible, constable, but at work. Tell you what - where are you?'

Leo arranged for Alan to meet Talya in a café – she was only in a small team, and could nip out for a quarter hour. Driving to meet her, Alan was annoyed that he had accepted the offer – Nicholas would alert his wife on the importance of sticking to their story.

Natalya Nicholas was most pleasant. Alan even commented on it. 'What's not to be unpleasant about – you're only doing your job and we can't have priest killers on the loose can we?'

She was indeed of Ukrainian extract – both her and Leo's dad's were DPs – Displaced Soviet Citizens who couldn't go home after the war because Stalin was killing them.

'But your husband seems to be proud to be a communist, Ma'am.'

She laughed. 'And rightly so, officer, but not a Stalinist! We're, well Leo really, he's a *Trotskyist*!' She twiddled her imaginary goatee and raised her eyebrows, but the young detective obviously didn't get it. 'Stalin ruled the USSR and Stalin *killed* Trotsky – they're not all just commies. Leo's a died-in-the-wool Marxist. In 1938 his dad was fighting for Trotsky and the Third International's hope of leading the international working class to political power. He was oppressed by the Poles who made him join their army!' She didn't notice Alan's eyes glaze over and continued, 'You're not a Toff are you constable? Don't you think the working class in this country are being oppressed by these public school Tory boys?'

Alan did think that, and though his Italian Granddad was proud of him being a Policeman, and telling him the Tories were the party of Law and Order, he had discovered that what they wanted was the law to focus on poor Benefit cheats and not on the off shore accounts of the rich.

'So you and Mr Nicholas are Ukrainians, well sort of, and belong to a wider community of East Europeans?'

'Well, our parents would, but it's getting a bit thin for us – we'd never even been to Ukraine until the Iron curtain came down. Then it was difficult – who would we find, what sad wounds might we open – so me and Leo were just tourists and basically reminisced about what might have been.'

'Friends?'

'Yeah – got a few. Oh Commies, eh?' She mocked surprise at what he was getting at. 'Excuse me! What has this got to do with the priest?'

Alan was not happy about her levity on this serious matter, it set an alarm bell ringing. 'It's to do with suspects, alibis and who can back them up, Ma'am.'

Talya bit her lip. 'Mm.'

'Who does your husband associate with – commie or otherwise?'

'Mm. Well he has a big team of youth workers – he likes them and they seem to like him. Someone's always got a birthday, anniversary and such like. Leo's one of four and I have a brother and sister, there's a whole gang of cousins, niece and nephews...'

'So – tell me, then – out of all those, who will Leo most associate with - say three or four best friends - excepting yourself I hope!' Alan smiled.

'Mm.' She held her chin. 'Other than family – he's close to his big sister Geo – Geovana. Oh and he has a drink now and then with an old college friend, Jan Princip.'

'That all?'

She turned down the corners of her mouth and shrugged her shoulders. 'Not easy constable, sort of dobbing in my friends and family to a police investigation of a murder. It is a murder investigation by now I suppose?'

He didn't answer that – he didn't know himself – so he took some contact details and let her get back to work.

Holly was at the side gate for the Convent garden. It was a pair of wrought iron gates to get a vehicle through. She was to one side peeping every now and then at her Dadda. He was engrossed with tape measures and sticks over by a far wall. She couldn't make out what he was doing unless it was planting a hedge. It seemed a bit stupid to her to be planting stuff in winter. She looked at her watch: March the eleventh. She pulled up her collar. It didn't seem like spring to her.

Brien didn't seem to be skulking around like a guilty killer, but then she thought that was his way with trouble – ignore it and it will go away. If he had come to her rescue – some hope, stupid idea – and if he had tackled Hu and maybe, just maybe it had come to violence, could he have shoved big Hu out of the window?

He had never said anything to her about their 'affair.' For the couple of years after she stopped him – no more little wifey – and before she went away, he never showed guilt, remorse – anything. He simply carried on as if everything was normal; as if he was normal; as if she could ever be normal ever again.

She even wondered if he ever felt it had been wrong. He must know that was why she left. But why had she left it two years without saying anything? Two years? Ten more like. Nobody listened. She decided not to shout - wasn't her own husband a total perv – much worse than her Dadda – maybe?

Poor Mammy – she should have guessed, but then she probably didn't.

Had someone pushed Father Hu out of the window? Brien really needed to know this. Ginny had gone on endlessly about Hu's betrayal of all that she and Brien held sacred in relationships between man and woman. Brien felt that their 'elephant in the room' was that both of them had been of the dying breed who actually went to confession to a priest in a confessional box any more. Even Father Hu had bowed to the pressure of knowing the vast majority of his parishioners had not carried out their annual Easter Duty of confession and communion, some for decades, and gone along with the fad for 'Penitential services.' Ginny didn't feel her soul clean after these. Brien couldn't comment – his soul would never come clean again.

He thought a row of raspberry canes were a much more productive way of 'hedging' the ugly wall and as the top of each one was breast high to him, he tried to visualise and sense the centre of gravity, pivot point, lift and speed that would be needed for the big man to flip over the balcony.

After about fifteen minutes Holly abandoned her station and went to the old Nissen hut that Brien's friend ran his drug project from. She staked that out. She saw that the man's car was there – she had seen it at his house and at the church. He had driven it to the pub. She had followed him all the way to Worksop and the cabal met up there. They must have something going on – why go all that way except to not be seen together?

There was quite a bit of coming and going – must be quite a few druggies round here? How come she didn't see any? There was almost always one of them standing outside having a fag – their legal drug.

He was coming – the big man had two full carrier bags, swung into his car and set off. She panicked straight away as he went straight up to about forty five in the middle of town. Holly was never a fast driver. The traffic lights cut her off and she saw him disappear up the hill. She noted it was Gainsborough Road. Was he off to the scene of the crime – the Loseborough. That was it – she got it. How stupid – Gainsborough and … The light changed and she set off again. She did go up to forty and luckily too, for from the brow of the hill she just caught the man's car indicating left at the end of the straight. It was a narrower road winding a bit and she caught glimpses of his car – she was with him now. He indicated left again and headed down hill away from any housing on a single track road which seemed to become a farm track fairly soon. Her heart was pounding, the road was bumpy on her bottom. She winced and realised she was too close now.

It wasn't as if she was in a marked car like a police car or anything – or that he knew who she was anyway. He pulled up and negotiated a large puddle outside the entrance to an old works or factory. The wire fence gate was locked. Once she was out of his way she went past and round the bend at the end of the fence. She had some difficulty finding a space to stop, as there weren't any lay-byes or passing places in view. She went further on, spied a section of edging obviously used by vehicles to let others past, drove on, turned and came back to it.

She jumped out and ran to the fence to see if the man was there. His car was parked now and he wasn't in it. Where was he?

She looked through the wire fence – single story buildings – no windows, some boarded up; lots with no roof. Weeds had grown to the height of the building but only the stalks were left by the winter. Holly wondered if she could hide if he came back again. The other side of the lane was scrubby old bushes. There were also a few bits of bush the other side of the fence. Only some of them had leaves. She made a run for a couple between her and the entrance.

She could then see down the old factory driveway.

She heard a few whistles – a signal. She ran a little nearer to the gate and behind one of the bushes against the fence. She heard a metallic clanging. A sheet of corrugated iron fell from one of the huts and a head popped up. The big man came out from behind the hut.

How had he got there?

He was chatting with the head. She couldn't hear what was said.

She noticed the fence was full of holes.

A loaf was passed from one of the bags, then more groceries, a few cans. Why didn't he just hand the bag over? Another two youths appeared from further down the drive. They were handed some food. The man followed them out of sight. The first head clambered out and ran after them.

Holly dared not go any closer. She waited a while. The man reappeared, empty handed now and he was being followed by a small group of lads. They seemed to pleading with him as he strode away from them. Voices were raised now, but she still couldn't catch any words.

The man stopped by the first hut, looked all around and surely saw Holly, but didn't register. She checked her outfit - jeans, dark green bomber jacket …she lifted her navy baseball cap and swept her hair back under it. She crouched.

The group were remonstrating with each other and the man was shaking his head. He started back to his car, but changed his mind and went back. He looked all round before opening his coat and getting something out for two of the young men. They snatched it and ran off. Holly decided to run back to the bigger bushes half-way and hid herself.

'Drug project eh?' she said to herself. 'I know your game my man – groom them with food, keep them sweet and dependent on you!' The Bagman, was it? She had heard that somewhere, probably on television.

The people who had worked on Tobin's case were worse than useless for Badder. She desperately needed to get it out of the way – to not have Chocky chasing this red herring – yet another of his conspiracies. She thought it such an unlikely story, but she had no solutions of her own. Her first proper case and nothing was going to come of it – an unsolved … well what was it? The Super was surely not going to let them go on forever, and what would the Coroner make of it?

She walked out of the station. She looked up to the heavens and was not so sure that it was the bright sky that made her eyes water.

On the High Street she was seeing nothing in the shop windows and soon found herself scooping some sugary froth off a cappuccino.

What did she expect – that the police would follow the whereabouts of everyone they had investigated? She didn't. Tobin had left prison and disappeared off the radar. 'Prob'ly in Spain if he's got any sense,' was the best offer she had. 'Could have millions stashed away – we never got any of it back.'

She had put Tobin's name through to the Border Agency, but wouldn't hold her breath.

There was an adoring couple across from her and she felt a pang of envy. She needed her blork! She knew that Chocky would want to see the team when he got back – but it was going to be late evening for them all. She decided to let the men get off at a decent hour and hold out some hope of a day off at the weekend – even a separate day apiece. She certainly needed one herself and warmed at the Saturday night plans the flatmates had to induct her into the delights of Sheffield's

Eccleshall Road area: A whole gang of mates from Uni and Hallamshire hospital were gathering and several blork opportunities were promised for Iruna – 'on-a-plate you beauty!'

She had decided she was going to get slaughtered and she was going to get laid. She had mulled over the idea of doing both and thought the former might ruin the latter. She was *almost* a thirty year old virgin. No she wasn't. She had the requisite 'get rid of it' fumbling the summer after her GCSEs – it was a complete 'is that it?' event.

In the sixth form she thought that couldn't be 'it', so tried again with a sweet lad that had been after her for ages, but he seemed a bit of a nerd. He was surprisingly good fun, the nerdiness was actually shyness. She took it softly softly … and so to bed. It was okay, they even gave it a few more goes over a couple of weeks but she still felt it wasn't all it was made out to be. She felt no real love for him and it was probably mutual. They didn't even 'chuck' each other, they simply stopped bothering.

Then there was Justin … and Justin … and Justin.

The couple across the café from her stood up. The girl held her little bag with both hands and the look she gave her boy as he returned their tray … oh the look!

Iruna had to remind herself why she had moved North or 'oop Narth' as she was amused to tell her Thames Valley Police colleagues. She hadn't told them *why* she was moving. Racists among them thought she would obviously be going 'home' to Bradford.

She had had considerable success attracting girls - lesbians – but she thought it was time that she went and got what she wanted for herself – a 'blork.'

She was satisfied, she couldn't say pleased, with her decision to settle upon Doncaster. She was definitely pleased with her house-mates, Louise a teacher and Becky a bank clerk. Together they explored the nightlife, went to the cinema and even a couple of hikes out to the Peak District. She had decided against joining a judo club - that seemed a step backwards. An occasional jog round Lakeside and a very occasional swim at the Dome kept her trim enough for the demands of being a Detective – Detective Sergeant Iruna Bahadur. She was grinning and nodding to herself. 'Badder will do.'

However, she was frustrated about the widespread notion that you got a future partner by getting off with them at pubs and clubs – it seemed medieval. Even her Mum had left rural Ireland - run away from the fear of the 'Lisdoon' matchmaking festival that had Iruna's grandparents hitched – dance, dance, dance until a farmer snatches you. They had threatened to send her off to it if she didn't get herself a fella soon.

Iruna was sitting at the Lakeside with a clipboard on her knee. She decided she needed a profile of her target. She was struggling with the image of sandy hair and freckles. Sweet, not macho. Not big – neither tall nor hefty. She tasted a kiss – a gentle kiss and closed her eyes. A steely shock shot through her as she realised it was Teresa she was thinking of. Teresa who? She didn't even know. She thought of them meeting at Carfax – the dead centre of Oxford - and the feeling of unforced mutuality of the walk down High Street, past Queen's College under Victoria's watchful eye, onto Rose Lane and down to the Cherwell by Magdelen Bridge. Then the kiss.

Iruna wondered why she hadn't resisted. She hadn't joined in. She thought it was all rather sweet – a kind of 'ah bless' moment. She knew that Teresa had looked at her, but she found a serious interest in a passing punt and the frolicking three couples who were at risk of falling into the river. She broke Teresa's spell by nudging her and nodding at the frolic.

Teresa's surname was unknown to her: she had looked at her watch, said she was on the late shift and rushed away. She did peck Teresa on the cheek – yes she did – and raced off towards Old Tom and the Police Station on Saint Aldates. She jumped in her car and looked at herself in the mirror. She took a very deep breath and drove home.

There were no punts on Doncaster's lakes. She tried to bring up Teresa's face and could see the light hazel eyes. They were surrounded by the freckles, but Alan Prisco's freckles. She shook her head, but then thought about it. It was cute that of all things he was a policeman who couldn't get the word 'burglar' right – it was 'burglear' and her initial cock-up had been to lose an 'ambulence' – not any ambulance, but a 'particlear ambulence.' Very cute. He wasn't thick though – corrected her spelling *and* grammar in her three word sentence 'WHO DROUND HIM!' Sweet.

The flatmates had all got off with a blork at one of the clubs and one of them had had a quick shag round the back. She wasn't saying which one, but it was not Iruna. That was just not Iruna. But she did not want to start again in a whole strange place and sustain any impression that she was a lesbian. She found herself speaking rather a lot about Justin - 'long term relationship' it had developed into, but 'it was going nowhere.' 'Yes it hurt', 'it still hurts', 'but *men*!' – big-eyes and tutting all round. 'Nuff said.'

It didn't hurt in the right place, so Iruna knew she was right to move on … and a move up north sounded right. 'People up north are more friendly and down-to-earth.' It was looking that way.

Alan was only a bit taller than her – and Teresa. He wasn't macho. Was he married? Ought to be in a relationship, nice bloke like that. She had better find out and not waste anytime hanging around – he didn't look the sort of man to push himself, but a bit of a pushover for the wrong sort of woman. She might need to save him. 'Nice blork eh, Runa?'

On Saturday she was definitely 'out of here' by four o'clock – 'deffo Chocky!'

She fancied some chips for her lunch, but picked up a healthy looking filled ciabatta and slunk off back to the station.

Abe Grant was not going to be de-railed from his mission. With Hu Stannton out of the way, he knew the rest of the Housing people would be relieved not to have to care for druggies and their self-induced problems, so it was back down to The Tin Tab and the Big Society volunteers. And yet even more was going to be expected if Leo had to redeploy his paid youth workers away to youth club work. Sorting out his own son Ivan had been an 'if you want a job doing well' situation, and he was still doing it. Ivan was 'chuffed to bits' with his big screen telly and peace seemed to have broken out between him and Marina.

Scraping himself under the fence and giving the signal to the 'kids' at the old factory, he held out hope that here were a few more lost souls he might turn around the way he had Ivan and Marina. If it weren't for Tin Tab, Abe knew neither of them would have any need for furniture…

'You are a soft touch' Abe, he told himself as he went back to the car. 'Never give them money.' 'What Never?' 'Well hardly ever.' He smiled as he slung the car into gear. 'Bus fare to get to interviews.' 'Whatever.'

What if the Disclosure and Barring lot wouldn't let him carry on? That shanty will be demolished soon and the other volunteers … well they do what they can, bless 'em.

It wasn't quite the 'the awfullest beating he ever took', but after his meeting in Maynooth, Chocky felt he had been mauled by sheep. After attacking him for even questioning any possible wrong-doing, the priests were all *so reasonable* about what they did do. All the time they were giving *so valid* explanations that he felt like screaming 'but why?' or even the kids thing of 'yebbut, nobbut.' They could see his incredulity and were hurt by what he thought was purely internal head shaking.

'Father Hu, God Rest Him, was ours, one of us, he belonged'; and 'why wouldn't we want to persuade him of the error of his ways'; and 'we knew he would thank us one day.' They were so self assured.

But where were they on the evening of…? No, Chocky knew he couldn't ask them that. Of course, if they had conspired and things had got out of hand – he knew they would not have wanted to actually murder Hu – then they would have a string of alibis lined up. He could broach the idea of it being an accident with them – but they would not be anywhere near – they would not even have crossed the Irish Sea.

'Look-it Inspector,' said the man who seemed to have been Hu's personal tutor or mentor throughout his training, 'Hu was, man-and-boy, part of our community. He came first to us as a lad, went away to think about his vocation and came back to us before his University. He was already on his way, so we,' he looked to the other two priests for support, 'we thought mebbe we could trust, even test him, by telling him to come back even later. And, Inspector, so he did. You've seen him?'

Chocky didn't want to admit to only having seen him laid out cold on the mortuary slab, so just nodded.

'Fine young man, I can tell you.' He again looked for affirmation, then went on, 'I tell you we took a risk giving him such a loose rein, but it worked. He knew he was one of us.'

They all relaxed into their seats, hands washed of the detective. He said nothing, but continued to look round the group. One of the others, a gaunt older man felt moved to attack.

'So the young woman thinks we frog-marched him back and brain washed him, does she?'

This wasn't quite what he said, but it was what Holly had insinuated, so there wasn't that much reading between the lines happening here. He shrugged assent.

'Might this be a way of describing the same situation in less inflammatory language: Hu was due for his 'annual appraisal' as part of his holiday and visit to family. He didn't come and the mother rings us – us mind, not himself. He is not at the presbytery, but we contact him. He's away and we find he is 'questioning his vocation.' We know what this means – we've heard it all before, haven't we Fathers?'

They stuck out their lips nodding.

'We suggest it reasonable that he talks it over with us. He is reluctant, just wants to think. We do tell him he owes us, and lovely lad that he is, he of course does agree - but he wasn't for moving.' He turned to the Italian De Niro character next to him to carry on – 'The Enforcer', thought Chocky.

'So Father Tom here,' indicating the mentor, 'got hold of one of Hubert's oldest friends, one who went through training with him, now serving in a Glasgow parish, to meet up with us and Hu in England.' He stroked a hand over a fist.

The mentor took the baton. 'Hu was so pleased to see us, he burst into tears. Well you seen the big strong man he is, we were like a bunch of girls there. It can be a lonely life you see, and he didn't see it coming. In the end he needed a bit more company...' He looked down and coughed. Chocky thought the man was speaking from personal experience. His colleagues leaned almost imperceptibly in support. He looked back at the inspector. 'He wanted to come back here and have a bit of thinking time without influence.'

Chocky almost burst, but held his gaze.

'Well I suppose I mean the influence of the young lady, and peace and quiet in community with his brothers in religion hereabouts. He and I had a daily catch up was all. No water-boarding at all.'

They all chuckled and felt their brother had carried the day.

Chocky ascertained that the stay in Ireland was a peaceful couple of months and at a final meeting all agreed that Hu had had a momentary lapse and was keen to get back to the job in hand. Unfortunately, no matter how deep and fine the soil, no matter how much sun and water the plant gets, sometimes, someone will come and steal the fruit.

With great reluctance Chocky didn't feel he had much option but to agree. Despite just hearing new allegations of Clerical Abuse in Holland, he didn't want to feel bad about the church, but he couldn't help feeling bad about some of the people in it, and especially here in the Emerald Isle there had been too many who let down the laity like him. The green he now most associated with the isle was not shining emerald, it was more like mould.

With several hours to kill before he caught the once a day plane, he wanted to call Iruna, but held back because he had nothing of substance to say. He needed to replicate Iruna's white boards so set to work with pencil and paper over a pint and a pie. The Guinness tasted no better for being in Ireland.

As Iruna got back to her desk Alan brought the local paper in – Thursday, of course. It had run a profile on Hu Stannton the 'runaway Priest' with a by-line 'They didn't expect The Spanish Inquisition!'

'What's that supposed to mean, Alan?'

'It's getting at us Ma … er, Sarge…'

She took a quick look around. She stage whispered, 'I told you - Iruna when it's just us, eh?'

He smiled and moved closer so they could look over the page together. The smell of her was gorgeous. It wasn't perfume. It was her, plain and simple; no make up or falsies; clean – the genuine article. 'Chocky was on about 'Opus Dei', a secret sect or summat. The rag's got onto a Monty Python sketch.'

'My brothers used to like that. Me and me mum didn't get it – silly, what bits I saw. Is it a man thing?'

'Bit before our time but I remember out on the beat we used to get shouts about silly walks. John Cleese?'

'Fawlty Towers? Now that is funny!'

They giggled together. 'But this isn't, is it? Chocky's gonna go mad.'

'Well let's hope he's managed to completely scotch this rubbish on his little jolly.' She flicked the paper. 'Who do you think did it Alan?'

He perched himself on a desk near the whiteboard. She joined him. He had to squeeze up to not fall off the edge. Nice. 'That Leo … or Holly.'

'Not Leo *and* Holly?'

He turned to look at her. She was in kissing distance. He looked down and laughed. 'To be honest Iruna…' He cleared his throat, 'I 'an't got a bloody clue!' He put his hand over his mouth. 'Am I any use to you?'

They were almost nose to nose, now. She could smell him; him; his sweet breath. 'Tha's a leading question, Alan.' She elbowed him off the desk.

She gave him a hand back up. They were both a bit sweaty. She swiped her tongue across her teeth. 'Chocky hasn't mentioned them two conspiring. But seriously Alan, do you suspect her at all?'

'On'y in so much as a partner is always a prime suspect. We always avoided domestics when I was in uniform – you can't win. And we haven't to forget that two thirds of all murders are domestic in some way.'

'Yeah well that would include his mother and his housekeeper cousin in our scenario too, though wouldn't it?'

'And that Pauline is a scary piece by all accounts.'

'Her and Holly. In fact Holly is also … spooky.'

'Spooky! Funny word, Iruna.' Alan was being careful with the privileged use of her Christian name. 'Christian'?

She 'woo-oo-oo-ed' in his face. He wanted to grab her. She turned back to the board. 'Wow, furrst she were all out of it and Chocky's babyin' 'er an' 'at - sorry, I've slipped into Ox-furred – when we first met her she was zonked, completely out of it.'

'Wouldn't you be if you'd just found out your husband was dead?'

'That itself was a bit funny – how did she know?'

'What y'mean?'

'Well Chocky went to tell her – officially – but she said someone 'with a funny voice' had already phoned her about it. Chocky was about to kill me for letting it out without seeing her reaction, when he realised she meant a bloke.' She smiled as she heard herself not say 'blork.' 'You shoulda seen her. She looked as if she'd been beaten…'

'Well maybe she was!'

'Say that again?'

'Domestic – maybe she was beaten up – by Hu.'

'What, and she got the better of him and shoved him out the winder? Brilliant!' She threw her arms up and then round Alan. She pecked him on the cheek, then stood beside him staring at Holly and Hu on the board. Like she always had with Justin, her arm was linked round Alan's. She didn't notice.

He did.

'Makes more sense than bloody Monty Python!' They burst into laughter.

He told her about his appointment to meet up with Leo's drinking pal after school – 'he's a teacher' – but having spoken to Nicholas, it maybe warned him, but Alan couldn't see any light coming out of his 'particlear' line of inquiry. 'They seem like a nice bunch – that youth officer guy and his family – for commies!'

Iruna wasn't sure it was too strong a word but she felt Leo 'hated' the priest. The Irish Clerical sexual abuse scandal could have wound him up into a frenzy. 'You know one of the things about the traditional communists is that they believe any act is justified if it is for the greater good.'

That was a deeper observation than he expected of Iruna. 'Go on.'

'He reckons he is like a guard for children – 'Safeguarding', you know? And he did goad Hu Stannton, Devine backed that up.'

'Did you believe him about the blood on the door?'

'Frankly? I dunno.'

They laughed again.

In her recently promoted role, she started to feel that she shouldn't be letting them have as much fun investigating murder. They read over the local rag and found that the Da Vinci Code type sensation had nothing substantial to it at all. The press were scraping round the same way the police were. She asked Alan to mock up something for the press, especially the Sunday Red Tops before he went to meet Jan, but first speak to the local as they will be part of some national chain.

Leo knew that he had to expect the police to check up on him with his friends and colleagues. He was not so sure what impression he wanted them to glean. He needed people to know how much he cared about children and young people – more people ought to be concerned about the effect of austerity cuts on their own children, and their futures. Did he mind that they could find out how much anger he felt at the corruption in the management of some public services – including that of the Catholic Church?

Leo was still feeling wound up about the effectiveness or otherwise of the DBS relative to job cuts when he had met his friend 'Jan the Czech' for a swift one after work. There weren't many in the pub and they got the comfy settee in the snug.

'The Catholic Church is for bad people', he started.

Jan choked on his beer. When he'd finished wiping it from his nose and the tears from his eyes, his sardonic friend continued.

'Well, think about it - Baptists - saved. New Lifers - born again. Mormons - why, they're even going around saving their dead ancestors.'

'Ye-es?'

'Jehovahs - among the numbered few.' Leo moved to pluck a new idea from the ether. 'But look at the R.C.s - all riddled with guilt, forever confessing, but failing again, then feeling bad and having to confess again. B-A-D.' He eyeballed Jan.

Jan's mouth chewed down, lip curled, lips pursed then split and he snapped his teeth a couple of times. 'Zurely, the Catholics are good ones - or they wanted to be?'

Leo was warmed by his accent and considering he was Orthodox and wouldn't be offended, continued his anti-Catholic theme. 'Ah - my point entirely. Catholics want to be good, but in fact even they recognise they're bad ... and I agree with them.'

It was eyebrows this time for Jan - both on the ceiling; shuttered right-down over the eyes; just one up quickly - attacked by the other into his Roger Moore impersonation. The beady eye now pinned Leo...

Leo took a good swig, then inspected his beer; held it up to the light; sniffed the bouquet; sipped the froth; rested it and ... Reverie.

'Hey!'

Leo gave a little cough/laugh and smiled sweetly. 'You wouldn't believe the reluctance to be Vetted by the Criminal Record Bureau. You know all of us youth workers have to be. Well the volunteers who work with children have to be too.'

'Have to be?' asked Jan. 'Who's going to make them?'

'You're right, of course, they don't have to be, but woe betide any organisation that has allegations made and they haven't made sure of the people they are recruiting.'

'What is this funny talk 'woby tide'?'

'You're right – sorry – old fashioned talk – my mum used to say it. It means they better watch out. Under the next stage of the Safeguarding Scheme they need to Disclose any offences, they're Vetted and could get barred. In this great new Big Society, we really have to create partnerships with Voluntary Sector groups, who also do work with our clients – young people. If they aren't cleared they don't get any Grant Aid. Of course, there's not many who'll work with our sort of youth…'

'Not me.'

'… but ruddy bible bashers – on a mission. But - one bunch already in there are saints - the other lot know they're not - all bad 'uns.'

'Come the revolution, eh, Leo? But look it - which do you prefer, the complacent bunch or the ones trying to be good?'

'But they're still all bad, don't you see - all God botherers by day, boy buggerers by night.'

'Leo! That's below you. '

Leo held his glass up to the light. 'Lovely beer this one.'

'Just how many boy buggerers do - you - know?'

'Hundreds.'

'Ah well - in your job I suppose you come across a few more than most of us.' Jan ratcheted up the pitch: 'but I don't know any. You're like a doctor, you are, you only see sick people, so you think everybody is sick.'

'No I don't - I see a lot of sweet innocent children and a few adult predators - all wearing dog collars.'

'Sweet innocent children? I thought you were dealing with binge drinkers, marauding round the town centre, spliff-tokers, pregnant teenagers, VD…'

'STIs.'

'Vat?'

'STIs - we haven't had VD since the war.'

'Speak for yourself.'

'Czech - mate.' Leo gave the high fives.

'Bit American for you, that isn't it?' said Jan.

'Yeah, but the kids love it.'

'Anyway,' Jan continued, 'I thought you felt very highly about the church people who help out at your drug project.'

'Oh I do.' Leo felt bad all of a sudden. Wound up as he was about the lost forms, he had 'gone off on one' as the kids would tell him. 'Oh, Jan, you are so right. They're saints.'

'Didn't think you believed...'

'Haha. I need to unravel, don't I? I was making a very wrong sweeping generalisation. Picture those people who give out communion at church.'

Jan did.

'They don't see that they should be cleared. They think: 'But I only give out communion – if I were to mess about with kids, everyone would see me.' They do not realise they are being Huntleys – that bloke who murdered the two girls.'

'Everyone knows Huntley, Leo.'

He frowned, nodded, then chuckled, remembering that he himself had forgotten when Gina mentioned Huntley out of context. 'Yes, but do they know he had not been checked - Vetted? He was 'only the school caretaker, he doesn't teach the kids,' they said. They didn't think of what he said to the kids; 'you can trust me – I'm the school caretaker aren't I – I take care for you.''

Leo knew he could be seen to argue against himself if he wasn't more careful. The Disclosure and Barring Scheme was useful, of course. They did need to know if people had a record, but that was a minor part of keeping people safe. He was so peeved about the cuts to the real people who safeguard, that he was at risk of undermining the value of the record checks.

Jan picked back up. 'You mean he didn't have to be cleared?'

'No, but now they all do. It's his fault that maybe eleven million people will have to be cleared from now on, under the upgraded scheme.'

'That is ludicrous. Where d'you get that figure from? Eleven million - across Europe?'

'No – it's serious – just the UK.'

Leo took a quick look around to see he wouldn't be heard. 'Even I've got to get myself cleared.'

In mock horror Jan said: 'Ah. You mean your aren't? Seriously though – aren't you?'

'Half the teachers in the country weren't. If they were already teachers, no one saw the need to check up on them. Or me. Or the head of the Youth Service.'

'Wow. Will that make eleven million?'

'Yes. Absolutely anybody who works in the 'area' of Children or Vulnerable adults – like caretakers, librarians, maintenance people ... do you see? I said 'works' didn't I? Well it's not only workers, but volunteers too. Didn't you read about the football Mums thing in the press?'

'I heard something about it on the radio. If you take some kids from the team along with your kids more than once a month ... something. Sounded ludicrous.'

Leo wiped away his smile. He thought it cute the way Jan, so long in the UK, could still slip into Czechlish when excited.

'Vat vill stop them?'

'Vat vill *bar* them?' he teased. 'Don't you mean who will catch them? What will bar them from working in those sectors is any criminal record, nay, more than just the record, even people on List 99 – ones who've been accused...'

'What, not found guilty, even?'

'Ah, not only been accused, but had enough against them to seriously consider taking them to court, when the accuser backs off.'

'So if someone found out you had been accused of having sex with a girl on one of your trips, twenty years ago, but it had never got to court, you could lose your job.'

'Hey, let's move it away from me, eh?' Leo felt his collar. 'In theory if that happened to a colleague – the boss even – they would be sacked.'

'You must have some in your team?'

'Ouch. Jan. What did I just say?'

'Seriously. Dope? Teenage sex – nineteen with a thirteen year old?'

Leo had a think.

'The thing that's really eating me, is that all this CRB, valuable as it maybe, is purely an administrative exercise and it costs money. But the funding for people to do the Safeguarding – youth workers especially – is being cut. Around the country, whole youth services have been scrapped.'

He finished his pint. 'Oh Jan, what are they doing to me? Better go anyway. Let me just say that I do not include my lovely Christian people at the drug project in my rant. They're saints in their way – good old boys, and girls – in my way too.'

Iruna drew a doodle grid on a pad and started putting names in. She remembered sociograms. She tore the grid up and threw it in the bin. Now she spread names out on a page and made a sociogram – she ran lines to connect the people they knew were connected. So how about Leo and Holly? If Hu had battered her, would Leo come to the rescue? Oh indeed he would! So does he actually know her? The team had not made any links.

Iruna realised that she had only the single link for Holly – not realistic – she must know somebody. The conference guys were all linked, both separately and together.

They were all linked to Nathan Helliwell, too. The link to Brien was a bit tenuous.

The women? Iruna felt that Pauline Stannton should really know Holly. Every 'ex' needs to know who her bloke has set up with – 'what's she got that I haven't?' Iruna dotted a line between them.

Mrs Devine would know Hu, Abe Grant and his wife, but maybe not Leo Nicholas. Could she have wound Brien up to give Hu a hiding? He looked a fit bloke for his age. She smiled and wondered if a seventy year old would ever be 'a fit blork' for her.

Then there was the gay context. Where was Alan with the gay couple? Where was she with all this gay talk? A threesome with Teresa and the butch oarswoman?

She shivered – that was good, it made her realise that though she was attracted to Teresa, it was as a person – it was not about sex. Chemistry? 'Maybe, Justin,' she thought.

Back to Hu – a threesome would certainly ruffle up the sheet. She wrote and underlined the word 'sheet' – three times.

That led her to the Hotel possibilities. Could Suzanne the chambermaid have had anything to do with it? The chambermaid was good enough for Strauss-Kahn. The team had taken her story at face value: she said she found Hu, but had she in fact been the one to push him? Had he been with her in the bed and he got rid of the sheet? Why? Shame?

Had *she* got rid of the sheet? Why? Had she pushed him? She certainly made the effort to revive him. That didn't work – though his face was warm, it was from the jacuzzi and the forensics showed he had been dead for several hours.

Were drugs involved? Abe Grant and Tin Tab? Did Hu think he could fly? No, it would be in the toxicology. Focus Iruna.

Smoking: ash on the balcony, cigarette in the water, cigar singe on the dressing gown.

DC Mike Gatting brought the photo of Leo Nicholas onto his screen. If he was the killer, what was the Safeguarding all about? Could a man who cares so much about young people, kill an adult? It seemed that he believed in the old commie stuff about the greater good. They had lined up the Czar and all his family and shot them, even the children. But it's not so simple. Mike knew that among themselves they were always bumping off someone with not quite the same interpretation of Marx.

Was Leo Nicholas, despite being the image of Trotsky, actually more like Stalin? Gatting didn't like the look of him.

He brought up the record. No pushover those miners' leaders – hard men picketing against the 'Met.' Mike knew there were soldiers and … thugs in those uniforms too. They had body armour, helmets and shields, and even horses, but the miners had nerves of steel and bodies to match. And a judo expert to boot. 'To boot!' he laughed at his turn of thought. He grabbed his jacket off the back of the chair – he was going to visit the youth office.

First of all he was let in to the general office for several youth teams. He introduced himself as interested in the Safeguarding processes they used and partnership – with Social Services of course, but how about the police? One of the secretaries showed him the blank forms they had to go through, and in case he was checking up on their data protection, the lockable filing cabinet in the locked room.

He gradually wheedled his way to an introduction and entry to the 'Area youth office', where he continued the discussion with Leo's secretary, Gina.

Gina was alert to his ruse, but didn't let on. Of course her boss was the Young People's service lead on Safeguarding 'Red-hot, he is too.'

215

Mike got out his note book and pretended to discover that that would be Andrew Nicholas.

'Leo, he's known as, Officer. He's actually at a police Meeting today – 'Safer City'?'

'ASBO and knife crime I suppose!'

'Knife crime – don't tell me,' said Gina thumbing a set of accounts.

Mike frowned.

'Yes I kept the budget for the grant. Leo got loads of projects going out of that.'

Mike drumming his fingers on his pad looked at Gina. 'What do you think about the CRB, Ma'am?'

'Proper! And it's called Disclosure and Barring Scheme now. All right and proper as I see it. We won't let people set foot on the estates until we've got full clearance and two references. Had someone people back-out recently – clearance still hadn't come through after six months, she took another job.'

'Lots of projects, you said. Not all done by your youth workers?'

'Oh no – mostly by voluntary sector groups.'

'And you CRB them from this office?'

Gina tensed up at that. 'Er, DBS, no, not generally.'

'No? Who does? They do *have* to be cleared?'

Gina did not want to veer into that grey area – she liked things in black and white. She looked at the team diary on the wall. Leo was unlikely to rescue her. 'Leo funds existing voluntary groups and yes they have to be cleared – of course you will know – all the fuss lately. But … when I said generally, Leo has cleared one or two workers for the poorer orgs – not supposed to!' she whispered.

'I've had a bit to do with Users – drugs, you know?'

'Oh yes – stock-in-trade for some of our detached workers.'

'Detached?'

'Yes – out of the clubs – on the estates, not that we've got many out, what with the cuts.'

'Tin Tab?'

'Yes Tin Tab – that's Carol's.'

'Carol?'

'Yes, she's our Leader-in-Charge.'

'Funny name – where is it?'

'Quite a clever name really – it meets in the Nissen hut on Spital Hill near the Old Convent Church: in the war a stray bomb landed in the church garden and blew all the windows out and possibly damaged the structure, so nobody went in until time and money allowed repair. The wife of one of our local grandees was a parishioner. The government were throwing up Nissen huts all over the country and she bought some land and a hut for the temporary church. Tin Tabernacles went up all over the country in the eighteen and early nineteen hundreds and the hut was nicknamed after them.

'When some folk wanted to help youngsters with drug problems, NIMBYISM struck and they couldn't rent anywhere.'

'Nimbyism?'

'Not In My Back Yard!'

'Of course! Sorry. Carry on.'

'In the end Abe Grant and his friends persuaded the church to let them use their old hall. 'Tabs' is another name for some of the drugs they used – E's and LSD especially, so they laughed about Tin Tabs!'

'I've heard of Abe Grant - good bloke by all accounts?'

'Lovely man.' A gleam came into the old secretary's eyes. 'He's been retired for years now, but he works more than full-time for those kids.'

'What's there to work at exactly – I don't understand?' The DC was as disingenuous as he could get.

'The main thing is they get thrown out – of their own home and then out of the hostels, would you believe. One hint of them in possession and … on their ear.'

'Only right I say.'

'We know this officer, that's why we still do it – nobody thinks they are worth it as much as Abe and Leo do. We listen to them; let them have showers; get them benefit info; keep hostels sweet; finding them somewhere off the streets is the most important thing – they'll be injecting hard drugs in three months, else.'

Mike was warming to the two men. Not a lot, but like the rest of the team, he was feeling the pressure to eliminate some suspects from their enquiries.

'Do you think the sentiment arises out of personal experience?'

Gina showed her alarm.

'Sorry, it's a bit insensitive, but based on the 'set-a-thief-to-catch-a-thief' idea?'

'What was it you came in for Inspector?' asked Gina.

'Well actually,' he coughed, 'I was hoping to catch up with the youth officer about Safeguarding and police clearance – CRB, er DVS, etcetera.'

She shook her head. 'D, *B for Barring*, S. Well I'm very glad you didn't catch him,' she laughed, 'he is fuming about that at the mo.'

'Something else the commie is angry about! Who is he lining up *now*?' 'What – not about Child Protection?'

'Interesting way of phrasing it! Interested about Child Protection – fanatical almost – but not about CRB. It's almost a mantra with him that 'It's people not paper that protect children.' He wants a clear cut system that keeps a track of those barred – a 'Portable CRB' that is not dead the day after it's done. The Government have promised it, but ahem, the new government has put it on the back burner. More work for us admin, less money for youth workers. Seriously! County have diverted millions to keep up with the CRB system and … well Leo thinks there may not be a youth service by the time this Government is finished.'

Mike thought this might be no bad thing. He decided he had better make a move before his gaffers wound up the 'Safer City' meeting and Nicholas got back to call his bluff.

He stood and took a look around and wrinkling his nose at what appeared to be an old factory. He decided to count the eighty year old police station as a blessing.

'Bit hot on smoking, the County? Does Leo have to go out by the canal for one?'

'Pah!' was all the comment that clumsy remark deserved, but Gina did add, 'Colliers don't smoke – might set the pit on fire.'

Gatting felt it was a step too far to follow up by asking if Nicholas's interest in Child Protection was because he was abused himself.

When Leo got back Gina was out to lunch. He only had time for a few bites out of his sandwich before his deputy Stephen Hall came in for his supervision session. He indicated the need for 'a quiet word' and they decamped to one of the little damp smelling interview rooms.

Loyal Stephen was keen to update his boss on the firestorm blowing up about the police activity around Leo. Leo kept a glum face and let Stephen fill in some detail. He was actually quite happy with it all – happy not quite the word – but pleased that his action had unwittingly produced a lot of support. He wanted the support to be for the issues, but the personal support was not unwelcome.

The kids – especially those out on the street – had got wind of Leo being harassed. They knew that Leo and Hu had worked together for years, for them. He couldn't have killed Hu, or wanted him killed. The staff felt likewise, but were not naïve.

'And how about you Stephen? How do you feel?'

Stephen had heard Leo ranting about the clerical abuse, the Catholic Church is for bad people, and 'Father [spits on floor] Hu' having his cake and eating it. 'Well some of us know how bad you feel about Hu Stannton – like taking Tin Tab clients, yeah?'

'And defenestrating him, Stephen?'

'As ever, you got me there Leo – left school at fifteen, me.'

'Threw him out a window!'

'Oh Leo, no. That's exactly what I mean.'

'So I did?'

'Oh Leo, Leo,' poor Stephen felt moved to lean over and lay his hands on Leo.

'It's alright Stephen, I'm *kidding* you, but I think you are telling me that I might have a no-smoke-without-fire problem with some of the team.'

' 'xactly! Your giving them the bum's rush and they don't like it.'

'How many times do they need telling I could lose my career – not just a part-time job?'

'Careful, Leo – 'not just' is all some of them can get.'

Leo held his head in his hands. 'I know – you know I know. But is there any gratitude for the extra work I put their way and the support I do give them?'

He pulled himself round and assured Stephen that everything would work out in the end – maybe not everyone's job, but the Hu Stannton situation. He explained that he trusted Stephen fully to cover for him – he saw him jump at that and had to reassure him that he meant only to cover for any unforeseen absence, despite the fact that Leo could foresee it himself.

He led Stephen through all the various teams and their pieces of work, offering support and clarification at every point. Leo's focus on this alone convinced him of his innocence.

Next up, Leo may have to face-off similar uncertainties at tomorrow's Joint Management Team meeting. He had better have his Annual Plan corrected by the morning, too.

Alan was trying to give some non-judgemental consideration to Chocky's obsession with the gay sex thing. Alan's mates had always used terms like 'brown-hatters' and worse to show their unhidden hatred of gay men. He thought it a bit rich when he thought they all loved a bit of anal if they could ever get it. He had never tried it on with any of his girls because to him it just sounded painful – he didn't want anybody buggering him, or even a bit of finger for that matter. 'What's love got to do with it?' or rather what's it got to do with love, he wondered. He believed it was okay if that was what you both wanted – and the same went for men-on-men, if you were that way inclined. Live and let live. Alan wasn't inclined.

He didn't like the way Chocky had made the quip about sex in bed, not in front of Iruna. Dirty old bugger wanted her for himself and was trying to get one up on Alan.

It was *five years ago*, and he was so drunk he really didn't know if it was him who was spied having a knee-trembler out on the fire escape with that pretty Police Support Officer at the Christmas party. He didn't deny it, as the lads were actually crediting him with a success. Enigmatic grin. Nobody else claimed it though. She never let on one way or the other, but Alan gave up the chase in the New Year.

If he ever had the chance he would never 'do the dirty' on Iruna Bada-bada-boo. 'She's out of your league and anyway get her bloody name right lad.'

So if the pair of gay men fancied a bit on the side – one of them say, sneaks off and has Stannton. The other finds out and tackles Stannton about seducing his pal … but who drowned him?

Another option: one tries it on with Stannton who turns him down and gets pushed out of the window. Gay runs back to mate who sneaks out and finishes Stannton off to stop his lover being recognised. Do either of them smoke cigars?

Alan enjoyed the couple he had tried over the years. Would Iruna approve? The two girls he had most fancied had gagged on the burnt taste when he kissed them. It had been a near death experience for him to give up the coffin nails, but he had done it. Sweet kisser now. But what if she enjoys a sly puff?

Chocky thinks there's a sly puff or three on Iruna's whiteboards!

He didn't tell her he's not so good with words. He texted Mike to do that for him – *please?*

The Desk rang up to Badder to say a very excited Holly Stannton had come in. She stage whispered it to Alan as she passed and he shouted to her to hold her – he needed a word about the phone.

In the interview room the considerably taller Holly held onto Badder's shoulders and revealed her morning's discovery. 'That big guy from the Drug Project…' she nodded to Badder to fill her blank.

Nathan Helliwell came into Badder's head, but he was no way a big guy. 'Sit down please Holly. Tell me calmly what you are excited about.'

Holly told of her morning's 'observations' – 'Brien's got something to hide – too calm altogether, but that big old man – I can't remember his name…'

How did she know any names at all? 'You mean Abe Grant – he's the leader of The Tin Tab we gather.'

'Yes, that'll be him. That charity thing is all just a smokescreen, you know? It's a cover for his pushing – pushing drugs – he's a fucking dope pedlar - I seen him!'

Badder sucked her teeth for a moment. 'You saw him what, Holly, take something out of his pocket?'

'Oh come on detective, what's an old man doing scrabbling round under fences at a derelict factory – giving a secret signal, supplying the druggies with food, then sneaking little packets out of his inside pocket.'

'Sure it wasn't money? You said they were begging him – begging is usually associated with, like, money?'

'Do you think I'm naïve? He looked around to see he wasn't being observed – all very, very shifty.'

'Do you give money to beggars, Holly?'

'No never, they just spend it on drugs.'

'We-ell?'

Holly had a think, she started to sink, but wasn't giving up. 'Grooming! Fucking perverts are always being nice to get what they really want later. I know about this stuff,' she coughed into both hands almost covering her face. The squeak came back into her voice, 'he gives them a few loaves and cheap tins of beans and sells them drugs, keeping them in need of constantly topping up his pension.'

Badder thought it quite a good story – Jackanory. She restrained her smile. 'I asked if you gave … and you gave the right answer…'

'Right answer? You playing with me?'

'Don't you see: a Drug worker would never give them money – he knows what you know?'

'Officer!' Holly shouted, 'my point exactly!'

Iruna had a little wobble. Was her explanation going to be at all convincing – even to herself. 'But, I tell you Holly, this man is loved – everybody loves him – he works day and night with these like, outcasts, Holly, and maybe *he* would break his own rules, they are *his* rules, you see, and give them money because they need it. But because they are rules, he checks he is not being watched breaking them? Get me?'

'Ha! What a load of twisting, convoluting old bollocks, if you don't mind me saying. What's he got on you?'

'More to the point we've got, er, nothing on him.'

'You sure? What's your hesitation?'

His record and being a lifer of course. But that was from before she was even born – a lifetime in the life of a lifer. All clear. 'We are working on some clear leads,' she lied, 'and you will understand that it's a process of elimination. Mr Grant is not at the forefront of our enquiries, but…'

'Got some clear leads have you? Come on then – Hu is my husband – tell me what you got.'

Holly stood. 'We are the professionals, Holly. You loved your Hu, so leave it to us to find his killer. I can tell you that we have ruled out accident and suicide…'

'Got some sense then!'

'… but my colleague DC Prisco wants your help with a detail, if you can give us a just a minute.' She checked how Holly took that as she left the room.

When Alan entered the room Holly was relieved that the woman hadn't sent in the 'heavy mob.'

Alan wanted her to explain about her phone records. He did not like what she had to say.

He thought he would take a supplementary question about smoking. She offered her open handbag and insisted he smelt her hands. Nice.

He looked at the dormant recorder, recognised that she was not under caution and let her go.

Mike was also looking into smoking and got a useless response from the receptionist at the Loseborough. His charming build-up to the question had been a waste of time. She and Suzanne the housemaid had been at the hotel for several years, they weren't friends and smoking is so strictly forbidden - 'it's a question at your interview these days – and you don't get a job if you smoke' - that she would 'be amazed, *amazed*, if any of the staff smoked at all.' That's maybe, then.

His list was reduced to just Abe Grant as the only smoker and then 'only roll-ups.' Surely a cigarette smoker would also enjoy a cigar – especially a freebie, or a gift. Did the hotel sell or supply them – business conferences? His return call received a definitive 'no.'

He thought about trawling the 'shirt-lifters' but left that to Alan and did his work for him on a press statement. What he did was fill his paper bin with no press statements. What have they got to state?

As he was driving out to meet Leo Nicholas's pal Jan Princip, Alan Prisco was thinking of his own granddad who came over from Italy after the war. He wondered how anybody in Britain could be racist – it really was sheer ignorance and stupidity. 'I'm pure Anglo-Saxon' they cry, 'just like Her Majesty!' He dearly wanted to ask them why they don't just fuck off back to where they came from then, but the German/Danes were so ignorant they wouldn't get it.

He imagined that Princip and Nicholas would have maybe communism in common.

'Quite the opposite, Inspector. In fact *we* are quite the opposites. How you say it: 'opposites attract'? Leo and me we fight about communism – with each other I mean.'

Leo had met Jan at University and his general intrigue with all things Eastern Bloc, attracted him to the Slav. He liked that Jan saw himself as a Communist, but that Stalin and all the USSR presidents were no more interested in the common people than the Czars had been. This concurred with Leo's reading of the situation – Communism, more acceptably referred to as Socialism in the West – was still something ordinary people needed.

Leo had brought Jan home and made him feel welcome in the extended community of families of DPs from the war. The irony for Leo was that Jan was effectively a refugee from the Eastern Bloc – an oppressed Christian.

Prisco was intrigued. It came back to him that his granddad used to row with other Italians about Mussolini, but he had decided to opt out as politics were breaking up families all over Europe – and the war had done enough of that.

'So Leo seems to believe in the greater good, like anything is justified if it's…'

'Yes I know what you saying Inspector,' he chuckled, 'he would seem to be a bit that way. Not a big fan of the Tories, he's not. Simple one that, considering his position.'

'Trotskyist, you mean?'

Jan snorted. 'Aye well, not Stalinist, we agree on that one – wouldn't you? What kinda name's that *you* got Inspector.'

Alan's turn to laugh. 'Dead right. So you're Czech and I'm Italian, yeah?'

Jan nodded. 'I'm Bohemian, but I'm not *a* Bohemian!'

Alan shook his head. He didn't follow that up. 'Tell me about Leo and the strength of his politics. You met at College?'

'Ya I know Leo many years at Uni – we were both a bit older than most of our colleagues, and I teased him about selling Socialist Worker. 'If only he knew what I knew,' stuff.'

'Socialist, eh? I've always thought about Nazi equals National *Socialist.*'

'Exactly. That's the kind of area we always strayed into. Stalin – leader of *Socialist* republics! But Leo hates Stalin, who killed his hero Trotsky. Like Marx, he loves the proletariat and hates capitalists. But to be fair on Leo, he is more like an anarchist – he really hates the … bosses, dictators, power seekers, etcetera, who always seem to Leo to become corrupt.'

'Power corrupts – is it corrupting him – he's a manager?'

That stung. Jan sat himself up. He frowned at the constable. 'Now listen Inspector, Leo is my friend, he is that because I like him. He is sullen, gloomy, sarcastic, arrogant, proud. Magnanimous, kind and funny. Doesn't like voicing his feelings, and maybe he would do something, say cruel, rather than speak his heart out in words - very good man, and I have met plenty bad men. He loves people wanting to get on with life without some power seeker taking, well taking even their *lives* off them. Like children: you know he's Safeguarder? Don't I know it! He thinks the county under the Tories are directly – not indirectly for our Leo – directly abusing children by taking away the very people who are guarding them. He hates this CRB thing – you know this?'

'Carry on,' said Alan, smiling.

'Well just like Stalin and Trotsky being 'communists', and hating each other, Leo actually sees the CRB – the main institutional tool of Child Protection - as being a risk to children..'

Alan frowned with his whole body.

'Yes, the bosses think it is enough. So they have diverted millions – several millions apparently – out of services to young people just to make sure they get the CRB forms in. Yes, you see the CRB is an … enquiry, enquiry is what it is, to see if person is criminal, but only that day and only if he been caught! Next day it mean nothing.'

Alan felt all the talk of hatred of bosses was leading where he wanted to go, but Hu Stannton wasn't Leo's boss, wasn't anybody's boss as far as he could tell. 'So he's not a big fan of paedophiles?'

Jan blinked. He nodded. He shook his head.

Alan waited – he hoped the Czech would introduce paedophile priests without prompt.

Geo was a big friend of Jan's. One of the reasons Jan was so close to Leo was because from the very first time Leo had brought him home, Jan had been smitten by his big sister Geovana. With their age gap, romance was not to be, but a warm friendship was sustained. He thought a generalisation was all the detective needed to know. 'Leo got a lot of background in child protection, you know. Nobody, even criminals don't like nonces, eh, Inspector? He got it everyday in his work. These young girls so sexy – media tell 'em they gotta be – all the time, everywhere.' He hutched himself forward and adopted a whisper. 'You Police? You tracking this Jelly guy, yeah? You know all about, yeah?'

Alan was thrown. He didn't know if this was going his way. 'Quickly then.'

'Oh if you don't know maybe it's not my place.' He decided on a prompt. 'The flower sellers' pimp guy?'

Alan's face crumpled up.

'They call him Jelly? Monitoring this guy – I think he's called Lee, James or John Lee – J.Lee - Jelly, see?'

'Mr Princip, I don't see where this going.'

'Frisco…' Jan mused. 'You Italian, Inspector?' He was wondering what he could say that would least hurt Leo's case. 'Catholic?'

'Naah. Even me granddad gave that up. But I'm with Leo. This Irish Priest stuff does my head in.'

'And Leo's.' Jan bit his lip but saw the policeman register. He decided he would try to help Leo with his worry, but would he be digging the hole deeper? He decided against the Italian priest detail – it was very personal and not in a criminal record – so he continued about the flower sellers. The detective was fascinated but it was obvious he was searching for something else – something about the priest.

'We are trying to eliminate your friend from our enquiries about the 'pampering session' he laid on – you have heard about it?'

'Oh yes – very tragic.'

'Did, er, Leo tell you about it?'

'Course, yes. Pretty damn cut up. Spoiled a good idea, didn't it?'

'Bit stronger than that for Hubert Stannton and his family.'

'That his name? What actually happened?'

Alan couldn't tell if Jan had craftily steered him into this corner; whether he was fishing for detail, or actually did not know. 'We are trying to clarify that. We were hoping you may have some detail about the build up … because you see, Leo has told us, and the others guys have confirmed, that he goaded Hu and that Hu got him mad, angry. You're his friend – had he discussed him with you?'

Jan did not want to lie. 'Was this the guy who used to be…'

'… a priest.'

'Oh, I was going to say on The Tin Tab committee - and moved to the Council housing department, and sort of 'took' some of the key clients with him. Leo was pretty mad about him. Is that what he goaded him about? The hotel thing was for The Tin Tab guys wasn't it?'

'When did you see him last?'

'Just a quick one over the weekend.'

'How was he?'

'Okay.'

Alan thought he would have to break cover. 'Did he get on about the paedophile priests?'

'No – no mention of priests, though I did think the Stannton guy, sorry RIP, was the runaway priest.' Jan thought then that Leo had possibly studiously avoided mention of his hobby horse.

He looked at the Inspector. He didn't want to drop Leo in it. 'I suppose he entertained you with his ongoing revolution? Well ya … he does set a high value on himself and, it seems from some of the things he tells me from his safeguarding work, not without a certain justification!' He coughed a laugh into his fist. 'But seriously, I don't think he could actually kill. Do you?'

Alan thought the whole thing a bit forced.

He wanted to check out the youth Club and the times Leo was actually there. He took a circuitous route via Masterton, up to the Loseborough, noting timings, then back to the station.

Alan and Mike welcomed the text from Badder telling them to have an early night, but to get their act together for a serious make or break meeting first thing in the morning. Alan popped his head round Chocky's office door to check Iruna was okay. He hoped she might invite him in to share her planning for Chocky, but she didn't even look up, simply nodded. What had Chocky done?

Sergeant Bahadur was feeling so tense in the build up to her DI's return from Ireland. She was scolding herself: what had she to be so worried about? It was her first 'real' case as a Sergeant, but Chocky had held the reins after the first few minutes of the investigation. What was it her old boss used to say: 'the first three minutes of every relationship set the tone for all the rest'? She had lost the body. She had to call for reinforcements.

That really was not her fault. The fact was that after a week of investigation it appeared that somebody was likely to get away with murder. She had no belief that Chocky would be returning with a gang in chains.

She had to explore what she considered to be Chocky's fixation about anal sex. It was homophobia, pure and simple: all that Catholic stuff – he couldn't get away from it. She thought of her mother for a moment, but then Teresa entered the picture - again.

Iruna liked Teresa. If they had exchanged contacts, where would that have led? Maybe not 'Oop Narth.' But she had consciously avoided giving Teresa her number; she didn't want her to make contact. Was Iruna herself homophobic? She laughed mirthlessly at the likelihood: 'takes one to know one, Iruna.' Not true, not in this case. Was it also wrong to regard Chocky's suspicions simply as homophobia, or was Iruna excluding a real suspicion in a form of inverted homophobia? She was also uncomfortable with the notion of *heterosexuals* consenting to anal sex. She shivered.

She had better come to some open-minded opinions on Hu Stannton's situation: Jez Fylde seemed to be a prime suspect for Chocky; he had no alibi, but they had no DNA. The two PCs put some store by the gay couple staying at the Loseborough; they were each other's alibi, but they had no apparent motive.

Nobody seemed to want to consider Hu's wife Holly in the equation. Iruna had to. Holly had openly admitted to the blood – they had intercourse just before

Hu left home on the Wednesday – Holly putting down her marker? 'Oh, no Iruna, not a red marker!' Seriously, it could be possible, but would they have had both … it did not bear thinking about. Not for Iruna.

Had Holly lied about simply driving around, she knew not where? All these damn telly programmes following people on video. If it were realistic, Iruna would have sown this up the second day. She took consolation in 'Crimewatch': even with all the video technology they had, the culprits still looked like ghosts. Grenley bypass has 'average speed cameras' all the way, but not where it crosses the road from Clayford, and that road meanders through several low tech villages. They had tried the garages and the town centre videos with no useful sightings. There are two car parks at the Loseborough, one with a video that steams up. You would hope that the perps would not know that, however. 'However' – a word that might haunt this investigation.

If he, she or they planned the killing, they would make the effort to avoid detection, and so not even park at the hotel. If it was all a horrible accident – which to Iruna seemed most likely – something should show up on the reception and/or the car parks.

Holly? No.

Grant, Devine and Nicholas are all seen leaving reception as they had declared. Devine's car can be seen leaving the main car park. The back car park is in a London smog in the subsequent ten minutes.

Any suspicion of the conference team rested on them not actually leaving the car park, or in Brien's case, returning. Iruna could see that all three could conceivably have motive: Devine not wanting his conviction for child Sexual Abuse getting out of the confessional; Grant afraid of losing his life's work if the ex-priest let on about his conviction forgotten thirty years ago; Nicholas with his 'anything is justified for the greater good', coupled with both his anarchy and hatred of Child Abusers hiding behind priestly vestments. If it was him she even felt some sympathy.

Banging her head on a brick wall for so long had clouded her vision so she decided to take a little jog into the park and along the river to the supermarket. Night had fallen. It was a crisp clear evening promising frost, but even the last quarter of the moon enabled Iruna to chase her shadow. Commuters taking the short-cut through the trees, despite it being the end of the day still seemed to have a swing in their step. Promises, promises? Coffee and a cake in the café along with bit of people watching, distracted her from some of her stress; a nice looking lad catching her eye and smiling, helped some more. She held his gaze but he returned to his newspaper. She found the dozy disco hit 'Saturday Night' tapping her toe.

She jumped as she shambled back into the briefing room to find Chocky silently staring at her whiteboard. He tapped it with his pen, turned and walking up to her, he took her in his arms. She didn't resist. He smelt of some sort of booze. He stood away and indicated her to sit.

He seemed abject in his apology to her. 'I don't know if my involvement has helped you at all. Red herrings are flying; wild geese are deep-sea diving and the Super's going to pull the plug.'

That surprised Iruna as there did seem to be a lot of leads that needed following up.

Chocky gave a quick rundown on how the Maynooth thing did have to be followed up, but the explanations all seemed so reasonable. He didn't waste any more time on detail. He didn't need Badder to tell him that the lads hadn't come up with anything from the gay fraternity, or else she would have texted.

'Evidence Runa – we have got diddly-squat. Where's that sheet? That'd definitely incriminate somebody, that's why it's been hidden.'

'We *have* thought of everyone haven't we?'

'We've thought of too many: we should've focussed on the two main suspects, the youth officer and the wife.'

'But we still haven't got any evidence on them … well except the blood on the door.'

'I wasn't happy with my first impression of Holly Stannton, were you sir?'

Chocky pouted his lips.

She went on, 'so a 'man with a funny voice' had told her that her husband was dead; she was stupidly lovey-dovey with the corpse; you hinted she maybe a drunk…'

'Did I?'

'Well in passing – it was certainly an impression you gave me going over that first time.'

He scrubbed his chin. He didn't think Holly had even had a drink – quite focussed even. 'In case you're wondering, I did have one can of beer on the plane! What other impression did you get from me?'

'Delicate – aching? She said she and Hu had a row. If it was on the phone, it was a very short one.'

'Yes, but if he had shouted her to, say, tell her to leave him alone for a minute, sort of thing, first ever cross word even? Could have been a shock – then when I arrived, Hu hadn't, and she had received the funny phone call.' Those footprints on the balcony were the cleaners weren't they?'

'Yes sir.'

'And the slip marks didn't reveal any kind of prints? Bit weird that if they were Hu's they didn't show as some sort of print. The lads get anything from the trail of smoke? There's ash on the balcony and a cig in the jacuzzi. Was Hu having a sly one when someone pushed him?'

'Coulda been Suzanne.'

'What, she lied about not smoking? Someone is! Cigar too, eh?'

Chocky thumped the desk, threw his head back and said 'Sergeant Bahadur, will you forgive me please, if I say … 'fuck, fuck, fuck'?'

She waited a little before asking if they hadn't been too nice to the suspects; would a bit of pressure work – arrest maybe.

He climbed down and sat nodding at her. He stood, did a turn and resting his fingertips on the desks said, 'It's our last resort. Book 'em Danno!'

Friday 12th March

After a welcome 'half day' off and a good night's rest, Detective Constables Alan Prisco and Mike Gatting were in the canteen early and discussed their edginess at what might happen next. Mike being the more experienced was ready for the team to be scaled down and thought he might be 'dumped' on Badder to steer the young sergeant though an ongoing investigation, but probably alongside another investigation.

Alan was miffed that he hadn't come up with something to help Iruna on her first case. Mike revealing 'his hand' started him calculating how he could be the one to work alongside her.

They agreed that they hadn't come up with anything but shit-creek - no pun intended - reference the anal sex. Neither of them liked what they regarded as homophobia on Chocky's part, but they had no better explanation. Mike thought the wife's behaviour was strange: her rant at Badder revealed a woman who was a long way from being the prim and proper 'vicar's wife' and possibly would enjoy a little more from the Karma Sutra than a nice ex-priest could think up. Alan thought that was just talking dirty.

Mike got a pound coin out and waved it at Alan: 'Wager?'

'What, about being wound up?'

'Nah! Whodunit?'

Alan shook his head. It was demeaning both to the deceased and to justice. Mike thumped him in the shoulder. Alan left half his bacon butty, stood up and stuffed his shirt into his trousers. Mike stuffed the bit of sandwich into his ample mouth and followed Alan upstairs.

Badder followed Chocky out of his office and set a paper down in front of each of them. It didn't take much studying, being a list of all the protagonists and the three words, 'blood', 'smoking' and 'anal.'

'Cards on the table, everybody – the Super's, well, I think the Super wants it left as accidental and given me only until tomorrow on this case.' He sucked his teeth. He felt like he was throwing water over a pack of young puppies. 'Badder will carry on with it with at least one of you lads. But …' He looked out of the window and back to the team. 'Evidence is what we're short of. We're long on possible suspects, but none have motives for murder. It doesn't look like an accident or suicide … so it's more like we are looking for …'

'A reason, Chocky?' said Badder. 'That's the thing – it's maybe a reason to be angry with him, but a motive to kill him?'

The three subordinates looked for Chocky's thoughts on that. 'With the Coroner – see, he drowned, but she wants to know why - a reason for death. The inquest is opened and adjourned, of course, but at this rate, it's got to lead to an open verdict and that reflects badly on her and on us. With all this … stuff, we can't solve the mystery.'

'What about looking down the telescope the other way, sir?' was the abstruse suggestion from Alan. 'Well I mean can we kinda like work out something by not looking at who feels *bad* about the priest but who feels *good* about him: who loves him, who cares about him …'

'Working through to leave who hates him, eh Alan?' suggested Badder.

'Yeah, like that.' He looked at Mike who seemed to have switched off. 'What you think?'

He didn't.

'Okay, so our prime suspect is the one who's supposed to love him – Holly - and of course his mother,' said Chocky.

'And Pauline too.' Mike was listening after all, 'but she is the woman scorned – used to love him and now hates him! Have we given her enough thought?'

Alan didn't like the appreciative smile Iruna gave Mike. 'I got the impression she mothered him, maybe even more than his actual mum, if you think about it. She has probably lost the most in this situation. She loved him as her young cousin, and gave up marriage for him.'

Mike snorted.

Alan continued, 'She devoted her life to him. A mother lets her caged bird fly, and Pauline Stannton then took him on for what, seven or eight years? She could see it being her whole life's work, snatched from her by another woman.'

'Yebbut, if she's going to kill anybody, why not Holly?'

' 's true, Runa, Sarge, but it wasn't Holly who hurt her, was it?'

'No Alan, good point. Sir?'

Chocky cleared his throat. He really did not want another suspect brought into the frame. He had considered the priest's housekeeper and discounted the idea. 'Alan. Mike. Iruna.' He looked at them one at a time. He brushed his knee of dust. 'The thing is, sorry to say, at this stage … without evidence, the last thing I need to take,' he tapped the list with his finger, 'is yet another name on this list. Unless … unless we can ramp up the MO and Motive for one or two of these, we are dead in the water, tomorrow.' He clapped his hands together. 'I'm not finished, though. Badder and I have come up with a last ditch stand: pressure. The bully-boys on the telly would get them up against the wall, roaring and spitting in their faces. Well Badder's gonna try aren't you duck?'

They weren't laughing but it did lighten things a little. They waited for him to continue.

'We're going to arrest Nicholas and Holly and give them a real grilling – tell them that they did it and how…'

'I didn't think we knew that,' frowned Alan.

'There's the risk - we don't. But they might break cover. One of them might break. But! Before that, we are going to arrest Suzanne … the chambermaid – cleaner.'

That shocked the two constables.

'Two things she's not helping with – the smoking, and of course the sheet.'

'I can see the smoking bit,' said Mike, 'you mean she might have lied – ash on the balcony, fag in the jacuzzi?'

'That's it.'

'But she won't take the blame for the sheet.'

'She might feel she has to,' said Badder. 'It was her who, reluctantly, told us about it, yeah? Maybe she's invented … well, come up with a story, eh, Chocky?'

'It has legs. See, she found the body, but did she put it there?'

Mike whistled. 'Nice one! Bit of a jolly freshened up the grey cells, there sir.'

Chocky could take that from a man of the same generation.

'And the chambermaid was good enough for that millionaire banker guy.'

'Dominique Strauss-Kahn,' said Badder. 'Yeah I thought of him.'

Chocky smiled. 'Right, then, we'll arrest Suzanne for wasting Police time in the course of a murder inquiry. Pretty serious. Seem right, sergeant?'

'Yes sir. And Nicholas and Holly for … *attempted* murder? Work on the idea of a row getting out of hand?'

'Aye, and I want to know where Jez Fylde is too, because if we haven't got anywhere with the others … look I'm sorry guys, but I want to bottom this anal…' he groaned and put his head in his hands. 'Yes well, you know what I mean.'

They agreed that Alan and Mike would bring in Suzanne and find Fylde. Chocky and Badder would arrest Leo Nicholas and Holly Stannton, and they would let them all chill in the cells. The whole team would spend time on the interviews one way or another, making good use of the two way mirrors. By four o'clock, they will have made a decision for Chocky to take to the Super on Saturday morning.

Badder had a quiet word with Chocky to explore the idea that she may get some support from the DCI – she had been very supportive to Iruna. Chocky didn't say so, but he thought that a bit naïve. 'She's been supportive all along Iruna. You'll have seen her popping in now and again?'

'Yes she was looking at the boards one time. She nodded at me before she went out.'

He rested his hand on her arm. 'If they do downgrade it, they *will* leave you with it. Then you can turn to the DCI for all your support – and you'll get it.'

As ever, Leo arrived early for the youth service Joint Management meeting at County Hall. Unusually he was not buzzed up to Conference room two, but was asked to wait in reception. Two of his Area officer colleagues, after giving him cold greetings and a funny look, were waived through to the lifts, ahead of him. He was looking vacantly at the girl serving at the coffee stall. He hadn't done wrong – management can't do anything with rumours. His line of vision was interrupted by a belt buckle, a suit. Wyndham Leyton, Director of Young People's services, waited for Leo to acknowledge him.

Neither of them rushed. Leyton waved him over and set off walking away from the lifts. Leo did consider ignoring the ignorance and staying put, but followed the boss as he opened a grand door and led him into the Council Chamber.

Leo reminded himself of the opulent panelling, and rich, new blue carpet and velvet seat cushioning. The maroon it had been for as long as he could remember had been deemed 'Red' by the incoming Tories and replaced. The bas-relief of steel-men and miners had been replaced with a windmill, trees and ... horses.

'Now look Leo, this hoo-ha you are mixed up in ... '

'I am not mixed up in any hoo-ha.'

Leyton tutted and was about to point a finger but thought better of it. 'Your current involvement with the Police has drawn the attention of the newspapers and ... don't interrupt me please ... drawn the attention of social media, and I'm sorry to say of our Elected Members. They, that is to say we, are of the opinion that all-in-all it is bringing the County Council into disrepute.' He did raise a finger. 'We therefore wish you to take 'Garden Leave' on full pay until the whole thing has blown over. Understood?'

Leo took a long hard look at his shoes. 'Are you *understanding* ... that a very good friend to myself - and to the youth service – is at this moment lying on a cold slab in a mortuary?'

'*We* do not know that he *was* your friend and the *police* seem to be questioning it also. Anyway!' he held the finger up again.

Leo narrowed his eyes at the offensive digit.

Leyton lowered it and leaned well into Leo's personal space instead. 'Anyway, I have said what I have said and it is an instruction. We do of course hope it all blows over in your favour, but until then, you will stay away from all Council premises.' He turned to pull the door ajar.

Leo saw the detectives peering in.

Leyton turned back, passed an envelope to Leo, and strode away.

The three men thought they would let Badder try to soft-talk the chambermaid into some sort of giveaway. She was trembling and crying – you couldn't set the dogs on her in that state. However Badder had agreed with the approach of getting her to admit to something she lied about already.

'I know you need to relax, Suzanne, but I'm sorry I can't let you smoke.' Suzanne blanched.

Badder pushed the coffee cup towards her and a couple of sugar bags. 'Do you take sugar?'

'I don't take coffee.' Suzanne folded her arms. She swept a fist across her running nose.

Badder swapped the coffee for her water bottle. 'But you do smoke, don't you?'

She shot a look across the room. 'No – I – do – not.'

'It's hard giving up, isn't it? How long have you been trying?'

Suzanne sobbed.

'We know you did smoke – and until very recently – but you have been denying it to us.'

'I have not!'

Badder realised that this was true; this was Suzanne's game. 'Ah, I see. You haven't have you? So, you are admitting that you are playing games with us,' and leaning across the table, 'and wasting police time in on a murder inquiry! When did you give up, Thursday 4ᵗʰ March ... around ten o'clock?'

Badder could see that Suzanne was rumbled, but rather than waiting for her to mess them around some more she seized the advantage. 'You found the body that morning, didn't you, Suzanne. You found it because you put it there didn't you?'

Suzanne yelped and jumped up. Badder came round the table to her side. She felt dominoes falling for her. 'You had wild passionate sex with this lovely hunk and it all went sour, so you seduced him over to the window and shoved him out, that's it isn't it?' Into her face, 'Isn't it?'

The men were a football crowd before a penalty. Alan beside Iruna had his hands clamped between his knees; Chocky and Mike outside, mirroring each other's clenched fists.

Suzanne pushed Badder and ran for the door. Finding it locked, she turned and looked at Badder – shocked. Alan stood but knew Badder could handle violence – better than he could. The other men couldn't see Suzanne.

Badder had no idea what she had achieved, if anything. 'Come and sit down please Miss?'

Suzanne handed herself round the table and strained down into the chair. 'Wha-at did you say?'

Badder let her interpret what she had already heard.

Suzanne realised that this was a bit more than not letting on about smoking. She took a breath, but it was another sob. The detective let her take her time. She looked at the tape and its red light. She started to speak but managed a squeak. She ripped the top off the water bottle and took stock. 'Now look here. 'I don't smoke' is all I said. I did not lie. Now you're accusing me of murder?'

Badder pursed her lips and swung her head.

'You are aren't you?'

Badder stayed mute.

Mike had turned away from the mirror groaning.

'Well I don't smoke and you can't say I do.'

'We can say that you deceived us; that you intentionally diverted us away from any suspicion of you and we wonder why. What have you got to hide?'

'I've got a lot to lose when you lot bugger off an' leave us to pick up the pieces. This is my job. Me 'usband's pissed off with internet pussy and I ...' Her voice broke to a whimper again. 'I 'an't got ... I got me Mum ... and nothing else round here. I can't afford...'

233

Badder took a quick look at the mirror. Alan smiled encouragement – fool. She lay a hand on the table. 'Just tell us the truth, Suzanne. The police need to work with the *truth.*'

Suzanne reached for the apron pocket where she had kept her ciggies for years. She crossed her hands in her lap. 'Not fair that. Not fair saying ...' and quietly '... dirty stuff.' She sat.

Badder left her alone with her thoughts.

'I need a ciggy,' she gasped.

'I know, Suzanne.' A nurturing motherly voice at last. 'And I'd give you one if you told me the truth ... and that smoke detector wasn't there.'

Suzanne looked up with dry clear eyes. 'Houldsworth has sacked two other girls for smoking. I had a good little thing going. Up on the higher floors, on the balconies, nobody could tell. I paced meself. Get a couple of smokes into every shift.' She gave a wan smile. 'I enjoyed the getting one over on the old sod as much as the cig itself, see?'

Badder apologised to her for implying that there was more to it, but they knew she had lied about the smoking, so what about anything else? Suzanne told her story exactly as she always had, except that now she admitted that that yes she had nipped into the room, fully intending to have her smoke. She had lit up, had a couple of puffs and then saw the body. She didn't know what happened to the cigarette, and yes she could possibly have let it fall into the jacuzzi. 'But I thought DNA would show if it was mine and you would have told me straight. But you didn't, so I thought 'least said', like.' She sat meek and contrite.

Badder felt that Suzanne was probably telling the truth. She was a bit short on motive. However, in case there was any comeback, she pointed out that the scenario she had put to her was a distinct possibility – that rich banker been in the news - and they were not completely finished with her yet. She kept her powder dry regarding the sheet as a lead in to accusations of a sex romp. She left Suzanne back on the verge of tears and went out to confer.

The men rounded on her, congratulating. Mike thought it wasn't such great shakes, but 'one down, three to go.' She told them why she didn't mention the sheet, yet.

Chocky thought it would reduce the Leo Nicholas opportunities for cynicism by owning up that he was 'Bad Cop and Badder...' The solicitor raised a brow, but the inspector ploughed on: 'So we have arrested you on suspicion of the murder of Hubert Stannton sometime during the evening of Wednesday 3rd March. We feel you have simply tried to obstruct our enquiries to distract us from your guilt. You have given us a motive – even explained how it happened and your alibi is weak – you don't actually have one for the full period.'

'What, you mean I can't prove I spent a half hour on the toilet reading 'War and Peace'?'

'Your wife did have the tea you made for her – near enough nine o'clock at night by the time she got in. The youth Club was in chaos and we can't nail the time you were there – and neither can you.'

'Ooh – don't know positive activity when we see it, don't we? Noisy children equals naughty children; bring back the birch. So you know I was there. The Chair of the committee will surely know what time he was there. Some of the kids…'

'Don't give us all that! It's a crafty alibi – have loads of people see you, but in the confusion none of them can be specific – indeed you could be a generic youth worker: they knew one had been but couldn't even describe you.

'Masterton is en route to-and-from Grenley for you. The only time you need to cover with an alibi is maybe as little as fifteen minutes. We know that you did sneak up that fire escape, the night *of* the murder, *not* the night before; you went back to Hu Stannton's room and finding him in, resumed your hate-filled taunting and goading. Him having trained a lifetime to be peaceful, it's not working – you can't wind him up. Grip marks on his body show he was man-handled commensurate with judo throws.'

Leo looked at Badder. She nodded: 'You threw him out of the window, didn't you?'

Leo held her gaze while he wondered if the car park video would have caught him moving close in to the building. It wouldn't get the Fire Escape – definitely not. It was a car park video and he didn't park there. They were bluffing. He bit his lip and started nodding. 'Is that the story I told you before? I mean I would love to have done that – rid the world of one more of the men-in-black, the snakes. You get me thrown out of work; you tarnish my career for a second time, just to help cover up the institutional abuse that the catholic hierarchy have cornered the market in. I spend my life trying to get decent conditions of work for men, decent opportunities for young people to move up the social scale,' he was spitting this out between gritted teeth, 'decent care for children trashed by their own parents – and priests of course - and the system,' jabbing the table with his finger, 'the party of law and order, aided by the wrong arm of the law, just steals the jobs off us to put even more money into their banker friends' off-shore accounts.'

'You pushed him then?' They could feel his leg vibrating under the table.

Leo just looked at his solicitor. 'We off then?'

'No you are not! You are going to explain to us what is wrong with our accusation or we'll charge you.'

Leo was running his own tape along the corridors of the Loseborough. No there were no video cameras there either. There was one in reception – that's why he didn't just nip in there. There was one in the bar and on each car park. Bluffing. He raised his brow at the brief. 'Shall I let them?'

The solicitor leant in and had a word.

Leo resumed, 'Two great blokes came along with me and Hu Stannton…'

'Don't try to accuse them; it's you we've got for this.'

'…they work alongside my team to help the young people whom your inadequate arm simply wants to criminalise for paying into the coffers of your cushioned drug barons. They turn in hour after hour, Abe Grant takes calls at night you, know.'

'So do we.'

'But he doesn't get a lovely overtime rate – he gets nothing but love and praise from the kids. He founded that charity because nobody cared…'

'We hobbled him from becoming one of your drug barons – he's a lifer! You can't give us that.'

Leo didn't want to own up to knowing about Abe's record, not with having vetted and not barred him, so he twisted his mouth as if that were a non-sequitur. He thought he was still on firm ground.

Alan and Mike from the dark side could feel his confidence. Alan willed Iruna to turn on some charm.

'Leo, you're not helping either yourself,' she said, 'or us; Hu Stannton's mother; or even abused children with all this. I don't get it - the heat, the hatred – you don't know he abused kids, come on now. Get rid of this suspicion for us so that we can catch the real culprit.'

Leo thought of his teenage mother and that serpent slithering over her in his sacristy. His real motive – revenge. He didn't need that – not yet. He put his hands up and took a deep breath, looked chastened. 'Okay, okay. No more messing about. I did as I said and that's it.' He turned to Badder. 'Sorry if my righteous indignation has maybe put you off the scent – if you are any good I don't believe it should have – so, unless you can prove differently, let's all get on with it.' He stood and began tucking his shirt in.

'Sit down! You have overlooked a vital piece of evidence which shows you are not telling the truth. So one more time with the missing bits … or else.' Chocky clanged hand-cuffs on the table. Melodrama might work.

Mike and Alan winced. 'Whose are those?' said Mike looking to the custody desk.

'No I tell you what – you *prove* it.'

Chocky didn't want to lie, but he felt sure about the video camera. 'You have overlooked the fact that the car parks are both covered by surveillance cameras.' This wasn't working – or Nicholas was a real pro.

'You think so?'

'Consider it for a moment will you, Leo?' said Badder.

He smiled at her and put on a comic thinking face; stroked his chin; looked across the ceiling. 'Done that.'

Chocky stood and gestured Iruna to the door. He remembered to stop the tape and went out. 'Get me a coffee! Whisky in it. Slimy git.'

Alan, Mike and Iruna looked shell-shocked. This was getting nowhere. They agreed to put Nicholas back in the cells and took a break before tackling Holly. Chocky suggested it was Iruna's turn to be bad cop, and Alan to try the knight in shining armour if, when, Holly appeared to buckle – as inevitably Badder expected her to pretend to do.

Badder wasn't sure how Holly was going to take to being actually arrested. A peep through the cell spy hole gave no clue. Holly's slump could be deflation; could be resignation.

She smiled at Alan then sucked her cheeks in and wiped it off her face. She dug him in the ribs and went into the interview room.

Badder slapped the file down in front of Holly making her jump. She remained standing as Alan sat. She walked slowly round behind Holly and her solicitor. Arriving next to her she leaned down and whispered 'You had a row with him and it all went wrong didn't it, Holly?'

This was true, but she didn't think they could arrest her for it. She had always been aware that they could probably place her in the room, but ... well only the bed really. How come they hadn't accused her of something already? There wasn't much she couldn't agree to so far. The solicitor nodded. 'Suppose so, Miss.'

'How wrong Holly – take us through it.'

'I'm not going through it again – but how much more wrong do you think it can get but my Hupee dying?'

Badder nudged the table. Holly winced. The Solicitor frowned.

'Here you are then; tell me all that was said in the row.'

Holly whimpered.

'Pack that in – tell me!'

'So I phones him and he thinks I'm checking up on him. Well I was wasn't I, but not like that, not in a bad way, in a good way, not a bad way, see? Not in a bad way – I wanted him. I wanted him home again. I told him that and he ... he swore.'

She looked into the sergeant's eyes – very close to hers. She could smell her breath, it wasn't curry. She didn't like curry.

'Holly!'

She started to whine, 'I never heard him swore, swear, ever. I mean I heard...' She gave a snuffly giggle, 'Well you know about me,' and she put her hand on Badder's arm. It was smacked away. Badder sat down and leant in to her – staring.

''Fucking checking up on me, y,bitch!' he said. Bitch? Me? He apologised straight away, but then straight told me to fucking leave him alone for five bloody minutes, he did.'

Badder wasn't sure she believed the priest would have it in his vocabulary, so was either mucking about or coming down to the level he suspected Holly was at. 'Those words, Holly? A priest?'

' 'xactly, Miss! I thought I'd got me ... well after all the fucking perverts who had me ... well I thought I'd got a good 'un, but fuck me if I hadn't slipped up yet again.'

'Now come on Holly,' cut in Alan, 'this is a bit hard to swallow.'

She looked at the pretty boy. He would probably be the sort she should have gone for. Just the nice side of plain, but strong and manly in a non-macho way. 'You can't see people's faces on the phone can you Inspector? I thought Hu might have been putting it on – my language, for me to understand, kinda – yeah I did wonder about that. I been wondering about that every minute, sir. Could he 'ave been, Miss?'

'Did you ask him?'

'I told him that wasn't very nice. 'That's not vey nice Hupee, baby', I said. He shrugged me off and ...'

'He shrugged you off, Holly?'

'Yeah, y' know what I mean.'

'No. Tell me.'

Holly had arrived at a crossroads. No way she was going to admit being in that room – not when they know he fell from that window. She knew she was their prime suspect. She had to stay out of that room. Could they prove she was there?

The only piece of evidence Badder had on Holly was the sheet – and she didn't have that. Holly wouldn't know. She took a leaf out of Chocky's book. She sat back and looked Holly straight in the eyes – and waited. 'The bed ... the sheet, Holly.'

'Oh God!' The colour drained out of Holly.

Alan felt it drain into his face – this was brilliant.

Holly clutched at the thread of her last statement. 'You know - kinda huffed and hung up on me. Only a couple of minutes. Well I just sat and waited – waited all night I reckon.' She didn't mention bed – hers or any other.

'Okay. You've got us there Holly – you did tell us about the phone call and we have checked it – both ends. It wasn't long enough to have a row...'

'You married Miss? In love? A row – being shouted at? Called names? What's a row when the man you love shouts and swears at you for the first time? I call that a fucking row!'

Holly opened the file and carefully studied the first page. She held her finger to a line of text. 'The very first time my inspector spoke to you Holly, you said, and I quote, 'My Hu died ... and it was all my fault.' I suggest what you say happened in the phone call was not *all* that passed between you. I suggest that you phoned to simply find out he was still there.'

Holly wasn't biting.

'When you found out he was still there ... think of his bed, Holly.'

She set off crying.

Alan clenched his fists under the table. Chocky had his hand on Mike's shoulder.

'Miss, that's cruel ... making me think of my husband ... like that. His bed. Someone else ... and him dead now.'

The team slumped, except Badder – she'd seen this baby talk before. She slapped the table. 'Someone else! Someone else Holly? Come on – think of the sheet. Where's the sheet Holly?'

The whole set up could have been a tableau, frozen in time. Chocky's fingers dug into Mike's shoulder; Mike thought he was going to grind a tooth off; Alan's nails cut into his palms; Badder's stare was fixed on Holly, whose only moving part was her brain and the cogs were going so fast they couldn't be heard.

She had them! They haven't got the sheet. She whispered to the solicitor asking if he thought they were trying to plant it on her. He told her to say nothing. 'Nobody knows,' she thought.

'Good question, *constable*. Where's the sheet?'

Chocky was disappearing out of the end of the corridor when she and Alan left Holly. They found him looking haggard and forlorn at his desk. He was spinning his pen on the desk. 'I thought you had it Runa. You did brilliantly, but we've got a right pair of slippery customers, here.'

She wanted to cry. It showed.

'No, none of us could've done better. You were hard enough on her, but Alan wasn't needed to save her from you – she just didn't crack.'

'That bloody babyface stuff, sir. It's not real. Not real is it Alan?'

Alan had a supportive arm across her back. 'No way – it was *her*!'

She turned full on to him. 'Really – you feel that strong about it.'

'Hell, yeah! See the colour drain out of her when you first mentioned the sheet...'

'Yebbut, then I cocked it up and let her know we ent go' it!'

Without a word the team had let Badder get out, and each went separate ways.

Regrouping in the canteen and before moving onto Jez Fylde, Chocky wanted opinions – gut feelings – hunches. Whodunit?

'It was her,' blurted Alan. 'Same as I said to Badder.'

Badder looked to Mike.

He was swaying his head weighing it up.

'Can we keep either or both of them in overnight?'

'I was going to ask you that, sir,' said Mike. 'I can't slip a cigarette paper between the pair of them. But we haven't approached the,' he sighed, 'well the anal sex, have we?'

It was all getting too much for her. Badder felt like crying again. 'Wise up girl!'

'Show of hands,' said Chocky. 'Who says we bring Fylde in?'

They were all reluctant, but all, including the inspector slowly raised their hands. Mike added, 'but let's keep the other pair in for a while, eh, sir?'

'Okay, we'll do the same as we've done with them, we'll accuse him of having sex with Stannton, come down really hard – you and me Mike. Sparing your blushes, Iruna, Alan, but let's give him a butch-male shake-down, shall we?'

Saturday 13th March

It was an ill wind that blew Detective Inspector John 'Chocky' Blundell into work on the Saturday morning. The shakedown idea on Jez Fylde had failed to crack his story. The DI had let the constables have the weekend off, but Sergeant Iruna Bahadur insisted on being there, at least until she found out whether or not she was going to be working with Chocky next week or have the DCI overseeing a severely reduced investigation.

She spent her time tidying up the whiteboard and putting it to one side. She would be applying herself to it for at least a few minutes everyday until a hint, the tiniest hunch, wheedled its way off the board and into her consciousness. On the computer she sorted the files for each one of the individuals that were still under suspicion, duplicating copies of any detail related to each individual, so each one would have every mention of themselves in their file.

She was amazed how many there were: obviously the 'conference' guys and their wives – that was already eight? Yes eight Iruna – Stannton may yet have killed himself. Then there was the youth work woman Simone Dunne - highly unlikely; the gay couple – no; Iruna was not discounting Suzanne the chambermaid; hell hath no fury like Cousin Pauline – possible; the barman Fylde – keep an open mind; Nathan Helliwell she was very worried about, but … his file took some closing; the Maynooth Mafia's did not.

Everything Leo really wanted to know about, he really could not ask – how did Hu Stannton actually die? The family would want the body and the Coroner would want to release it, but what would be the verdict? He did not tell anyone of his suspension. He didn't do the garden. After not a second of sleep, he just could not. Talya would leave him alone in the garage. He considered getting a stainless steel exhaust for the Moggy Minor. He lay on the floor underneath the car, spanner in hand, and found himself in a fitful dream: Hu Stannton was pleading with him in Italian. He couldn't understand him, but knew that if he applied himself, he could get the drift, because until he got to school, Italian was his mother's tongue. He didn't want to apply himself. He wanted Hu to go away; no he was not going to Vet him, he was going to stand on his head and push him down into the flames of hell. He saw his mother pleading with him to stop, the mother who betrayed his father with that snake. He went to stamp and banged his knee, woke with a jolt and bashed his head on the gear box.

Holly got home and switched on the television. She channel hopped – she didn't want it to stop on a station. She got a glass of wine and came back. She could see nothing except Hu smiling at her from the cold, cold slab in the mortuary. 'Y' Lummox, Hu.'

She was in bed for nine thirty, unwashed, and she slept. She woke and showered and returned only to find birds shouting her awake and the sky a little brighter, she thought it was the moon but getting up she found the dawn was coming. 'You don't care, Holly. You don't care *enough*.'

Alone in the world – but she was not.

Ginny Devine rooted her husband out of bed at first light. He was driving her mad with lack of sleep – him lashing out, jumping awake, twitching all the night long. She got him to take her to the market and maybe on to that nice garden centre, see if there's anything new for the season – there will be. 'And we can have lunch – and carrot cake, Brien?'

Brien looked at her, a stranger. He had returned to her bed after 'the change', but by that time it was too late. It was good old fashioned winceyette pyjamas for him and a grandma nightie for her – a wonder she didn't get a night cap to go with it, (and a chastity belt?). They kept to each other's side of the bed after a very chaste goodnight kiss – except when he lashed out.

If only he could tell her who he was lashing out at. It was Dorian Grey, only the face on the canvas was his own, his young freckly face, nary a wrinkle, lovely wavy chestnut hair, fine smiley teeth. Smiley. He thought of the hair – he still had it all – and the teeth too – though they had all but exchanged colour. The face mutated into an eyeless mask framed by a full head of wild blonde hair, wet hair, gently waving in the water – Hu Stannton.

The Superintendent laid a photograph of a scrap yard before him. He hadn't said a word. She placed another on top of it - a close up of a crushed white car. Chocky leaned and peered.

'Yes that's blood, Chocky. These metal thieves are feuding, methinks. The crusher operative was too late to pull back as he saw the jaws close on the first car of the day - an unprocessed, good looking Merc. It had been placed there overnight. I need you to get onto that Chocky.'

Chocky was almost relieved that he didn't have to explain himself, but of course he was wrong. He would have to accept, and then admit his reluctance and … his failure.

Abe rang Brien to see if he wanted a cuppa. He didn't. He wasn't sure if the Garden Centre story was true or not. What were the police up to? He wasn't ringing Leo on a Saturday morning – poor lad kept daft enough hours without Abe breaking into his weekend. He wanted Father Hu buried – surely his family did too, but not quite for the same reasons. He was a calm person, so Rowena would suspect something and quiz until she found out – not like the police, more like a shrink – 'tell me about'; 'what I'm hearing is'… If he was edgy he couldn't tease her, the Coddy stuff didn't cut any ice. He went fishing.

Leo found the keys to the narrowboat and decided nobody would come looking for him there. He left his phone in the Moggy and disappeared in a cloud of smoke and dust whipped up by the Subaru.

He had a mug in one hand and the wet tissue in the other cooling his black eye. He heard the lapping of the water on the boat sides getting excitable – rain was coming.

Who was in the frame? He was, of course. He thought the wife might be – Hayley, Holly? He bet it was her scuttling away from Hu's room. Surely the Police would have found out and done something. Maybe they had done something.

He did have a faint niggling that Simone Dunne may have found Hu. For all the blue rinse, twin-set and pearls, Leo knew she was a local lass with pretensions. Steely pretensions? Her heroine Maggie Thatcher got way with murder, why not her?

Leo was sorry that Abe's record will have put him right on the spot. Always calm was Abe, always. How deep those still waters went, was an enigma to Leo. He had wanted to get in, and indeed he felt Abe had let him in. 'You alone Leo, Coddy and my priest. I need to trust you so I want you to trust me, and that means things might come unstuck – druggies will say anything, anything but the obvious truth – and when they do, I want you to know you can trust me because you hold my darkest secret.'

Dark indeed. And how about Abe's friend? Because Abe trusted Brien, did that mean that Leo could too – no questions asked? He didn't need to ask – Brien came out with it. Smoke and fire? He showed some smoke, but how big was the fire? He only got Probation, for what, a single slip, donkey's years ago?

Who would forgive Abe and Brien? People would forgive the Lifer, but not any sort of child abuser – nonce. Equal Opportunities. Leo could forgive them both. He was above that kind of thing. He, Leo Nicholas, was more equal.

After listening for a few moments, Iruna went to knock on the DCI's door, but held off. She turned away. She wanted to 'chew the fat' with her, just build the relationship a bit more. The DCI had encouraged her, was very warm to her. She thought she would just say hello and see how it went from there. The DCI was bound to ask about the case and Iruna thought she could pull a few faces, not say much, and see if the boss would pick the ball up and run; maybe reveal something about her own background, her own tricky case. They'd have a coffee.

She turned back and knocked. No answer.

For some strange reason – probably a lazy cleaner – the Super's waste paper basket was sitting in the middle of the floor, unencumbered by any obstacles to him scoring a try with it. Chocky needed to kick something. Not the Super, not Iruna. Himself?

It was a frustrating meeting. The Super knew they weren't getting anywhere with the Stannton case and there was not a serial killer stalking the women of the town, or picking off the clergy, he 'probably jumped, Chocky, come on?'

Did she want Chocky to tell that to the Coroner? He did not believe it, nor did the Super, but 'there's nothing to lose, nothing to gain. Call it quits, Chocky.'

Chocky thought there was a lot of losing going on. People, the media - who thankfully had found little more than he had, so were pretty mute – people wanted answers. Poor Holly – if it wasn't her – Hu's Mother, even the Lifer and the Paedo – if it wasn't them – they all needed answers. Real people's lives go into a vegetative state over the unanswered death of a friend.

The Super eventually accepted Chocky's offer to take on the case of the crushed carcasses – car and man - but allowed for him to touch base with Sergeant Bahadur each day. She would need to continue to chase the many leads they had and 'to find that bloody sheet.' The Super recognised that the sheet did imply guilt, would hold clues, and could not be ignored. She did not want to hold onto the body any longer. She did not know what the coroner would make of all the leads and no clues. They weren't going to propose accidental death – it was not in question. She wasn't going to have 'misadventure', and it was still a bit too soon for the 'person or persons unknown' conclusion. 'Fuck it Chocky!'

'My own sentiments, in different words, entirely, Ma'am.' He moved the basket out of harm's way and went to find Badder.

Chocky shutting his office door held an omen for her; she thought she was going to cry. She 'bloody well was not going to cry.'

He took her by the elbows and told her that she had his full support and the Super had assured him of that. They would continue the case together, but Badder would do all the leg work with one of the lads to help her. Of course she had the general back up of the station, the Desk, Switchboard, Evidence Officer…

She hoped he was going to say Alan. She had lain in bed last night wanting him to hold her.

'… and one of the lads can be with you and/or me, as and when, you know?' He smiled a knowing smile. 'Have you got a preference which one?'

'Mike Gatting please sir?'

Mary Blundell was ready for her Sweetie from Thornton. Chocky arrived home before noon on Saturday, crestfallen – just as she had anticipated from last night's silent supper. She harboured him from the storm and soaked him into her. She got the gist of regret that he had let the enthusiastic young sergeant down and would be returning creaking and rusty, one step behind the metal thieves.

She insisted on a break. He conceded. He promised to simply report on Monday and then have Tuesday and Wednesday off - they would get away.

She had a treat prepared for him.

Iruna flung herself down on the settee and the flatmates immediately pumped her up with a 'concoction.' They promised a great Saturday night in store for her on Eccy Road, no-holds-barred, meeting up with old friends from Hallam and Sheffield Uni and crashing at Louise's brother's place. 'Just lead me on', she pleaded. She was lucky she had not found out that he was another Justin until they met in a roaring pub, or else she would have *travelled* in dread. Already well primed, she purposely misconstrued him as a Dustin, saying how strange it was that such a famous star as Hoffman had so few people named after him.

He in turn did not *purposely* misconstrue her: 'Rooney, you say? Irish, yeah? Thought so.'

Justin immediately crashed away to regale an old mate, returning to her like a satellite – only more often. 'Yeah, I can see it – you got that Spanish Irish look.' He caught his sister ear wigging and whispered in Rooney's ear, 'my favourite look' - so extremely loud and incredibly close that she heard her guard fall with a crash. He was not her type at all. In another few orbits she saw him bite a girl's ear and kiss a bloke. He had lovely tight buttocks.

'Hey, how'd you know? Nobody else ever guessed?' she yelled.

He studied her afresh. 'Black hair and blue eyes – guys from the Spanish Armada, wrecked on the west of Ireland and marrying the biddies – Black hair meets blue eyes.' He kissed her nose, blinding her.

He had gone again so he missed her say, 'that's my Mum, that is.'

Next orbit, she wanted *two* sentences out of him and reaching to grab him, she tripped him and they collapsed in a scrum. Her judo could easily have saved her, but she didn't want that – she wanted to land on him.

She did land him, and at breakfast next morning his teasing continued as if she had not wrestled him into a post coital coma less than six hours before. Alright with her - she didn't need him in her future. He had helped her get rid of her thirty-year-old-virgin-almost-complex, 'wham bam thank you man!' He had recognised a side to her no one else ever had, and that completed her. He was off out to meet the lads for a Liquid Lunch, to carry on where he left off, leaving his sister to clean up his place. Iruna thought he wasn't even going to say goodbye. He hung on the door, beckoned Louise over and wriggled a pointy finger: 'Roo-ney! Harrr!' and in that incredibly loud whisper he confided to his sibling 'She offered her honour; I honoured her offer.' He turned and tripped down the path roaring, 'it was honour and offer all night long.'

'Bastard' she grinned to the mates. 'That's the last he sees of me,' she thought.

Monday was a settling day for all: Chocky logged on with the metal team, taking Alan along with him to the scrap yard and leaving him with a few tasks while he was in Sheffield; Badder and Mike went out to the Loseborough for a final check before handing the room and jacuzzi back for normalisation. Houldsworth the manager was mightily relieved, saying the owner was on his back every day and had men standing by for a complete refit and redecoration to lay the ghost of the room. Badder felt Mike sneer at him, but shivered in herself.

On Tuesday Mary Blundell, determined to distract him from his sense of failure, had dressed her husband in her Valentine present of a new shirt and the reluctantly dabbed Aramis aftershave, before taking the wheel for the drive to Sheffield. She had U2, The Police and Sting, random, old and new, on a play list for him to relax to – and she smiled at him nodding before they hit the motorway.

He awoke to see a brown sign for Kelham Island and smacked his lips. His lovely Mary had thought of everything. 'Yes but that's not all Chocky.' She knew he would want to crawl round all five pubs, but needed a build up to her surprise – 'We need to fit them all in before nine thirty.'

'Nine thirty!'

She smiled and he frowned. 'What have you got up your sleeve Mary Joseph?'

She decided that they would have an early dinner at the Milestone – 'you know I don't fancy eating in one of your mucky pubs' - and if he wanted to save the best to last – he usually did – they would need to get to the Fat Cat for nine o'clock, for his favourite beer and then...

He knew she would laugh at his sniffiness over the 'gastro-pub' notion, but having warmed up at the Wellington, she could see the smile in his eyes as he salivated over the menu at the Milestone. As the waiter was peppering his steak his phone went off and Mary's finger went up. 'Iruna.' He forwarded the call to answer, but seconds later the message tone tolled.

'Oh go on.'

His face lit up and he went to stand. 'They've found it!' He sat back down and whispered across to her, 'they've found the missing sheet – our vital clue.'

Has ever a man enjoyed his steak more?

Mary thought a tease was in order. 'When did you first see Anthony Sher?'

'Are we going to see Anthony Sher?' he looked at his watch – plays don't start at nine thirty. He mused. 'The Golden Years!'

'Got to be – it's when you met me.'

'Naa – 'cos I first saw Sher at the Liverpool Everyman.'

She laughed because of course she knew, she simply wanted to set him off.

'We didn't meet in the seventies did we?'

She tilted her head reprovingly. They had actually met at a disco at the Catholic Chaplaincy while at Liverpool Uni, but after he wound up the Baptist in her about being a 'prod' spy, the evening didn't exactly end in a clinch - certainly not the romantic kind. She later recognised the young policeman who consoled her after her cat had been strangled and dumped, but she didn't remind him until he had proposed almost two years later.

'Ah. That's best forgotten. But was ever a boy so smitten...?'

She knew where he was going and it was good – but anywhere was better than the case. His English teacher taking the class to follow a season at that seminal season at the Everyman Theatre, sowed the seeds for the boy's major in English Literature at University – and a lifelong love of theatre.

'Of course us lads would be looking out for Julie Walters and Kate Fahey, but it was Anthony Sher – you knew he was in it but it took a while to find him – he was a chameleon: a Chinaman in 'Good Woman', the Fool in Lear, and so on through the season, I couldn't believe that the body in the embodiment of Enoch Powell was actually Sher – he was amazing. Hooked!'

Mary smiled at her man in his element.

A cloud passed over him. 'Where did we see him in Macbeth?'

'With Harriet Walter at Stratford – now that's a woman taking the plaudits, Chocky, how she delved the depths of Lady Macbeth!'

Chocky was still occluded by his thought. 'Out, damned spot. Out damned spot!' he gasped.

'Chocky!'

He got excited. 'No, see,' he reduced to a whisper again, 'great coincidence – we have been searching for at least a spot of blood – we need...' he looked around something like a crazed man – Sher again, '... we need just one spot of evidence, don't you see?'

'Chocky, you are *not* at work now!'

Mary saw that he was agitated by his news but she led him on, through the imperitive Pale Rider at the Cat – and onto the Museum next door.

'Museum Mary ... at this time of night?'

It was just his sort of thing - an exploration of some of Sheffield's historical moments re-enacted by people who were saved by ... The Ghost.

Securing assurance that he would not abandon her and her plans for Wednesday to shoot back to find out who owns the DNA - 'no it won't come back 'til Thursday', she laid her cards on the table – tickets to see Sher in 'Enemy of the People' at the Crucible on Wednesday night.

He ordered up a bottle of champagne to round off what had been a sweet, sweet night. 'And here's to Saint Paddy – it's his feast tomorrow. Did I tell you that Iruna's half Irish?'

At the same time the next night, with a couple of Saint Patrick's Day Guinesses after the show, she couldn't stop him babbling on about his own 'enemy of the people' – one of the suspects in their case. This time she didn't stop him, she couldn't knock that enthusiasm – it was what she most loved about him. He had to side-step on tiptoe round the factual detail to tell her how this guy – just like Dr Stockmann, Sher's character: 'He wants to save the world, especially young people, but seems to be out for blood. The thing is, he is probably a great manager - not like authoritarian Police bosses – he wants to be democratic. Guess what? His people want him to pipe down. They are under a threat of Redundancy – public sector cuts see? He wants to fight the bosses, and them to join in, strike, whatever, but they want him to stop drawing attention to them.'

'An enemy to his own people, eh? Wants to fight you too, I bet?'

'Too bloody true! Sorry. Yes, we've had some right ding-dongs. He's a suspect because he seems to have insisted – and he owns up to – goading our victim to action so that he can fight him.'

'And he's suspect because he ... succeeded?'

'Spot on, DC Mary!'

'Spot?'

'Damned spot.'

Thursday 18th March

Chocky left the Super's office with a begrudging slap on the back and permission to go full-steam ahead with the Hubert Stannton murder enquiry. Badder was greatly relieved and set off to find the Detective Constables.

'Hold your horses, Iruna. Let's just be sure we do have some evidence on that sheet. Tell me all about it – how did you find it?'

'Well you probably know that the Loseborough owner was champing at the bit about his losses in not being able to let that room. He sent men in first thing Tuesday to strip it – everything that moves – except the bed ironically, but I suspect he will sling the mattress – I would.'

'Who would ever tell?'

'Ah well.' She wobbled her head – old Ghandi again. 'Anyhow, a refurb was probably due – bit old fashioned I thought.'

'Old fashioned clientele I imagine.'

'He's bringing that room right up to date, anyway – to try to attract the social network savvy younger ones and executive toy-mad jet setters…'

'What, jetting into Gainsborough for a G8 Summit?'

They laughed together.

'Yebbut, nobbut, that's when it fell out.'

'*Fell* out!' shouted Chocky. 'Fell out when we couldn't find it. Where was it?'

'Pretty crafty, sir, Chocky sir. It was very neatly folded and packed in a speaker apparently?'

'A speaker? Oh I think I get it – a speaker is essentially a box with the actual speaker bit screwed inside. Aha! The fronts come off some and you can choose to have the works on show,' he chuckled, 'sort of Pompidou centre - or hidden. Maybe the SOCOs … ahem, *we* should have thought of that.'

Badder left him to his own obscure references, but agreed. 'We were lucky one of the men dropped it on the stairs and it fell apart. If it had happened in the skip, we would still have nothing, but it was obviously a sheet – folded up real tight apparently – so he handed it to reception. Fortunately that dopey girl realised the significance and bagged it for us.'

'First reports?'

'Yep – blood, hairs, er … other stains. Hope to get forensics to us before lunch.'

He looked at his watch. 'Any guesses?'

She hemmed. 'Haven't we done enough of that – it's only a few minutes now.'

Chocky and Badder were sitting staring at Holly with looks of disappointment and dismay. Chocky was clicking his Parker and Badder was chewing her lips. Holly kept giving big, very big, blinks.

'So what are you doing back here Holly?' said Chocky.

She was obviously nervous but not a wreck. She looked down at her hands and back up. 'I really don't know what can have changed Inspector.' She looked at the sergeant for a clue.

'You went to the Hotel, to the Loseborough, didn't you Holly? It's not fibs, Holly, it's lying to the police and … well you need a very good explanation.'

'I have Miss, I have got a very good explanation, but you'll think it's me that killed my Hu, but I couldn't … I didn't.' She started to cry weakly. 'I have got an idea.' She reached down to her bag and the detectives leant over to see what she was going to produce. It was a pack of tissues. She looked to and from each officer. 'It's a bit delicate, see?' She looked Chocky in the eye. 'Inspector, would you mind if I just told the lady?'

Badder baulked. 'I'm not sure…'

'Woman to woman?'

Badder wasn't scared of her, but didn't trust yet another of her feminine wiles turned onto her; they worked on the men, but she wasn't sure of herself. Chocky looked at Badder, brows raised, and nodded. He glanced at the camera and the two way mirror. 'If I agree Holly, I don't want any soft soaping. Bloody well get on with the truth, the whole truth, yes?'

She blinked again and nodded fiercely. The tape was still running as Chocky closed the door quietly. Badder picked up her chair and went round to the other side of the table to remove that barrier and sit side on to her suspect. She threw her pen onto the file and folded her arms.

Holly started, 'You got a fella, Miss? Well you've had a few I'm sure – you know what they're like I'm sure.'

Badder nodded.

'But like, been in love and that, sort of let them do what they like, yeah?'

Badder was non-committal.

'Well I've had some bastards I can tell you, want you to … well do anything, you know what I mean? I was naïve at first, and stupid girl that I was, I thought it was for love, but that perv Rupert was pimping me. I cottoned on pretty soon, but everything was lovey-dovey you know? I was pretty, and pretty nice to 'em, so I never had any real problems – just got fed up with the lot of 'em. Men. So I had nothing to do with 'em for, well a few years actually. I had a friend, a girl, flatmate and that, we looked after, and looked out for each other and for a while I thought I would never want another man. Course she gets a bloke in the end and there I am – first like a raspberry, then a fuckin' lemon.'

Badder noticed her own leg was tapping. She coughed.

'Yeah sorry.' Holly coughed too. She sat herself up.

Badder thought she was beginning to identify with Holly's situation. 'Can I assume that all this was in London, and that you decided to, well, move out - fresh start?'

Holly gave her a really appreciative smile. 'That's it Miss, exactly.'

For a moment Badder thought she was going to stop there, that she thought her story was told.

'But then...' Holly had a finger pressing down on the table and was twisting it. 'Then I made a kinda plan. What sort of bloke will treat me nice, I wonder? A nice bloke I think. Then I think that *I need* to be nice for a nice bloke to like me. I think of going to church, maybe even confessing me sins and that, yeah?'

Badder smiled and nodded. Thinking of Dustin, she knew it wasn't the route she had set upon; but then thinking of Alan - well maybe. 'They don't come much nicer than priests, eh?'

'No it wa'n't like that Miss. It's like I dolls meself up and kinda hangs around this church like, yeah; and well, you shoulda seen him: wasted or what!' She looked across at the door.

Yes Badder had seen him. Without animation to guide her, he seemed just the sort of handsome bastard who would do anything he wanted to the women who let him. But it's difficult to judge character from a corpse. 'Tall, er ... *light* and handsome, eh?'

'Yes and very, very nice.'

It was a pregnant pause: was Badder about to find out after all. She hadn't needed to even mention the sheet.

'Until, you know.'

'We do know Holly, but you have to tell us.'

'You guessed the phone call wasn't the complete falling out, didn't you? Well I did find him. First I watched from the garden – you can just walk into that place. I went to the car park...'

'Hold on Holly – did you *drive*?'

'Yes. Oh – yeah, car park. No. No I drove past – I've never even seen it before – and the lane has a turning space at the end. I parked there Miss. I walked up and had a mooch round. That's a funny saying init? One of slimy Rupert's I bet. Anyway, one of the car parks just goes onto the garden. It's nicely lit and some people had lit up out there. I stays in the shadows for a while and watch. Then I sees my Hu in the bar – that's where the people have come from. He's at the bar having a laugh with the barman and I'm pretty pissed off about that, after what he's just told me on the phone. Lucky for me I'm not in my house gear. I check out if I'm okay for a posh bar. All the people I could see seemed more or less in party clobber. Ha – another of Rupert's! What's happening to me, I'm regressing?'

'You're doing brill. Go on Holly. Did you think about mingling?'

'I did yeah, but I wanted to see who Hu was preferring over me. The bar was clearing, I reckon everybody was maybe off to dinner or summat. There was still a little click at the bar – couple of nice birds giving my Hu the eye by the look of it –

but the barman had his ear, I could tell. He musta been funny. Suddenly Hu finishes his pint and raising a finger, sets off away from the bar. The barman has a quick word with the birds and follows him out. 'Aye aye,' I thinks, but he just crosses over and goes towards the reception. I walked straight in the back door and turned at the bar entrance – it was the stairs. I can hear Hu going up so follows him. I see him turn onto his floor and peep which door he went to. After a minute I creeps along the corridor and stops a sec listening at his door. Nothing. I walks on to the end and have to get my breath back – from excitement – I can manage stairs alright.'

Holly stopped to check out her audience. She stood up and stretched, looked at herself in the mirror – and into Alan's eyes, if she only knew it - smoothed her skirt and sat again.

Badder was fine and also shot a glance at the mirror for reassurance. This was the moment of truth – what cock-and-bull story would it be?

'So what was that signal to the barman, I thinks? Was he going to be coming up those stairs any minute?'

Mike nudged Chocky and Alan. 'Mincing Fylde after all?'

'Well I couldn't care about him seeing me, he didn't know me from Adam – or should that be Eve? – so I sets off back towards Hu's door. I thought I could hear the telly, but it must have been the opposite room or something 'cos when I went in it was off. But Hu was on! He was on me – right up to me gritting his teeth and, well - growling really. His eyes – oh his horrible eyes – his lovely blue eyes could've been yellow devil eyes, you know the goat thingy they do in Horrors?' She shivered her whole frame.

A chill went through Badder.

'A fight! It was a domestic!' whispered Alan.

Holly shook her shoulders and stretched her neck. She rubbed it with her hand. She stretched her lips across her teeth. 'Well here goes Miss.'

The men leaned in to the window.

The next bit was told in a hoarse whisper. 'Hu spits all this verbal at me. I dunno what to think, I never ever seen him like it. It's like someone I never seen. I don't say anything for a minute, but when he lets me go, like he wasn't holding me but, with his gaze and that, yeah? Well I was released. I takes a look round. Bit fuddy-duddy, but swish for fogies. Lovely big window so I opens it. I been standing outside for ages so it felt like an oven in that room. It was a cool night but clear and pretty. I stares at the stars a minute but he drags me in. He's a *bit* more reasonable – calmed down a bit. We talk a bit of sense.'

Her voice is back to normal pitch.

'I puts my hand on his chest and says 'what's a matter my Huey, baby?' Well that lit his fuse – He's not my baby; can't I leave him alone for one minute? He's shouting now. Haven't I got a life beside him; where'd I come from anyway; have I got nothing better to do than be checking up on him? I'm all the while trying to butt in that it's only love, I *love* him, I want him; I *want* him; I want *him.*' She sobbed.

Badder let her arms down into her lap and leaned in a little. 'So you made out on the bed.'

'What?' she shouted, blinking and stammering, 'What you say?' Holly did not want to say anything about the bed – she knew they realised she had been up there, but they never mentioned the bed so they mustn't have any evidence. 'No! No-no, no. He's fucking got hold of me now, shaking himself and shaking me. I can handle meself Miss – I had a few blokes at close quarters – I knees him in the knack…' she went into a squeal '… an' I runs outta there.'

Badder stared blank at Holly and waited for her to realise that wasn't going to wash.

'Wha-at? What's a matter, Miss? I did - I ran out and went home.'

Badder folded her arms, crossed her legs and sat back. After an eternity while Holly messed with tissues and looked at and away from Badder several times, she eventually said, 'So what was so 'woman-to-woman' about that. Which bit of Hu pushing you round couldn't you tell my Inspector?'

Little Miss Holly pouted her lips. 'Well I didn't want to tell about fighting with my man…'

Badder slapped the file. 'Stop buggering me about Holly – I've had it with this baby stuff. That's not what you wanted to say, now come on!'

She stared at the detective for a moment. She blurted, 'He *buggered* me.'

Badder knew what she said. She choked up for a second, but there was so much snot mixed up with it, she needed the tape to hear it.

'It was her!' said Chocky bashing the Constables, then bending over, he cursed the floor.

Badder had her hand on her mouth. She didn't know if she could go on. She wanted to. She put her hand out to Holly but withdrew it: Hu may have abused her, but she killed him. Which is worse? Badder knew which she thought, but a court would say differently – so would her male colleagues. She looked plaintively at the glass, but held up her hand. She was going to get it out of her.

'Oh Holly – that's horrendous. I know it is just so … I'm so sorry, but,' she glanced at the tape again, 'please give me some detail? What – he shoved, grabbed, er…?'

The sergeant was all awash in Holly's eyes making it easier for her to tell of her ordeal. 'It was like he'd practiced, it was so swift, Miss. He grabs my hair with one hand and the quilt with the other and with a single swing he pulls it off the bed, and me on – face down. Well I don't know if that was his original idea, 'cos he just froze for a second, and then it was a frenzy. He debags me and jumps straight in.'

She squeaked again and wiped her nose. She inspected the officer for a moment and continued. 'I haven't had a baby Miss, but we can guess at the pain, yeah? Well I tell you, he ripped me up. I reckon I screamed but was so choked no sound came out. It was all over in no time – the excitement. Men, eh? But he froze again. I wait, thinking he's going to fuckin' kill me now, so I keep still and quiet – probably sobbed or summat. Anyway he gets off ... and real quiet like. I kinda cringes and waits. In the end I takes a peep and he's not there – he's in the bathroom I reckon. Well I gets up, pulls me pants up and scarpers.'

Badder allowed her to recover a little. She stood up and walked a couple of steps away and looked back at the wreck. She mimed 'get us a cuppa' at the mirror.

Holly was beached and oblivious.

After a wait of several minutes during which time Holly was like someone coming out of a coma, a Woman PC brought in some tea and biscuits and withdrew. Badder played Mum, whilst wondering about how to determine the veracity of Holly's statement and how much more detail she could get. She obviously felt it was a lot to own up to, and will not have admitted it before for fear of incriminating herself in a murder. But did she murder him? The window story seemed a bit far-fetched to Badder – why did she really open it and wouldn't he have shut it again? This out of character behaviour by the ex-priest – and only relatively recently defrocked – may have been a shock to himself and he threw himself out. Was he already out of the window and not in the bathroom? Did she check?

'Well Holly, that was so much to have bottled up inside you this last fortnight. It must have been hell.' Holly was rocking herself almost imperceptibly. 'You say he was in the bathroom.'

No reaction.

'Had you thought he may have gone out the window?'

Holly stopped and looked up. 'Uh? Window?'

'He fell out of the window, didn't he Holly?'

'Did he?'

Badder's hand said 'you tell me.'

'I don't know! I wasn't there. You trying to make me say I pushed him. I didn't!'

'There isn't only pushing is there, Holly?'

Badder felt she had confused her. She didn't want to lead her; she wanted what Holly had to offer. She waited.

'What kinda like made him ... you mean without actually pushing? Made him throw himself?' she had a twisted face.

'Well how about that? Did you?'

'Well ... I can only see that, if he maybe felt so guilty about what he done to me. I mean, like I said, it was a different Hu who ... set about me like that. I didn't know he could do that – and I must suppose ... I don't know. He couldn't o' *jumped* out the window.'

Badder sat looking at her.

'What, Miss? What you want me to say? Oh yeah – I didn't see him – I didn't see him jump or fall out the window.'

'Now that is a clear statement: you are saying you were not involved in any way with him falling out of the window – careful now.' She pointed to the tape.

'Yes I am saying that!'

'It seems to me that you are also denying that you fought with him after what he did, and maybe in the … tussle, say, he fell out of the window.'

Badder was surprised that Holly needed time to consider this. Maybe she was an innocent victim after all.

'Yes I bloody well am – he frightened the shit out o' me and at the first opportunity I ran.'

Could it have been the barman – could he have been coming up and hearing someone in the room, bided his time? 'Was anyone about – in the corridor, the stairs, the foyer, when you went down?'

She sat blinking and looking round with her hand on her mouth. 'I know I sorted me top into my trousers and kinda brushed my hair before I went to the stairs. I told myself to walk out calmly as if I was supposed to be there, you know. I didn't want any receptionist seeing me or anything, so I went back the way I came. There were a few … yeah a few fogies in the bar; the barman wasn't, a girl was serving; I didn't see her look at me; there were no smokers; the garden … that was deserted too. I saw a car coming down the lane and it went past – there's two car parks i'n't there? I think the car went past and into the other, 'cos when I got onto the lane I heard a car door slam as I walked back to my car. That was a long walk I can tell you – I hurt, you know, I really was hurt.'

Badder wondered if a medical examination would help evidence. As the blood on the sheet was Holly's and she admitted it – there were some of both their hairs and no one else's on the sheet as well – she didn't see the need for any more intrusion. She looked to the mirror. She sat back. She finished her tea – cold.

As she went out to the men, puppy dog Alan threw his arms around her. Though she was smiling at Mike and Chocky, she appeared unresponsive and Alan dropped his arms.

'That was a marathon run Iruna,' said Chocky, 'very well done.'

'Right!' said Badder, 'who believes her?'

Mike coughed and looked at Chocky who was nodding. 'Good question. Let's send in the WPC with fresh tea and biscuits and all have a minute eh?'

On the way to the canteen Mike was chewing his lips thinking that this was no victory – they were no further forward at all. He felt they were going to get no further either, so he was all for disbelieving Holly's Jackanory. Alan was warmed by Iruna's secret pat on his side. Chocky knew they still had all to do. Iruna was thinking of her Mum for some strange reason – 'Rooney!'

'I don't think you could have got any more out of her – I mean I don't think she had anything else to say.'

'Really, sir?' said Badder. 'You Mike?'

'I – don't – know. Prima Donna is my way of seeing her – we've seen her act up in so many different roles, haven't we?'

They all did have to agree. After talking through what she had revealed, they had to move on to what they were left with. If they were going to accept her testimony – whodunit? Alan thought Chocky would go with the gay theory, so started that ball rolling. Motive was the problem there: if the blood had not been Holly's, then the gay liaison theory was worth investigating, but Chocky pointed out that they actually had nothing but prejudice to go on otherwise. Alan pulled a long 'that told me' face at Badder.

They seemed to reach an impasse and they noticed Alan getting agitated. 'Okay,' he said, 'how about this: what's she doing here? I don't mean at the station, I mean why did she move up here?'

They all stared at him. Was he going off on one?

'Seriously. She's got no family or owt up here, she didn't come for a job, as far as I can see, and without either of them, why would anybody want to come to this shit-hole?'

'Steady on, Alan – I come from round here and frankly don't like your tone.'

'Oh come off it Mike! Answer the question.'

'It's a good one,' said Chocky. 'I think it's time to dig a bit deeper. Her story doesn't necessarily exonerate her from all guilt you know.'

Feeling for the 'sister', Badder felt this a bit heavy handed. 'If we believe he raped her – anally too - why on earth not?'

'Who did she tell?'

'What?'

'Who did she call for help? She reckons she's all alone in the world. I don't suppose she called Rupert – but, well we've all been to domestics and she was at least very close to him once.'

'But he is not even on our radar, sir,' said Alan.

'I realise that son, but it's just an example – who else could she turn to for help? You said it – what is she doing round here? She may have stuck a pin in a map, but let's find out eh?'

They kept her in but Badder insisted they treat her well – get her favourite takeaway for tea.

Holly was standing holding her buttocks and staring at the wall. Why had Hu turned on her, turned so nasty? It was obviously her own fault – she made him do it. She had told the young detective, but had never told herself. What else did she need to hear? Why did Hu do it? What was it he said when he calmed down? She had never gone over that bit of their encounter. Yes, he wasn't really speaking to her, he was almost talking to himself. Leo winding him up, who's he think he is? She'd never heard of him. Abe's a good man but he and Brien didn't stand up for him.

Brien! Dadda. Hu and Brien together. Did Hu find out about Brien and her? Had Hu found out that she wasn't the sort of girl a priest should marry? Did he know she'd … well been round the houses. Confession? Would Hu have heard Brien confessing, and confessing what he had done to her? That wouldn't turn him against her, would it? Maybe if he thought she was a spoilt thing – second-hand goods. She hadn't made out she was a virgin, but Hu had heard a few confessions – he didn't expect that of her.

She thought of Rupert Spiro and their threesomes. She loved the idea – sometimes another man, other times a woman – always friends of course – to start with. Then it was another couple – swinging together; it developed into orgies. Always at least some rough-house she didn't like, but … for the rough there was plenty of smooth.

Her and Rupert used to talk them through – until he let out his sordid little scheme. He was charging! He was making a thousand a time for what Holly thought was a bit of sharing fun. A thousand a person. With booze and food – 'our house-parties'! He was making ten grand a night. 'I'm making that Spiro! And you didn't think to tell me! You're whoring me!'

She looked at the interrogation room chair. It gave her a sore bum.

Alan took Chocky literally – who did she call? He re-examined the phone records. Hu Stannton did seem to be everything to her. She made few other calls. Almost every call was a mobile, but the call after the one to him, just around six on that night was to a local landline. It wasn't BT registered. He asked the evidence officer to track it down for him.

Chocky got a warrant and sent Badder and Mike to search the house. 'What we looking for?'

'Anything.'

Even that was a tall order. The house was not pristine but it did look hardly lived in. There was a guitar and some pop and folk music books. A small bookcase was not yet filled with Richard and Judy's and a stock of new looking Penguin classics and a random selection of coffee table books. Mike felt a bookcase would tell you something about the owner – not this one. Upstairs was no different – Holly's clothes looked pretty trendy and she had four times as many as Hu – the detectives had a laugh about his needing only a habit until a couple of years ago.

'It's not as if we are looking for a piece of lead pipe or …'

'… a candlestick in the billiard room? No Mike.'

'Have you seen a photograph even?'

'Well I suppose we are looking at a couple who have both run away from their previous existence.'

'Creepy though, don't you think?'

She wondered what he would make of her room – of course 'hers' was actually at home in Blackbird Leys and it would tell a story. No come on, hers at Lakeside would tell a whole lot more than this place – Snaps of Baba and Mammy,

Mick and Paddy (Mekhal and Padman – and their kids of course!). She looked at Mike huffing around.

'What are you smiling at?'

'Nothing – friends, family, life – they haven't got one, have they?'

'He hasn't,' grumbled Mike.

Chocky wanted to know who drowned Hu. Bloody stupid name – with a name like Hubert – stupid enough to start with - why hadn't they nick-named him Bert? Even if it was true that Holly had nothing to do with him falling, could she have done just as she said - Fylde shoves Hu out and she finishes him off – holds his head under water?

No, that didn't hold water. What about the cigar? Jenks was sure the dressing gown was singed and there was ash present – definitely not Suzanne's cigarette. Who was to say it wasn't there before the fall – just caught by a cigar in the room? No – smoke detector would have got it. Hotels are pretty strict on not smoking in rooms, too. But out on the balcony – like Nicholas on the fire escape?

Friday 19th March

As the tape was running, it was Brien Devine sitting opposite Chocky and Badder on Friday morning.

'You are under arrest on suspicion of being involved in the death of Hubert Stannton,' said Chocky. 'Have you anything to tell us?'

'Oh I do. I had nothing to do with it!'

'It will go much easier on you if you tell us why you received a telephone call from Mrs Holly Stannton on the evening of his death.'

Brien looked to his solicitor who nodded. 'I did not.'

'We have searched her phone records and she rang your house phone at four minutes past six.'

'Would that be on a mobile phone, Inspector?'

'It would.'

'May her husband have used it to ring me?'

Were they rushing things again? Chocky looked at Badder and decided to attack. He stood over the man and bellowed 'she used it to ring *you*!'

Brien felt on fairly firm ground – they wouldn't have any kind of transcript or recording to back up this allegation. 'But I do not know Mrs Holly Stannton. Why would she ring me, unless she was fishing for some information about poor Father Hu's death – and God Bless that poor woman too?'

'Don't give me that!' Chocky snapped. 'We know you held Father Hu in very high esteem.'

'Are you forgetting something – a time lapse, mebbe – leading to a memory lapse?'

'What?'

'The Father Hu I knew was my parish priest and he left us two years ago.'

'But you are the treasurer of The Tin Tab committee, are you not?

'I am that.'

'Well he's carried on visiting The Tin Tab in his new role as a Housing officer.'

'I have heard about that – good man.'

'Come off it – you'll know all about it, have seen him, kept in touch – the works.'

Brien knew this to be untrue, so sat his ground.

Chocky banged his fist on the table.

Brien flinched but was not cowed. He looked to the solicitor who shook his head.

Badder was thinking about the evidence they hoped to confirm with a text from Alan, who was at that minute searching the Devine household. She decided to gamble on an affirmative. 'We have not brought you in out of some kind of whimsy, Mr Devine. We have evidence – more than the phone call, and as Inspector Blundell said, you are doing yourself no favours in wasting our time with your denials – please help yourself by helping us. Tell us again and in as much detail as possible the *truth* about the evening after you left the Loseborough Hotel after your 'conference.'' She was finding it very difficult to change her mind from the man whom she had met before – devout, repenting a long ago offence – he would say 'sin', so would her Mammy. She believed in forgiveness. It was not 'once a Paedo…' with Iruna. But she recalled he did not think he could be forgiven – therefore he had nothing to lose. She checked her phone was not on silent. She had to plough on.

'Okay, Mr Devine, I want you to speculate why your phone number was rung by Holly Devine's phone.'

Of course he knew and if he even indicated that he knew the phone had been called, he was for the drop. 'Surely. Now then, say Father Hu rang, the Missus answered and that was no use to him.'

'Alright – but will Mrs Devine tell us that?'

He had to consider that. She would of course tell the truth – she had not answered the phone. Can they tell the call was even answered? He decided to continue to bluff. 'I couldn't say officer.'

He was trying his very best to appear unruffled but knew he was only partly succeeding. He needed something – that Hamlet moment.

'You have told us that you do not smoke and your wife has confirmed it.'

Now he jumped – was the whipper-snapper reading his mind? It wasn't a question, so he didn't answer. The phone on the table buzzed and the woman looked at it, smiled and passed it to the miserable looking man who lit up.

Chocky waded in. 'You lied! You holy Joe, you, hiding behind your praying and your 'lovely man' stuff about 'Lovely Father Hu' – you've been lying to us all along! Our people have searched your house, Mr Devine. What do you think they have found?'

'The Missus has a mobile phone?'

'Get away! She says she didn't hear the phone at all – so you must have answered it.'

'Who's to say it was answered at all? You didn't find that by a house search. You are blundering around in the dark.'

He didn't know how much of a raw nerve that word hit in Inspector Blundell. 'You lied about smoking Devine! You smoke cigars, don't you?'

He laughed, he hoped convincingly. 'Ah, me Hamlets! You know I hardly think of them as smoking! Silly me! Well I apologise officer – I smoke about five of those little cigarillos a year. I suppose you found them in an old jacket, did you …your people?'

Chocky was not convinced. Brien's change of colour did not help him. But indeed he owned up. Could he have forgotten? Chocky looked at Badder. He turned back to Devine. 'Your wife knows about the cigarillos?' he sneered.

'Oh God, no – she'd string me up, so she would. Like I said, I will have one very occasionally, out on a walk mebbe. Not let the smoke linger on me clothes!' he chuckled - a mischievous little boy.

Badder had had enough of people charming their way round Chocky. 'You lied to cover up the fact that you were there when Father Hu fell out of that window.'

Chocky shot upright, she carried on. 'She phoned you and you went to help her out. You finished him off... ' Chocky shot her a look so she stopped.

Brien was ready for this – he had been ready for a fortnight. He stood up and looked from one to the other of the detectives. 'You are out of your minds. You cannot possibly show that from anything I have said or done.'

'Siddown!' It was Chocky facing him down. 'We can and we will.'

He called an end to the session, stopped the tape and asked the solicitor to wait a few minutes with the suspect.

Once out of the room Chocky rang Mike for more detail. There wasn't any. They had found Hamlets; Mrs Devine was as surprised as they were chuffed; they had a few photographs of Devine's daughter Colleen. She might have something to do with all this. There was nothing else to go on. Chocky kicked his waste bin. Badder held her head in both hands and squashed her cheeks and eyes, groaning.

They got the boys to fetch Holly back in and put Brien in the cells.

'You phoned Brian Devine at four minutes past six on the evening Hu died. Why?'

Holly knew they would find the number on the phone so she had made a plan. 'It was Hu's – he had the number of the guys from The Tin Tab in our phone – why wouldn't he?'

'Our phone!' shouted Chocky, 'Your phone! He had his own – remember we found you had phoned him from *your* phone.'

'Oh come off it officer. You got a wife, yeah? You mean you haven't got her work colleagues numbers in your phone – case you can't get hold of her.'

She had wriggled again! Of course he did have Mary's office number and even a couple of colleagues' numbers in his phone. 'But Hu had his own phone with him – why would he use your phone and ... anyway! Stop messing us about – you phoned Brien Devine. Why?'

Holly simply stared at him. An insolent look if ever he saw one.

They put her in a cell.

The team gathered to scratch heads, together.

They had the packet of Hamlet cigars on the desk, alongside pictures of the cigar singe on the dressing gown, of Holly and Brien, and Colleen's from the house. Badder had turned over the photos of the stained sheet. There was a lot of lip chewing, sighing and the required head scratching. Nobody wanted to hazard any more guesses or air any more hunches.

'Are we agreed that both Holly and Brien have lied to us?'

They all nodded at their Inspector.

'So Holly initially lied that she had been to the hotel, now she's admitted that.'

'Is she lying about the phone call?'

'She's not telling the whole truth, Mike?'

'She's a wheedling little liar – I wouldn't trust her as far as I could fling her.'

'We could ask Mrs Devine straight out about the phone call?'

'Go on – try it Alan,' said Chocky.

While Alan was doing that, Chocky asked Mike to tell him about the photographs. 'Dunno, sir. Dare I mention the word 'hunch'? Where is Devine's daughter? Did she really run away?'

'Is she buried in the yard, you mean?' said Badder.

'We know she isn't,' said Chocky, 'because she made allegations about him, but didn't follow through.'

Mike had two pictures next to each other – the one they had been using of Holly from her wedding snap and one of Colleen looking about fourteen – formal school portrait – nice and clear. He got a piece of paper and tore a little hole in it. He laid the hole over the child's face. He did the same with another piece of paper – a bigger hole this time, to fit the larger format photo of Holly. He whistled and turned the pictures for all to see.

'She never heard the phone.'

'Thanks Alan – knew she'd say that, didn't we. Wow!'

'What are they, Mike?'

'You tell me Alan. What do you see?'

Mike had made triangular holes in the paper to hide all but the eyes, nose and lips on the two pictures.

'Couple of the snaps we took from the house.'

Badder pulled the two nearer to herself and smiled. 'Never!'

'But we know she's not!' said Chocky.

Back in the interrogation room, Chocky asked, 'Who is Holly Dean?'

She frowned. 'Funny sort of question – 's me – you know it's me. Holly Dean, becomes Holly Spiro,' she threw a mock spit, 'then Mrs Holly Stannton.'

Tell us a little more about Holly Dean – where were you born?'

'I was born and brought up in London; trashy parents – boozers; left home at sixteen; never looked back.'

'Where are your parents?'

'Dunno. Bet at least one of them is dead in a gutter.'

'It's not true is it Holly? That's not your name is it, er … whatcha called?'

'We can't find a record of your birth Holly,' said Badder.

'Is it my fault that you are such rubbish detectives?'

'That is not the point – if Holly Dean was born on your birth date, there would be a record and a birth certificate.'

'Yes, I reckon that's true – but just because you can't find it…' That insolent look again.

They knew from the DNA that she was not Brien's daughter. The photos were just an amazing coincidence – a pretty girl and a similarly pretty woman. They didn't want to make any more foolish and rash accusations. They had to let her go again.

They tried to get some more out of Brien – there had to be some link between him and Holly Stannton/Dean. He stonewalled – yes he supposed Hu, for some strange reason could have given him a call, tried to find Abe to get to a mutual client maybe.

'But the timing! Very soon before his death and not long after you had been with him for two days.'

'Yes it is strange, but I didn't speak to him – and I don't think the wife did, else she'd 'a told me.'

They had no reason to keep him, but sent for his wife and kept him until at least they had her side of the story.

Holly had now admitted that she went to the hotel. They originally thought Leo Nicholas had too. Could Brien have been there as well? No, you couldn't make it up.

They didn't think they had any grounds to arrest her, but Ginny - Mrs Virginia Devine - was most cooperative, just like her husband, she was keen to help find the killer of 'poor Father Hu.'

They weren't sure how to approach it, so all the team were on – Chocky and Mike watching from outside, letting Badder and Alan – 'the sweet, not so threatening ones' Chocky had irritated both of them with – do the talking. They also thought they had been given a very unimportant job. 'No, Alan – we are all on the lookout for lies – you two inside and us two through the mirror.

It was evident that Mrs Devine had little clue as to the seriousness of the situation, especially with regard to how her husband might really be involved.

'Now, Mrs Devine, Ginny…'

'Let's stick with Mrs Devine, Miss.' Firm, but sweet.

'… there was a phone call to your house just around the time we think Hu Stannton died. Alan here asked you and you said that you had not heard it. Okay, but you may still know why your house was called.'

She smiled ruefully. 'Now I am not a detective Miss, but sure you see how funny a question that is: do I know why someone phoned me, when I don't even know anybody did?'

Badder looked to Alan. 'It is funny, yes Ma'am,' he said, 'but you must realise we know something, and someone who lives at your house knows something and we are trying to find out exactly who and what the significance of that something is.' Alan coughed and stroked his chin before continuing, 'It's like this Mrs Devine, Mrs … er, a phone relevant to our inquiry was used to phone your house at six-o-four on the evening of Mr Stannton's death – we know it – fact.'

'I see that, but I didn't hear it and Brien says he didn't either.'

The detectives both looked long at her.

She became uncomfortable. She looked in her bag; looked at the mirror; looked at Badder; got a tissue out of her bag. 'Not my Brien?'

'Really.'

'Why would he lie?'

They let her think about that one too. The nose wipe would indicate that she had given it enough thought.

Badder changed tack. 'I know it's a very sensitive subject, but can you tell us about your daughter, please – her childhood…?'

Ginny was surprised, but couldn't see any harm in it and even warmed a little to talk about her lost child. 'Lovely wee thing – apple of her dadda's eye.'

'Not yours Ma'am?'

'That's cruel young man. A daughter is the apple of every mother's eye – that's taken as read. But she was so sweet and so pretty – you seen the pictures, you took them away. I didn't understand that.'

'But she ran away – what did she run away from?'

'She did no such thing – she grew up.'

'And where is she now?'

Ginny knew that Colleen was alright; healthy and happy; settled, maybe married; probably not had any childer – yet. 'She's working in London. Fashion, design, art galleries – she loves all that kind of thing.'

That was a lot more than the detectives were expecting. 'How do you know this ma'am, you visit?'

'No, no we get a regular update on the telephone you know.'

'Regular? Like a fortnight ago, perhaps?'

'Ah well, she's been busy of late … yes, busy, see. Hasn't been able to ring for a bit. Mebbe jet setting to New York – 'locations' she used to talk about, you know.'

'Used to? So when exactly did she last ring you?'

Ginny did not see how this had anything to do with them, or the death of the priest.

Nor did they. They did however have a mysterious woman in their sights, and the Devines were the parents of another woman, one whom they had not seen for many years, and who would be about the same age as Holly Stannton. The connection was niggling at the team. They asked the date of birth of Colleen, and though it was the same year, it was different date. 'Why did she leave, Mrs Devine?

'Itchy feet. Headstrong.' She looked at the young man and almost whispered, 'Sex?'

Alan coughed. He needed more.

'Well you know you young ones – it's all about sex – I seen it on the telly. Well me and Brien we weren't letting our little girl go down that track – but despite our best efforts to protect her, we think she did anyway. We had some therapy and that sort of thing, God Almighty!' She wiped her face. 'They said we were suppressing her natural desires, Holy Mother o' God.' She wept.

They had to get more out of her, so Badder gave the 'cuppa' sign to the mirror.

'Just tell us a bit more about her before she left – at sixteen was it? What was she like doing her GCSEs?'

'Ah there you have it! Learnt more about the ways of the … boys, than Geography and History. Wild she was – went before she even got the results – good job, else Brien woulda skinned her alive. Nothing! Well Art and Drama – Art and Drama! – Cs. She left us a note, we were sure she'd be back, tail between her legs, soon enough. She called us up a few times and I begged her to come on home, but she'd hang up when I got going. I set Brien on to her, but he said she wouldn't talk to him. I used to see him on the phone – he'd be telling her how we missed her, listening; asking her to come on home, listening; but he said she was just refusing to talk on the other end.'

Ginny was visualising the situations. She looked at the detectives a couple of time before continuing, 'After the first couple of years he said they were mischief calls because no one was there, but I worked it out that if he answered, our Colleen wouldn't speak and just hung up. It got to be if it was a silent call, he'd hand the phone to me and go and hide.'

'Why did she leave, Ginny – your opinion?'

'We gave her everything, but it wasn't enough – it wasn't what she wanted. She wanted dancing, wild parties, short skirts – you know I did wonder if she met one o' them rock stars. I heard about Groupies and it frightened the daylights o'me. You know who I picture her like? Mandy Rice-Davies.'

The Detectives looked at each other and shook their heads. The tea came in.

'Before your time, but she crops up on the radio now and again. Mandy – not our Colleen. She was out in London at sixteen – Perfume Affair it was - sex and drugs and rock and roll don't they say?'

'We've heard of that,' she smiled. 'But coming back to the phone call – it wasn't a call from Colleen that night?'

Ginny was nonplussed. They knew she didn't know there was a call. Hadn't she just said that if it was a silent one, then Brien would have passed the phone to her? She was beginning to wonder if maybe Colleen had talked to Brien after all this time. But he would have said. He was very jittery since Father Hu had died – but who wouldn't be – only natural. What are they going on about Colleen for? 'Are you telling me? You are aren't you? You know who it was from and I don't even know we got one. You had better give me a clue as to why I am here and what you might want me to say. Is Brien in trouble? He wouldn't have threw poor Father Hu out the window...'

They did need to give her a clue. 'Father Hu's wife phoned your number.'

'His wife!'

'Mrs Holly Stannton. You know her.'

'I do not know her, the hussy. Brien told me she was called Holly. Never seen her. He ran off wit' her! Poor priests – women always running after them. I suppose we have to be resigned to the fact that a fine young man like Father Hu would be a great catch – suppose Brien is right about him holding out that long. Oh if only he could've overcome this hurdle – coulda made bishop – cardinal...' She went all dreamy.

Badder restrained herself from adding 'pope.' 'Now Mrs Devine – you know who she is, she knows, well at least who Brien is...'

'Why's that Miss?' she snapped. 'Why's she know my Brien?'

'From The Tin Tab.'

'The Tin Tab – is it there he met her – a druggie?'

'No, no, sorry Mrs Devine, Hu was involved in The Tin Tab...'

'Back then.'

'No – still. He got a job with the council, and he helped to get young people into accommodation. Brien would know this.'

'Well I never – well I never knew that!' She sounded convincing.

Badder was convinced that Brien would know Hu; the explanation about Brien's number in Holly's phone was plausible; but why would Holly *or* Hu have rung Brien at that particularly fraught moment in their relationship? She looked to Alan who flicked his brow and sighed.

Another impasse.

As they were leaving the interrogation room, Badder indicated Alan to see Mrs Devine out, 'and let Brien take her home,' while she returned to hover over the waste basket. She got a glove and pen out and bagged the tissues from the bin for analysis. 'Just a hunch.' She didn't tell anybody.

On the way out that night, Alan felt Badder trailing him to the car park. She got to her Mini and after a quick glance round, called him over, bundled him in and Coopered him off to a big Village pub in Tickhill just outside Doncaster. He took her home in a taxi.

Saturday 20th March

Brien repented, but he had asked no forgiveness. For almost twenty years he was still repenting his sin – the sin that most people now seemed to feel is the most unforgivable crime. He knew they were right and expected no forgiveness. He asked God on a daily basis to not think the worst of him – he thought his many years of repentance had possibly worked his passage out of Hell's fire, but he still expected a long time in Purgatory.

He wasn't suffering yet – was that acceptable? People round here, yes even in London, thought he was a good man. He thought of himself as a good man – he was a very good man, except for his one catastrophic fall from grace. He blamed God for that and they were in constant dialogue about it. God had made him a man and his Ginny a beautiful woman – and was she not also his Eve?

God had given the earth and all its beauty to man to enjoy, and that included Eve. He honoured the Lord and his creation, but why did Brien have to leave Eve out of it now?

He had not, and could not ask his Colleen to forgive him. He had never even mentioned it. He knew she had realised that he was not the good Dadda after all. She rang and listened to him listening. She probably wanted to hear a sob, but he pitied only her – not himself. So how could a man who believes in forgiveness not forgive himself, nor even seek it?

Colleen had at last asked for his help. Well hadn't she? She had gone away without a word, and not a word since … then she pleads with him; an ultimate sacrifice from a man whose soul is lost. He could not refuse. So if he had lost his soul anyway, could he lose it more? Lost is lost is lost…

Jesus said that no one has greater love than the person who laid down his life for his friend. So Brien, in carrying out Colleen's implicit request knew that, despite those twenty years of repentance, he was ultimately laying down his life – his eternal life – for her.

Father Hu – all the confessors, ever - told him that he was of course forgiven, but he didn't want to hear that. But still – hedging his bets - he just wanted to know that Jesus's man here on His Earth had heard him say he was sorry and that he would be repenting. He said his penance and of course he meant every word and served the church and God's people in any way asked of him. Almost. He had Disclosed to Leo, who had Vetted him and so, wasn't he barred? But he had offered – what more could he do? The repentance would continue but the forgiveness would not be forthcoming – he knew it.

He needed some advice. He decided to seek it. What if he didn't like the advice? He wasn't sure he could trust the confessional any more after Father Hu. Father? More like son in reality. What a turnaround. Brien would never have thought it - could not think it now. After all his faith, he was just another priest to betray his calling.

Right! The other thing Jesus said was that he who scandalises the mind of the innocent – anyone who shows an innocent that wrong is right – may as well have a millstone round his neck and be thrown into the deepest sea. Didn't the priests say that that person is the only one that Jesus ever condemned? Had Father Hu even reiterated it? Whoever said it, Brien heard it and knew that in saying it, Jesus was indeed condemning Brien Devine. Much as she wanted to be, Colleen was *not* his little wifey. He grabbed his head in his hands and pulled at it, down, down. He peeped up at his crucified Lord.

But Colleen was Hu Stannton's real wifey and he had … buggered her. Now that's not right; it was a scandal.

So Brien was right to do what he had – she had asked and he had done it. Was it right?

He needed to find out and that meant travel – he wasn't going to risk going local and getting turned in. He thought the priests of today would maybe have to turn in a murderer who came to their confessional. Brien wasn't that bad. Brien wasn't a murderer.

Ginny needed a treat – maybe a shopping trip, get her hair done, nice meal, a show. Not London, nowhere South – he was known all over the south – not fame, not infamy either - he had been the paymaster of thousands of good Catholic Irishmen all over the South. Sheffield? They'd never been. He would go to the Cathedral while Ginny was at the hairdresser. You get confession anytime in a Cathedral.

When they got back home the phone was ringing as they came in the front door. Ginny picked it up – silence. 'Another of those call-centre people.' She went to put the kettle on and Brien waited for the phone to ring again.

That evening Alan and Iruna were in a pub again - this time his local. The place was buzzing after the great excitement of the Arsenal v. West Ham Match. Badder had given up wondering why people didn't support their local team – a billion Chinamen supported Man U – who was she to quibble? Her brothers had given up on Oxford United. She told Alan that Paddy had turned to Arsenal, so he would be in the pub rejoicing, and Mick would be looking for Liverpool to stop the enemy - Man U - from taking the top spot off Arsenal next day.

It had been great fun for her to be in the midst of testosterone-filled young men in their element, and to be swept out of the malaise of the investigation and into Alan's arms as Arsenal had a man sent off and they would lose. But even with only ten men they still didn't lose.

They were relaxing alone together and it was lucky she had such a hangover that morning that she didn't need any more fuel. Alan had scoffed his requisite post-match pint, pie and peas, and Badder's steak was remarkably good for a pub meal.

He was at last getting to know the girl 'with the made up name' from a 'posh city darn sarf.' It was hilarious: her mum was an Irish nurse who fell for the handsome Indian who broke his hand at the car factory. He was anti religion after his granddad suffered in the partition of India creating the Muslim state of Pakistan. Mum was likewise fed up of the Irish-bashing over the IRA stuff, and with the Catholic hypocrisy. Iruna didn't let on that she had already told Chocky about her Mum - proud of her Irish heritage - and though Dad wanted the kids to have a name reflecting their Indian heritage, she did the registrations – and the spellings. So Mekhal was Mick to her and Padman was 'well you can guess.'

'So is Rooney gonna help Man U beat us tomorrow then?'

She paled. How did Alan make the same connection as that bastard brother of Louise's. 'Wha-at?'

'Iruna – Irish – Rooney!'

She laughed but didn't know what was funny – except maybe Mick, Paddy and Rooney?

'So where is your Mum's joke with your name, then? Come on?'

She was getting it. 'Ha! Oh yes, she had the last laugh. Dad wanted me to be called after his Granny A-runa – A-R – it's a lovely name too – to do with the rising sun and that. Mum was okay with that, but in respect to the old country she spelt it I-R! To be honest most people call me Runa anyway.' She pecked his nose.

The lime and lemonade was a bit boring and after lasting since well before the meal, as Iruna took the call, she discovered it was also warm and flat. She choked on it. 'Brien Devine's body has been found in a river!'

She and Alan had fetched her car from Tickhill that morning and she had driven him to his local. She had some difficulty persuading Alan to not come to work 'in that state.' It was the luckiest hangover *she* had ever had.

She parked in the supermarket car park, the far side stretch of which was cordoned off and floodlit. She could see the top of the SOCO's tent over the hedge. There was quite a gathering on the flyover looking down on the scene. A PC escorted her to the dark side of the riverbank and brought Chocky over to her.

'This is bloody funny Runa.'

'Suicide, sir?'

'No way – it's hardly a foot deep. His head's smashed in on the rocks. You ... you could have a look...'

'Oh leave it out Chocky,' she said, tapping him on his stomach. 'Come on.'

They were stopped by the SOCOs a couple of yards from the tent and given galoshes before being shown a careful stepping route to overlook the body. The tent was partly into the river to hide from the prying crowd. Brien Devine was lying flat with his arms outwards and his mouth and eyes were open. His injury was not evident. Badder noted his hair was smart and slicked into place as usual, but the rock beside his head was bloody.

'What do we know, sir?'

'Well nothing as yet Iruna. Another fine day – lot better than last year, else we'd probably have snow prints - so no wet foot prints and I don't think any fresh bits here. There is all sorts of stuff – lots of dog-ends and duck shit under the bridge – but not so much out here. People park-up here, pop into town – market today – then come back on that footbridge you can just see over there, to do a proper shop in the supermarket.'

'Witnesses?'

'Not to speak of. Dog walker found the body – the main path to town cuts across back there, so not many coming past here. Actually, thinking about it, the Supermarket was open, but town and market were shut, so I think maybe it would only be very few around at this time.'

They came out and peered around. The opposite bank had a good stand of wintered trees for a hundred metres before some houses could be seen. It was a similar distance to the car park CCTV – central and unlikely to catch anything over in this corner – or for that matter through the bushes, leafless as they were. Standing nearer the shop, they could see a camera stanchion on the far side of the flyover. They went back that way and decided that both the supermarket and the town CCTV would be useful for cars coming to the area. They went across the footbridge up to the main road and back round the towpath. Chocky peered up at what looked like it may have been an old mill-house to see if it had security cameras – not outside.

'So what does it look like to you, Iruna?'

She thought it a bit unfair of her senior to put her on the spot, but it was vague enough and she decided to take it as a compliment, him respecting her opinion over his own – he wouldn't put her down if he did disagree. 'It just looks like he's fallen backwards, Chocky.' She mimed arms flinging out for balance, and head going back 'like a rocket.'

'Aye and a rock hit! Sorry – inappropriate, but true. It's a fall of maybe a metre – add his height, making it a fall for his head of about three metres – some speed and potential impact.'

'Yebbut, why did he fall backwards and what was he doing here sir? Any evidence that he had been shopping? Where's his car?'

'Just over there look. SOCO got his keys for me. Car was locked, no shopping, no ticket – don't need one after six, see?'

'So – was he pushed or did he jump?'

'Didn't jump backwards did he Iruna?'

'No sir-ee!'

'By the way, where were you – he didn't spoil your Saturday night did he?'

'Yeah, in the pub, but lucky it wasn't last night.' She held her head. 'Needed that drink Chocky.'

'Those drinks!'

'Haha, plenty many drinkies – sore head this morning, but meant I didn't fancy any tonight.'

'What were you doing in a pub, then?'

'Nice steak, sir.'

'Anybody I know?' he smiled.

'No sir.'

Chocky pointed out the duck muck to the SOCO – maybe footprint, trail even. Someone would doubtless have some on their shoes, too.

They then went to the Devine house, and ascertaining that she didn't know where her husband had gone 'of a Saturday night', told Ginny Devine of the discovery of the body.

She was strangely tight lipped about it.

They said they couldn't state it would be Brien of course, but were pretty sure. She sustained a blank look.

They told her she would be asked to identify the body, but not yet, as it was still at the scene – 'probably tomorrow?'

Iruna was worried about her lack of response and tried to offer some succour. She offered a support worker, but Ginny refused. She put on her coat and indicated the front door.

They looked at each other. Iruna raised her brows and Chocky nodded at the door, but immediately turned back to Ginny. 'Mind if we take a quick look around please, Mrs Devine?'

She took a deep breath and rested her wrists on her waste. 'Ah, get on with ye!'

Badder headed for the door, but realised Chocky was going back into the little kitchen. He swept his head around the tiny back lobby and returned to her.

They told her someone would be in touch about the identification and they would definitely need to speak to her on Monday.

Ginny followed them out of the house and locking the door behind them all, she grumbled something about seeking her own support '... from the Monsignor. And if he's in bed, I'll dig him out!'

Once inside the car Badder said 'What was that all about?'

'Queer wasn't it?' he said. 'And I just wanted to see if there were any mucky duck prints or boots by the back door.' He shook and scratched his head.

Iruna shook her head at the DI's choice of words.

Sunday 21st March

Ginny didn't quite know who to turn to for support after a cold reception from her parish priest Monsignor Green. Her surmise was correct – he did not appreciate being disturbed at that time of night.

Abe Grant was Brien's pal and she knew he was a good man. He would help her.

When they saw the body together, Abe was very moved and cried openly – she was very surprised – an observer might say stunned into silence by his distress. Ginny stood with her hand across her mouth, looking at the mortal remains of her loyal, but pretty useless husband. She thought he would be where he had always wanted to be – and that was not with her, but with his carpenter pal Jesus.

No thought ran through her head about why he was lying there. Their life together was running before her eyes. All that sex he wanted. All those babies she wanted ... to live. The dead babies were his; he was with them now. Then her Colleen had gone and left her. She never said, she never asked, she never did find out, but she thought Brien must have done something – must have scared her off, must have expected too much. He did expect too much of Ginny, and she was glad when he eventually gave up.

She realised Abe was 'carrying on a bit' so she put her arm round him to comfort him. She didn't expect the big man to blubber like that. He was lost in the unfairness of the whole thing: good men like Hu and Brien meeting terrible ends – an end he had caused. He knew about crushed bodies - he knew it every day. It was unnecessary and was always somebody's fault. In these cases it was his.

Abe had his own suspicions and decided to ring Leo. He didn't get the response he was expecting. He thought Leo, wise, canny Leo, would have a logical explanation. How come he had invited a coterie for the pampering and that two of them were now dead in mysterious circumstances. Leo was scared about the intimation of such a call. Was Abe wondering if he was next? Though he thought this just daft, he did not intend to be as cold as he was to one of the few people he held in the very highest regard.

Regaining some of his usual composure, he thought Abe might see something in the issues around Simone Dunne. He knew it irrelevant, but felt the need to obscure himself by putting up a little more smoke.

In turn Abe did not see the connection and felt he was wasting his time on the phone.

Leo immediately rang the police but failed to get hold of any officers working on the case. He realised that Abe's apparent suspicion about the 'conference' group being gradually knocked off, pointed at Leo of course. He considered directing the needle of suspicion towards the Lifer, but could not do that to such a friend. He knew they would come for him again.

He decided to water the seed he had already sown - he left Inspector Blundell a message asking if Simone Dunne had been helpful in the Stannton case.

He also thought it maybe the professional thing for someone in his position to offer some support and consolation So, who to: he didn't know Mrs Devine at all; or Hu's wife – and Hu was dead. Who else was there? He kicked himself for not being nicer to Abe.

He met with his girls – Talya being one – along with their boyfriends for Sunday lunch. He had to let their buzz and banter wash over him, and wash flavour out of the food too. He felt Talya constantly nudging him and checking him out, but there was no way he had a ready smile that could convince her.

Chocky heard the story of a second death in the 'murdered priest' case on the BBC News. They had put the cases together. Thank goodness the body was too late for the Sunday Tabloids. Who would come up with the 'Loseborough Four'? He was not enjoying a relaxed Sabbath. He had Holly Macbeth stalking the battlements of his darker moments ranting about her 'damned spot.' The Ashkenazi Anthony Sher needed no chameleon traits to take on the role of Leo Nicholas as the 'Enemy of the people.' But Brien Devine: why that mild mannered man? Why him. No it was not an accident.

Monday 22nd March

Chocky was not amused to have two particular messages on his phone on Monday morning. The one from Leo winding him up about Simone Dunne: stupid fool - did he not realise that such a suggestion was simply a slur and would more likely sustain their suspicions of Nicholas's own guilt, however tenuous?

Another from the Bishop asking for '… something to work with that is not tittle-tattle', was fair enough, but very high handed. The police could only work with facts, and the hierarchy – albeit the church's – should understand that.

He was however intrigued by the message from the pathologist at the mortuary: She thought it worth mentioning Mrs Virginia Devine's reaction to seeing her husband's body.

By ten o'clock they had Mrs Devine and Holly in custody, plus Leo Nicholas. They also had taken several bags of shoes for forensic duck muck.

The team of detectives decided that at the very least, they had two 'typical' domestics on their hands, and so had the surviving partners of maybe two unrelated rows in custody.

They wondered about their conspiracy theories and decided that Holly pushed Hu and called Brien – for some strange reason – but considered that a bit far-fetched.

On the other hand maybe Ginny pestered Brien into tackling Father Hu about his womanising. She took him back to the hotel and it all went too far. Having waited outside, she realised that if Hu came round he would finger her husband so she finished him off. 'What about the cigar, sir?' asked Alan.

'He maybe lit up on the balcony and had it in his hand when he shoved Stannton.'

They were not sure why they had Nicholas in custody, but it was too much of a coincidence that two of his conference guests now lay dead. They were keeping him away from any contamination of the investigation.

They split up, Badder and Mike took Ginny while the other two took Holly.

Badder suggested that Mike might make most headway with Ginny if he adopted the respectful 'Madam' approach and get her story of this telephone call.

It soon became clear to him that both calls were taken by Brien and he had responded by action – he had left the house, and his wife, as a result of the calls.

Badder sensed that he was leaving out a perhaps more obvious line of inquiry – that Ginny had in fact killed her husband in a row, possibly, but not necessarily, to do with the Stannton affair. 'Tell us about your husband Brien,' she said, 'and what you were both doing on Saturday.'

Mrs Devine was not a bit helpful, denying all knowledge of either phone call.

Along with the message from the mortuary, Badder felt Ginny was being disingenuous, somehow. 'I want you to explain why there were two mysterious telephone calls to your house – we think they were from the same person – from Mrs Holly Stannton?'

'Like I said before, I didn't hear the first call and neither did I hear the second one. Seriously, I do not understand why you are … well almost torturing me with your insinuations.'

Mike stepped in: 'Your husband appears to have been pushed – maybe not very hard – but pushed all the same. It looks just like a row sort of thing. In all cases of suspicious death, I'm sorry to say Mrs Devine, we have to suspect the wife or partner. Brien was pushed off a … muddy riverbank. We have taken shoes from your house for forensic examination, and if it comes back that you have … material on your shoes, then it will point very strongly to you having pushed him. So…?'

Ginny pursed her lips and took a breath. 'So … what, officer?'

'So where were you?'

'At home watching television all night.'

Badder struck out: 'Holly Stannton looks very like your daughter Colleen.'

Mrs Devine blanched and a made a clucking noise in her throat. Her eyes welled up.

'You knew that didn't you!'

Ginny burst into tears and wailed. They let her, but it went on too long – she seemed inconsolable.

Mike became uncomfortable and suggested a tea break.

Alan Prisco opened the batting with Holly. She had not seen much of him so he may get something fresh out of her. They now accused her of again phoning the Devine's – this time it was Brien who was dead an hour later.

She knew they could get nothing on her so she continued where she had left off: deny everything and make them prove it. They would know it had been very difficult for her to tell her story, they surely wouldn't think she had made that up. They knew the blood was hers and they now knew that it tied up with the forensics on Hu. She lifted her phone onto the table. 'I didn't phone anybody.'

'Callbox, Holly. You knew we would check your mobile.'

'Why would I bother with a callbox – do they still exist even?'

'Because you thought we couldn't trace it.'

'And can you?'

Alan was unfamiliar with her quick wit and this flummoxed him. 'You're denying you called the Devine's at all?'

'No.'

'What? You saying you did ring?'

'No.'

Alan turned to Chocky who indicated him to carry on. He had to think what the two apparently contradictory negatives could mean. 'You are not denying you rang …so, tell me what exactly you are saying 'no' to?'

'Your questions, er, constable?' She looked to Chocky, who again looked to Alan.

Alan checked his notepad. 'I think I see: you are not 'denying' that you called the Devine's, but you are saying no you did not ring. Am I missing some clever little word play here? This is about two deaths, Miss.'

'Madam to you.' She smiled at Chocky. 'Holly to you, Inspector.'

'Okay Holly, Alan here is also a detective trying to find your husband's killer - your - husband's - killer. However, we believe you when you say he anally raped you and we think that makes a strong motive for you to kill him.'

Her face straightened at last. 'You are accusing me of stuff and I am saying prove it! I have said I do not know about the first phone call and now you have another I don't know about. It's even more tenuous – I have a phone here and you say I phoned from a callbox.' She leaned over to eyeball Chocky. 'I wouldn't expect this sort of nasty behaviour from you Inspector.'

'Alright then Holly, nice man that I am, I am saying you called the Devine's to support you, but in fact, Brien went and …had something to do with killing Hu. Now whether that was your intention, we cannot prove yet, but we are definitely accusing you and we need you to be clear about what you are denying – but own up to your actual involvement – it will all come out in the end, you know.'

'Hu raped me. I ran away. That's my story and you prove I am lying.'

Alan and Chocky started at once, but Alan deferred to his Inspector.

'Holly – you are lying about the phone calls.'

'Like I said – prove it.'

Chocky wondered if they could maybe get some 'Spooks' technology and place her mobile phone in the vicinity of the public callbox. They weren't exactly the Met. But Holly Stannton was a ghost – a spectre, maybe a vampire come to drink the blood of a priest. Silly – but in fact the person before them was phantom – a figment of the girl's own imagination. He had to leave her there. He was not letting her go, but almost wondered if she could simply seep out through the walls of a cell.

Leo told the detectives his version of what may have happened – how he had got the 'conference' together to exterminate vermin – a paedophile, a murderer and a sex abusing priest. He should have got hold of some Zyclon B and had he known in advance, the basement showers had a real Auschwitz feel to them.

Chocky was not impressed and let him have his 'little joke.'

Badder felt sick to her stomach. She was not entirely sure they had told him about either Abe Grant's or Brien Devine's records. She thought he may have dropped himself in it, but decided to take the chance to confer.

'So we now have it on record,' Chocky pointed to the recorder, 'how you pushed Hu out of the window and now how you ...well, would have liked to have killed them all. So Abe Grant is next. How did you lure Brien to his death?'

'You couldn't make it up, could you Inspector, but like me, I bet you're going to try?'

'Leo, you play this cold hearted 'anything is just for the overall good of the race', but we find now hundreds have signed up on Facebook to support you, to witness to the great work and many opportunities you have provided for young people. You seem like a very caring guy.'

'I am that – but not about you lot. I care about Abe – and I cared about Brien too. I didn't know him as I do Abe, but there was a man who...' He suddenly realised he could be incriminating himself for real.

'Yes Leo?'

'I have to tell you that I have reason to know, good reason to know...' he saw the look on Badder's face, 'I am a Safeguarding Manager in Young People's Service. I have to clear people through the CRB, the Disclosure and Barring Scheme you know. I do NOT have to clear our Voluntary Sector colleagues. However...' he again checked the sergeant, 'however, they sometimes, well often ask me to – saves their organisation, charity, you see.'

Chocky's fingers were drumming.

Leo noticed, smiled and raised an eyebrow.

'Whatever you are going to say, your management has suspended you, and your staff want you to pipe down. Get on with it then, and it better be good.'

'Abe and Brien are just two of them.'

'Oh, so they stupidly told you of their record and – here it really is – you turned that against them. Many true words spoken in jest – your Auschwitz rant is true – isn't it?'

Badder thought that was going a bit far, but it was true that Leo Nicholas had two hatreds – authority and abusers. 'So what is your plan for Abe Grant?'

Leo jabbed the desk with a finger and through gritted teeth said, 'Abe Grant is the salt of the earth - one of the finest men I ever met. He apparently did kill his wife, but took the punishment many years – decades – ago. I would bet my life on it that you have nothing on him at all since he came out of prison a new man. Now Brien I do not know, but early signs are that he is cut from the same cloth. Like doctors can maybe think society is sick, because all they see are sick people; you lot think society is evil because of all the criminals you meet everyday; me I get daily updates on the activities of paedophiles in our community, so I could, yes could, feel men are all creeps. But I don't.'

He saw that both detectives were with him. So 'easy does it' now Leo. ''s right isn't it? But you don't do you sergeant? Came into the police to do good?'

She smiled at him.

'And I know you are a good man, Inspector – I've tried your mettle, sorry, but your colleagues have sorely tried mine.' He rubbed his head. 'I do not want to believe 'Once a Paedo, always a Paedo', and do want to believe that Brien was a reformed character – well maybe only slipped the once anyway – and Abe recognised that man repenting – their word, but I am okay with it – so he was fine by me. As I understand it, officers, you are not investigating his crime, but him as victim … and I didn't kill him.'

Chocky wouldn't say he was happy with the situation, but he did not want any more cat-and-mouse with Leo Nicholas, nor to give him any clues to help him build his own defence of killing Brien. He looked at Badder and they obviously concurred that Leo Nicholas had about wrapped up the interview.

While they were winding down in the canteen, there was an almighty clattering on the stairs, the door bashed open and Alan raced over. 'I've got it! I've found it! It was her all along!'

Chocky didn't want to quash Alan's excitement or to knock back all his effort, determination and success in finding crucial details that had been eluding them throughout the investigation, but, as ever, his findings did appear to leave as many questions as answers. And the lack of an identity in the 'it was her all along', was sustained.

Starting with what Alan had found, he let him put it to Holly Stannton.

It sounded like Alan was clearing his throat, but Chocky smiled when he realised it was the opposite: Alan was trying to slur his speech 'Kholly De-ean, eh?'

'Mm. Yes sir?'

Alan flicked his eyebrows and smiled. 'Sounds like – Kholly De-ean - sounds like…'

She was a little paler.

'There is no record of Holly Dean – well not one that is you. You are not Holly Dean are you? Would you like to tell us who you are?'

'No. I think you should tell me who you think I am. Have you been looking up the correct spelling?'

'Oh give over Holly!' said Chocky, 'Tell us about your life as Colleen Devine.'

She thought she was doing so well. Where could she go from there? Was she going to say she killed both men? Too late for tears, but she couldn't stop the blood from draining out, from draining out of her face and mingling with the blood of her Dadda and her Husband in her heart. She loved them both. They both loved her. But … they were both men and couldn't help it.

Savages. When would women cease to need men – boys? Boys never seem to grow up, to take nature's route to maturity – to increased hu-man-ity. They had abused the child, they had pimped the beauty, they had buggered the woman, and all in the one woman who wanted to be neither Colleen Devine, Holly Spiro nor Holly Stannton. The names tarnished her. She splayed her hands almost in supplication to the young detective. 'Sounds like Holly Dean, officer. Well done.' She continued to look into his eyes and gradually broke into a pleading smile. 'If you want my life, you can have it.' She turned to Chocky. 'Want it?'

'No Holly – Colleen...'

'Don't call me that! Holly it is.'

'We don't want your life Holly, and we are not going to take it away from you, but two lives have been taken away and we...' he turned to Alan with a smile, 'we want to know why their lives were taken away.'

'I may have been ... that other girl, but it was a childhood, and it was taken away from me. I was accidentally given a new name and Holly Dean is who I am – Holly Dean has had a good, but very short life. I hope I can be Holly Dean again and carry on ...' She suddenly stood up and shouted, 'where's that woman, that Paki – I want her to hear my story?'

Chocky waved at the mirror and Badder walked in. The silent solicitor had nothing to say, but was visibly uncomfortable. Alan shouted for another chair and Mike showed up with one.

'You don't need that,' shouted Holly 'fuck off out – and you two,' she told the detectives. She pointed at the tape, 'That thing's still going,' she considered her solicitor, 'and you can get out too.'

When all was quiet again and she had Badder sitting next to her, she asked her name. 'Oh that's pretty! I was a bit rude just now, I'm sorry, you no doubt heard me through the mirror,' she chuckled at the notion.

Badder joined her, 'No I don't mind Holly. I am not averse to a little bit of positive discrimination.' She felt inclined to take hold of Holly's hand, but with all eyes on her, albeit unseen, she resisted. She waited. After all this time and such a trudge through the mire, the end looked in sight and it didn't look so bad – not for her anyway. But if this was Colleen Devine – what relation was she? She wasn't Brien's daughter, the DNA proved that. Her hunch! She needed the DNA off Ginny Devine's tissues. Ginny Devine – butter wouldn't melt; but a mother's revenge – Hell's Fury. Who scorned whom?

Holly took a huge sobbing breath and started, 'Look Iruna, I told you that Hu ... y'know, I don't want to keep saying it ...'

'I know Holly – but just tell me what happened.'

'Oh it was just like I said, er ... you don't want me to tell it again?'

'You called Hu, found he was still at the hotel, drove over and tackled him. He didn't like it and attacked you. Can you maybe tell us more why you think he did that? Maybe his mindset will help us to understand what happened next, yeah?'

Holly had to think about that. 'I'm not sure I can Miss. He hurt me see, Iruna, and I wasn't actually thinking about him any more, I was thinking about me, y'know like?'

'Yes, yes that is fine if it is ... the truth, Holly?'

'Mm. Yeah, yes it is the truth.'

'So you ran out of the hotel. Then what?'

'I went down the Lane to the car and as soon as I was away from the place I just cried, cried and cried – out loud and that. I stood by the car for ages – I couldn't sit down, y'know. But it got a bit cold and I had to get in the car. I lay the seat right back and set the engine going to warm me back up. I maybe had a little sleep – y'know, nodded off. I know I jumped – awake like and decided to call someone.' She stopped and looked at Badder who waited.

'I' she squeaked again, 'I don't really know anybody any more. I got a few friends down London, but they weren't going to help me up here – 'sides I don't want to go running back with me tail between me legs do I?' Recalling her ordeal, she pushed her hands into the hollow of her back and stretched.

Badder wondered if she would make up some story about the number in her phone.

'My Dad abused me when I was a kid, see – I didn't mind at the time, like – it was nice actually, I loved him so much and he loved me,' she checked Badder who managed to look blank, 'gradual like - tender, gentle … but I found out at school that it was against the law and well…' she sobbed. 'Well I got to thinking it had to stop. I played a few moody wobblers for a couple of years and then just walked out. Just walked out and into Holly Dean.'

'From Colleen Devine?'

She nodded. 'Mm'

'Now we've even got a problem with that, Holly…'

Holly looked confused.

Badder wondered if Holly was maybe adopted and didn't know it. She was worried about putting any words into Holly's mouth. She thought of her own dad – yes he was surely her dad. What was Brien to Holly? She decided to leave the genetic relationship until later. 'So, er, Brien and Ginny Devine are your parents?'

'Mm.'

'For the tape, please, Holly?'

'Yes, Brien and Ginny Devine are my parents.'

Badder looked at the mirror.

Holly followed her gaze. 'Yes I had a problem with that too.'

'But you rang them for support – for help, Holly?'

'Mm.'

'What did they say?'

'Nothing really.'

'Come on Holly, help yourself.'

Holly was shocked. What had she done now? 'Miss! I needed help, sort of. Needed to tell somebody – that's all, an' I did, that's all. That's all I did, Miss, honest Miss.'

It was so pathetic. It choked Badder. Holly still hadn't got the whole story out so Badder couldn't stop, yet.

Chocky was champing at the bit – he wanted to get straight to Brien to see what he had to say about the phone call. But all was still very unclear. He willed Iruna to go on.

Badder wanted her DNA sample to come back and help her with the next step. She checked that she hadn't missed anything on her phone. 'So who did you speak to Holly?'

She whined an answer through tears. Badder could hear and waited. 'I told him what Hu had done, that he had, y'know, Miss.'

'So you spoke to Brien? Your Dad? Your Dad who abused you?'

She nodded. 'Not easy is it?'

Pointing at the recorder, Badder said, 'You told Brien Devine that Hu had sexually assaulted you.'

'Thought you got it – what I said before? Yes he did abuse me, I know that now, but then I loved him and I knew he loved me. He was gentle and that – not like they say now – not like rape. Nice then, but woagh yeah, it fuckin' changed me for life ... for love ... for men, yeah?'

Badder's head was shaking. 'But getting one abuser to help with another, Holly?'

Holly nodded vigorously. 'He thought I was accusing him - the stupid old man - so I hung up on him.'

Yet another turn. Badder held her breath and at the other side of the mirror Chocky was biting his knuckle. What if Holly killed her dad but had nothing to do with the death of her husband. But surely they had to be linked somehow, however tenuously.

'He didn't believe me, y'know. He seemed shocked an' that, reckoned he didn't know who I was. Where did that fuckin' leave me, eh, I ask you Miss?'

Badder was now completely confused and wondered if this was helping the investigation at all. She decided they all needed a break and asked Holly if she minded – no, she needed 'the loo' – so Badder swished out, ushered the men out of the corridor and upstairs and sent a WPC to support Holly with fresh tea and sympathy.

Badder needed the whiteboard. Alan handed her an ice cold cherry cola from the vending machine. He had noticed that that was her drink of choice. She took an almighty swig and it frothed up though her nose. She belched, cried and laughed – just what she needed. 'Come on Alan – sort the pictures out now!'

She whipped her phone out, listened a moment. 'Yes! Ginny Devine is Holly's real mother but Brien isn't!'

Mike smiled but restrained a comment. Alan and Chocky laughed out loud.

'What? Oh yeah – idiots – you know what I mean – that's why we couldn't get anywhere with Brien. Somehow he seems to have abused her, but he is not her real father.'

'She may not know that, Sarge.'

'No, course not Alan, but she seems to have loved him as her 'Dadda' at some point and she definitely spoke to him after Hu raped her.' Addressing them all, she asked, 'You think she called *him* … or her Mum?'

'So, you sly thing, you got a DNA sample off Ginny, eh?' said Chocky.

'Tissues from the interview – okay innit?'

'Course! Clears a nice new path for us. So should we have been looking at Ginny all along?'

'Why not!' said Mike. 'We haven't looked at her at all – you didn't look for her on the videos did you Alan?'

'Don't even know if she's got a car or how she dresses.'

They had established that Holly Dean – Mrs Hubert Stannton – was in fact Colleen Devine, however she had covered her tracks. They had Ginny Devine in the station – she was definitely Holly's natural mother. Brien was lying in the mortuary. He had been lying about the call, too, it seemed. They had to acknowledge that Brien must have been either Holly's adoptive father or step-father. Mike pointed out that a lot of incestuous abusers were step fathers.

Rain lashed at the windows – a welcome break after a long dry spell, even in winter.

Should they hold on to Leo Nicholas? At that point it was looking like a family affair and needed a long look. Holding Leo might just be stoking up more trouble for later and the hours were running out anyway. He tried to cadge a brolly off them.

They agreed that it looked like Holly had rung her 'dad' who weighed in and killed the man who raped her. They also agreed that the obvious had been dogging them for too long.

Possible scenarios thrown up by the fresh details included Holly not speaking to her *dad* – he wasn't her dad after all – but speaking to her Mum and she killed Stannton. They knew almost nothing about her, and despite looking like any other old lady, she was bigger than Badder, and she could have been a wrestling champion for all they knew.

Ginny would know that Brien was not Holly's father, and maybe the call told Ginny that her husband had abused her daughter and she went for Brien.

Holly admitted that she had been at the Hotel; had had a row with Hu; who had sexually assaulted her; so why should she not have been the one that shoved him out of the window that she admitted opening? Riddled with guilt and at the highest pitch of emotion, she rang home and set another ball rolling: that's what they had to find out next – what ball?

They went back to Ginny and she consistently denied that she had received a call. Once they had accepted that, the detectives regrouped and decided they needed to tackle the paternity issue. They needed to be sure of their facts – they couldn't allude to Badder's clandestine DNA sampling. That would not be difficult as they could point out the known fact that Brien was not Colleen's father. They still had to tread carefully as a very emotional situation could ensue if Ginny were to deny that Holly was Colleen and assert that Colleen was Brien's daughter, Ginny hadn't 'gone' with anyone else!

A strange and eerie scenario also occurred to the team – to bring mother and daughter face to face after … half the daughter's lifetime? They were worried about the ethics of it and could not see how it would help. Holly would probably accept that Ginny was her mother, but the reverse may not apply. They could not admit to the DNA Badder had got from the tissues, but if necessary they could now take an official sample and come back with the results.

Back with Ginny, Badder referred to her final comment to her – that Holly looked like Colleen. She now laid the two photographs before her. Ginny had done her crying about the notion and studied the photographs very carefully for some time, occasionally stroking them and talking to them. 'So who is this?' she asked.

'That is Mrs Stannton, she was calling herself Holly Dean. It sounds a bit like Colleen Devine if you slur it, doesn't it?'

'It's been a long time, officer. She is a very pretty girl. Why are you telling *me* this?'

The woman in front of the detectives was the recently widowed wife of a possible murder victim. She was holding herself together very well, all things considered. She could of course be the murderer, but just as likely was not. How to give her this shocking piece of news. 'Your husband Brien was, I'm sorry to say, but sure you know … was a suspect in the violent death of Hubert Stannton.'

'Father Hu,' she whimpered.

'We have spoken to you about two telephone calls to your house. They are very important as they were made by Hu's wife. Now if you didn't take the calls, somebody did, so it must have been…'

'Brien. My Brien.' She spoke to the photos. 'Was that your Colleen, Brien?' Whether he answered or not, the detectives didn't hear. Ginny sought confirmation from them.

'Are you still denying taking the calls, Ginny? If you insist then we can tell you what we think. However, we would really like you to tell us what *you* *t*hink.'

'I did hear you say that I knew that … that Father Hu's wife was our Colleen. That's just ridiculous. Why? It would be *such* a coincidence. How even? She lives in London. She doesn't know Father Hu.'

They waited.

'She has phoned me. Colleen. Colleen did phone our house. She knows we are there for her if she ever wants to…' She sniffed hard. She blinked hard.

'You *do know* something don't you? Did Brien know?'

'No! He would have told me.'

'He gave us the impression that you were very angry about Father Hu running off with a woman.'

'I was, I was indeed – it's utter filth, is what it is!'

They let her own words sink in.

'Aaw! Aw no! He couldn't … he couldn't tell me because I would be saying that about our…' and she cried aloud some more.

They had to proceed. Mike knew that 'Softly Softly' was a most aptly named and iconic detective series. He leant in, a strong shoulder to cry on – metaphorically. 'You didn't know Mrs Stannton, you just had a strong belief about a priest … well he wouldn't go for a horror, now would he? She must have been a lovely girl for him to even be attracted?'

Badder smiled at Mike and Ginny, dragging at her cuff as she had her knuckles to her mouth, was attentive to what he had said. Badder passed the tissue box.

'That's better, Officer. It's true isn't it?' She looked at Holly's wedding portrait again. 'She doesn't look like a horror, no. She looks nice. She looks like a woman in love.'

'It's from her wedding picture, ma'am.'

'Why didn't you come to me, Colleen? We love you. You are our child, we will always love you.'

Badder noticed that Ginny was talking to the adult photograph at last. 'So you agree that she could be your daughter?'

'Is she?'

'Ginny, this is very hard, we know. You have just lost Brien and this could all be such a shock…'

'But you said she's not Brien's, so how come?' She sat back exhausted.

Badder bit her lip and fingered the photograph again.

'Ma'am,' said Mike. Holly nodded him on. 'Ma'am, *she admits* she is really Colleen Devine.' He was acutely aware that Brien wasn't the father, but felt very sure that he thought he was. 'Was she adopted, Mrs Devine?'

Ginny looked up for a flash, and then continued to look down again. She was still. 'But anyone could just turn up and say that … there was that Frenchman impersonating a dead boy just a few years ago.'

They let her try to argue that out for herself.

'She ran away, that's what. What would she come back to marry a priest for. Sex! Sex was what drove her away. She wanted to be a little sex pot like all them young ones. I seen it on the telly.'

'Now look Mrs Devine,' said Badder beginning to run out of patience. She knew what it was she wanted to hear.

'Sex was all he wanted in the end, but he was no good.'

The detectives sat up and listened.

'Brien, poor man. His sex was killing me, and our babies. It was him killed them.'

Badder felt her heart turn three hundred and sixty degrees. What more could be thrown into this mix. He was a paedophile – was he killing their babies?

Ginny was mumbling away. Mike said, 'just a bit louder for the tape, Ma'am.'

'Brien and me. Lovely together – it was wonderful, then the babies started to die. We both wanted one so much. I lost …I lost nine babies, Miss,' she drew Iruna with her gaze. She turned to Mike Gatting, 'This next bit is very difficult for a woman to say, to admit…'

He turned to move. Badder indicated him to stay, then so did Ginny. 'It's alright you being here, but just try to understand me … please?' He nodded. She went on, 'we had all the tests – not as good as these days, but they were getting there, you know. Well…' she checked Gatting sitting back writing notes. 'Well it was Brien's sperm…' she coughed. Gatting hadn't moved. 'The babies had a genetic defect – they were never going to survive … and they found it was Brien's genes, not mine.' She let that sink in; let them realise what she had to do. 'They only told me and I never let Brien know, poor man. I told them that we would give up and they hadn't to tell him. But he wanted a child so much. Great dad he would be – he was!'

Yet again she coughed, swiped her face with her hand. 'Well don't think bad of me Miss, sir, but, well … Brien worked away a lot – firm took contracts wherever they could get them, and he'd be setting up offices and pay systems, you know. Well I don't suppose I look like the kind of woman – I'm not! I'm not that kind of a woman – but I seen it in the fillums – I found myself some very nice men, up for conferences and that, who just wanted a chat - away from home, with a … respectable woman, you know?'

They were nodding at her. Whatever next? Ginny the High Class Hooker?

'We'd have high tea, maybe the odd cocktail. I would give them a wrong number and never hear of them again. But I wanted to find one, one who … would father me a child.' She blinked hard but her listeners did not disappear. 'Wasn't going to tell him of course!'

Badder was thinking this all very sensible – probably went on all the time nowadays. She wouldn't put it past being standard practice for lesbians.

'I was scared in case it wouldn't look like our child – like me or Brien. So when I thought I had got the right idea – I did,' she smiled, 'I found a fit fellah, good head of hair like my Brien and seduced him.' She chuckled. The detectives smiled. 'He had to be someone who came up to London more than once – I wasn't sure to catch straight away. I got his number, but always used call boxes to ring him. I caught with Colleen and never rang again. To Brien a daughter!'

Great story, but not a lot to do with the bodies of two men - not yet. So Badder said, 'and Brien just found out?'

'What? Brien found out? How?'

'No sorry, I was thinking that was maybe what happened at the river.'

Jumping to conclusions. Ginny was not going to be cornered. 'She pointed at Holly's picture. 'She never knew. She didn't tell him … oh!'

'Oh yes, Mrs Devine?' said Mike.

'Oh no, officer. Not what you think, not me. I did not push my husband in the river.'

'So why did you tell us that long story,' said Badder, 'such a tragic, but actually quite nice story? You must have been thinking … we thought you were leading up to how Brien died.'

'No Miss. You asked me if she was adopted. I thought I had better tell you the truth, strange as that may seem. But anyway,' she squinted at the photographs, 'I'm not saying this is my Colleen – even if she says she is.'

Badder was stumped yet again. She knew her own forensic sample was inadmissible. It was useful in confirming one of their suspicions – Holly was now definitely Colleen Devine, but they were not in a position to reveal their knowledge. She had hoped that the strange circumstances and her own story would lead Ginny to own up and come out – to maybe even confess to one or both killings. She needed support and advice and closed proceedings for the day.

Released from custody, but not from all suspicion, Leo had taken a diversion to stake out the Boss, Wyndham Leyton - at the wrong house yet again, a different one from Saturday night: he wanted to be sure of the man's duplicity – was it multiplicity? – before he took action. He hadn't told Talya about suspension from work, so she wouldn't see anything strange in his being out at odd hours – youth workers were proud that they were out working with 'difficult' young people when everyone else was off duty.

Engine and lights off, Leo didn't see DC Prisco's lights go off behind him. On the news he heard there was talk of a fundamental review of Police was needed – Oh Yeah! But he forgot it when he heard that Further Education Colleges had to cut a quarter of vocational courses because of central funding. More kids on the street.

His mind turned to wondering how different he was from Dostoyevsky's Raskolnikov: like him Leo does not regret his Crime, yet unlike him, he does not accept need for his Punishment. Leo felt so alone in a world where socialism, true socialism, had become a dirty word - Thatcher, now Cameron besmirching the name of Trotsky. Leo has saved the world, his bit of it – especially women and children - from an icon (to him) of the paedophile predatory priest. He cannot carry the whole revolution, but true to himself, he will not give up the fight and is prepared to carry on alone.

Leyton's car was outside yet another of his mistress's houses – and Leo knew the cuckold to be an honourable man. Enough seen, he decided to drive on home.

So what punishment would Leo deserve? He has killed an ex-priest. The priest had seduced a young woman – it was Leo's mother all over again … and again. When would it stop?

Poor old Abe Grant had killed a woman – he had not seduced her, they had fun together and during that childlike, but illicit and reckless fun, Abe had killed her by accident. In himself he couldn't accept the accident, he would only accept his own guilt. He took his punishment – nine years in prison and a life conviction for the culpable manslaughter of his girlfriend. For thirty years he had served young people, who in their reckless use of drugs may repeat his folly. He brought in Brien to help him and Leo had concluded that, like Abe, he was a one time offender with maybe decades of repentance behind him. But Leo had no evidence of that.

So who had killed Brien? He checked his own hands on the wheel – not even a bit sweaty. 'Mani fredde, cuore caldo,' cold hands, warm heart, his mother used to say. He had no chance to find out if she bore any resentment towards her boyfriend the priest. His dad didn't, why should Leo? Maybe he didn't, he simply wanted to do something special for her, for her memory, now she had gone. It made him feel better, too. She might not realise it, but Holly Stannton was better off without the snake. But Brien – what was he to do with it?

Tuesday 23rd March

Holly and Ginny had been kept in custody overnight – each under suspicion of the murder of her husband.

The detectives had agreed that they needed the forensics on Ginny to officially confirm what Badder's unofficial sampling had proved. They would then *tell* Holly that they knew that she was in fact Colleen Devine, and see if they could get both women to clarify who killed whom and why.

They had to run a gauntlet of pressmen with renewed interest in a double murder in a church based scandal. One of the nationals had found a reference to Brien Devine's child sex abuse conviction and they were all baying for more blood. Now they all knew that Stannton's wife had been arrested for Brien Devine's murder and that she was in fact Devine's long-lost daughter. Had she suspected Brien of killing her husband? Was it her whom he had abused? Now an adult, had she tracked him down?

Alan teased Iruna that they were her paparazzi, so she had to take him outside to finger-wag him to back off - or else. He was shocked, but didn't have time to show it, as she was off back inside. The only clue he heard was '… not at work…'

The forensics weren't in, so the team were all at their computers: Chocky was trying to tie up early stuff and clear it away – the anal sex and gay stuff, checking out his own homophobia 'I would have expected better of you John Blundell'; Iruna was wiping and re-routing flow-lines on the whiteboard; Mike was getting anything he could on the Devine's and Holly's other contacts and relations, such as her ex, Rupert Spiro, whom he found in prison for living off immoral earnings; Alan was festering about Leo Nicholas – he couldn't get round the fact that it was his little conference that had started this whole thing off.

Iruna ambled into Chocky's room and after a few minutes going round the houses she realised they were mirroring – both with their feet on the desk and a coffee mug in both fists. A phoney war. Did they both have the same idea? Neither wanted to ask.

'Nice little trick with the tissues, Iruna.'

'Yeah, thanks Chocky. Think it'll *do* the trick?'

'I somehow can't get round a conspiracy though, can you?'

'I don't know. I think it possible that someone pushed Stannton out of the window, then went down to check he wasn't going to come round and accuse her.'

'Her?'

'Well no, sorry. Just that we got two women in custody, sir?' She didn't want to say that she was convinced of this and that she didn't think there were two involved.

'Still – *her* though? One of them?'

'One of them has got to have killed Brien hasn't she? I mean, Leo Nicholas wouldn't, well would he?'

Chocky scrubbed his chin. 'But isn't he more of a killer? Can you really see either of these setting out first to kill Hu Stannton?'

'Well, er,' she squeezed her eyes to. 'Hu raped her … what happened next?'

'Are you leaving Leo right out of the picture? He set it up and I … well do you believe he didn't creep back?'

Iruna swept her feet down. Going over this old ground irritated her nearly as much as Chocky's homophobia. But then she chuckled, 'speak for yourself, Iruna!'

'What?'

Teresa's pretty face flashed before her. 'Nothing Chocky. It's just a bit of a … a treadmill. We've just got to wait and see.'

Badder pushed Holly's photograph towards Mrs Virginia Devine and said, 'This is your daughter Colleen.' She waited.

Ginny looked at the picture for a good while. She slid it toward her. Eventually she slid it off the table onto both hands and gently lifted it to her lips. 'You turned out well, Colleen; got fine cheekbones – my mother's.' She stroked the picture. She placed it carefully back on the table. 'Well officers, what do you want me to say?'

'Simply the truth, Mrs Devine,' said Badder.

'You've just told me a truth that I have been wanting to know for sixteen years.'

'But Mrs Devine, it is not a happy truth. We believe one of you killed Hu Stannton and one of you, maybe the same one, also killed your husband Brien.'

Despite a whole night in the cells, she did not appear to have taken any of that on board. She didn't think the woman in the picture was her daughter and didn't really know anything about Hu Stannton since his apostasy, so she had been absorbed by what had happened to her husband – and what he had to do with Colleen leaving home. 'Well I might have killed Brien, but...' She suddenly realised that she didn't want her daughter to be a killer.

'But...?'

'I might not have.'

Chocky leaned in. 'Did you, though?'

She had a think about it. She looked at the photograph. 'Butter wouldn't melt.'

'It would, Ma'am, Ginny, I assure you it would.'

'Are you accusing her of killing my Brien?'

'No we are accusing you of killing your Brien and want you to explain why we are wrong.'

Ginny wanted to save her daughter from pain. She wanted to say she had killed Brien herself. 'Yes I killed Brien.' She looked down into her lap.

'So tell us how it happened then Mrs Devine,' said Badder.

Ginny coughed and rummaged round her brain. 'We went to the supermarket and had a bit of a row. He said he was going to walk home. I raced after him and

289

he stopped dead and … and I bumped him into the river.' She was completely devoid of emotion.

Chocky thought of a little girl making up a story – telling a lie.

'Where exactly was this please Mrs Devine?'

'Beside the car park wasn't it! The river goes right past the car park.'

'Was it or wasn't it?'

'I just said.' She was definitely a petulant child.

'It's a big car park – runs from the flyover, past one trolley shelter along the main car park, behind the Garden centre section then on along past another trolley shelter and the back car park, then the tar path stops and the muddy path starts. That's why we collected the shoes and boots.' Badder looked at Chocky and gave a quick flick of the side of her mouth. He nodded.

'Yes there, there where it gets muddy.'

Leading her witness, Badder continued, 'at the back of the far car park where it's very dark, yes?'

'Yes that's it Miss. Lucky because I let out a scream. I would wouldn't I?'

'Probably, if you *had* done that.'

'Yes well I did.'

'You didn't, though. Brien was found about a hundred metres upstream from there, almost under the flyover.'

Ginny was staring at the sergeant, her lips pouting.

'So you have just confirmed to us that you did not kill your husband Brien Devine,' said Chocky. 'It remains for us to discover whether or not you had anything to do with the death of your son-in-law…'

Ginny screamed.

'… Hubert Stannton.'

As the detectives left the room Badder looked back and saw Ginny fixed in an Edvard Munch mask.

It was Chocky's basic instinct that mother and daughter ought to be reconciled. Some reconciliation it would make at that point! It seemed obvious that Mrs Devine did not know her daughter any more – didn't even recognise her. She would no doubt recognise her voice from regular telephone conversations, but how would the introduction go: 'This is your daughter. She just killed your husband'? Maybe not Chocky.

The team agreed that it must have been Holly who pushed Brien. They decided to interrogate her about that.

She had been well looked after and therefore didn't look like she had spent the night in the cells. She didn't look like a double murderer – does two make a serial killer?

The detectives now knew what the real relationships between the various protagonists were. However they did not know whether Holly had any knowledge of her real parentage; they suspected that unless she had done some sort of paternity test, she would not know that Brien was not in fact her father. She didn't need to know this – he was for all intents and purposes her father – from the moment she was conceived. She would naturally turn to him for help.

'Holly when you left the Loseborough Hotel after the horrible row with your husband Hubert Stannton, you telephoned your parents.'

She looked into Chocky's eyes. She expected him to say more.

'You did, Holly, you said you did.'

She looked to her solicitor who raised her brows in question. That was no answer. 'You do not. You do not know that.'

'You are not going to continue to deny it, are you? Now come on. You rang them for some support, didn't you? You usually speak to your mum don't you, but it was your Dad who answered – and you told him what had just happened.'

Holly was nodding. 'No I didn't.'

'But you were nodding.' Chocky's voice was pleading now. 'You were nodding while I said that?'

She looked down at her hands then willed them to shift her better onto her seat. 'Dadda.'

'Your Dadda, Holly. What did he say?'

'He didn't know I was Hu's wife. He didn't know! Ha!'

'So he didn't know who it was calling him, is that what you're saying?'

'Oh he knew who was calling, I was always ... I used to be always calling ... 'my darling daughter Colleen', he said. I couldn't believe he didn't know it was me married his precious priest. See, I sort of asked him about the priest when I first came up here. I went to see my dad at his regular place – at his bloody church. He teased me about the priest – didn't want me to find out who the hunk really was – said he was called Father Von Trapp. Sound of Music my arse!'

Chocky resisted a smile. Badder didn't.

'Reckoned he didn't recognise, on the phone, no - on the phone he said he didn't recognise me *that time*, yeah?'

They nodded.

'Well I was pissed off, wasn't I. Thought 'I'm getting no bloody help here', so I slams the phone down.'

'But you called him back?'

'Yeah, I already called him back. He just said he wished I had told him.'

'Told him what exactly, Holly?'

She looked at the Inspector as if he were an imbecile. She folded her arms and sighed, 'what the fuck?'

Badder intervened – perhaps a feminine touch was required. 'Holly, now you are confirming, you are not *denying* what you told us yesterday, so we need to be clear what happened and why. If you did phone your dad, did he do something, maybe something you didn't expect ... maybe?'

Holly rubbed her lips with a finger and nodded at Badder. 'Yeah. Yes, that's what I wondered.' She was frowning now. 'I wondered if he'd gone and done for my Huey, see?'

'Indeed I do, Holly.' Iruna saw Chocky smile. 'I do wonder if he maybe went to tackle that man who hurt his daughter, yeah?'

'Yes Miss, that's it...'

'And did you find out? Did you find out that your dad had...?'

Holly chewed her lip. 'Well I'd been following him, him and his fat friend...'

'Abe Grant?'

'Think so. I did ask. Sounds right. He was pushing drugs to them youths out at that derelict factory and meeting up with my dad in the pub and that – right bloody shifty pair of conspirators, them two.'

Thinking Chocky was maybe right about a conspiracy after all, Badder was shocked to find the lovely Abe Grant re-entering the frame at last. 'So you followed them to the Loseborough?'

Holly stood.

'Sit down, Holly.'

The Solicitor also indicated the chair and stroked a hand down Holly's back.

'Sorry,' Badder went on, 'what did I say wrong?'

'I never said I followed them – *to the Loseborough!*' she shouted. 'I just followed the people who went there with Hu for that conference thingy, but not *to* it.'

'So where, Holly?'

'Just said didn't I? Pub and that.'

Was she running them off on a tangent again? 'Holly – help me a bit – pub *and that?'*

'Their houses, that factory, the church and that.'

'Okay, Holly, say we believe that you did not push Hu out of the window. But we do believe somebody did, somebody did push him, Holly...'

She bit her lip again and was nodding.

'You think it was Brien.'

She continued to nod.

'Can you *tell* us what you thought at all, Holly?'

She picked at a fingernail. Then she checked her other hand. 'Who do you think it was Miss? It was him wasn't it?'

Leo Nicholas was sitting in his car reading what an awful paedophile Brien Devine had been, then further down the page he read that they were not saying that at all. The headline was a surmise, but the story had the facts – well the five The Mail had made out of two and two. He found that the police had arrested two women for the murders of Hu Stannton -'runaway Priest', and Brien Devine -'Paedo.' They surmised that they were the wives of the respective men, but were not willing it to be explained away as simple domestics, they were building it into a paedophile sex exploitation ring. Of course a lot could be conjectured from the facts that both the priest and Devine were Irishmen, and that the priest's 'young wife' - *'his own age'* thought Leo – was Devine's daughter.

Leo had a sharp moment of regret about not sharing his Police experiences with Jan. How could he not? Easily – he might let out the truth to such a friend. What would Jan think of him? What was all Leo's CRB, Vetting and fucking Barring anger about a system not protecting children, but people like him – him and his youth workers doing the actual protection, and here's Leo running his own revolution. His people were being thrown out of work – his own job could not last much longer. And like Trotsky said, people only really reveal themselves when they are thrown out of the normal conditions of their life - only then do they have to fall back on their reserves.

He thought of how he did the double take when he first met his Natalya – good enough for Leon, good enough for Leo. She opened the window of his life. 'Life is beautiful. Let the future generations cleanse it of all evil, oppression and violence, and enjoy it to the full.' So, better detectives than the police that the press were, they had also uncovered the fact that another of Mrs Stannton's ex-husbands Rupert Spiro was in prison for living off immoral earnings. Now they had her bang to rights for dobbing in her exploitative husband *and* shoving off her abusive dad.

Leo tried to visualise the woman fleeing from Hu's room that evening at the Loseborough. From the fast but awkward gait, almost a stagger, he thought it may have been an older woman. Maybe that was why they had Mrs Devine in custody, too. Did they suspect her of pushing the priest out of the window?

It had taken quite a shove to get Hu over that parapet, Leo thought it would need to be a fit woman. That little sergeant would know the technique – but it wasn't her.

Hu had been readying himself for the shower when Leo sneaked in on him. Hu hadn't locked the door after the woman, and Leo heard the water rush start up. It was quite cold in the room. The French windows were open. Leo went over to look out. Fine night. He pushed the doors wide open and coughed. Hu stood into the bathroom doorway.

'Buona Sera Reverendo Padre,' said Leo addressing his mother's abuser.

Hu walked towards him, nonplussed. 'What are you doing here?' He wrapped the dressing gown tighter and went to force his way past Leo to shut the windows. Leo jabbed the near frame out of the way. He turned. He pushed Hu on his way. Hu hit the balcony, winding himself.

Leo saw him red-faced and sweating. No wonder after the row he had had with the woman – the bully. No woman could hold out against a man of his stature. What was the window doing open anyway? Had the woman escaped the priest's clutches at a crucial moment? The priest could not be found to have yet another woman in his room.

Hu took a huge gulp. He came for Leo. Leo face-palmed him back again. Nice rugby move. He followed through with a sweep to the legs. Hu was gone.

Leo bobbed down. He bit his knuckle. He looked across to the running shower. He picked up a glass, took it out of the plastic bag, gloved his hand with that and filled the glass with water. He turned off the shower. He traipsed spilling water across to the window. He splattered the marble. Maintaining the low profile, he made a couple of slip marks with the heel of his hand. He returned the glass to the sink. He sloshed a ready pasted tooth brush over the rim and into the glass of water and left it. He went out of the fire escape door he had not come in. Door shut, he pocketed the plastic bag.

Leo felt himself agreeing with The Mail for the one time ever and siding with the abused young woman. They would let her off with a suspended sentence.

The perfect crime Leo.

Holly told the police that she had concluded that maybe her Dadda had needed to make up to her. She didn't need to have a woman-to-woman any more. She told them straight out. Yes she did think that Brien had done for her Hu. As a kid her and her Dadda had been very close. Her Mammy and Dadda did not sleep together, she never did know why, but she used to sleep with her Dadda sometimes – she was his little wifey. Her Dadda used to make love to her and it was – she checked out the Inspector – it was lovely.

This went on right into her secondary school years, and then she found out it wasn't right. She told him and he pleaded his need. 'Well it is, isn't it, Inspector? You men – you can't do without it, can you? Anyway he just told me it would stop and told me he could go to prison for what he'd done. I didn't want that, did I? I loved my Dadda.'

It was pouring out of her. The detectives listened in stunned silence. 'All the same, it prayed on my mind, I wanted boyfriends and I wanted more of that love-making – but not with my dad – oh, no! Then Boys? They couldn't do it – Wham Bam – you know it!'

Badder knew it. She knew it wasn't good enough.

'I had to go. I couldn't tell Mammy and I didn't need to tell Dadda. So when I rang him, well, you know like, well…'

They could see she had at last run out of steam. 'You think he did go and tackle Hu?'

She nodded.

'Do you think he pushed him out of the window?'

She looked straight into Badder's soul. Badder thought 'WHO DROUND HIM!' 'You pushed him out of the window, though, didn't you Holly?'

She continued to look Badder in the eye, but was now shaking her head with a frown. 'No-o. No I didn't – he did.'

'You thought Brien Devine killed Hu and you called him to the riverside. You pushed him in didn't you?'

She nodded.

'For the tape, please Miss? Did you kill Brien Devine?'

'Yes.'

They all let out their breath.

They left it at that. They didn't know what sort of a crime they were working towards or what they could make stick with the Crime Prosecution Service. Badder didn't want Holly charged with anything much, and Chocky was thinking Holly shoved Hu in self defence and her father ... well he deserved it.

They had to keep her in, but had to let her mother Ginny Devine go. Ginny pleaded to see her daughter, but they were still unhappy with the circumstances and refused her.

Chocky tracked the Superintendent down to the supermarket – that supermarket - and on the nearby riverbank, told her the outcome.

Friday 24th March

Standing under the arbour at Rufford Abbey, Leo wanted to see the Inspector arriving – and that he was not accompanied by squad car. He hadn't noticed the man in the jacket and jeans standing under a huge beech tree – Chocky also wanted to see his quarry break cover.

Nothing was revealed.

Would Leo run away? No, he won't run away on me by a law of nature. He's a moth to my candle? - he'll keep circling around me, circling around me, freedom will no longer be dear to him, he'll fall to thinking, get singed, he'll keep on making circles around me, narrowing the radius more and more, and—whop! He'll fly right into my mouth, and I'll swallow him. Tasty!

Leo didn't flinch when the Inspector came up to him – had he known all along?

'Away from possible prying eyes,' said Chocky, 'and out of uniform.'

Leo set off along the front of the ruin towards the lake. Chocky fell in beside him.

'You know this place?' asked Chocky.

'Course I do – pits all round here – I was the NUM rep. Bit like pushing water up hill – Notts was full of scabs. You could say it was them that actually closed down the coal industry.'

Chocky was pleased to have hit a nerve so soon. 'So you blame them for the rest of your life?'

'Naagh! Not their fault. Men are sheep – aren't we?' He went into some length about leading people and arrived at the question of the Black Sheep. 'It's always a bad 'un, isn't it – a Black Sheep? But you know it's a black one that the shepherd chooses to lead the flock?'

Chocky thought it about time to ask what he wanted to see Leo for. He wanted … he needed Leo to know that he thought him a murderer.

'Interesting choice of venue, – part of the Dukeries – all those billionaires – by today's standards – profiting from the efforts of men hewing and choking on coal under their very parlours. Czars waiting for a more just reward.'

'Now there you have it Leo – Revolution?'

Leo stopped and cocked his head at the Inspector. Comrade Dostoyevsky came to mind again. An 'extraordinary' man has an inner right to decide in his own conscience to overstep … certain obstacles – poor Brien. He looked around. It was still early spring so there weren't crowds even on a free entry day. He did not want to be trapped. 'Is that what you brought me here to talk about?'

'Well in a round about way,' he also took a look around, 'yes – and your part in it.'

Leo was not sure that the Inspector knew where he was digging. How much would he guess: the name not 'Andrew', but 'Leo' and why? Union man so probably Socialist. Ardent Socialist, so probably a commie. A 'Commie Bastard'? Leo had felt no ill-feeling towards the Inspector. Why was that? Empathy? 'So you know I was arrested for Picketing. Is that it?'

Chocky smiled, bit his thumb and kicked a stone. He looked across at Leo as they continued towards the lakeside. A gaggle of geese, ducks and moorhens anticipated a feed and sailed towards them. 'I quite like you, Leo, if that's not too forward and shocking a thing for me to say.'

Leo did not think he was being hit on by a gay – that would have shocked him.

Chocky went on immediately, 'I wanted to know … I want you to know that I believe you killed Hu Stannton.' He was smiling and looking straight ahead.

Leo thought the man was studiously allowing him to react, to adjust his position, but without scrutiny. 'Would that benefit the whole of humanity?'

'Perhaps not the whole of humanity, Leo?'

'So you are agreeing that his death could be regarded as a benefit – a good thing.'

'You caused another man's death too. Is Brien part of your collateral damage?'

'Of course it could be seen as acceptable – but only if it is essential for the practical fulfilment of the idea.'

'Was it?'

'Was it my idea, Inspector, Chocky?'

Chocky knew the moth was moving away from the flame. He knew Leo didn't kill Brien. 'Getting back to Stannton - you told us how you did it…'

'Could have done it!'

'… but left us to prove it.'

'And you didn't.' Had they got some other piece of evidence?

'No we didn't. So, Leo, Help me clear up the investigation, will you? Your explanation of what happened really helped us clear it up. Have you a similar notion about why, that's the thing – motive? Why was Stannton killed? No, you didn't kill Brien Devine. However, you hated everything the priest stood for, very popular stance at the moment. But you aren't a tabloid rationalist – you have much higher motives.'

Leo had given up preaching, got down off his soap box, given up even telling people that they were being exploited – someone more important than Leo had told them that they were a land owning democracy – they were *not* being exploited. He had given up telling anyone his politics. 'So what's your angle, Inspector? No, I don't think you are being forward and no I'm not shocked. I might be surprised if … but I'm not surprised that you quite like me. How come?'

'How come you're not surprised?' he laughed.

Leo pursed his lips and flicked a brow.

'You really care about people – you've set yourself up as their guard. For instance, my colleague, Sergeant Bahadur, was really moved by your obvious compassion for the young druggie in hospital.'

'What? How did she know?'

'Yes, thought so. She came to get you, but you were so moved that she left without you even noticing her.'

For the first time to Chocky's knowledge Leo smiled broadly. 'You're disarming me, Inspector. Not sure I am comfortable with that. Come on then, give me something.'

Chocky indicated his civvies – his jeans, 'Just me, Leo, John Blundell, in me jeans, no wire-tap, no following surveillance – call me Chocky and tell me why you aren't sad about Brien Devine's death.'

'Brien Devine, eh?' Leo coughed. 'I am. I was. I was sad that he had died. But then … yes, then I thought,' he gave Chocky a studied look, 'I thought … did you say, or did I conjecture that you are also a Catholic?'

'Ah, but don't jump to any funny conclusions, Leo.'

'No, I won't. So tell me this - should *you* be sad about Brien's death?'

A smile worked its way into Chocky's eyes. 'Hm. Playing religion against me?'

'Press are going on about him being a Paedo. Haven't you Catholics had a bellyful of Paedos cutting under your radar?'

'Leo – a Safeguarder!' spluttered Chocky. 'I know he did have a conviction, but the press…'

'Yes I know. Just checking. I actually reckon he was a very good man – better than me. He totally served his church. Old Abe tells me he's been doing that for … what, decades or something. I spent a couple of days in his close company and was fully at ease with the sort of hard working … would you say, 'penitent'?'

'I might, but go on.'

'I can't *pay* people to do what Abe, Brien and his friends do for the so called dregs of our society – day and night. But here's a funny thing – I hate that Catholic Church as an institution – not as a collection of people – a billion of you, is it now? Nine hundred and ninety nine million of them are very good people expecting – nay hoping for a reward after this life.'

Chocky was nodding and smiling. Leo knew his enemy.

'At the Loseborough – stupid name – we happened to have a discussion about Latrun.'

Chocky was frowning.

'The good thief – on the cross next to Jesus?'

'Demian, or something, I heard, not Latrun. Dimas?'

'I've been there,' he bragged, 'tank museum – Latrun in Israel is named after him. But anyway, his name doesn't matter. Your old mate promised him Paradise that day, didn't he? And now Brien?'

'Haha! Nice bit of logic … but still a shame.'

'You are following me, but you're not following your religion.'

'What?' said Chocky, 'he killed Stannton out of love for his daughter and … sort of … died in the process.'

'Sort of!' He jabbed his finger and laughed at the Inspector. 'You get it don't you? You've got to agree with me.'

'But *you* killed Stannton.'

Leo stood hands in pocket, one eye shut against the glare of the sun. Inscrutable.

'If you killed Stannton, then Brien was killed unnecessarily.'

Leo was stirring his finger round. 'Ah, but he would have got every Catholic's greatest wish, wouldn't he?'

Chocky was cornered. In many a battlefield, Chocky knew that he and Leo would have been on the same side. He really hoped that Leo would give him the tiniest lead or detail on which to rebuild the case against him. And he knew that Leo would know, too. What he liked about Leo was his wish for a better world, but not with his means of attaining it – not with killing.

Chocky was not going to get fat on moths today. 'Can I buy you lunch?'

They were at the far side of the lake. Twenty more minutes for the Inspector to wheedle something out of Leo. Leo knew they would have to drop the 'investigation' by the time they got within earshot of the café. 'We'll see. But I know you have to agree that no one except Holly is a real victim round here…'

'So you insist Brien was collateral damage, and not a victim? Whoever killed him sent him to Heaven? Preposterous!'

'You mean wrong, or not?'

'But you are not religious, so in your terms he was an innocent, and as you said, repentant sinner who could maybe have enjoyed a decade or more of life, with even a reconciliation with his long lost daughter.'

'No, no!' said Leo. 'If Hu hadn't have died, she would have remained lost to both of them. Do you not think that an end may justify the means as long as there is something that justifies the end? You can't have it both ways.'

'Is that you, or…'

Leo was flicking his Trotsky.

'Of course,' Chocky continued, 'some means do justify the ends. So tell me about the end in this case … and the justification of course.'

'You wanted to know if I could have a deeper motive, Chocky? Now there are some details of the case you haven't told us, aren't there? Like, what did that bastard priest do to that young woman of his?' He looked around. He now knew that it was her he saw leaving the room, struggling from the room, staggering from the room. There was no one in earshot. 'Did he abuse her?'

Chocky said nothing. He nodded.

'So…' Leo was tapping the air, his lips pursed.

Chocky's heart leapt into his mouth. He stopped himself biting his lip.

'... a priest abuses a young woman – and gets away with it.' Leo took a deep, deep breath. 'And I get a sister.'

Chocky readied a whistle, but held back. 'A motive? Your motive?'

'Motive enough for thousands and thousands of young people across the Catholic world, I think.'

'And you are their agent.'

'I am a victim and I am their Safeguarder. I have spent a career – a second career after Thatcher took away my first one – trying to enable young people to lead fulfilled lives, safe from abuse – be that sex and violence, or simple exploitation in the workplace. Society is riddled. Your good will – I believe you have it – is exploited daily by corruption in your own Police and political management. Systems and organisations – albeit Catholic Church, County Council or Political party, always harbour people with selfish desires for power and the exploitation of others. Across the world, these austerity measures are trashing the very people that the commercial sector *can't* exploit, Public Service Employees who look after the vulnerable. The youth service that I joined no longer exists...'

'But you are a manager in it!'

'In name only. The capitalist economy does not understand how much need there is for non-commercial services like mine. It does not understand that we step in where education has failed – drugs, work, crime, and yes arts, sports and leisure - and it fails a lot the world over. Me? I am a tool to get rid of the workers – then they get rid of me. The countdown is on ... but the explosion won't happen 'til I'm long gone.'

'That the next atrocity in your revolution?'

'That demeans you. The time bomb is the poor exploited and uncared for in society, put in a silo and a lid put on. It will blow.'

Chocky whole heartedly agreed with the man – but he wasn't going to let on. 'Why do you stay, then?'

'Because I am at least a friendly face delivering the chop. People understand – they don't blame me.'

Chocky caught a mouth-watering waft from the café and stopped. 'Leo. Thank you for daring to meet me. Do let me buy you lunch – they are sometimes free.

Leo's wrinkled nose was not impressed by what he discerned as rancid chip fat.

'Let me just say that I think you took the law – or righteousness as you see it – into your own hands.' Chocky's smile was a little reassuring. 'I believe you threw Stannton out of a window – attempted murder. Though he *may* have been finished off by person unknown, it was you who made his wife unhappy, causing her to kill someone else – that being her own father. This in turn deprived a wife of a husband in her retirement.'

Leo wasn't going to argue with that. His stomach was churning and he decided to insinuate a hunger. 'That is your belief. I appreciate your candour. The meat maybe a little unsavoury, but you have seasoned it well … and moving on from metaphor, I accept your offer of real food. Do you support Everton, Chocky?'

Chocky's jaw dropped.

'Catching flies, Inspector?'

After

Mother and daughter met for the first time after sixteen years on the steps of the courthouse. They did not have anything to say. There had been so much unsaid for so long, how could they say it without recrimination? Who could blame who for what? Who knew the whole story? They hugged.

Mother was looking at the woman who killed her husband and had 'got away with it.' The jury could not agree that Holly had killed Hu, but they did think she had killed Brien. However, they did not think there was any intent. It seemed the defence's claim - that her only fault was not to stop to help the man she had pushed - had swayed them. There was the added bonus for Holly that she saw he had not actually fallen in the water – just onto the bank and it was only a short fall – he would surely get up and brush himself down. At least they believed that she thought that the man who killed her husband had also abused her as a child. Disgusting. How could they?

Daughter was looking at the woman who caused her father to abuse her. This woman had helped her with her periods, yes, and Holly's words for her, were most choked by the fact that she continued to be the little wifey well into the time she could have been a mother herself. How ever did Brien get away with that? If she were a real woman, she would give her man what he needed and he would not need to take it from elsewhere. Then she must have known what Brien was doing and … let him. She was sympathetic to her Dadda. She had no sympathy for her Mammy.

Mother and niece looked over this scene and had plenty to say.

Hubert Stannton's mother thought there had been a complete travesty of justice – she couldn't see any wrong in her Hu - how could that siren say such things about the good and holy man?

Her niece Pauline Stannton had lost the man in her life to a seductress and murderer. She was sick to her back teeth of people accusing the priests of abuse. Hadn't they given up that sort of thing? Nobody forced them – except the evil temptresses and she was looking at one of them.

Leo gave his condolences to Abe over the loss of his good friend Brien. Abe was remarkably philosophical as he had not known the historical Brien who had been shown in court, but the man he had known for many years was a kind, thoughtful, devout and generous man, evidently repenting whatever he believed he had done. It was Abe's feeling that Brien's final act – if indeed it was him - was a magnanimous one, erroneously but selflessly giving up his chance of Heaven for his daughter. 'He laid down his life for a loved one, Leo – 'This Day you will be with me in Paradise' - isn't what Jesus told your old friend Latrun, Leo?'

The Detective team was generally satisfied rather than ecstatic at the outcome. They felt justice had been done, even if it wasn't the law which had meted out the punishment. They had a young woman who had apparently been abused as a child, pimped as an adult, then had her 'nice' husband, in a seeming fit of madness, turn on her and anally rape her. In a complete turnaround, her childhood abuser had come to her rescue – so he thought. She had to admit to setting him off by her phone call to him, but she really did not expect him to go and kill her man. When she eventually met him for the first time in half her life, she had no strong basis for communicating her anger, so she lashed out. He probably simply staggered back, his head unfortunately hitting one of only a few rocks on the muddy bank.

Detective Inspector Chocky Blundell felt strongly that a couple of years Probation was a fitting 'punishment' for Holly – it would function as rehabilitation for her and would do her good.

Detective Sergeant Iruna Bahadur felt no punishment was required for the poor woman, but concurred with Chocky that in effect it was more a support than a punishment.

Detective Constable Mike Gatting was a little peeved that Brien Devine had effectively escaped proper justice, and that their team had been pipped to the post by Holly.

Detective Constable Alan Prisco's heart was pounding – bursting out of his chest – and he could only think about the Super's understanding and offer of a move to another team, so he would not be mixing business and pleasure. It was a key condition that would allow him to accept Iruna's offer of a proper love affair – 'only if you are serious and open to marriage, Alan?'

Badder gave all the men a hug and thanked Chocky for sorting out the 'fine mess she had gotten into.'

Chocky took them all for a slap-up meal at the Mussel and Crab, where he said the Super was standing a drinks tab and taxis home. He didn't tell them that the Super had agreed to let him keep tabs on Leo Nicholas whom he believed had pushed Hu Stannton off the balcony, even if it was Devine who finished him off.

Leo had to anticipate a long watch on the dark car park at County Hall. Wyndham Leyton did not keep regular hours - that was his way of keeping his wife in the dark. Leyton was just like the bankers profiting from the losses of millions of savers. As the shares were going down in value, the punters needed to sell, and of course the bankers did that for them – and took their standard commission. They profited from sales whether or not the vendor was profiting or losing. Leyton was profiting from all the jobs he was cutting for his masters. He was carrying out a 'thankless task' for them and they would thank him handsomely. He was getting his reward in this life, all right.

Leo's team was more than decimated – it was not one in ten: after two years of natural wastage followed by the latest savage cuts, Leo's team was now less than half what it had been ... and a lot more cuts to come. Then what of Leo's job? They couldn't sustain a manager with such diminished responsibilities - except for the one who did the diminishing of course – promotion for him.

No, Leo didn't believe in God. Leo didn't believe in the next life - all we get is here. Leo had an unshakeable faith in the importance of fairness: everyone deserved an equal opportunity, an equal opportunity to experience - to experience what?

Leo was quite clear - he understood evil - storm and flood, earthquake and tsunami, dictators and revolutions. What goes around, comes around. You get rid of Hitler and you end up with Stalin. But Hitler and Stalin both had a choice, and they chose evil. Did they have a balance - some happy times some sad? Did they give as good as they got, as good as they could?

Those two poor schmucks Abe and Brien had given half a century between them. What good did they get? They had taken what they thought would be the best – rapacious. It wasn't given them, they took it – both took a woman's life away. How bad was it? Leo couldn't judge. He wouldn't assume to judge.

But that bloody God bothering priest - he had only good and he had been given it – laid on a plate for him. He had received love, respect, veneration - adulation even - and he had told people they would get love, respect and ... happiness, if they did what he told them.

It made Leo's Red blood boil to hear poor, sick, oppressed people promised happiness in some ridiculous other life. Leo didn't want to be the judge of the two secret schmucks. Leo felt his indignation was righteous, and so was having his own silent revolution.

He swung his sock cosh round in a circle – he needed to get the heft of it - not too much sand to make it difficult to swing, but enough to ensure maximum cranium crushing impact.

If he did carry out his judgement, would he be 'giving' sadness?

If he did, would he 'give' joy to the world? Father Smarm had had his fair share of happiness - and not much to up-skittle it. He had given happiness and he had got happiness, he had promised happiness and now he would be finding out if the schmucks would be getting any of that promise.

No he wouldn't. He wouldn't find anything. He wouldn't know anything. There isn't anything after this life. He didn't even have the long lingering agony of cancer or loss of himself in dementia.

After a lifetime of comfort, respect, love of family, love of his people, Fr Smug wanted more. No! Yes, he did have his cake and ate it.

He had a very short journey to find out – the 'no road' to the Pearly Gates. Well, he would find out nothing. He wouldn't find out anything. His happiness would've continued for a lifetime - then stopped in an instant.

That's heaven on earth.

Leo felt a chill round the ankle of the bare foot. He had weighed up the risk of being found with only one sock on and decided it would take seconds to replace it – who would notice anyway – he wasn't in short pants! The other option would be to carry a spare sock for the cosh, but he would have to dispose of that quickly. He would still have to dispose of the pair he had on, but he would have time to do that away from the scene.

Leo thought of Abe and Brien. Gullible they may have been, but at the thought of them, warmth spread through him. They were good men.

They didn't think they were good.

They were riddled with guilt.

They were complete suckers.

They had spent fifty years repenting.

Abe was enjoying a loved life on this earth.

Brien had all the love he was getting. He would have felt good supporting his daughter – he would have been on a mission and died a martyr. Heaven – for him! Leo felt no remorse for bringing about Brien's demise. Anyway hadn't Leo provided him that opportunity to redeem himself. In a revolution there would always be collateral damage – unfortunately Brien was in Leo's revolution and he could not have planned it better.

Leo was going to be a match for Wyndham Leyton – Leyton was no way his equal - but Leo was going to get even with the pig.

Leo looked over the county.

He looked over the town.

He looked over the good Abram and his loyal friend Brien.

Holly had tempted Hu.

Leo had cast them out of their Eden.

He saw what he had done.

He saw that it was good.

Acknowledgements:

Thank you:

Barrie Purnell, David Graham, Bernie Gatt, and Diane Murphy for text editing.

Bassetlaw Writers and Retford Writers for forbearance and their constructive criticism which has helped shape this novel.

My early readers and reviewers, including Chris Warren, Colin and Cecilia Baird, Margaret Lees. Michael Yore, David Graham, Dominic Murphy, Sue Donahue and Peter Naylor-Morrell.

George Gatt ex-Thames Valley Police and Coroner's officer for procedural details and 'OSINTOT'.

St Joseph's, Retford for the Tin Tabernacle, the original church.

Wendy De Burnay for Retford Jail.

D.J. Saunders for the cover photo and artwork.

Losehill House Hotel & Spa, Castleton for the Jacuzzi.

All the wonderful Youth Workers and Teachers I have worked with over the years in Potters Bar, Merseyside, Humberside and Nottinghamshire. I hope this does you credit.

All the young people my teams have kept safe over the decades.

Also by Kevan Pooler

WMDs - Dynamite, Nuclear Power and Sex.
Their 'inventors' bemoan that their finest inventions
have been turned into Weapons of Mass Destruction, but which is
the worst?
Our hero listens but does not hear.

A year later he is in Africa helping childhood ex-Boy Soldiers
to regain a childhood through the language of Circus Skills.
Will he discover from personal experience which WMD is the worst?

www.kevanpooler.com

Also by Kevan Pooler

HALF A MILLION PRISONERS OF WAR IN BRITAIN

**A love story: man for woman, man for child, man for mankind.
What Daddy did in the war.**

Released from Strangeways Prison, his sentence as a Conscientious
Objector commuted to exile as a farm labourer, Eric Chapman, ex Sheffield
cutler, is intrigued by the Prisoners of War he is billeted with.
Befriending Palmiro 'Pam' La Banca leads him to explore the 'Officially
Secret' world of the 168,000 Italian POWs who built the first 80 Standard
Camps in the nationwide system.
Estranged from his pregnant wife, Eric seeks friendship among Britain's
enemies.
By the time 402,000 Germans are added,
he realises he is the only one interested,so sets out on a quest to record
the POWs' experiences in Britain.
Then came the Ukrainians.
The complete story of the POW camps in Britain 1940-1950
www.kevanpooler.com

Kevan Pooler runs a Nottinghamshire writers' group and is a School Governor, ex-Safeguarding Trainer, English Teacher, Friar and Youth Officer.

Born in Oxford to Patrick Murphy and Edith née Pooler, he spent his teens training to be a Franciscan Friar. He 'missed the sixties,' but has been trying to catch up since.

Being Editor of the college magazine and Social Secretary helped him to beat Peter Hitchens and Andrew Linzey to President of the Student Union in Oxford. From that experience he discovered that Youth Work was a career.

After unqualified success in Potters Bar, he decided to train in Liverpool. He taught English and Drama on Merseyside and Humberside before returning to Social Education.

Following national recognition in Rural and Mobile Youth Work in Notts, he took on Mansfield District, one of the most deprived urban areas in Britain. His management of a multi-disciplinary team of youth workers in Sexual Health, Homelessness, School Truants, School Excluded and Knife-Crime, helped to secure the highest ever grant for youth work.

He could not stop the slashing of Youth Work budgets.

Kevan had accumulated so many stories, that he decided to turn to writing them up. Needing to hone his skills he joined one writers' group and started another. This has been running for seven years.

He wrote 'Apple?' working title, 'A Lethal Weapon Too', in response to the Weapons of Mass Destruction debate, child soldiers in Africa, and rape as a weapon of war.

This was followed by 'Barred?' a crime thriller set in a youth project, questioning quite who is safeguarding young people and should some of them be barred.

Kevan then returned to a Youth Work anti-racism project started in the late 1980s, where he saw the kind treatment of WW2 Prisoners of War as a starting point for our multi-cultural society. Finding little widely accessible information, it took four years to research and results in 'Convicted for Courage', a full social history of the POW camp system within the UK, contrasted with the treatment of Conscientious Objectors.

Kevan lives with his wife in Nottinghamshire. They have four grown children.

www.kevanpooler.com